THE
OMEGA
OBJECTION

SAN ANDREAS SHIFTERS

BY G. L. CARRIGER

The San Andreas Shifters
Marine Biology (available free via Gail's newsletter)
The Sumage Solution
The Omega Objection
The Enforcer Enigma

BY GAIL CARRIGER

The Finishing School (YA)
Etiquette & Espionage
Curtsies & Conspiracies
Waistcoats & Weaponry
Manners & Mutiny

Delightfully Deadly Novellas
Poison or Protect

The Parasol Protectorate
Soulless
Changeless
Blameless
Heartless
Timeless

Supernatural Society Novellas
Romancing the Inventor
Romancing the Werewolf

The Custard Protocol
Prudence
Imprudence
Competence
Reticence

Claw & Courtship Novellas
How to Marry a Werewolf

THE
OMEGA
OBJECTION

SAN ANDREAS SHIFTERS

G. L. CARRIGER

GAIL CARRIGER LLC

GAIL CARRIGER, LLC

Version 1.0
ISBN 978-1-944751-16-6

*This one is for the librarians out there
(Goodreads and otherwise), without you nothing
would ever be properly organized.*

CHAPTER ONE
Saucebox

"What do you mean you didn't sleep with him? You've been chasing his tail for six months. You got cold pussy at the last minute?" Isaac stared in awe at his friend.

"Isaac! Don't be crass."

"Babycakes, I'm always crass and you love me for it."

Clara giggled and bumped against him. "I totally do." Her eyes were big and worshipful on his face. It was only a little creepy.

Clara was human, so she didn't understand why she liked Isaac so much. Isaac had learned not to mind. It wasn't him, it was what he *was* and he couldn't do anything about it, so he might as well enjoy the results.

"You going to tell me why you turned him down after weeks of flirting?" Isaac adored contrary women. He didn't want his cock near them, of course, but he loved to talk about their sex lives. Mysterious alien creatures that they were.

Clara rolled her eyes and looked cagey. "Well…"

Isaac perked up. That meant there was something seriously wrong with the dude. All this time trying to get him into bed and what? "Ooo, lemme guess. He kisses like a dead fish? He's kinky in a bad way? Smells wrong?"

Okay, maybe not that last one. Humans didn't seem to care as much about smell as Isaac did.

Clara laughed. "Sugar, you have no idea. He's got this—" She stopped in her tracks (and mid-explanation) and stood frozen on the busy sidewalk. Her big blue eyes were wide and staring at the club. They were across the street from Saucebox, the sacred space where Isaac and Clara practiced their nightly ritual of group counseling, liquid courage, and interpretive dance. Otherwise known as *bartending*.

Clara and Isaac were two of San Francisco's best and most popular bartenders.

It's not arrogance if it's the truth.

Clara was clearly distracted by something very shiny. "Oh, *my heavens*, would you look at the new bouncer?"

Isaac laughed. "You going to put a hand to your head and faint?"

"*Land's sake!*" Clara always stepped up to play her part if given the right cue. "Stop looking at me, honey-child. Look at *him*. Does he bat for my team or yours? Oh, *please* say he's straight."

Isaac squinted across the street. "Can't tell at this distance."

Clara gave him an incredulous look. "You're joking. You could stand on the top of the Empire State Building and ID every gay man in New York City."

Isaac grinned at her. "I'd sure try."

"With your spit."

"Can you think of a better gay litmus test?"

They wove their way through the mostly stopped traffic. Stopped not for the bouncer, but because it was San Francisco. Such ruthless jaywalking made Isaac feel like he belonged in the city.

"Holy shit." Isaac finally got a good look at the bouncer of questionable sexual orientation. "We are in so much trouble."

"I know, right?"

Isaac had been against the idea from the start. Having a mingle-with-shifters event at Saucebox might prove profitable, but it was asking for trouble. Especially for him. Adding a bouncer who looking like *that* into the mix? Insanity.

"That's what our boss thought would work to tame shifters? Is he crazy?" Isaac shook his head. "He'll put most of them into heat."

Clara glanced at him wide-eyed. "Oh, you think that's how it works? Do you, human-boy?"

"No, but the way some of them behave around specimens like that..." Isaac let himself trail off suggestively.

"Or specimens like you?"

"It'll be ten times worse around that mountain demigod come down from Olympus to bean us with his laurels." Isaac tried to collect his scattered thoughts. It was going to be one hell of a long shift.

Their usual guy, Oscar, was also on the door. Oscar was a big friendly black dude, darker than Isaac but still apt to engage in those weird bonding things that humans did around race and gender. Isaac had learned, if not to appreciate it, at least to participate. Oscar wasn't gay, but apparently, within the confines of co-worker status, that wasn't as big a deal as it might have been under other social situations. They were both dudes. They were both black. They were both in San Francisco working for the same club. Thus, *bonding*.

Humans were weird. That would be like shifters bonding over fur color.

However, Isaac was making an effort to understand the species in general. After all, he'd chosen to live amongst them and until recently his skin color seemed to work *not* in his favor. As such, he considered learning to interface with Oscar as helping him with his transition.

Now, if only the new bouncer would just glance up at him, and…

Oh, just look at those eyes. Big, brown, and wicked.

Isaac's inner wolf, who hadn't paid attention to anything in a long time, picked up his metaphorical head in interest.

Isaac mentally slapped him. *Down, boy!*

Clara nudged him. "Ain't that the most delicious hunk of brisket?" She always rediscovered her Southern roots when there was a super hot guy around.

Isaac swallowed on a suddenly dry throat. *Delicious* didn't even begin to cover it. His wolf licked his chops.

Isaac knew, given what he was, that he should probably not have a *thing* for really big dudes. But that's the problem with life, you can never control the *thing* that puberty gives you. Isaac had friends at the club who'd come into their maturity in the '80s and almost all of them had a *thing* for spandex. (For which there is no excuse. Except, of course, coming of age in the '80s.) Isaac, for whatever reason, had a *thing* for massive guys. Perhaps it was because he was a pretty big guy himself. Perhaps it was a latent revenge fantasy of wanting to take advantage of the very type of man that once made his life miserable.

The new bouncer was really fucking big. He was six and a half feet at least – all of that muscle. He had brown hair to go with the brown eyes, but with smooth, milky skin, like he didn't see the sun often. If at all.

Isaac stopped paying attention to where he was putting his feet, and in one of his more graceless maneuvers, tripped over the uneven pavement and pitched forward right at the two bouncers guarding the door.

Huge strong hands caught him, and his world was all about a pair of thick-lashed chocolate eyes.

"Alright there?" Deep, mild voice, calm, and not easily riled by anything.

Isaac stared at the big man now holding him up and

wanted to wreck him in the best possible way.

Those pretty eyes crinkled at the corners. "I hate it when the sidewalk jumps right up at me like that." *East Coast accent?*

Those amazing hands steadied him back to his traitorous feet.

Isaac found his voice. "Bipedal motion has always been a problem for me."

Big rough fingers cupped his jaw. "Yeah?" A thumb pad traced the bone under his cheek. "Ever considered trying out a quadruped?"

Isaac loosely registered Clara's disappointed sigh behind him. Part envy, part resignation, part romantic drivel.

Well, there it is. He definitely plays for my team.

At which juncture, Isaac finally remembered to breathe. On his inhalation he smelled the man, started coughing, and freaked the fuck out.

Saucebox's new bouncer smelled amazing – like warm brandy and lemon and nutmeg and freshly killed rabbit laid out at his feet for a courting gift which meant…

Werewolf.

His wolf, the idiot, was doing some kind of happy tail-chasing thing, which made his pulse flutter and his human self feel slightly woozy.

Isaac jerked away, still coughing, while simultaneously trying not to gag.

Clara slapped his back. "Oh sugar, you're such a spaz."

Isaac's eyes watered. He carefully did not look at the new demigod-mountain-werewolf-dream-creature. Instead he caught Oscar staring at him like he'd grown a third arm.

"Oscar," he said, on a wheeze.

Oscar grinned. "Isaac."

Clara pushed forward and stuck her hand out at the new guy.

"Hi there, sugar, I'm Clara. This klutz here is Isaac.

We're your bartenders for this evening."

The chocolate eyes finally left Isaac's face. "Hello Clara, I'm Tank." He was almost pretty in profile, if pretty was welded of steel and could crack long bones with his teeth.

Oscar explained what they already knew. He was like that. "Tank's on board tonight to help with the boss's little shifter experiment."

Which totally made sense – hire a werewolf to deal with shifters. They basically specialize in group activities and busting chops. Except, of course, that there weren't supposed to be *any* werewolves in the Bay Area. That was one of the reasons Isaac had moved to the place.

Tank was either a loner, which was dangerous, or part of a pack, which was *really* dangerous.

Involuntarily, Isaac jerked away from the man. He had to hope it wasn't pack. His wolf whined and Isaac clamped down on the muscles in his human throat to stop it from leaking out.

Clara shook her head at Isaac, mouthed *What on Earth is wrong with you?* and then grabbed his hand and dragged him inside.

Isaac wanted to keep right on walking out the back door, into the alley, home to his shitty apartment where he would gather up his stuff and move on to a new city. One that *really* didn't have any werewolves.

Instead, he allowed her to lead him through to the far side of the club. He waited until they were well out of earshot. Which he knew with werewolves was further away than humans expected – all the way inside, behind the bar.

"So, what's a werewolf doing in the Bay Area?"

Clara gave him a funny look.

Oh shit, that was out of the blue. She wouldn't have known Tank's species. She couldn't smell the wolf in him. Plus, Isaac never really asked about the shifter community.

He was nice to them, and they adored him, but he tried hard not to be curious.

Isaac shrugged. "I figured that's what he most likely is."

"Did you?" Clara was a good friend so she let him dig his own grave.

"You know, all big and hot and growly. Plus, the quadruped quip. Aren't werewolves supposed to be like *the fuzzy best*?"

"Well, he certainly fits then. But gay? I've never heard of a gay werewolf. Have you?"

Isaac blinked. *Well, yes, intimately. Me.*

He avoided the question. "There's never been a werewolf in Saucebox before. Not since I was hired on." *I would know.*

Clara shrugged. "Wouldn't be surprised if that means there weren't any around 'til now. Then again, seems every shifter and his cousin comes in here eventually, always asking for you." She paused her organizing of the mixers, gave him a head tilt of query. "Why is that?"

Isaac shrugged. "I'm a likable dude?"

It was one of the reasons their boss had decided on a mingle-with-the-shifters special for this evening. Since Xavier hired Isaac a couple months ago, more and more of the local shifters had started frequenting his club. At first it was just a barghest or two. Dogs always managed to track Isaac right away – proverbial tails wagging. Then the kitsune found him, because foxes turn up like bad pennies. They brought along drama, excitement, and junk food. Turns out those plastic-packaged powdered doughnuts at gas stations that Isaac thought no one ever ate… kitsune love them. They thought everyone else loved them too. Xavier put in a vending machine. Once the kitsune found Isaac and the doughnuts, well then *everyone* else came in to talk to him.

They didn't know why.

They never knew why.

They couldn't smell what he was, because Isaac had no scent. The ultimate protection. Isaac smelled human, because he lived with humans. On purpose. Or he smelled like the bar. Or he smelled like the city. But he never smelled like wolf. And didn't have his own signature scent like all other shifters.

For a shifter to figure out what he really was? Well, that would take frequent exposure to werewolves. Like the one guarding the door right now, massive and gorgeous and giving him the occasional puzzled glance across the wide empty expanse of the still-closed club.

Run. Run run runrunrunrun. That was Isaac the human freaking out, not the wolf. The wolf lolled a tongue at him.

Isaac didn't run, he started the nightly ritual of setting up his bar and resolved to ask the next kitsune he saw why the hell there was a werewolf in his city. Well, another werewolf, besides him.

In the meantime, he went back to quizzing Clara about her failed sex life.

Tank watched the dark-skinned human walk away from him. Isaac moved with part style, part freneticism, managing to be both graceful and abrupt, like some modern dancer. He was wearing black jeans that were just the right side of too tight. When he slipped behind the bar and that perfect ass disappeared from view, it was one of life's great disappointments.

Tank tried to rip his eyes away, except now he focused on the way Isaac's shoulders perfectly filled out his black t-shirt. Tank never thought he'd meet a man as beautiful as Isaac, not in this lifetime. And for him, lifetime meant a bit longer than most. But there Isaac was, cleaning the spouts of booze bottles.

Isaac was tall and slender, but not too much of either. Tank really liked that, because with little guys he was always afraid of crushing them. Besides, those pixie types took one look at him and went belly-up, or, more properly, ass-up, and Tank wasn't into that. Isaac was over six foot and all lean muscle – unlike Tank's own galumphing form. Tank wanted him draped over his own body, like a tablecloth.

Theodore Depeine hadn't had to earn his nickname, it was given to him early. All the males in his family were huge and submissive to pack hierarchy. His dad used to joke that if packs could be thought of as football teams, the Depeine males were the defensive line. Big enough to be Alpha but without the necessary genetics, tough enough to be enforcer but without the inclination to aggression, too big to be Beta and without the need to constantly compromise. Workhorse werewolves – just hook up the plow, strap on the battle axe, sit back, and relax. We got ya covered.

His dad once said, in a rare moment of reminiscence, "Back before Saturation, when we were fighting the human's wars, Depeines were the foot soldiers."

Around the table at the time, Tank's brothers hadn't even paused shoveling down meatballs.

"Cannon fodder," suggested Tank, a little bitter about his lot in life. Shouldn't they want to be *more*? Doesn't everyone want to be special?

His dad only shrugged. "Someone has to be." *Accept your lot in life, son— support rank, background, always reliable.*

Tank understood his place in the universe. To live his life without shaking the roots of reality – hold the line, protect the rest of the pack by being massive and immoveable. Then produce a litter of baby defensive line for the next generation's team.

Which is how, since it turned out he actually wanted to

be more than just cannon fodder, Tank ended up in San Francisco. The bisexual thing didn't help either. He wasn't convinced he could form his own identity with the San Andreas Pack, but he sure as shit couldn't do it with his family around.

"Who's that?" he asked Oscar. Eyes on the muscles of Isaac's forearms as he rubbed down the bar top.

"Like what you see? Clara's pretty game. You'll get lucky if you pay her some respect."

Tank's gaze flipped to the female bartender. She was giggling at something Isaac had said.

Tank wasn't one for talking much over his preferences. Not that he was embarrassed, just that it wasn't anyone's business but his own. So he only grunted in acknowledgment.

Dating a human was never a good idea anyway. They smelled wrong, like prey. But he might have to make an exception for that pretty, pretty man. Although Isaac hadn't really smelled of anything. Weird that. Regardless, the problem was, would the human want to date a werewolf?

Half an hour later, the club officially opened.

Tank didn't bounce often. Generally, Judd or Kevin leaped at the chance. After all, they were enforcers, it was kind of their thing. But Judd already had a gig, and Kev had a date or something freakish like that, so Tank said he'd take it on. The San Andreas Pack had recently started up a small but remarkably popular security-meets-bodyguard-meets-private-muscles firm, called Heavy Lifting. That's who the Saucebox query had come in for. Tank would do his part, it was a pack obligation after all. Now? Well, now he was really glad he'd wolfed-the-fuck up.

Since Heavy Lifting started, Tank had acted security to VIPs often enough to know the drill at any nightclub. The first few hours were boring and slow, open for one or two regulars, and waiting for the beautiful creatures to show up.

However, Saucebox quickly proved itself aberrant. It had an unusually steady stream of visitors, mostly shifters, coming in after work to grab a drink and a snack before heading home. Oscar explained that Saucebox's food was actually pretty good and that the head honcho, Xavier, made sure his kitchen catered to the varied tastes of the local supernatural community.

"Especially these days." Oscar nodded at a pretty bakeneko paying the cover charge. She skulked past Tank, giving him a wary look.

"Just here for the door, darling," Tank tried to reassure her. But his voice was low and growly and if you're six foot plus it's impossible not to loom.

She winced and moved faster.

Cat shifters.

Oscar said, "The boss is pretty savvy. When your kind started coming more and more, he saw a niche in the market that no one else was stepping in to fill."

Tank nodded. "He's trying to turn this place into a shifter hangout? Hence this evening's festivities. Smart."

Oscar nodded.

Tank sniffed. The club smelled good enough but nothing so that it'd tempt *his kind* in such numbers. There must be some other appeal. Outside of DURPS (the Department of Unnatural Registry and Processing of Shifters), he'd never seen so many supernatural creatures of different species in one place.

"Why'd it start, then? What was the original draw?" Tank nodded to a couple of familiar faces, Gladiola and Chrysanthemum, as they trotted up. He wasn't even slightly surprised to see them. They always knew the latest hot spot. The two kitsune and their respective leash of lovers were friendly with his pack. There was mutual barbecuing on occasion.

Gladdy pounced on him. "You!"

He hugged her back, careful not to squeeze, she was such a tiny thing. Chrys pounced after and dared to give his neck a little lick.

"Hey, now!"

The two kitsune grinned at him while they forked over the door fee.

Gladdy had her hair green with black stripes for the evening and was wearing layers of black in different weights and textures, with thigh-high lace stockings and a very short skirt. She took fashion seriously. Chrys was similarly dressed, standing slightly taller than his mate and with more leather than lace. His hair was plain glossy black, although he was wearing about as much make-up as Gladdy. Tank thought it looked better on him.

"Looking fine as fuck, you two." Kitsune liked to have their hard work appreciated and Tank never skimped on a compliment when one was due.

"Aw, thank you, darling! You sure you don't wanna play?" Gladdy pursed her pretty lips at him.

They'd been trying to seduce him (well, to be honest, they'd been trying to seduce most of the San Andreas Pack, on and off since they met). With kitsune this was more general compliment than actual intent, especially when flirting with werewolves. But it was flattering.

Tank waved them inside with a smile. "Don't you two ever stop?"

"Where's the fun in that?" Gladdy wanted to know.

"Aren't you going to check our IDs?" Chrys grinned, pertly.

Tank laughed. Gladdy was rumored to be in her nineties and Chrys was probably around sixty or so. Both older than he was. "Oh, go on in, you troublemakers."

The kitsune flounced past him, both of them with far more sway to their hips than necessary.

Oscar coughed. "You handled that better than I usually do."

"They get tetchy with you?"

He nodded. "I try to be professional, you know?"

"There's your problem. You gotta flirt a little with kitsune, even if it's only with Gladdy."

"But isn't he her husband or mate or whatever?"

"Yeah, but flirting for fox shifters is like shaking hands, common courtesy. I mean, they understand sexual preferences, so Chrys wouldn't expect it from you, but ignoring all outreach entirely comes off as a douche move. Like you can't see any value in either of them. Were they seriously courting you, there'd be a whole series of negotiations, for safety reasons alone, given how big you are." Tank shook his head. "You probably took it too seriously. Just smile back, throw one of them the occasional wink. Doesn't take much."

Oscar squinted at him. "One of them going to lick me?"

Tank laughed. "No, he did that because we're friends."

"This the same with all dog shifters?"

"Foxes aren't dogs."

Oscar grunted.

Tank shrugged. "I wouldn't worry too much. You don't have my instincts. They'll give you a pass."

"Apparently." Oscar looked a tad insulted.

"Wasn't meant to criticize, you can't help being human."

"Charming."

Tank winced. All too often he put his foot in it. *I'm a big blundering fool who ought to keep his head down and just do my job.* "Sorry, dude, no insult intended."

"Are all werewolves as arrogant as you?"

Tank considered that seriously. "Most are worse. Except Betas."

"Maybe next time we need shifter muscle, I'll ask Xavier to request your pack's Beta then."

Tank hid a smile. "Trust me, that's way more than you need. I promise to behave myself from here on out. Keep my mouth shut."

Oscar seemed to shrug off Tank's blunder at that. "So, you want to know why all these shifters started coming into Saucebox all of a sudden?"

"Was it all of a sudden?"

Oscar jerked his head in a nod.

"So why?"

"Watch the bar and you'll see pretty quick."

Tank shifted position so he could still stand sentry at the door but had a clear view of the bar at the back of the club. The place was still pretty quiet. Just a few early birds (well, early cats and dogs and foxes).

Isaac was behind the bar. Smooth movements under that tight shirt with sudden jerks of the head as his attention was caught or when he slapped down a shot glass. His face was animated, his generous mouth often smiling, his pretty pale eyes flickering about to see what was needed.

Clara was working food mainly, pulling it out of the old dumbwaiter and setting it in front of those who chose a nightclub for dinner.

Even though Oscar said the food was good, it struck Tank as an odd choice. After all, the Mission was stuffed with amazing restaurants. Why eat at Saucebox when there was killer Korean next door? He shook his head. Takes all sorts.

Gladdy and Chrys made a beeline for Isaac. The bartender waved them to take seats, and poured them each a shot glass of the Omnivore Special. Tank recognized the color from when he'd had the tour. It was hot sake mixed with tuna water and wheat grass. Tank swore he could smell it from where he stood. Oscar swore it was beyond nasty but that the kitsune went bonkers for the stuff.

"Isaac invented it," Oscar explained.

"'Course he did," said Tank.

Isaac tapped in a food order on the special screen, without asking the kitsune what they wanted. They were clearly regulars. Then he leaned forward on his elbows, chin in hand, and gave them his full attention.

How glorious that must be, to have Isaac's full attention.

The foxes proceeded to talk nonstop in a focused manner that reminded Tank of a job interview. It all seemed very intense.

Oscar said, "And there it is. That's why they come."

Tank considered this revelation. "To talk to a bartender?"

"To talk to *that* bartender."

CHAPTER TWO
Counseling Kitsune

Isaac leaned back from the counter, indicating that the session had ended. Across from him, the kitsune couple he'd been counseling wore relaxed smiles. Nice to see them happy.

"You staying for the mixer?" Isaac asked.

They shook their heads. They were one of his regular pairs, came every Thursday after work to see him and check in. They'd found him early on and adopted him right away. Or, better put, insisted that he adopt them.

Isaac straightened, gathered up their shot glasses and empty plates, and then gave the countertop a perfunctory wipe with his cloth. Sure, he'd been talking to them and not serving, but Clara had his back. It was quiet, not yet seven, and everyone knew to leave him alone when he was sympathizing.

Xavier had learned real quick that the early crowd came to his club, drank his stock, and ordered his food with lucrative regularity for one reason, and one reason only, to talk to Isaac.

Xavier was a savvy businessman. He knew that while most clubs made big money on the weekends, a man earned his true living off his midweek regulars. So he'd given Isaac a raise, as many early shifts as he would take, and steady hours. Word spread from there.

"We should get home. The kits are waiting on us." Gladdy smiled fondly. She was thinking of their cadre of co-habitating friends and lovers, not her actual children. Of which, Isaac once learned to his amazement, she had *nine*, all long since grown and fled the den.

He took a deep breath. "You two are doing so much better. Don't you feel it's time you took a break from me?"

Gladiola looked crestfallen. "You're breaking up with us? But you're our *favorite* bartender."

"You two don't really need me anymore." They'd been going through a rough patch in their mating – drama drama drama – some cheating, some lying, mostly semantics. He'd helped them sort it out easily enough. Now they kept coming back to him out of habit. And possibly affection. But not necessity.

"But we *like* you." Chrysanthemum give him a big-eyed look of pathetic fox cub left out in the rain. Blink blink blink.

Gladdy got onto her knees on the bar stool so she could reach and grab Isaac's hand. "We *like you,* like you. I mean, if you don't want to be our bartender-meets-shrink anymore, we'd love to take you out to dinner."

Chrys added, "Or just to bed. Bed's good too." He gave Isaac's long form an appreciative once over.

Isaac's smile did not waver. *Here we go again. Curse of my birth, everyone wants me, except that they actually don't. Not me, not really. They want the way I make them feel. They want the wolf I bury inside. Social addiction.*

Gladdy had put it best when they'd first discovered him. "Being around you is like swimming in warm comforting pudding."

Isaac reached gently down to extract his hand and petted each kitsune on the head, knowing they needed the physical reassurance of his undemanding affection alongside sexual rejection.

"I'm honored and complimented, but I must decline." He was careful with his sincerity, although they were both so small, such an encounter would no doubt be fraught with technical difficulties.

"Monogamous?" wondered Gladdy.

Isaac didn't respond to that. It was natural to be interested in the private lives of authority figures, he supposed. Even if that authority figure was only the bartender you'd adopted as psychiatrist because he listened really well and helped you with your weird marriage without judgment.

Isaac was much more sympathetic to shifter problems than any human ought to be. He could tell them truths without flinching. After all, he'd moved to the Bay Area and started this new life so that he could be honest about his sexuality. Honest about his shifter identity, *never*, but honest about who he slept with? Sure. *Funny that I traded one for the other.*

"Gay," he said, by way of explanation.

Gladdy nodded, face a little sad. Not too much. It was no ego hit to her and didn't affect her sense of self. She wasn't threatened by his admission.

Chrys said, "Well, I'm game. Gladdy won't mind, so long as she can watch. Isn't that one of the things we just took weeks with you to figure out?"

"He's right. I'd enjoy the show." Gladdy gave her mate positive reinforcement, just as Isaac had coached her.

Kitsune, thought Isaac, *ever the optimists.* He tried to come up with a polite way to let down the two foxes. "Thank you, but no, that's not what I'm looking for."

Chrys said, "Well, we sure hope you find whatever it is you *are* looking for. And if you ever want to talk about it, we're all ears."

Gladdy gave herself the illusion of two large fox ears for a split second to illustrate her mate's point.

Isaac smiled.

Chrys continued. "Thanks for everything. I think you might have given us forty more years together, if not more."

Gladdy was equally gracious. "You're so good with us. For us. I never knew a human could do that."

Isaac played his human role well. Never let his wolf out. He'd gotten the reputation for some latent savage mage ability as a result. New clients always assumed, whenever they came up to his bar, that that's what made Isaac so good with shifters. Savage quintessence, smoothing the world around him, making him easy to talk to.

It was a good enough explanation. Utterly wrong, but it kept them from questioning him too closely. His wolf growled. He wanted to be given credit for something. Isaac growled at his wolf.

Gladdy shook her head in wonder. "The way you are, the way you comfort, it's amazing."

It's instinct. Nothing but fucking instinct. "I'm just a really good... bartender."

The kitsune gave him a toothy smile. "It's more than that. But you keep your secrets, honey. Have a fab evening. We'll be back, if only for kisses."

Isaac chuckled. "I never doubted it for a moment."

He watched the two fox shifters wend their way out through the evening crowd. The club had filled up while they talked.

Saucebox had the general feel of an upmarket gallery, although more mellow lighting. White walls, big art, black dance floor that was a bitch to clean, and mirrors everywhere. No disco balls for Saucebox. Xavier didn't do kitsch, or cheap, or corny. The lighting was recessed and subtle, except over the bar where the bottles glowed in backlit glory. And everything that needed lighting had it, especially the till, because money and alcohol were taken seriously.

The kitsune paused at the door to have a long conversation with the new bouncer. They clearly didn't mind that he was a werewolf. Isaac narrowed his eyes. In fact, Chrys was all over the man mountain. The little kitsune looked like he wanted to climb Tank, licking him all the way up and then nibbling all the way back down again.

Isaac's wolf didn't like that idea at all. Isaac didn't like it. Agreement for a change. Then Isaac didn't like *that*, and he didn't like that he didn't like it. *Argh!*

He hated that his well-constructed little world now included a werewolf. One who, if he wasn't gay, sure was tolerant.

Warm chocolate regard met Isaac's frown over the glossy black heads of the two kitsune. Tank looked somewhat sheepish – trying to extract himself as politely as possible. It was as if he were reacting to Isaac's inadvertent jealousy.

Which made Isaac feel a little better, and hate himself a little more.

Tank watched in awe as, over the course of about three hours, Isaac chatted with a stream of troubled shifters. Many of them left before the mixer even started. All of them looked a great deal better, emotionally, on their way back out.

"Nice chat?" he asked Gladdy and Chrys when they paused to say goodbye.

"He's sooooo good," enthused Gladdy. She patted Tank's cheek. "Not that you need him, sweetie."

Tank shifted uncomfortably. *Seems I need him rather badly, just not like the rest of you.* "What's that mean?"

"You're so stable, big guy. Nothing ruffles you."

Good old Tank, boring and dependable.

Chrys grinned. "Hey now, Glads, maybe Tank's got troubles. Still waters run deep and all."

Gladdy glared at her mate. "No need to trot out a cliché." She turned back to Tank. "Didn't mean to insult you, sweetie. Figured it was kind of your thing. All solid and," she floundered, "big and firm."

Tank nodded, resigned. At least he was doing his family proud, even on the other side of the country. "That's my heritage, *big and firm*. So, Isaac helped you guys?"

"Always. I was thinking of suggesting that maybe..." She stopped herself. "Hum. I better talk to Alec first."

Tank was curious about any possible intersection between Isaac and pack, but if it was something worth his Alpha's attention he could only say, "Yeah, always best to start with him."

Gladdy nodded. "I'll talk to him on Sunday. We're coming over to yours for roast venison." She licked her lips. Tank could see the flash of fox there, behind her lovely face, vulpine sharp and full of mirth.

Saturday was full moon, which meant his pack would be hunting. They'd special dispensation from the park service to cull the local deer population on full moon. Afterward they always did a spit roast. It was Marvin's idea to get the community invested in having a pack through food and socialization. (Marvin was a merman with a head for marketing.) At first, just Max's ex-co-workers from DURPS showed up, which included Gladdy, but once the kitsune spread the word it basically became a *thing*. Now a handful of local shifters and their assorted friends and lovers all followed the phases of the moon closely, and started salivating just after full.

"See you in a few days, then." Tank grinned at them.

Gladdy and Chrys bounded off into the city, tiny forms with mighty strides and angry clothes. Tank envied them their confidence in such an urban forest with all its acrid smells and forgotten folk. San Francisco was a pack without cohesion or Alpha, a stressful place for a wolf. The kitsune, however, were comfortable as only scavengers can be around so much risk and opportunity.

Tank couldn't help it, his gaze was drawn back to the bar inside the club.

Isaac's tall form flickered under the diffuse lighting – quick, quick, quick, then still and focused. He smiled in small uplifts, one corner of his mouth, but he wasn't cheerful. It was more welcome mixed with self-deprecation. He had a new shifter sitting in front of him, talking in earnest and at length.

"He never stops, does he?" Tank didn't bother to keep the awe out of his voice.

Oscar was distracted by a trio of mermaids paying their cover. The ladies regarded both him and Tank with interest but no fear. They had a very poor sense of smell, merfolk, so it's possible they didn't know Tank was a werewolf. Or it's possible they didn't care. They also had some stellar supernatural defenses in the savage mage arena, especially the ladies.

Oscar, riveted by the stunning women, grunted at Tank's question. But when the mermaids made their way inside, he said, "You're fascinated with our boy, aren't ya? Just like all the other shifters who come panting after him."

Tank winced but soldiered on. "They all just come to *talk* to him?" *Or do they all want to fuck him, too?*

"Seems like." Oscar's eyes stayed on the mermaids as they swayed into the crowd, liquid beautiful.

Tank felt himself tense a little. It was just this side of too odd. Why *were* all these shifters coming specifically to talk to this one human male? Not that Tank could deny the attraction. But surely not everyone wanted those pretty lips on them the way Tank did. Not *everyone*. Tank, after all, could think of a million more things to do with Isaac than talk.

"I'm gonna do a pass around the floor," he told his

fellow bouncer.

Oscar snorted. "Sure you are."

Tank made a show of being intimidating muscle, moving by stages toward Isaac's section of the bar. It looked like he was on a break from counseling at last. Or, more likely, it was now too busy for that level of focused attention – the psyche-office was closed for the night. The bartending side of Isaac's job now took precedence.

"Hey." Tank leaned one elbow on the bar, gave Isaac a long look and a slow smile. Isaac smiled back. Tank glowed under it. That smile was a real one.

He swiveled so he could watch the floor but still keep an eye to Isaac in his peripheral. The man was now fussing with the till.

"Hey," said Isaac back.

"Gonna come greet me proper, now that you're safe behind your counter?" Tank coaxed.

Isaac's eyes went big but he slipped over to Tank quick enough, almost like he couldn't quite help himself.

Tank thought Isaac's eyes might be gray. The pack's Magistar adjunct, Max, was Asian (well, *mostly* Asian) with the bluest eyes Tank ever saw. Tank had thought when he first met Max that it was the most amazing combination. Until he met Isaac. Brown skin and gray eyes were just about the hottest thing ever.

"Hello, pretty one," he said, putting his hand, open palm up on the bar top.

"Said the wolf in the fairy tale." Isaac's breath caught, but he slid his own big hand into Tank's even bigger one.

"Little red riding hood, are you?"

Isaac shivered.

Tank tugged him a bit, getting him closer, needing him closer. He kept hold of Isaac's hand while he bracketed Isaac's face with his free one. His skin was butter soft.

"Your eyes gray?" he asked.

Isaac blinked at him. "Uh huh."

Tank pursed his lips. "Fairytale got it wrong, I want *you* to eat *me* up." *Best to be clear on this kind of thing from the get-go.*

Isaac's lovely eyes flared hot and aggressive – *oh, he likes that idea.* The human pressed down on Tank's palm, pushing it into the cold granite of the bar top. Tank's breath hitched, wanting all the textures of Isaac's skin thrusting into him.

Isaac leaned a moment on his one hand, giving Tank his weight, giving him something precious and dominant. Then he seemed to realize what he was doing and flinched back.

Tank had a horrified moment of feeling like he'd offended him. Too much too soon and too unexpected. "Only joking."

"I don't think you were." Isaac still looked frightened.

Tank was resigned. He hated that about himself. He was so big he scared people. It wasn't what he wanted – to loom and threaten. He wanted to use his body as a foundation, something for a lover to build on, glorious or cozy, safe or generous, he cared not what so long as it might be a home. No one seemed to want that from him. No one ever saw his size as welcoming.

"You met a werewolf before?" Tank asked, needing to know where the mine fields might be.

"Oh, yes." Isaac shuddered, flinching away from some memory that Tank suspected would haunt them both.

Tank took a cautious sniff. Human, but stale, like Isaac was wearing someone else's clothes. There was no other smell under that overlay. The scent of the bar was on him too, and tendrils of the people around him. But Isaac had no real scent of his own. It almost felt to Tank like nose-blindness. Another oddness about this mysterious man.

Isaac, consummate bartender, moved away to tend to a needy customer.

Tank maintained his position. He saw Xavier, the

owner, appear on the edge of the dance floor. The man gave him a nod. The shifter-meet-and-greet scheme seemed to be going well. Not that Tank knew what normal attendance was like at Saucebox on a Thursday night, but the place was now packed.

Xavier tilted his head at someone and Tank was instantly alert. There was a man pushing through the crowd. His eyes were intent on the bar and his expression was not friendly.

Tank's hackles rose and he moved to intercept.

Soon as the man was close enough to smell, Tank clocked him. Fur and flesh, hearth and home, blood of the hunt but less wild than wolf. Black dog, then. Big, although not as big as Tank. And hunting.

Hunting in Tank's territory.

So now both of them were hunting.

"You sure it's Thursday?" Clara danced around Isaac, flicking the tap for a local IPA.

Isaac stood next to her, coaxing a stout into low-foam submission. "Sure doesn't feel like it."

Clara shook her head in awe. "This mixer was a killer idea."

"Don't say that to Xavier, his ego doesn't need any boosting."

"I think he's probably figured it out for himself." Clara switched to a new glass, another IPA. Humans had horrible taste in beverages.

Isaac glared at the club. "You know this basically just gives tacit permission for humans interested in dating shifters to come hang out."

There were fewer shifters (even in the weirdo Mecca of the Bay Area) than there were humans in the world, so a shifter-only event would have low turnout. But throw it open to humans too? A hundred years after Saturation and humans still found supernatural creatures *exotic*. Thus, the club was packed not just with shifters but also tail-chasers. And the flirting between the two was off the charts.

"It's a meat market out there," Clara agreed.

"Fur market?" suggested Isaac. He turned away, braced a new bottle of wine on his thigh, and cranked the cork pull with a satisfying pop.

"Don't be prejudiced," yelled Clara, moving down the bar away from him, "Some of them have scales."

Things were actually going really well, apart from that one hiccup with Tank. *God, so hot.* How had Isaac forgotten himself so quickly? Forgotten all his hard-won lessons. The chief of which being: avoid werewolves at all cost.

But Tank seemed so perfect. His hand under Isaac's had been firm and sure, but pliant and oh, so willing. No doubt Tank's body under Isaac's would feel much the same. Isaac wanted to press down onto him, into him – full length and both of them naked.

His wolf had been, for one moment, sublimely happy.

And then he'd remembered, *Tank is a werewolf.* And things had not gone well after that. He'd pulled away. Tank saw it and was hurt. A small careful beginning crushed, as it should be. Isaac knew he could have been nicer about it. He was nice to everyone else, but not to werewolves.

Isaac was well aware it had been a coward's retreat. But his world was once more made up of careful smiles, and serving, and making others happy in order to disguise himself. There was safety in that. He'd forget about Tank.

Until things went very badly indeed.

Because Hayden turned up.

Isaac's first warning was Tank, who swung into motion away from the bar with remarkable speed for such a massive man. Something or someone tipped him off, or perhaps it was just instinct. Isaac was watching him out of the corner of his eye (had never stopped watching him, truth be told). So, when all that mountain stillness unfroze, Isaac turned to track why.

And there was Hayden.

Isaac hadn't ever slept with Hayden. But it wasn't for Hayden's lack of trying.

Isaac had always figured that his self-imposed regulation, avoid werewolves, applied to weredogs as well. Hayden had taken to single-handedly disproving this a good rule. The barghest had come to him weeks ago with relationship problems and it took Isaac ten minutes to realize they were self-inflicted.

Hayden was one of those men who seemed so reasonable talking about himself. But when he talked about his exes and his inability to keep a boyfriend, it was always the other guy's fault. With a more reasonable person, Isaac might have laid this out before him and said, "What I see is one common denominator. You. So perhaps there is something in yourself you might fix, before fixating on someone else."

Unfortunately, Hayden was not at all reasonable. In fact, he was highly unstable. So what Isaac had done instead was decline to see the man again. Hayden took this as acknowledgement of a desire to sever professional relations so they could have personal ones. Of course, Saucebox was a club, not a medical facility. So Hayden could keep turning up. Which he did. Trying to buy Isaac drinks ("I'm working"), trying to take Isaac on a date ("I'm *so* not interested, dude"), and finally trying to force Isaac into sex one evening in the men's room ("I'm stronger than I look").

His wolf fucking loathed the man.

Frankly, Isaac had dealt with worse, and he didn't want to cause trouble. But Clara was not so reticent, and she mentioned Hayden's harassment to Xavier.

Xavier was not pleased. "Why the hell didn't you tell

me this was going on?"

Fortunately, Clara had only mentioned the *verbal* shit Isaac had been putting up with. She didn't know to mention the bathroom incident. Isaac kept that to himself, because Xavier *also* wasn't stable, although in a different way.

Yet now Hayden was here, and Hayden was angry, and Tank was intercepting him.

"Barghest." Tank barred the man's path.

Hayden's lovely chiseled lips drew back in a snarl. "Werewolf."

Tank's eyes flicked up briefly to check with someone across the room.

Xavier. Of course, he's here for this. Isaac burned with embarrassment.

His boss was a slight, angular man, with a face both mean and beautiful, black limpid eyes inherited from his Filipino mother, and intricate full-sleeve tattoos that told stories of lost islands in a language Isaac wasn't meant to comprehend. Xavier preferred his vodka cold and neat, his food fried, and his women leggy. He liked all three expensive and was protective of his passions. He also did not hold with anyone messing with his club or his staff. Whether Isaac liked it or not, when he joined Saucebox he became part of Xavier's weird dysfunctional family.

Xavier gave Tank *the nod.*

Isaac began pulling the expensive shit down and hiding it behind the bar. Just in case the fight got ugly. Also, it gave him something to do while his wolf went quietly bonkers.

Tank said, "You're not welcome here."

Hayden reared back. "Excuse me?" Then he tried to dodge around Tank. "Isaac, snuggle-muffin!"

Hayden had underestimated Tank's speed based on his size. Isaac suspected that happened a lot.

Tank blocked Hayden's path easily. "I'm asking you nicely."

"But Isaac's my boyfriend. I just need to tell him something."

Tank put a hand to the man's chest, steady rather than threatening, and then swiveled to catch Isaac's eye.

Isaac shook his head in denial.

"You little shit! You're mine!" Hayden lurched at him.

Tank wrapped his hand in Hayden's tight shirt, no doubt grabbing chest hair with it, and held him back. There was the sound of tearing.

"You asshole, this shirt is a Coda & Zucchero!" Hayden did something important in finance downtown and liked to dress that way.

"Walk with me." Tank's tone was low and calm, but he dragged Hayden bodily along in his wake. The dance floor cleared before them. Tank lumbered toward the front door.

Clara came up next to Isaac, mouth slightly open. They watched Tank swing and toss Hayden out into the street, Hollywood movie-style. The werewolf then stood, arms crossed, barring the entrance, like some stone sentinel. No way would Hayden get back inside.

"That was anticlimactic," said Clara.

"That was effective, is what it was," said Xavier, coming up to them. "I liked it." His eyes gleamed. "You alright, Isaac?"

"I'm cool, boss."

Xavier gave him an evaluating look.

Isaac tried to look unperturbed. What he felt was creeped-out and humiliated. The dog shifter had clearly fixated on him. He'd caught Isaac's scent or decided Isaac was his precious bone (well, no boning and no scent, but whatever the allegory). Hayden had decided he wanted to own Isaac, and Isaac hadn't any way of protecting himself from intent. If Hayden had a pack and an Alpha, Isaac might petition for discipline. But a large part of Hayden's problems stemmed from his solitary living condition. Stray barghest weren't as unstable as lone werewolves, but they certainly weren't stable either.

Isaac did have one recourse, of course. Hayden didn't know he was a werewolf. But a black dog of Hayden's size against a wolf of Isaac's temperament and rank? His wolf was eager to try, innately aggressive or not. But Isaac hated to shift. And he hated to fight. Plus, he didn't want either known by his coworkers, and Hayden kept coming at him inside the club.

If anyone found out Isaac was a werewolf, they'd ask about his pack. And then about his birth. And then about his records. And they'd demand all the things he did not have. And then he really would have to run.

Again.

CHAPTER THREE
The Wolf in the Man

The barghest was no trouble. Tank hadn't thought for a moment he would be. The man wasn't anything important, not Alpha or even enforcer level. If it came toe-to-toe between shifters, all status markers being equal, it was merely a matter of mass. Under those circumstances, Tank mostly came out on top, especially with dog shifters. Werewolves were bigger than barghest, and Tank was one of the biggest of his kind.

The black dog knew this too, it was just that he wanted the bartender so badly. While Tank could hardly fault the wanting, the stalking and the demanding were disgusting. So Tank was delighted to toss the dude out.

The idiot lingered outside the club, spitting vitriol like he was the injured party.

The patrons, lined up to get inside, had seen it all before. They, no doubt, took comfort in witnessing a bouncer effective at his job and were entertained by the spectacle. The shifters amongst them understood the dynamics without requiring an explanation. Those who could smell knew wolf versus dog. Those who had other senses knew equal rank meant victory by size. Any with a feel for the social layout of supernaturals in the Bay Area had heard that there was a new wolf pack in town, and knew that there was no dog pack to speak of. The outcome was inevitable.

Wolf won. By rule of backup alone. But also by rule of sanity. This wasn't going to escalate. It was merely cleanup. So the shifters watched with expressions of mild interest and approval.

The barghest finally got tired of yelling and stormed away.

Oscar grinned. "You handled that easy."

"Helps that I am what I am."

"No doubt, man. No doubt." Oscar clearly forgave Tank then, for his arrogance earlier. It would have been a hell of a lot harder for Oscar to manage an angry barghest. The regular bouncer was big and strong, but he was only human.

Still Tank wanted to explain. "Stray dog won't take on a whole wolf pack."

Oscar looked around, confused. "But there's only you."

"Here, right now, there is. But he knows, just like all these others know, there're more of us. And there's only one of him. Dogs are good. Smart. Hunters and trackers." He shrugged. "But wolves are better. In the end, he doesn't want to piss me off, not because of me, but because of what I represent."

"Man, you shifters are weird. It's like some biker gang or protection racket."

Tank shrugged. "My pack does actually ride motorcycles on occasion."

"Oh? Whatcha ride?"

"Sirius Roadster." Tank liked his bike, mainly because it was practical and big enough for him. "Gets me from point A to point B with no fuss, but I'm no motor-head to care all that much."

Oscar nodded. "I ride a Creature Six myself. Good bike."

"Yeah? Shaft drive, gotta love it." Tank grinned at him. *Shaft drive, get it?*

Oscar didn't follow the innuendo.

Straight men. Bah.

They talked bikes for a bit while they ran the rope.

Xavier came by at about midnight, when they'd let inside most of whom they were going to. The man-in-charge wanted to tell them that they were at capacity.

Oscar smiled. "Real good for a Thursday, eh boss?"

"You're telling me." Xavier's harsh expression warmed briefly. He turned to Tank. "You coped with that, whatever he was, nicely."

"Barghest, and thank you, sir."

"Barghest?"

"Black dog. Kinda like a werewolf only a lot uglier."

Xavier's dark eyes gleamed in amusement. "Shifters got so many layers to their interactions. It was the right thing to do, by your people's standards?"

Tank bristled. As if he wouldn't kick *anyone* out who threatened Isaac. But then he realized what Xavier was really asking. The man was trying to understand this world he had invited into his club. Creatures in his space.

Tank nodded. "Yeah. We're peers, same social rank. But I could easily have won a one-on-one fight. So he didn't lose face when I ran him off. He also hasn't any excuse for being a coward. No Alpha VOICE, no Beta calm, no enforcer muscle. He left because I made him. That's hard to come back from. He won't come hunting me, either. I got pack. But..." He let himself trail off.

"You're worried about Isaac once he leaves the club." Xavier followed Tank's concern perfectly. "I'll pay you time and a half to stay after closing and walk him home."

Tank almost bristled. He'd do that for free. He'd have waited and tailed the man secretly anyway, to make certain he got to his place safely.

"Wait. He *walks*?" Tank hadn't meant to shout it.

Xavier wasn't at all perturbed. "Yep, the idiot. Through the Mission at three in the morning. Fucker thinks he's immortal. Like he's one of your lot."

Oscar said, "I'd wait for him, if he'd let me. But I said I'd see Clara home and they're not really in the same direction."

Tank said, "I'd be happy to walk Isaac back to his place."

Oscar gave him a look. "Thought you'd say that."

Xavier nodded, still grim-faced. Seemed his natural expression. "Good. I'll tell Isaac, that way he won't protest as much."

"He won't like it." Oscar looked like he slightly relished the drama. "He'll see it as interfering."

"Why is that?" Tank wondered.

Xavier shrugged. "Too used to taking care of himself. Doesn't mind looking after others, but when someone tries to look after him? It's interfering with his hard-won independence."

Tank scrunched up his nose. "Foster kid?"

Xavier shrugged. "No idea. When Isaac wants to tell me about his past, he will. You watch yourself with him." He gave Tank a look, no doubt sensing Tank's more than platonic interest. *Perceptive bastard.*

Tank shook his head. "I've no plans to join his throng of admirers." *What can I offer? Big dumb lug like me?*

Oscar snorted.

"No?" Xavier changed the subjected abruptly. "I'll be talking to your pack about bringing you back on the regular for this thing, Mr Depeine. It seems popular enough for me to make it weekly and you seem to fit in well. You up for it?"

Tank blinked at him. "This ain't my normal scene." He was going to say that Judd or Kevin might be better suited long haul, but then it might be one of them walking Isaac home. So he held his tongue.

Xavier narrowed his gaze. "If you commit, I'll consider offering Heavy Lifting a retainer for VIP work as well. You know I own the Minyas Hotel?"

Tank felt his eyes widen. "So this isn't your first shifter rodeo." The Minyas was a swanky waterfront establishment that catered almost exclusively to supernatural clientele. Everything from salt water on tap to a raw food kitchen. Any shifter with any kind of money tended to stay there. It'd be a great security contract for Heavy Lifting. Alec would be pleased. The pack would be elated. All because Xavier wanted Tank on Saucebox's door once a week?

Tank said, "I'll mention to my Alpha that you'll be in touch."

Xavier continued to stare at him, waiting.

Tank inclined his head. This man had negotiated with Alec before – he knew what the Alpha would ask first. "I'll tell him I'm willing."

Xavier slapped him on the back. "Good man. Now, I best get back to it." He returned inside.

Oscar said, "Alec is your Alpha?"

"Yeah."

"He a big tough guy, like you?"

"Nope."

"Huh."

"Yeah, that's what most people say."

"How's that work, then?"

"Ain't always about size."

Oscar laughed. "It's more about how you use it?"

Tank thought of his Alpha's slim elegance. Alec wore fancy wireless glasses (that he didn't really need) over his kind hazel eyes. Alec left paperwork all over the dining table and got excited about color-coding microorganism charts. But Alec also emitted a quiet oppressive power, and he could freeze them all with a single barked word. Alec would never do it but for their own good, but the point was

– he could.

"Yeah, that's what it's about."

Oscar grimaced. "Not sure if I want to meet this Alpha of yours."

Tank nodded. "Good, that's how you should feel."

"Man, you werewolves."

Tank changed the subject. "How often does that kind of thing happen?"

"Boss man making unilateral decisions about our lives? All the time."

"No, not Xavier. Isaac and the stalker."

"Depends what you mean by *that kind of thing*. You see how he is? Shifters just love him. Hell, even humans seem to love him. He's one of *those dudes*. Wears charisma instead of cologne. Might drive me crazy, except I like him too. He's a good dude. And we ain't competing for the ladies, if you see what I mean."

Tank did see. He tried not to be too excited by the outright confirmation of Isaac's gayness and by the fact that later that night they'd get to walk through the city together. His chest felt stretched and tight with anticipated pleasure and fear. To have the bulk of Isaac's attention all on him might be more a burden than even a man his size could withstand.

Isaac was not pleased with Xavier's interfering.

"I can take care of myself! I don't need a fucking werewolf to walk me home. Isn't that like throwing me to the wolves to protect me from the dogs?" They were out on the sidewalk. The club was closed and the patrons were gone, so Isaac could afford to be grumpy in public.

Xavier didn't bother to humor him. "I've paid him overtime for it, and he said he'd be delighted. Stop fussing."

"Great, now you're paying someone to look after me. Like a goddamn babysitter."

"Well, you *are* acting like a child. Look, here he comes. Now behave."

Tank trundled up. He had a leather motorcycle jacket slung over his shoulder.

Isaac nodded at him, too angry to say anything, and brushed past him to begin walking downhill. His wolf perked up and inhaled in delight. He whined softly at the loveliness of Tank's scent.

Tank lumbered after him.

Isaac forced himself to breathe in other things instead. The putrid odor of a city with too many people and not enough public restrooms, but also the damp newness of a fresh day, and the salty encroachment of a high tide. It was one of the many reasons Isaac loved his job. He was nocturnal by nature, and there was something about wandering home in the small hours when everyone was still asleep. Like the whole world belonged to him with no one else in it.

Except walking next to him, messing with his world, was Tank's hulking presence, new and unsettling.

Tank kept messing with the smell, too. He smelled so good, Isaac's wolf wanted to turn it into his own.

Charming, he thought, *the wolf without a scent wants to steal someone else's.*

Even after a long night at the club, pressed against the sweat of others as he cleared out the crowd, Tank still smelled of himself – warm brandy and citrus spice cake, fresh meat and hunting fur. Isaac's wolf felt safe and wild, intoxicated and comforted, and hopeful.

Run run runrunrun.

The wolf's need for the man warmed Isaac's blood even as his need to flee a fellow werewolf vibrated his human muscles.

Damn it, full moon must be soon. His wolf was always

harder to control around full moon.

Tank made running feel less like escape and more like a test. His presence was a coil of seduction that spoke directly to Isaac's wolf.

Run to me. Run with me. Run together.

Instead they walked together. As humans. One of them pretending. The silence between them surprisingly companionable.

Tank inhabited his human skin to perfect werewolf completion – solid and comforting, supernatural and other, and *safe safe safe* in a way Isaac's head could not believe was real, but his wolf knew to be true. It was also coupled with *want want want*. Never before had those two things coexisted for Isaac – desire and surety.

Isaac lectured his wolf. *Too much risk.* Learned wariness. Isaac argued, until both of his selves were exhausted and he allowed Tank be *there there there* and simply enjoy it.

Tank kept darting little hopeful glances at him from under long dark lashes. As if he had no idea what to do or what he looked like or how much Isaac wanted to tip him over and jump his bones, almost literally. His wolf was eager to taste – cock or blood, it was hard to decide which.

They walked in silence because Isaac was confused. Because Isaac had never been pack or home or safe. Not ever. So he could do nothing more than wrestle with the perfection of those possibilities. They were just as real as Tank's scent, alluring and terrifying.

Isaac found himself inching closer as they moved, inhaling deeper. He brushed against Tank, let the backs of their hands touch, pretended not to notice when Tank looked at him more directly, startled and eager.

They reached Isaac's rundown old apartment building, with the garbage blown up against the gate. Walking stopped, and tension vibrated between them like the pack tether Isaac had never had. Running wasn't possible –

either away or together. Isaac was so troubled by that fact that when Tank gave him one more shy look full of hope, Isaac reached and pulled safety to him.

It was as if, by grabbing Tank's massive shoulders, Isaac was stealing a little of Tank's scent for himself. Isaac's wolf chuffed in pleasure. Isaac felt foolish just stand there, inhaling Tank and holding on to his shoulders, so he leaned against him. Huge arms came around his waist, not gripping tight, just cradling him in warmth.

He let out a hopeless little sigh and raised his head to kiss. Tank waited for it.

So Isaac licked the seam of Tank's mouth, wondering if he tasted of brandy and citrus and spices. He nibbled, questing. Tank yielded with the smallest of sighs, opening to his query. It was a sweet benediction colored with spikes of light and want.

Isaac wanted so fiercely. He wanted everything all at once, his hands on Tank, and Tank's on him. Flesh sinking into flesh. Skin under his lips and tongue and teeth.

Or was it his wolf that wanted?

Isaac found himself pushing Tank to lean back against the warped old gate. So Isaac could press against Tank from chest to thigh. Isaac was hard. So was Tank. Big there too, it turned out.

Tank let him, of course. Part of the safety in this werewolf was that Tank would let Isaac do anything. To him. With him. Isaac sensed it – his human and his wolf were certain in Tank's nature.

Isaac couldn't stop himself. He ate at Tank's mouth using lips and teeth and little murmurs of encouragement to keep the big man still. He ground against him, hips undulating without any intent, just need. So much need.

Under him Tank panted and yielded, not passive but welcoming and eager. Taking it all, letting Isaac run his hands over stupid clothing. *Why is there clothing?*

Isaac tugged and shoved and ripped the annoying fabric

aside until his hands were smoothing over Tank's skin, glorious and warm. The breadth of the big man's back was all muscle under Isaac's eager palms. Isaac dug his fingers and short blunt nails into that tempting expanse. Tank trembled and arched against him.

The werewolf's mouth opened under his. Tank opened, exposing himself and his needs. Ready for anything Isaac might want. Isaac had never thought he would find such a man. Large in his giving and submissive in his desires. Isaac had never thought he would find such a wolf, one who shivered under his touch and yielded as if it were not against his nature – not against everything that werewolves stood for.

As if Tank didn't want to turn the tables and dominate.

As if Tank liked it.

As if Tank would let Isaac take and take, and would never stop giving because there was so much of him. With so much to give.

Isaac's wolf gloried in it all. Isaac's human body was flushed and fierce with animalistic desire. A sense of profound ownership crashed over him. Was this what Hayden felt for him? Danger then. Wanting too easily corrupted. Was this some taste of a shifter's need? Danger there too. In depending on anyone else for sanity or happiness. Was this what it meant to have pack? Danger in connection and the pull that would become loss of self.

Runrunrun run, said Isaac's human side while the wolf within panted with desire. *Stupid wolf.*

Isaac pulled back, and moth-like, Tank followed, pushing away from the gate. The big man's eyes were closed, his head lowered, his lips kiss-swollen and glistening, slightly parted. So perfect. Isaac thought it was the most beautiful thing he'd ever seen. And the most dangerous.

He reached around the mass of muscles and brandy-scented temptation, fumbled his key into the lock. A big hand steadied his, thumb caressing his knuckles. The lock clicked open and Isaac was through, slamming the gate in Tank's face. The werewolf didn't flinch. It was almost as if he expected rejection.

Tank stood there, on the other side of the gate, and watched as Isaac unlocked the front door.

Tank stood there, huge and patient and raw and breathing a little too quickly, until Isaac was safely inside.

Tank stood there still, when Isaac closed the door against him.

Up the many stairs (because the elevator was broken) and inside his shabby little apartment, Isaac found his stomach hurt, and his lips tingled, and his own skin smelled like warm brandy, citrus spice cake, fresh meat, and hunting.

He should have showered. But he didn't.

He should have packed his measly belongings and run away into the dawn. But he didn't.

He stripped and curled in the center of his bed. Wanting to be his wolf so badly, needing the comfort of his own lost fur, but forcing himself to stay a human. His wolf was not to be trusted.

Eventually Isaac slept, as he had when he was a child and he wasn't allowed to run, dreaming of a freedom he didn't have and a scent that wasn't his, and wondering if the two were the same.

Tank couldn't stop thinking about Isaac. He walked back to the club, now dark and empty, retrieved his motorcycle, and thought about the smoothness of the bartender's skin and the warmth of the man's eager mouth. Tank thought too much about that hard and eager cock pressed against his own. He thought about how Isaac had pushed him, demanded he yield, and how glorious it was to do so. How unlike a human. How unlike most men who found Tank attractive.

When men looked at Tank, big and hulking and bumbling, they didn't ordinarily think… bottom. Mostly Tank drew in the pretty ones (not that there was anything wrong with that, just that Tank wasn't interested in being anyone's Daddy, least of all a lover's). So far as Tank was concerned, nothing beat being taken. He'd rather be lonely than in charge.

The roads belonged to Tank on the ride home, too late for returning night owls and too early for morning traffic. He thought of Isaac's counseling sessions, everyone so eager for that soft calm voice and sweet kind face. *They call him the shifter whisperer.* Tank amused himself. Isaac of the tight t-shirt and pert ass. Isaac with his firm touch and frightened body language. Isaac, who'd closed off and gone from Tank before he even shut the door.

The pack house too was quiet, everyone else home before him and already in bed or out running the nearby parklands. Tank paused at the front door, sniffing the air. Kevin's large cream and rust wolf-form ghosted out from behind a bush, checking to see who'd entered their territory.

The enforcer emitted a whine of greeting. No challenge, just *hello pack mate*.

Tank waved.

Kevin chuffed a query.

Tank shook his head and mimed going to sleep.

A snort of disapproval from the enforcer met that. *Why not run? It's a beautiful night.*

But Tank wanted to dream of soft skin and gray eyes, and a man whom the world was telling him might one day smell like his.

CHAPTER FOUR
Trickle on Trappers

Tank was in wolf form running sunset patrol the next evening. It was Friday and he imagined Isaac already setting up his bar in preparation for the weekend crowd. He hoped Isaac was safe and that Hayden didn't come back.

The pack was mostly home, anticipating a communal dinner before they went off about their various nighttime social engagements. Tank was feeling restless and antisocial, so he volunteered to run the perimeter while the others prepared for exciting evenings out with friends, lovers, or bacon. According to taste. His own plans included a game night with Max, Bryan, and Colin. The others had dates, or in the case of Alec and Marvin, a date night. Tank's plans did, in fact, include bacon. All game nights should have bacon.

He smelled her before he saw her – sun-dried hay and mossy riverbanks – and veered toward the front of the property in response. She was being respectful, had done nothing more than exit her car, letting her scent ride the wind and alert the pack. The scent was familiar. The big SUV was familiar too once it came into sight. The large brash female who stood, impatient but knowing, was a friend.

She was alone for a change. Trickle usually came to visit with her wife, Pepper. She'd started out as Max's boss, but upon becoming his ex-boss, had graduated to being Max's friend. And then, of course, she became everyone else's friend, because anyone who could put up with Max could handle a wolf pack easy. Pepper was absorbed shortly thereafter, as the obligatory human appendage. Except everyone quickly realized that Pepper was brilliant and vibrant and lovely in all ways, not to mention an amazing chef. The San Andreas pack wasn't stupid enough to ignore such gifts. In fact, Pepper and Lovejoy were already talking about a food truck venture together. *Do it raw! Sometimes we wiggle, sometimes the food does.*

All this meant that in the end, Trickle had become the appendage and Pepper a pet of the pack.

Tank suspected eventually Alec would just give up and invite them both to be de facto members.

For now, however, Trickle waited politely next to her car as an intruder in their territory. She was massive. Kelpies came that way – it went along with only one name and a river smell. She was fair in complexion and hair, with a propensity for men's suits during the week and vests on weekends.

Tank liked her. They shared that thing that came with being over-large in a world built for smaller folk. Mainly a mutual disgust over the questionable stability of deck chairs.

Tank ran to greet her, rearing to his hind legs to put both paws on her shoulders and lick her face. This would change her smell enough so the others knew she had been welcomed. Not that it mattered too much with Trickle, but so far as Tank knew, this was an unexpected visit so best to err on the safe side.

She confirmed this. "Hi, Tank. Sorry to drop by unannounced."

"Why *are* you here, woman?" A voice came from behind and above them, the acrid sweet smell of quintessence wafted down, mixed with the comforting mellowness of home.

Max. Pack. Mage. Power.

Max's tone was sharp.

Max's tone was always sharp – it mattered not whether friend or pack or lover. In fact, Tank suspected that the more annoyed Max sounded, the more affection he felt. With his mate he was practically waspish.

Max slouched down the steps to greet Trickle, his lips twitching as if he were trying not to smile.

Max and Bryan didn't live with the rest of the pack in the big house on the upper part of the property. Instead they occupied the funny little grandma unit above the garage near the street. This despite the fact that the house and grounds actually belonged to Max. He had a right to the biggest and best room, but he preferred his small private space. So Alec and Marvin had the master suite in the big house, while Bryan and Max denned in a tiny second-story studio apartment. Since everyone was happy with this arrangement, Tank never questioned it.

Bryan bounded down the stairs after his mate. He was in wolf form, which meant it likely they'd been practicing their Magistar skills. The Beta bounced up to Tank and bunted against him, pleased and playful. Bryan was a big wolf too, mottled white and kind of bear-like, all pert-eared fluffiness. But Tank was still bigger, so was gentle when playing with him.

"My, but Tank really is enormous." Trickle crossed her arms, looking between the two wolves as they nipped and tussled.

"That's rich coming from a kelpie." Max frowned at his former boss. It was not an angry frown, it was a Max hug.

"How's retirement then?" she asked, grinning.

"Nice to be my own boss."

"I bet it is." Trickle didn't pry into Max's Magistar duties. If he did anything of note, he'd have to come by her office at DURPS and file the paperwork anyway. Luckily, quintessence had been quiet recently. Nothing major for Max to fix or destroy.

Although Tank realized that this might be a reason for Trickle's unexpected visit. Official Magistar business. He prepared to return to patrol, no cause for him to hang around if this wasn't pack-related.

Max seemed to be of a similar mind. "You visiting us *officially*?"

The kelpie grimaced, uncomfortable. "The opposite, actually. I shouldn't really be here at all."

Tank perked up.

Max nodded. "DURPS doesn't know? Come inside, Tank can guard."

"Nothing like that. Nothing for you. Nothing *that* bad." She grimaced, aware of the harshness of her words.

Max only shrugged. It was true. Things had to be rotten to need a Magistar.

Tank and Bryan stopped playing and stood, ears pointed forward, tails still, attentive.

Trickle looked at Bryan rather than Max. "It's actually a pack matter. I thought it might be best if Mr Fluffy McBetapants came along while I talk to your Alpha."

Bryan inclined his head and then shifted form. As a human, he was big and muscled, a dirty blond with a hairy chest and hazel eyes. Not Tank's type but unquestionably fine as fuck.

"You're worried it might upset Alec?" Bryan's deep voice was warm and easy. It showed not a hint of stress. He was Beta. It was his business to be calm.

Tank preened. They had the best Beta. What other pack could boast one that was *also* a familiar? Bryan even fought on occasion, and Betas really weren't meant to be fighters. But then Alphas were, and Alec preferred not to.

Alec and Bryan, brothers, had a strange childhood. Bryan, a nascent Beta, spent his youth protecting his geeky awkward younger brother, a nascent Alpha. In the end, they formed their own quirky pack, and Tank got to be one of them, with all their weirdness and oddly arranged ranks. Tank felt both proud and inferior. Really, who was he to hang out with the special ones? Yet he loved his oddball pack.

He barked, tail up and wagging, and started to lead them through the grounds toward the big house. Alec was already there, home from work. The Alpha would help Trickle fix whatever was worrying her. It's what strong packs did, helped their friends.

Bryan laughed at him and followed. Leaving Max and Trickle to bring up the rear.

Bryan, of course, was still naked. Tank turned to check if the kelpie and mage were coming, just in time to see Max leer at his mate. "My, but that man has a gorgeous ass."

Trickle ginned. "You know, I once doubted your taste."

"Foolish child." Max sniffed.

The very old kelpie laughed at the very young mage. "I admit to no particular interest in the gender as a rule, but I agree with you on purely aesthetic grounds."

"See? That's all you had to say."

Tank could practically smell Bryan's embarrassment. He resolutely kept walking.

Trickle shook her head and rolled her eyes. "Boundless power and the training to use it haven't improved your character one jot, oh great and wondrous Magistar."

"Improve? This?" Max wiggled his fingers at himself. "Surely you jest?"

"You're impossible."

"No, darling, just unlikely."

Bryan shook his head at his mate and his friend.

Tank chuffed. *Such silliness.*

Tank always thought of Max as being made up of

sharpness – high cheekbones and tilted flinty-blue eyes. He was all sharp cutting glances and sharp cutting words. Sharply dressed too, covering himself from throat to wrist to ankle. He was beautiful, but dangerous and fragile, like a sword made of cut glass.

They were at the front door.

Alec opened it before any of them had a chance to. Either he'd sensed the tethers of pack approaching, or he was heeding some Alpha premonition, or most likely he was heading out to his car because he forgot his laptop. Difficult to tell which, as Alec was equal parts Alpha power, wolf ability, and absent-minded professor.

Alec Frederiksen was a lean, almost delicate-looking man, the kind who seemed best suited to lab coats and sweater vests, although he was wearing a t-shirt and jeans at the moment. He had a sweet, open expression and the kindest hazel eyes you ever saw.

"Bryan?" He didn't even blink to find his brother naked on his threshold. "You and Max done for the day? How nice." He swung the door open, gesturing them inside. Bryan went to the coat closet in the hall where they kept extra bathrobes and pulled one on. For the sake of Trickle's non-existent sensibilities.

Max hesitated. Tank wondered if the Magistar would ever get over hating the big house, the bad memories even after all the remodeling. Finally, he shuffled inside.

Alec noticed Trickle. "Oh! Ms Trickle? Are we having a shindig tonight? I thought that was Sunday." He turned in confusion to his Beta. "Bry, it is Friday today, isn't it? I went to the lab earlier, I'm sure I did."

Since Alec could go on for a while in this vein, Trickle nipped it in the bud. "I dropped by unexpectedly, Alpha. My apologies. It's just that something interesting happened at work today and I thought you ought to know about it."

"Oh yes? You couldn't call?" Alec, confused, nevertheless gestured the kelpie into his den. Then suddenly his eyes sharpened and he tilted his neck back to stare up into the eyes of the taller woman. "I see. You *couldn't* call, could you? Phones might be bugged. This something to do with Max and Bryan?"

He paused. Frowning. "No, not Magistar. You brought it to *me*. A pack matter? Tell me, please."

Tank interrupted with a whine. Did Alec want him to stay or keep patrolling? He bumped against his Alpha's long legs, meekly seeking comfort and direction. Trickle was tense. His Alpha was tense. Max was tense. So Tank was now tense.

Bryan was not, but then, that that's why he was there. Beta. Bryan dropped a hand to his brother's bony shoulder and squeezed. The Alpha relaxed.

Tank whined again. *What do you want me to do?*

"Stay, Tank."

He let out a small breath of relief.

"Speak, kelpie." Alec's voice went hard. The true power of it wouldn't work on a non-werewolf, but the dominance was there. It said Alpha, and even a kelpie would listen to that.

"It can't be known to have come from me." She looked nervous.

Max shrugged. "I'll take the blame, if someone needs to." There were plenty of things a Magistar couldn't do. Like listen in on private government matters, but most people didn't know that. Including the government. If whatever Trickle told them got out, Max would just say he'd learned of it in some mysterious Magistar way. He'd wiggle his fingers in the air and look coy. They were welcome to try to come after him because of it.

Trickle let out a breath of relief. "Shifter Bureau of Investigation visited my department today."

Alec nodded, biting his lip.

Tank let out an involuntary whimper of worry. *Why was the SBI sniffing around?*

Bryan's hand was back on his brother's neck.

Alec pressed fingers to the top of Tank's head.

Tank instantly felt better.

Alec's voice was cool. "Trappers, huh? They were asking about werewolves?"

The kelpie nodded.

"Did they subpoena our pack records?"

Another nod.

"Should we expect a visit?"

Trickle shrugged.

"Do you know what they're after?"

The kelpie tilted her head. "Hard to tell with SBI. You know how they are."

"No, actually, I don't. Most werewolves avoid the government as much as possible. We paid our dues in the war. They generally don't ask much of us now, so long as each pack stays off law enforcement's radar."

"Thus SBI poking about makes you nervous."

"SBI makes everyone nervous."

Bryan said, "What are they like?"

Trickle shook her head. "Cagey. Private. Dangerous. You know, trappers."

Alec grimaced. "They trying to catch one of mine?"

"You know any other werewolves in the Bay Area?"

Alec took a breath. "Okay then. Thank you for telling me. We'll take it from here. Tank, round up anyone on patrol. Bryan, go fetch the others from their rooms. Pack meeting, now."

Tank was out the still open door before his Alpha ended the order.

Tank had never met SBI before. He'd never cross a trapper willingly. But just knowing they were sniffing around made him try to recall any possible wrongdoing that would bring the bureau to their door.

By the time he returned, Judd and Lovejoy in tow, the kelpie was gone and Alec was sitting in the den with the rest of the pack, looking grave.

Max paced the huge windows. Could be he was worried about SBI, could be he just didn't like being stuck inside his old house. The windows were new, floor-to-ceiling beauties that took advantage of the house's position on the top of an ocean-side hill, looking down over the San Francisco Bay. They'd been ridiculously pricy, and a bitch to install, but the resulting view was amazing.

Colin was the last to join them, back from school. He looked worried when he came in, finding the whole pack assembled. Perhaps he thought it was some kind of intervention.

Judd looked up at their youngest member, comforting him instinctively with relevant information. "SBI is sniffing around."

Colin's pretty face suffused with equal parts relief and a new worry. He dropped his backpack and sat next to his brother.

The living room of the pack house was modern and open plan, composed of a big round dining table and a state-of-the-art kitchen as well as den. The sunken sitting area around a massive fireplace was all comfortable scratch-resistant black leather couches (werewolves, after all) with outrageously bright throw pillows (that Marvin rotated regularly) and nubby blankets, cowhide rugs, and stainless steel tables. Alec liked things simple and comfortable. Marvin liked things contemporary and frothy. They compromised. The rest of the pack didn't care.

Tank, still in wolf form, as it was doubtful he'd have much to contribute to the conversation, curled up on the big hide that served instead of a carpet. He was happy to have his full pack around him, despite the reason.

Alec sat on the big couch with Bryan on one side and Marvin on the other. As was right and proper, Beta and Alpha-mate. Marvin was a merman, not a werewolf, but he was still pack. He smelled of salt and sea and fish, not unpleasant, because he also smelled of Alec, which meant home.

Max stopped pacing and sat behind Bryan, hip perched on the back of the couch, a hand on his mate's big shoulder. Quintessence wafted off both of them, a little acrid and slightly too sweet, but tempered by Bryan's own wolfness, which was earth-warm and forest-comforting.

The pack's second set of brothers, Colin and Kevin, sat on one of the little couches. Kevin was the stronger wolf with enforcer rank. He looked it too, bigger and bulkier than his younger brother. His hair was a darker red and his face more open and eager.

Tank curled at Judd's feet across from them. Judd was their other enforcer. A strong pack *always* had two. From where they sat, Tank and Judd could watch both Alec and the front door across the room, guarding. Judd could also keep an eye on Colin and pretend he wasn't. Lovejoy flopped next to Judd, eyes bright and interested. Very little upset him, even trappers.

"I need to know, gentlemen, if there is any reason SBI should be hunting us? Any reason at all, from before we moved here. I've never asked too closely about any of your histories." Alec glanced to Judd at that. "But now I must be prepared. Is one of you the reason they might be after us?"

Everyone tried not to look at Judd.

The enforcer shifted uncomfortably, running a hand over his close-shaved head in a nervous gesture.

Tank, Alec, Bryan, Kevin, Colin, and Lovejoy had all splintered off the same pack, the Boston Red Paws. They'd known each other, at least casually, since they were children. But Judd had been a loner, and he just *felt* so much older. Suspicion fell on him simply because he had more of a past, more possible reasons for the government to be after him.

Then again, they'd all spent time away from pack,

college years, or drop-out years, when they might have gotten up to no good. They all had reasons for leaving Boston, too – reasons that might come back to haunt them.

"Max and Marvin are exempt, of course," added Alec, into the silence.

"Why's that?" asked Colin, seeming annoyed by everyone giving Judd funny looks.

"The SBI asked DURPS for *werewolf* records."

Another long silence. No one admitted to anything.

"Well," said Lovejoy, nudging Tank with his foot. "At least we know it's not Tank."

"Oh yeah, why's that?" Kevin was willing to help him try to cheer everyone up.

"Couldn't get a gooder wolf."

"*Gooder* is not a word, numbnuts."

Tank let out a pathetic sigh – the long-suffering victim of their banter. *Yes, I'm boring.*

Everyone chuckled weakly.

Judd said, "Look, we all have mistakes in our pasts, even Tank the Paladin."

Tank slobbered on his foot.

Judd wiped his foot on Tank's furry stomach and continued. "But I doubt anything so major it would bring trappers down on us. Perhaps it's something simple? Or a case of mistaken identity? Or perhaps they're tracking a loner that strayed into our territory?"

They looked at each other.

"I haven't smelled anyone." Kevin had been the last to run a wide patrol.

Tank growled his agreement.

Bryan didn't speak often, and when he did he was careful with his words, measuring each one so as not to waste a syllable. "Bay Area is big."

Lovejoy followed his meaning. "Exactly. Our territory is mostly North Bay. Some loner could lurk down in Silicon Valley, or over in the Oakland Hills, and we'd know nothing about it."

Max threw up his hands up. "If none of you will admit to doing anything bad, then there's no use in speculating. Either SBI has the guts to come to our front door and ask directly, or they don't. Can't do anything about it until we know what they're really chasing."

Alec glanced over his shoulder at the mage. "I'm not saying we have to take action. This is me warning my pack that we must be on our guard. But also that I don't want any surprises."

They all looked at one another again.

Colin said, finally, "Could this be a setup? False accusations?"

Tank whined. He hadn't thought of that. They were an odd pack, for werewolves. Most of them gay, several in inter-species relationships. No doubt they made the higher-ups nervous. Especially with a Magistar pairing. It's possible someone in the government was gunning for them. Alec had moved them to the Bay Area because of its open acceptance. But that was local, SBI meant the feds were involved. The federal government was way less accepting.

Alec winced. "Fair point. Good thing we dotted all our i's and crossed all our t's with DURPS."

"And good thing we have a few of those paper-pushers on our side," said Max with the profound confidence of a man who'd once been one of those paper-pushers. They had friends in bureaucracy and that had to count for something. Trickle and Gladdy both still worked at DURPS.

Colin said, "Unless they decide it's a mark against us. Accuse us of bribery or something."

"Trust you to look on the dark side." His brother sighed.

Colin grimaced. "Just because they wear suits and flash badges doesn't mean they can't be bullies."

Everyone was staring at him. Colin flinched, realizing

how much he'd revealed, and then quickly added, "They aren't after me, I swear."

"Course not, pup," growled Judd.

Kevin gave his brother a pat. He stopped quickly. Colin didn't like to be touched too much. "What do you want us to do, then, Alpha?"

Trust Kev to bid for action.

Alec nodded at his enforcer. "Double up on patrols. Keep your noses open for loners in our territory. Each of us is to go about his normal life and business as if he were under surveillance, because we probably are. We've a hunt this Saturday." He looked at Colin. "Mandatory attendance for everyone, no excuses." He flicked his eyes to Max and Marvin. "That means you guys too. Just be home, stay safe, guard our backs. Nothing much more we can do, really. Just don't give them any excuses."

The pack all nodded. Even Max.

Alec turned to focus on the mage. "Don't do anything drastic, Max. We play it safe for now. You taking any major action, even if it's the right one, will only make us look defensive."

Max grimaced, but nodded. "You want me to lay any traps? Bryan and I can fix small enchantments now. And we've nothing else on our plate."

Alec considered. "Not yet. We'll keep our guard up the wolf way. If they come looking for werewolves, we give them model werewolves and model citizens."

The pack all nodded.

"Alright, boys, it's Friday night. Let's have some dinner and try to cheer up, then you can all fuck off and have fun."

They did all try.

Tank wasn't sure about the others, but his little gaming group had a pretty somber night of it. He lost his campaign to conquer the Empire and the bacon was overcooked.

CHAPTER FIVE
Packing Surprises

It was strange – the mountain demigod had been at Saucebox for only the one night and one yummy kiss, but Isaac ached with his absence.

Clara's grin was huge when he grumbled about facing up to a Friday with only one bouncer. "Missing your new tasty treat already?"

He distracted her by grabbing her hand and admiring the new manicure. "Oooo, sparkles!"

"I'm getting my disco diva on."

"Don't know why you bother. They only get chipped and covered in alcohol."

"Gels, sugar. They last *forever*. I'll take you some time."

Isaac wondered how nail polish would work on a werewolf. Not that he'd ever find out (even if he got gels, he never shifted). Sparkly nails on Tank? *Ooo, why is the idea of that huge buff dude with nail polish so very hot? Wouldn't it be cute to see a wolf with pink disco claws?*

He and Clara argued companionably about the relative sexiness of different nail colors and shapes, agreeing on very little except that a French was déclassé.

Isaac was preparing for his next counseling session

when something happened to throw his whole evening schedule off. Or more to the point, *someone* happened.

He heard her before he saw her.

"Isaac, darling! I neeeeeeed you."

Lavish Wellington strode across the dance floor in heels so high any other person would have had to mince. Not Lavish, of course. Lavish never wore anything she couldn't kick ass in.

"And I'm here for you, babydoll." Isaac came around the end of the bar and opened his arms.

Lavish flew into them.

"Why does she so clearly love you more than me?" wondered Xavier, walking up.

Lavish looked coyly at her boyfriend. "Because it's Isaac. Everyone loves Isaac more than you, darling. Isaac, hon, I had the *worst* week. I must tell you *all* about it."

Isaac knew what to do. He extracted himself carefully and went to make her a kir royale with an orange twist and a maraschino cherry.

He placed it in front of her as she assumed a stool. "Tell me all about it, sweetheart. Xavier, give us twenty minutes."

His boss rolled his eyes. "But we have reservations."

"So you'll be late. You probably own the place."

Xavier shrugged. "No, but I'm thinking about buying it, so they'll wait. You girls have fun. I'll go do some paperwork or something." He kissed Lavish fondly, careful not to muss her makeup, and then drifted away like a good boyfriend.

Lavish smiled after him. "I do adore that man."

Isaac chuckled. "And he adores you. Now tell me."

Lavish began to wax eloquent, almost poetic in her ire, concerning her clients, her co-workers, and the barista across the street. Isaac made sympathetic noises in all the right places.

Lavish was a high-powered lawyer of some pricey

corporate ilk. She was, in fact, exactly the opposite of Xavier's normal type of girlfriend. Except her height. (Xavier liked women tall enough for him to require a stepladder.) For one thing, she was brilliant, and for another, she had more clout than he did in certain circles. These things made Xavier uncomfortable, and made Lavish last longer than any of his other lady friends.

Eventually, Lavish (unburdened, relaxed, and three royales sweeter) set off with Xavier to some hugely expensive meal.

The shifter whom Isaac was supposed to be counseling, a lean sweet-faced vanara who worked tech and had come all the way up from Silicon Valley, waited patiently. Isaac turned to him with an apologetic smile.

"Boss's girlfriend," he explained. "What can I get you?"

"A local stout, whatever you recommend, and some good advice."

"Well, I can vouch for the beer, but the advice is less reliable." Isaac, served the shifter his stout, and readied himself for a session. *Open and friendly expression, check. Calming energy pushed out, check. Sympathetic ear, engaged.*

"That's not what I hear." The man was stiff about the shoulders, twitchy, uncomfortable but not emotionally overwrought. Not a romantic problem, then.

"So, what's troubling you?" Isaac's evening officially began.

The vanara was not too bad off. He was having a hard time socializing at a new job, kept wanting to stroke his coworker's heads and stuff like that. Isaac recommended relaxing at a shifter spa for help with tension, and suggested a few social tactics for better fitting in with humans – baking some nice banana bread for his team that kind of thing.

Clara nudged Isaac's shoulder as the man left, steps

light. "Another happy customer. And cute."

Isaac smiled. "Oh, you know me, just trying to help."

"Yeah, but no one ever listens to *your* problems?"

"Moi? I don't have any problems."

"Uh huh. You mean, you don't wanna share them. It's fine. Keep your secrets." But she was clearly a little hurt.

Isaac yearned to console her. Of course he did. It was what he was. His wolf ached to nudge up against her. But Isaac was strong enough to resist his own nature, especially if yielding meant exposing his past. No one could be trusted with that, even Clara, whom he genuinely liked.

Gladdy came mincing in then. The kitsune didn't have an appointment. She was visiting Saucebox for a drink with the girls, nothing to do with Isaac. Still, she looked a bit subdued so he checked in with her while he poured her an Omnivores Forever shot.

"What's up, buttercup?"

Gladdy sipped the tiny drink. "Had a lover named Buttercup once. Pretty little thing."

"Rough day at work?"

"Oh, you know DURPS. Paper-pushing. The usual."

"Why so down, then?"

"My boss was weird all afternoon. Something happened this morning. Some visitors or whatever from higher up the food chain put her in a crap mood."

"Your boss is a kelpie, right?"

"Uh huh. And I know they're always pretty grumpy, but she was different today – like, *seriously* worried. I'm hoping we don't have layoffs coming or something like that."

"I doubt it's that bad. You know kelpies. Plus, you'll be fine. You've been there for decades."

Gladdy nodded, finished her drink, and ordered another.

"Those your friends there?" Isaac passed it to her and nodded toward the door where a small, noisy group of mixed female shifters and humans wandered in.

Gladdy brightened and went to join them.

Isaac wished his job was always so easy.

He only had the early shift that night. He was off at midnight, leaving Clara and the third bartender, Lance, on for the rest of the evening.

The city was alive and buzzing when he hit the street. He should have been more alert, kept his nose in form, because Hayden got the jump on him and he ought to have smelled him coming.

The barghest slammed into Isaac and shoved him up against the wall in a side alley with that speed all shifters have, especially the bigger predators. Isaac's wolf reacted, but sluggishly. Stupid creature was pining for something.

Hayden was up against Isaac before he could blink. The barghest used all his muscles to hold Isaac captive, trying to mark him, first by rubbing his mouth against Isaac's cheek and neck, but then his teeth flashed. Not canines, thank fuck, the man was no Alpha to have a third form, but still the claiming intent was there. Isaac was having none of it. He was still a werewolf, and while he may not rank, he bet that his wolf was just as big as Hayden's dog.

His wolf perked up and growled. Too little, too late. Isaac internally cursed at him to shut it. His human side was perfectly capable of handling this.

Instead of shifting, Isaac brought his knee up as hard as he could. It was the only leverage he had. Hayden cried out, doubled over, and dropped back. Isaac brought his other knee up into the man's nose hard enough to break it.

The guy was a shifter. It'd heal easily enough, but it'd heal faster if he shifted and instinct would tell him that. Clearly, he wasn't as good at controlling his beast as Isaac. Plus, full moon was tomorrow night. He succumbed to the urge.

The barghest shifted right there in the street. A profound indecency, what with no major threat and it being

Friday night in San Francisco, full of raucous humans.

Isaac didn't shift himself. It was ingrained in him to clamp down on his wolf and suppress the need that came along with the threat of a fully formed black dog. A lifetime of training and discipline kept him human. It was as if he had no other form at all.

His beast stirred, wanting to be free, to take over, to eat his humanity. His wolf was becoming a problem. It seemed that the less Isaac shifted, the more difficult it became to dumb down the creature within, as if his human form had forgotten what his wolf felt like and wanted to revisit it. It hurt worse than anything to hold back. It hurt more to stifle his shift than it did to actually give in to it.

But even stifled, Isaac was still a werewolf, and faster than any human could be on two legs. He was also built like a runner, long and lean with a big stride. So he took off.

The black dog chased him, of course, but Isaac was faster. To run was to encourage the hunt, but Isaac hadn't any other option. The club was closer. He might have gone back, but instinct drove him home. His wolf took over what he could. Isaac's brain clouded with fear and instinct, driving him downhill toward his lonely den and his shabby apartment.

He ran, missing the comfort of Tank's big form. Wondering at any moment if the big werewolf would step out of the shadows and rescue him. He snorted at his own idiocy.

Like some white knight.

Like some pack mate.

Like some mate.

Isaac made it, just. He fumbled with the stupid lock, but was inside and slamming the gate behind him in time.

The barghest hit it hard. A huge shaggy black creature, part wolfhound, part monster, teeth like a hyena, breath like a cesspool. The gate dented and rattled. Isaac feared for its survival. But it held. It was one of the reasons Isaac rented that particular apartment.

Isaac didn't stay to see if it would continue to hold. He ran the steps up to the front door, and was through and slamming it shut behind him. Up the stairs, he crashed into his third-floor apartment. It was empty of all his human roommates – Friday night, after all. With that door triple-locked behind him, then his bedroom door dead-bolted, Isaac dove into bed. He was fully clothed and covered in spilled drinks and street grime. But safe. One more night, safe, and still human. Or human enough to pass.

The San Andreas pack was tense all Saturday. Fortunately, nothing out of the ordinary happened to justify it. The SBI never appeared on their doorstep to arrest anyone. No one was found while running perimeter. The pack was safe.

The full moon hunt that night was subdued, especially when compared to their normal monthly jaunts which had a tendency to be bouncy and joyful. Still the pack brought down a beautiful buck. It was, at least, a successful hunt. The wolves took pride in their abilities.

Max and Marvin met them outside as they returned in the early morning. The mates didn't often stay awake to greet them, but tonight they felt the need. On full moons, the mage and the merman usually hung out at Max's place, drinking white wine and eating smoked salmon frittatas and binge-watching *Scotland's Next Top Alpha* (arguing about whose kilt was the longest) until one or both fell asleep.

They'd formed an odd friendship – the aggressively cheerful merman and the prickly mage, but a friendship nonetheless. Tank thought it a very *good thing*. Marvin reminded Max that there were joys in life, and Max reminded Marvin that there were losses. Full moon, when they were inevitably left behind, was a time for sympathy and bonding. No doubt they complained about too much body hair in the shower drain, and *how come every meal had to include red meat?* It was a mark of concern that tonight the two hadn't drunk themselves into silliness and slumber. Even they had felt the need to stay alert and on guard.

Bryan ran to his mate and pressed against his legs. Max leaned over and ran his hands reverently through the thick cream-colored fur.

Alec was a little more coy, but no less pleased to find his merman waiting up for him. A quick sniff-check to ensure Marvin was safe, and then a simple head-butt of love, while the merman fondled Alec's silky ears.

Tank felt a pang of loneliness, for there was no one waiting for him. In that moment, what he wanted more than anything was to run the bridge into San Francisco, to the worst part of the Mission, to check if the man without a smell had made it home safely. But that was a silly idea. There was nothing special about Tank, no reason for particular affection or regard, no reason for anyone to be waiting, or expecting him to check on them.

Tank shook off his melancholy, taking comfort in the rest of his pack around him, the fact that both the mates were safe and untroubled by SBI, and the pleasing thought of a barbecue with friends tomorrow.

His bed, when he sought it, was big and empty. So he stayed in wolf form, nose to tail, and let his dreams be of gray eyes, because he was a wolf who knew no better and might be excused some measure of yearning for the impossible.

Isaac pretended to be sick on Saturday night. This always happened when full moon fell on a work night. Xavier, thank god, had never put the two together. His best bartender was mysteriously ill about once a month or so, and Xavier only grumbled about scheduling.

He could suspect PMS, I suppose.

Xavier was annoyed by the inconvenience, of course, but not as much as he might have been on an ordinary Saturday night. Because full moon meant Saucebox's shifter customers were mostly elsewhere. Some because they wanted to be, others because they must be. For supernatural creatures, full moon wasn't a night for drinking and dancing (not at a club in San Francisco, at least).

Isaac spent full moon as he had every one for as long as he could remember. Barricaded in his room, desk up against the door, dresser pushed in front of the window, just in case. He had a bag of greasy junk food and a pile of meaty snacks. The cravings could get bad. Beef jerky was a godsend.

Isaac hated the full moon. Hated its call. No matter what he did, his body was wracked with chills as though in a deep fever. He was also super clumsy, like his hands were actually paws. His bones shook and his joints ached with a need he refused to satisfy. His wolf, trapped deep inside, howled with the pain of it. Both of them were miserable.

Sunday's barbecue was definitely *not* a quiet, unassuming affair. Frankly, gatherings involving werewolves rarely were. Luckily, Alec anticipated this from the start, so when the Pack had their first post-moon roast, they invited *all* the neighbors.

The neighbors, mostly out of curiosity, had all attended. Now the San Andreas Pack hosted Sausalito's version of an unofficial block party once a month. Of course there was Mitch, who left passive aggressive notes on their motorcycles and pretended he never got the invitations. He also liked to run the leaf blower first thing in the morning. But every neighborhood has to have a Mitch – it's basically a requirement amongst humans.

People began to trickle in at about five in the afternoon and just kept coming. Gladdy brought her entire leash, a motley yet cheerful assortment of friends and lovers and mashie nibblers (as she called the more esoteric of her relationships). Most among her retinue were human, although there were a few of the smaller shifters as well. They all tended toward bright clear eyes, t-shirts with hand-stenciled slogans, and questionable haircuts.

Gladdy shook them all off and went directly up to Alec, where he sat sipping a beer and chatting politely with Dr Werstmeizer (three houses down on the left) about concerns growing pit fruit in a coastal environment. Gladdy always said hello to Alec first. She was not (absolutely *not*) doing this to show Alpha respect. As she was fond of reminding them, foxes didn't have Alphas. No, she did it because she usually had a burr in her tail about something.

Tank was lurking nearby purely by chance, and he sidled over to listen in. Gladdy in a tizzy was always entertaining.

"Alec, darling, handsomest of werewolves, smartest of biologists."

"Hello, Gladiola, my dear. What do you want?"

They embraced briefly. Alec didn't have to stand, the lawn chair put him at the perfect height. The Alpha even permitted a tiny neck nuzzle from the kitsune. It was a great courtesy and she was clearly thrilled by the honor. He let her scent him! Not much, but enough for her to know she had attained rank in his eyes. Kitsune and werewolf were different in many ways, but not every way.

She got straight to the point, a novel approach for Gladdy. Tank suspected she was a little intimidated by

Alec's scent. Which was likely why Alec had permitted her nuzzle in the first place. Alec was crafty with his power.

"I want Colin to meet this friend of mine in the city. May I borrow him next week?"

Alec shook his head in confusion. "Colin is perfectly capable of deciding this for himself."

Gladdy went wide-eyed in feigned innocence. She tossed a lock of hair (green today). "But it's a *school* night."

Alec snorted. "It's college. He can do as he pleases. You persuade him, if you can."

"But I should like to know I have your blessing to try."

"What's wrong with this friend that this is such a danger?"

"Nothing! It's just Colin is so shy and difficult to socialize."

Tank shuddered internally. Imagine being set up on a blind date by a kitsune.

Alec nodded. "It'd be good if he got out more. Do you want me to chaperone?"

Tank muffled a laugh just imagining it. *Poor Colin!*

Gladdy's eyes widened. "Uh, no. I don't think that's necessary. I just don't want him to use you or pack duty as an excuse."

Alec laughed. "Oh, you know that boy too well. Fine, if you get his promise, I won't let him cop out."

Tank saw Judd, who was also eavesdropping, swallow hard. The enforcer suddenly seemed to find rotating the deer on the spit a vitally important duty.

Gladdy trotted off to find Colin, her posture battle-ready. Tank pitied the poor kid, he didn't stand a chance. He was about to be set up on a blind date whether he liked it or not, that was one determined vixen.

Tank went back to ambling about the gathering.

Those of the pack who were dating had invited dates. Tank felt a bit like a loser as a result and was trying not to sulk. Until it turned out that Kevin had accidentally invited two (who didn't know about each other). This caused a scene, food was hurled. Marvin got tetchy about senseless waste, the two ladies stormed out arm-in-arm, and Kevin ended up joining Tank in the losers' corner.

"That was one of your finer moments." Tank bumped the enforcer's shoulder with his.

Kevin sighed. "Sometimes I can't decide if it would be better if I were gay, poly, or perennially single. No, don't answer that, Solo Sucker. Your opinion doesn't count."

Marvin overheard and perked up. "Oooo, pick gay!" He batted his baby blues at Kevin. Well, baby *turquoises*, to be perfectly descriptive.

Kevin rolled his own green eyes in response.

Marvin was not to be thwarted in his effort to gay-i-fy the universe. "Everyone is doing it!"

Judd came over, grinning, an unexpected brightening of his normally somber face. "Yeah, Kev, join us."

"Come to the dude side – we have cock?" suggested Tank, as a slogan.

Trickle appeared at that juncture, apparently tired of Pepper and Lovejoy's perennial food truck conversation. "What are you boys giggling about?"

Marvin fluttered his eyelashes at her. "Cock, of course."

"Always good for a laugh," she agreed, sipping her wheat-grass soda.

Kevin gave her a desperate look. "Save me, lesbian, you're my only hope."

"Whatcha need, straight boy?"

"Wise words of wisdom from one who knows all."

"Two fingers, darling. Two."

Kevin propped his chin on his hand. "Tell me more."

"What?" Marvin wasn't following until Tank made a rude gesture. "Oh. Yech. Never liked oysters myself. What about you, Tank?"

The pack was generally obsessed with sussing out Tank's sexual orientation. Marvin in particular. Tank never felt right saying, "Sexual preference? Strong personality." So in answer he said, "Big fan of oysters and mussels myself, event the occasional scallop."

Marvin blinked at him, lost on the tide of metaphor.

So the banter continued for most of the afternoon and well into evening. The crowd thinned and evolved as some went home and others arrived – mostly those shifters who preferred to wait until after sunset and those humans who had no sense of punctuality.

Mana was one of the nighttime folk. By the time the drag queen of their hearts showed up, most of the venison had been stripped away. Lovejoy had saved her a chunk of the liver, of course. Because he was madly in love with her and everyone knows the organs are the best part.

Mana rewarded him by eating it all, then cupping his cheek with her small hand, staring up into his eyes, and whispering words that caused him to blush beet red and sit down abruptly.

Tank could not help but wonder if Isaac ate liver. Would it be weird to show up at the bar with an offering of barbecued organs? Yeah, it probably would be weird by human standards. Besides, none of the good bits were left.

"Looks like Mana thinks Lovejoy hung the moon," commented Max, noticing Tank's obvious envy.

"With his dick," added Marvin.

"Off his dick," countered Max, who was never one to let anyone be more crass than him.

Tank ignored them both and went to clean up the remainder of the potluck offerings.

The omnivore shifters had learned early on that a werewolf gathering was not to be trusted on the subject of vegetables. Gladdy and her crew always came with vegans in tow. They lived in the East Bay, after all. But it meant lots of bowls of grains, and grasses, and garbanzos and such. Vegetables were messy.

Tank didn't mind, but most werewolves found vegans innately suspicious. It had taken the pack a while to accept that the kitsune came bearing tofu. Tofu was not to be trusted on principal.

Anyway, it had kinda become Tank's duty to make sure everyone was reunited with their dishware before they left the party.

As things died down, Judd got their fire pit crackling cheerfully (this time without the spit over it). By ten it was just the San Andreas Pack and associated lovers left, settled around the fire in an intimate circle. Marvin sat on Alec's lap. Max nested close to Bryan. Mana leaned against Lovejoy. Even Colin had, cautiously, angled toward Judd. Everyone had paired off. Except Kev, of course, but that was his own dumb fault.

Mana and Marvin seemed to be engaged in a protracted attempt to persuade Colin he must visit a spa with them.

"This new shifter-specialty one opened up in Japan Town," Mana was saying. Tank had never seen her so excited about anything. "It's heaven! One side is purely for your human form, Korean style. They just scrub the top layer of skin right off your body."

Everyone listening grimaced except Lovejoy, who looked intrigued.

Marvin nodded enthusiastically. "I emerged... reborn. The other half of the spa is all about animal beauty. If your supernatural form has hair, they do the best fluff and blow!"

Max gave a funny startled cough.

Alec said mildly, "Babe, I don't think that term means what you think it means."

But Marvin was on a roll. "You should have *seen* Mana's coat. So glossy. And her tail was this massive puffiest of puffs!"

Mana preened. "Thank you, darling. I do like to be the

puffiest."

"I don't think *I've* ever seen Mana's coat," objected Lovejoy.

"What kinda fox are you, anyway?" Max was permitted the faux pas of asking about second form (he was human, after all, and didn't know better).

Mana arched one perfectly manicured brow. "Arctic, of course."

The group laughed. Tank thought it suited perfectly. Mana was bigger than the other kitsune he'd met, older, and likely with more tails. He could see her as a white fox, the rarer larger kind that traced its lineage back to China.

Marvin continued, "They did this buff and shine on my tail. I mean, my scales were polished to perfection. I swear, I've never felt so pampered. Colin you just *have* to come with us next time."

"Why me?" wailed Colin.

"Cause you're the prettiest," said Max with confidence.

"I'll go," said Lovejoy.

Mana patted him, "Of course you will, honey."

Tank and Kevin exchanged looks. This was so not their scene.

"Run?" suggested the enforcer.

"Please."

Kevin cleared his throat and announced to the cozy circle. "Hey, Alpha! Monster Truck here and I are gonna run the perimeter, if you're okay for a bit?"

Alec waved them off merrily.

They went to the big house to strip.

"I'll take the backyard and parklands, I need the exercise. If you'd stick closer to the front?"

Tank would rather it was the other way around but Kevin outranked him. The incident earlier when both girlfriends had un-girlfriended themselves seemed to have affected Kevin more than he let on. Well, Tank was equal opportunity, but he did find women more stressful as a rule. Not that he'd ever do two of anything at once – he liked to focus.

"You doing okay?" Tank pulled his shirt off, annoyed to find he'd dripped something greasy on it at some point that night. *What a slob. I can't even eat properly.*

"I guess. You know, I actually really liked Tiffany. Amazing tits."

Tank snorted. "Fine, no sympathy from me. Go sulk in your heterosexual man funk."

Kevin said with dignity, "I will. I guess you've decided you aren't one of us, then?"

Tank said, "Wasn't a decision."

"Well, yeah, I know that. I'm not totally insensitive. It's just we speculated, you know, bi or something. Because you never have much to say on the subject."

Tank raised both eyebrows. "Never have much to do on it, either."

"Well, you never talk about *anything*."

"I'm not as fascinated by discussing my sex life as the rest of you bozos."

"Fair point. You also never seem to date anyone."

"Perhaps I just don't invite them home because then they might meet each other and start screaming and pulling hair and shit... oh, wait, that's you."

"Touchy fucker, aren't you?"

"Go run, Kevin. I'll take vanguard."

Kev went suddenly serious. He was, after all, an enforcer. "You'll keep them safe?"

"Judd is *right* there."

"He's distracted."

Tank sighed. He was naked now and getting cold. He wanted to shift. "Yes, Enforcer, I will keep them safe." It was a vow to his pack superior. *Hold the line, defense. Pack protector, throw yourself on the grenade.* Then he shifted and left Kevin in a tangle of his own clothing.

The group by the fire waved as Tank's massive dark

form ghosted by them toward the driveway. Tank ached with longing and pride and love for them all. *Mine. Theirs. Pack.* Then he sped away, because it was also overwhelming.

Chapter Six
Rejection on the Side

Isaac slept most of Sunday. The full moon left him feeling like his skin was stretched too tight over his bones. He returned to Saucebox that evening, looking just as ill as he'd claimed he'd been. Clara sent him home early because the bar really didn't need two of them on a slow Sunday night.

Monday and Tuesday were Isaac's nights off.

Wednesday, Hayden tried to approach him inside the club again. Oscar was alone on the door and the barghest managed to slip past him. Oscar was a good bouncer, but no match one-on-one to a determined black dog. However, the barghest picked the wrong evening, because Isaac was deep in a counseling session and his patient was not at all patient about being interrupted.

Isaac's Wednesday regular was a berserker with woman troubles. Isaac had been seeing Kettil since the beginning, and managed to help him quite a bit in the romance arena. Kettil liked him, in the manner that bear shifters can *like*, which is kinda gruff and mixed with mild disinterest.

When Hayden interrupted the session, Kettil turned the full force of four hundred pounds of bear shifter on the black dog, crossed his huge forearms, and glared.

Hayden slunk off, cowed.

"He giving you trouble?" Kettil asked.

"A bit."

"Want me to take him in? He banned?" Kettil also happened to be in the shifter branch of the SFPD. Quite a few of the local bear shifters were, since the police actively recruited berserkers. They made decent beat cops, given the right incentives. (Limited exposure to bicyclists, regular bakery rounds, and absolutely no bocce ball. Bear shifters had weird pet peeves.)

Xavier showed up then, looking more grim than ever. "Yep, he's banned, and I'll press charges for harassing my staff."

"He touch you?" Kettil narrowed his eyes at Isaac.

Isaac grimaced. The last thing he needed was some kind of legal trial. Xavier, no doubt, kept a string of sleazy lawyers on retainer, but Isaac's past couldn't take that level of scrutiny. "Not in front of witnesses."

Kettil growled. "Pity. Don't matter much. If he's still hanging about after I'm done with you, I'll haul him in just to scare him a bit."

Isaac bit his lower lip. "I don't think that's necessary."

Xavier's eyes gleamed. "Well, I'd appreciate it."

Kettil eyed Xavier's tattoos suspiciously.

Xavier gave him a shrug.

Isaac suspected that not all of Xavier's deals were on the right side of the law, but his boss played everything close, and in the matter of Isaac's safety, apparently Xavier and the cop were in agreement. Because Kettil gave his boss a curt nod.

Xavier added, "We got extra muscle returning to the door tomorrow. I might try to bring him in most nights that Isaac is on. If this continues."

Tank, thought Isaac, not pleased by the joy and relief that suffused his body. *He's thinking about hiring Tank for regular shifts.*

His wolf rumbled in pleasure.

Isaac was compelled to protest. "I don't need a fucking bodyguard."

Xavier ignored him and explained to the berserker, "Been getting more and more shifters in here since I did that mixer."

Kettil grunted. "Started before that. Since you hired this one." He pointed at Isaac with his thumb.

"True that. So I think a shifter on the door with Oscar might be good for business, as well as safety."

Kettil nodded. "Agreed. You getting one of my kind?"

"Naw, all the best berserkers are on the force. Off-duty cops are way too expensive."

Kettil only grunted again.

"I got me this werewolf I like."

Kettil nodded, looking thoughtful. "One of that new San Andreas Pack?"

Wait a second, Isaac blanked out, *pack?*

"Yes indeed. Name's Tank."

So Tank's not a loner, he comes with family attached. I really should think about moving. Last thing I need sniffing around me is an Alpha.

His wolf whimpered, either in need or fear.

Kettil nodded. "I've not heard of him, but in my line of work that's a good thing. That pack's got a decent reputation, and werewolf is a good choice for a bouncer."

Xavier puffed up, pleased by the praise. "Well, I'll leave you to it, then. If I want him more than just Thursdays, I got some negotiating to do."

Isaac felt he should protest further. It seemed like Xavier was bringing in Tank mainly to act as Isaac's protector, which seemed a huge waste of money, but Xavier was already gone. Kettil looked at him expectantly.

"So, what exactly did she say when she dumped you?" Isaac asked, getting back to the big man's dating issues.

Alec stopped Tank as he was heading out the door into the city for his bouncer gig on Thursday.

"He wants you regular."

"Yeah, I know, every Thursday."

"Yeah, no. Now he wants you five days a week."

Tank grimaced.

Alec looked sympathetic. "I know, bouncing isn't really your thing. I offered him Judd or Kevin. But the owner's a prick and specifically demanded you."

"Because I'm familiar and didn't fuck up last time."

Alec frowned. "What happened last time?"

"Nothing out of the ordinary. One of the bartenders is real popular, got himself a bit of a stalker problem."

"Shifter or human?"

"Human bartender, shifter stalker."

Alec nodded. "That might be why they want you more frequently. I take it their regular bouncer is a human?"

Tank inclined his head.

Alec sighed. "You're not complaining as much as I thought you would."

This way I get to see Isaac, walk him home, keep him safe. "It's not like I got anything better to do," was what Tank said to his Alpha. "Plus, we want to finish the deck and buy those chairs Marvin's been cooing over. Extra income can't hurt."

Alec shook his head, smiling. "How did I get so lucky with you, Tank? Such an easygoing dude."

Tank smiled at the praise and at the pain, because *easygoing* was code for *dull*.

Kevin came wandering into the hallway at that juncture, scratching his naked chest. "Someone has to make up for the rest of us assholes."

"Too true," agreed Lovejoy, also joining them. Lovejoy was dressed for a date. Which meant his jeans were too tight, his shirt was unbuttoned too low, and there was too much gel in his hair. He was also wearing a gold chain and multiple rings. Lovejoy was not gay, but he was Italian. His current squeeze being a kitsune drag queen of diminutive stature and epically stylish proportions, he'd taken to putting in maximum effort for their dates. This generally seared eyeballs and amused everyone. Except said drag queen, who ordered Lovejoy around something fierce and was weirdly delighted by his Guido tendencies.

"Where you taking Our Lady of the Perpetual Feather Boa this evening?" Tank asked, hoping the couple was not intending to attend the mixer at Saucebox. He wanted to keep Isaac to himself for just a little longer. Admittedly, he was sharing the man with half the shifter population of the Bay Area, but sharing with pack was different.

"North Beach stand-up comedy thingy. Should be fun. Then a late dinner and a walk through the city."

"Very romantic," approved Kevin with a not-so-subtle shoulder nudge.

Lovejoy glared at him. "And what if it is?"

Kev held both hands up in a warding position.

Tank cleared his throat. "I'd best be off."

"You're okay with a five-night commitment for a while?" Alec had to be certain. It was his business to make his pack happy. Solvent, but *also* happy.

Tank nodded. "It'll do for now. We'll introduce Xavier to the idea of Kevin or Judd gradually, then maybe make the switch."

"What are you doing with the idea of me gradually?" Kevin wanted to know.

Alec explained. "Tank took that bouncer gig last week and the club owner loves him, demanded him back this week, and now wants him on a full schedule for the foreseeable future. Apparently, the club is having shifter issues."

"Why does everyone always like Tank best?" Kevin

flopped back onto one of the couches with an exaggerated sigh.

"Until they meet Bryan," amended Tank.

"True," acknowledged Kevin.

"Until they meet Marvin," added Lovejoy.

Alec smiled fondly at the mere thought of his mate. "True."

Everyone liked Marvin – he was just so pretty, and nosy, and bossy, and sweet.

"So what you're saying, really, is no one likes me best?" Tank made a face at them.

"They do when compared to me or Judd." Kevin would not let it go.

Alec snorted softly. "You're enforcers. You aren't meant to be liked. You're meant to be feared."

Kevin grinned. "Oh well, when you put it that way, grrrr arrrrr."

Tank patted him on the head. "Yes, dear, very fierce. Can I please leave now? I'm gonna be late."

"Go on with you," said the Alpha. "I'll draw up a short-term contract, say three months on this schedule? That work?"

Tank nodded. He was a little slow on the uptake, and a little slow on the take down, but three months had to be enough time to seduce a human bartender. *Or have him seduce me. Right?*

The Thursday mixer got started a lot earlier than they expected. Apparently, word was officially *out*. Xavier was delighted. But by nine that evening Isaac and Clara were already exhausted. They hadn't psyched themselves up like they would on a weekend. They should have. It was almost as busy as a Saturday.

Isaac slapped three shot glasses of high quality garum

in front of a school of mermaids, then tilted his head toward the party of human tech-bros responsible. The ladies speared the bros with blue, turquoise, and teal expressions of mild interest. They downed the fermented fish sauce, then ordered Pearl of the Sea cocktails charged to those self-same bros and went to join them.

Isaac shook his head, *suckers*. He began to mix the cocktails. Rum, anchovy syrup, clam juice, finished with a splash of Worcestershire sauce, and a pickled onion wrapped in nori for garnish. He carried the cocktails down to the now raucous party, along with three more IPAs for the human males.

"You be careful now, gentlemen," he cautioned, knowing the men would entirely ignore his warning. The mermaids reached for their cocktails, eyes gleaming.

Isaac wasn't sure how he knew that Tank had arrived, but he did. There was just this sense of safety suddenly washing over the club. His wolf, jittery since last night, quieted inside him. The bar, usually such a heaven of fun and productivity, had become a risk since Hayden fixated on him. But knowing Tank was here not only calmed his wolf, it made his human side less worried too.

Isaac looked through the animated crowd of sycophantic humans fawning over supernatural creatures – *the very definition,* thought Isaac, *of lambs to the slaughter*. And there Tank stood, Isaac's favorite werewolf. Well, Isaac's *only* werewolf.

Man, I'm acting just like a dumb human. For here Isaac stood, wildly attracted to the very thing most dangerous to his fragile, stupid little life, not to mention his well-constructed facade.

Warm chocolate eyes twinkled at him from the doorway. Isaac was desperate for Tank to come inside and swing by the bar and check in with him.

But Tank only nodded and resumed door duties.

Isaac was fluttery as a teen knowing the big man must

come visit at some point that night.

"Hey there, handsome!" said a familiar voice instead. Gladiola's small form popped onto a barstool that was mysteriously suddenly vacant.

Isaac smiled at her, automatically reaching for a shot glass to serve her favorite drink.

Then he smelled it.

Werewolf.

His head came up sharply and he looked not at Gladdy, but at the young man she was tugging along behind her.

The kid was tall – well most werewolves were bigger than humans. Even Isaac was over six feet. But this one didn't really look like any werewolf Isaac had ever met before.

The boy was just that, still a boy. Isaac didn't osmose this information from his appearance alone. It was hard to tell age with werewolves, who mostly stopped aging once they were bitten. No, he got *boy* from the look in the kid's eyes. There was nothing jaded or old there, just sadness.

If he hadn't smelled like shifter, Isaac would have carded the kid.

Oh right. I'm supposed to be a human. Smell doesn't count.

He asked for the kid's ID.

The driver's license put Colin Mangnall at only twenty years old and from Boston, so when Isaac handed it back he said, "You can have a soda, if you like."

The werewolf's lips curled, as might be expected. Wolves weren't wild about carbonation.

"Glass of milk would be fine," said Colin the boy-wolf. He had a nice melodic tenor and a quiet unassuming attitude. Isaac had thought Tank mild-mannered for a werewolf, this kid was practically self-effacing. Which is when Isaac figured out why Gladdy had brought Colin in to visit him.

Potential new client.

There's something wrong with him and Gladdy wants me to provide counsel. To a werewolf.

Isaac handed Colin a glass of milk and nudged Gladdy's drink closer.

"So?" he said, trying not to sound harsh.

Nevertheless, the boy flinched.

Colin really was a pretty thing. Fair-skinned, puffy-lipped, and blond – at least Isaac thought blond at first in the dim lights of the club. But with the smattering of freckles across his nose, he might be a strawberry blond. *Cute.* Not Isaac's type, he liked his men more… mountainous, but he could see the appeal. Although he was a little young for Gladdy's leash.

"This is a friend of mine, Colin. I brought him to meet you." So, not one of her leash, just a friend – if he were a lover, she'd own to it.

Colin blinked at Isaac, as if he too didn't quite understand what he was doing there. Or it might be the slight drugging effect Isaac had on eighty percent of shifters, especially werewolves. Well, most every werewolf he'd met until Tank.

If memory served from last Thursday, Tank belonged to the ten percent of shifters who wanted to screw Isaac. The final ten percent usually wanted Isaac dead.

Or that's how Isaac calculated it.

As neither Isaac nor Colin said anything, Gladdy opened negotiations. "Colin here is a werewolf and university student. He's a good pup. Part of Tank's pack."

The boy brightened notably. "Oh! You know Tank?"

Isaac nodded. "He worked the door last week, good sort."

Colin nodded. "Easy to be around."

"Why is that, do you think?"

The werewolf fiddled with his glass. "I don't know. I mean, I guess because he doesn't ask anything of me."

"But the others do? Your Alpha?" Isaac couldn't stop

himself from being what he was, from trying to help.

"He wants me better."

"You've been sick?"

"Not really. Weak, I guess. Pathetic, more like."

Isaac let that slide for the time being. "You aren't living up to their expectations?"

"I don't like shifting all that much."

I hear you, kiddo. "And the pack sees this as a flaw?"

"They don't think it's healthy." The boy paused, blinking as if he was emerging from swimming underwater. "Hey, why am I telling you this?"

"I'm easy to talk to."

"But I don't *talk* to anyone."

Gladdy, who'd been sitting back and watching the whole exchange with her mouth slightly open, said, "He really doesn't. This is the most I've ever heard him speak."

Unfortunately, reminding Colin of her presence had the immediate effect of clamming the boy back up. It also reminded Isaac that despite how instinctually he slid into trying to help, especially a werewolf in pain, he couldn't do it. Not for a pack member. Flirting with Tank was mildly idiotic. But counseling a werewolf was stupid in the extreme.

Isaac flinched away. He'd been doing that thing where he leaned over the bar, giving the young man the full force of his attention, cradling him with his gaze, helping him by becoming a vessel of utter acknowledgement of his existence.

The boy sensed his withdrawal and a flash of pain crossed his beautiful face.

Isaac sighed. Angry with himself. "Drink your milk, kid. Gladdy, a word?"

Gladdy slid off the stool and pushed her way through the crowd, meeting Isaac at the end of the bar.

Isaac lifted up the gate, walked through and crouched down to her level where they were mostly hidden by the masses. Clara would miss him soon, so he couldn't stay too long out of sight.

"I can't help him, Gladdy."

The kitsune looked utterly flummoxed. "But, Isaac, you help *everyone*. You've never turned anyone away. Even that asshole barghest. You gave him a whole session before you sent him packing. You only said a few sentences to Colin, already he's opening up. And he's such a sweet kid. His brood family – they fucked him up real bad. Please, can't you—"

Isaac was intrigued despite himself. "Not his pack?"

Gladdy's metaphorical fox ears went back. "No! Well, not this one, not the San Andreas Pack. The one he came from in Boston, I can't speak for them. But San Andreas rescued him, I think. Or his brother did."

"He's got a littermate here, does he?"

Gladdy nodded, brightening. "Kevin. Oh my god, he's the cutest thing. Pack enforcer."

Isaac tried not to flinch. His dad had been an enforcer. Before he fancied himself an Alpha and ended up running a cult.

I have to be firm here, he reminded himself. "Gladdy, no. I'm sorry but I *can't* help this one."

"But you could help him, couldn't you?"

Yes, I could help him, but no. "I can't, Gladdy."

"You mean you won't."

"Same difference."

"But why?" Gladdy practically wailed. "His Alpha is really worried about him."

"He's a werewolf."

"But Isaac! You're one of *us* now."

"*No.* I'm not."

"I mean an honorary shifter. We kind of tell each other about you. If someone is having problems we're all like – *go see Isaac.* Human dude, works at Saucebox. Worth the price of admission."

"I should start charging."

Gladdy looked excited. "You should! Get an office together."

"Sweetie, I never even attended high school. I'm not qualified to be a professional shrink."

"Oh." Gladdy looked crestfallen. "But could I pay you to help Colin?"

"I don't deal with werewolves."

"What? Why not?"

Isaac smelled Colin then and straightened, threatened, his instincts urging him to stand fully to put himself at some kind of advantage. Or in this case, on the level, as they were about the same height. Although Colin was a good deal thinner – too thin, really.

Colin looked at Isaac funny, as if disappointment had allowed him to cast off any soporific effect of Isaac's abilities. Isaac's outright rejection allowed the youngster to see him clearly, for one moment. His eyes were hungry and hurting.

Isaac wanted to reach for him. Sympathy rushed over him, drowning him in empathy and weakness. Every instinct he had was urging him to console and cherish. His wolf keened to be of use. To help and heal. To be whatever the boy needed. To tend to pack. His wolf wanted that so badly, more than he had ever wanted anything.

Except perhaps Tank.

Although that was different. That was just sex.

This was socialization, and instinct, and cohesion, and some dark crazy desire that would be Isaac's undoing. Had been his undoing too often before.

"I'm sorry Colin. I can't talk to you. I can't help you."

"Because I'm a werewolf?"

Isaac inclined his head.

"And you're a man without a smell?"

Such innocence. The poor kid had landed on the heart of the manner. Fortunately for Isaac, Colin was too young, or too ill-trained in pack ranking systems, to know what that meant. Or it's just that there were so few like Isaac in the world, Colin didn't recognize one when he encountered him at a bar.

One of the packs Isaac had met in the wild had said that. Said that females of his rank were rare but that males were practically unheard of. Said he was *special*. Wanted to keep him. Keep him forever. Then demanded to keep him.

Then trapped him.

Then caged him.

Isaac reminded himself of that. Colin represented a pack too. They would try to do the same. Isaac must hide what he really was.

Colin blinked at him – pained eyes, pale lashes. "You're scared of us. Scared of werewolves."

Isaac nodded.

Colin sounded sad and small, "That I understand. Me too." Then he turned and wandered away.

Gladdy gave Isaac a disgusted look. "That was badly done."

"You should have warned me, Gladdy, before you brought him. Told me what he was ahead of time. I would have said not to bother. I would have told you that I can't help children and I won't help pack. You shouldn't have brought me someone broken like that."

"He's broken like you, isn't he?" Sometimes it was brought home to Isaac how old Gladdy really was. Ninety years on this earth and even someone as oblivious as Gladiola Kitsune picked up on others' emotions occasionally.

Isaac inclined his head. "And if I don't know how to fix myself…"

The little kitsune nodded. "You can't fix him. I'm sorry Isaac, I didn't know. No more werewolves, I promise. But you know Tank, at the door, is one of them, right?"

Isaac nodded. "Yep."

"You're okay with that?"

"Yep."

"Because he's only a bouncer or because of Tank being all, well, Tank-ish?"

Isaac shrugged.

Gladdy sighed. "I'll warn him to be careful around you."

Isaac flinched. What could he say to that?

Then Gladdy too was gone.

Isaac returned his attention to his very busy bar.

"That was quick," Tank said, as Colin came back out only ten minutes or so after he went in.

Tank had been pleased to see him there. Colin needed friends and the mixer was a good idea. Gladdy as escort was a fine plan. But he also wasn't too surprised to see his pack mate leaving so soon. Colin had trouble adjusting: to the move, to the pack, to the Bay Area, to crowds, to being out, to being in school, to, well, everything.

Colin gave that funny half-smile of his, the one that never reached his eyes. "He didn't want me."

"What!" Tank was instantly upset on his pack mate's behalf.

Colin's eyes widened and he started. "Oh. No! Not like *that*. I mean the bartender. Gladdy said she wanted me to meet this bartender."

"WHAT!"

"Oh, god." Colin moaned. "I'm doing this all wrong. Gladdy just wanted me to *talk* to him. It wasn't like a set-up for a date or anything." He flushed.

Tank instantly calmed. "Oh. Like for one of his counseling gigs?"

"Is that what he does with the others?"

"He didn't with you?"

"Well, I think he started to. I mean he's good. Really good. Made me feel all, you know, calm and stuff. I just started to say things I normally wouldn't. But then it's like he remembered something bad and this wall came down and he dragged Gladdy aside and said he couldn't."

Tank was floored. "But Isaac helps *anyone* who asks."

Gladdy interjected, popping up near his elbow. "That's what I said."

"But he won't help *me*." Colin shrugged, trying to pass it off as no big deal. Although it's clear that it was. "Not that I need help, of course."

Neither Tank nor Gladdy said anything. Everyone knew Colin needed help.

Tank glared at Gladdy, and then he glared through the club at Isaac, who was oblivious, back to mixing drinks. "Why not our Colin? He's a good kid."

Colin rolled his eyes.

"Apparently, Isaac doesn't do werewolves." The kitsune looked a little coy as she imparted that bit of information.

"What?" *I sure hope he's open to doing at least one werewolf.* "What's wrong with werewolves?"

Gladdy shrugged. "He doesn't like them."

"He doesn't?" *Tell that to his cock.* Tank thought of Isaac pressed against him as they kissed. His body, at least, was interested.

Gladdy looked at him funny. "You're gonna have to fix this, Tank."

"Me?"

"Yeah. He doesn't seem to mind you."

"No one minds Tank." Colin sounded a little bitter.

Gladdy glared at Tank. "We want Isaac to stay."

"We do?"

"Yes Tank, *we* do." It was as if she spoke for the whole shifter community, which frankly, Tank had kinda assumed was Mana's job. Then again, Mana was also a kitsune. Perhaps it was a fox busybody thing.

"Okay." Tank agreed, wholeheartedly. Even if he was confused about the other stuff, he definitely wanted Isaac to stay. Preferably in his bed, on top of him, for long periods of time.

Accordingly, after Colin and Gladdy had left and the door slowed enough for Oscar to handle it alone, Tank started a circuit for the club. Of course, eventually his wandering took him toward Isaac's end of the bar.

"Hello, handsome," he said, hoping he didn't sound too eager.

Isaac flashed him a delighted smile at first, then seemed to remember himself and closed up.

He was pretty busy, so Tank just lurked and waited, keeping an eye on the crowd.

A blue-haired human male with a pale face and dark eyes sidled up to him. Tank assumed he too was trying to get Isaac's attention. For some strange reason, though, the man's focus was on him.

Tank gave him a curious look.

The man smiled and leaned toward him to ask a question, although the music wasn't all that loud (shifters had sensitive hearing). This one smelled totally human, and sweaty and eager – which was flattering.

Isaac interrupted by passing Tank a cold glass of milk. Tank laughed and took it.

"You're on duty," Isaac explained, his gray eyes flashing briefly at the blue-hair.

Tank nodded, his whole self focused on Isaac. "Not that alcohol would do much. Wrong metabolism. But I prefer the milk. Thank you."

Out of the corner of his eye Tank watched as the pretty blue man, looked disappointed and drifted away.

"I met one of your pack earlier." Isaac drew his attention.

"Yes. Colin." Dangerous territory, Tank felt, but Isaac

had brought it up.

Isaac began wiping down the bar near Tank, not looking at him.

Tank wanted those silvery eyes on him. He touched the back of the bartender's wrist, the hand holding the rag. Just one gentle fingertip. Isaac's skin was so soft.

Tank was careful with his words. "What happened, Isaac? What happened with Colin?"

CHAPTER SEVEN
A Confusion of Werewolves

Isaac tried not to enjoy the tiny contact too much. Tank's touch was so gentle from such a big man. Tentative.

"Werewolves make me nervous." Isaac dampened down on his own wolf, who once again wanted to bathe in Tank's scent. Roll all around on top of him, mark him with teeth.

"I make you nervous?" Tank stopped his caress and seemed a little upset, as if there was some implication that Isaac was comparing Tank to Hayden and his ilk.

"No. And that's weird. Because I know you're a werewolf, but somehow it doesn't matter."

"Something was done to you? Something bad by one of my kind?" A tiny crease appeared between those chocolate eyes.

Isaac inclined his head.

Tank considered a long moment before he spoke again. "You didn't know there were werewolves in the Bay Area when you moved here, did you?"

Clearly, I'm not the only one with the ability to perceive motive. Is Tank like this by werewolf instinct, or is it only with me? Isaac was thrilled by the idea of being Tank's only.

It also provided the opening he'd been searching for. "How long have you guys been here, then?"

"About six months. Everything duly recorded by DURPS. We moved in by the book. Alec is a stickler for such things. But being as you aren't a supernatural creature, I guess there's no reason for you to check the records of territory. It really upsets you, doesn't it? Us being here?"

Isaac hesitated and then, because Tank had kissed him and that was worth something, admitted, baldly, "San Francisco is known for its general openness toward queer folk, and supernatural folk, and interspecies dating. Werewolves *aren't* known for any of those things. In fact, in my experience, they are the opposite of accepting."

"Is that what happened to you? Some asshole wolves beat you up for being queer?" The big man's tone was soft and dangerous.

Isaac made a funny face. "Nooooo," he said, but he knew that he didn't sound sure of himself.

"My pack, we aren't the normal kind of werewolf. I promise."

Isaac was instantly on his guard and suspicious. "You're not. How's that? Not that I know a whole lot about packs, but you've an Alpha, and Gladdy says there's an enforcer."

Tank nodded. "Two. A proper pack always has two. One of ours is Colin's older brother."

Isaac crossed his arms. "That sounds about typical."

Tank clenched his massive hands. His expression was one of agonized self-doubt. Isaac could tell that the man believed he was doing this all wrong.

"It's true that, in general, werewolf packs aren't known for" – Tank cleared his throat, obviously hunting for the right words – "progressive social attitudes."

Isaac snorted. *Well, that's a very politic way of putting "homophobic assholes."*

Tank soldiered on. "We tend to live in trailers with the carcasses of cars and deer in our yards, bum about on motorcycles and complain about the *little woman back at the ranch*."

Isaac snorted again, this time in amused recognition.

"But San Andreas really is different. Alec, our Alpha, he's gay. He's not at all what you'd expect. He's kind of a nerd and kind of a dork. He's a marine biologist and his mate is a merman." This was all said in a rush, as if Tank felt he had to spit it out or he'd lose courage.

Isaac felt his eyebrows climb toward his hairline. "Your Alpha is *gay*? How is that even possible?"

Tank shrugged. "Well, I'm bi. You know that, right? I mean, we did kiss, but sometimes I surprise people with it. You know, 'cause I look like this, all huge and clumsy and unkempt, and then I'm like, hello, totally queer, and they're all…"

Isaac stopped him with a chuckle. "Yes, Tank, I figured. Your tongue in my mouth was a dead giveaway. I thought you might be in the closet or something."

"No closet's big enough for that."

"Could be a walk-in."

Tank snorted. "Well, I'm queer and so is my Alpha. So are a few others in our pack. It's kinda why we formed."

Isaac nodded. "I concede, that *is* weird. From what I know of werewolves. Go on?"

Tank brightened noticeably at the encouragement. "Well, we have a Beta. You know that's good, right? I mean not as good as having an Omega, or a Beta *and* an Omega, but still we have a Beta."

Isaac was proud of himself (he only flinched a little).

"And he's gay. And he's awesome. Best Beta ever." Tank's big chest puffed up with pride. "Betas keep the Alpha calm. Ours is awesome." He seemed to feel compelled to explain.

Isaac didn't mind – after all he was pretty ignorant of

werewolf pack dynamics. He hadn't been raised in a pack. He'd been raised in a cult. "Go on."

"Bryan, our Beta, never says much. He's just kinda grounding and sweet and golden."

"Like you?" Isaac was embarrassed the moment he said it.

Tank was still distracted. "Oh no! Bryan is a million times better than me. I don't rank at all."

There was a strange kind of desperation to his earnestness, as if it were vitally important that Isaac understand his pack. Isaac supposed this must have something to do with helping Colin.

Tank, obviously, would do anything for his pack. "Bryan is magical. And he's also a familiar. You know, a *Magistar's familiar*? Because his mate, Max, is this kick-ass super powerful mage."

Tank glanced up, caught Isaac's confused and slightly alarmed look, and back-pedaled. "But Max is a totally decent dude. If you excuse his potty mouth. I mean, Max can be a little curt but he's not intentionally malicious – well, not unless you earned it."

Tank paused, panting a little. The poor guy was talking a mile a minute and clearly not used to it. Fortunately, Isaac was accustomed to listening, and the bar had quieted slightly. The blue-haired bit of fluff who'd been making eyes at his werewolf earlier had scampered off somewhere to lick his wounds. As he should.

Wait, my *werewolf? That's not good.* Inside, Isaac's wolf gave him a smug look. *Mine. Yes.*

Said werewolf hadn't finished his milk. He was still trying to explain. Trying to make Isaac feel safe. "Actually, Max is kinda an asshole, but he's *our* asshole, and one-hundred-percent human, so you shouldn't have any problems with him."

Isaac allowed himself to be charmed. "Okay, let the defense rest for a moment and allow me to catch up? So, you have a gay nerd Alpha, a merman Alpha-mate, a silent Beta who's also a mage's familiar. I'll give you, that doesn't sound like any pack I've met or heard of."

Tank nodded. "Well, then there's me and Colin and Lovejoy. We're basically normal. Although Colin and I are queer. Lovejoy's straight but he's dating a kitsune drag queen, so that's gotta count for something."

Isaac felt as if he had completely lost control of the entire conversation at this point. *Where'd the drag queen come from?* So he just nodded. *This is getting weirder and weirder.* His wolf agreed. Isaac told his wolf to butt out.

Tank continued, "Our enforcers are normal and enforcer-like. Except that Kevin joined our pack in order to get Colin away from his family and Judd used to be a loner. And he's super gay too and old. We aren't sure how, but pretty old."

He brightened up suddenly. "Oh, Isaac, you know what you should do?"

"What's that, Tank, baby?" The endearment slipped out as Isaac let himself go with the flow. It could hardly get any more surreal, could it?

"You should come to one of our barbecues! We have a big one after each full moon. You missed the most recent one, but they're great. You could meet everyone casually, and test us out. See that we're decent dudes."

Isaac thought that was the worst idea he'd ever heard. His wolf thought it was the greatest. *Pack pack packpackpack,* he panted.

Isaac scrambled for an excuse. Tank had certainly made his point that his pack was different from, and less threatening than, any other pack. But it wasn't safety that concerned Isaac. Not entirely. It was wolf instinct. Theirs. And his.

He avoided any kind of barbecue commitment by asking another question. "You settled here, in the city?"

That didn't make sense. There was nowhere decent to

run in San Francisco proper. Not really. And one thing Isaac had learned about werewolves after he left the cult was that most of them ran wild on full moon. And city wouldn't countenance that.

Tank shook his head. "Across the bridge in Sausalito. Max, our Magistar, has this massive old run-down house and it's right up against parkland. He basically gave it to us so long as we fixed it up."

"What? Why?"

"Well, Max hates the place and we were having a hard time finding something to rent where we could all live together."

Isaac blinked.

"Not like that! It's just better, as we're a young pack, if we all live in the same space. Like frat bonding or something. So, come to our barbecue? You'll see we aren't all bad, I promise." Big chocolate eyes blinked at him, full of pleading.

Isaac couldn't come up with a good excuse so he said, "I'll think about it."

Tank gave him a tentative smile and ducked his head shyly. "I'll let you get back to work, then."

Isaac realized that bar traffic had picked up once again. He took a deep breath. Just because he was frazzled and confused didn't mean he couldn't do his damn job.

Tank drifted away, half his milk left behind.

Isaac's wolf keened that the other man hadn't been taken care of properly. His wolf wanted to hunt for him, provide more than just milk. *You're an idiot, wolf.*

Mine, said the wolf.

Tank got to walk Isaac home that night.

Well, to be more precise, he persuaded Isaac to climb onto the back of his motorcycle so they could ride there together.

Isaac was a delicious tangle of long limbs, draped awkwardly but perfectly against him. He folded himself up in an endearing manner, letting out a tiny sigh that might be joy or terror at the intimacy. Because intimacy clearly wasn't Isaac's thing.

The short trip was everything Tank loved about riding with a partner. The full length of Isaac's lean torso pressed against his body, strong hands on his hips. Tank wished it were longer but the few blocks flew by at such a late hour. He made Isaac wear his helmet, because Isaac was fragile and human and more important in all ways than Tank's own fat head.

Isaac's lips were parted and he was breathing funny when they stopped. His eyes were brighter than normal after he pulled the helmet off. Tank suspected Isaac enjoyed riding with him, too.

Tank licked his lips, eager.

The other man's gray eyes, under the waning moon and old streetlights, followed the action and dilated.

Tank had this glorious thought that perhaps this amazing man actually *wanted* him. Wanted stupid, big, oafish Tank, with nothing to offer anyone but endless stability.

"Come up with me?" suggested Isaac, looking surprised by his own words.

Tank nodded, mute with joy and luck. He slid off the bike and kicked down the stand. He was confused as to his good fortune, but not so much that he would second-guess anything.

Like a child, tentative and afraid of rejection, Isaac took Tank's hand. *Why should he fear anything? I will do whatever he wants, however he wants it.* Perhaps Isaac did not realize that yet. Tank would have to show him.

Their entwined hands were somehow sacred. Tank was taken back to his childhood, a lonely boy in the schoolyard, afraid of his own size already, and leery of the other children. They all seemed so erratic and unpredictable, high-pitched and terrifyingly frail. He'd forgotten the memory until this moment.

It had been Bryan, back then. (*Biff*, as he was called by their former pack. He'd asked them to stop with that name, now that he was a familiar. *Biff* apparently didn't have the required gravitas for a Magistar's familiar. Max said if *Biff* wouldn't do, how about *Bubbles*, and then called him that for a week. But Max also already called him Bryan so he was just being Max-ish about it.)

Bryan was Tank's age mate. Both of them had been still human, too young for the bite. Bryan's hand had meshed with his, and he'd tugged Tank forward into the schoolyard. Bryan, a child of the Boston pack, already bowing to his future responsibilities as Beta. *You are mine,* the firm grip had said to Tank. *You will be ours. And we will keep you safe. And I will keep them safe from you. Together.*

Isaac's grip was achingly similar.

Although, of course, the difference was that Tank wanted Isaac. Rather desperately. Wanted him with white heat and hard need and a permeating desire to yield. It was worse than any need for release, the need to give everything over to another.

Tank followed Isaac because he was being led and his place was to follow. And he found comfort in that. He hoped Isaac would not want him to push or to conquer. So many saw dominance in his size – saw aggression and superiority. But Tank was made to be used by a lover, to surrender parts of himself into another's keeping.

Isaac would learn soon enough. When it came to sex, Tank was all things gentle and never demanding. No doubt, then Isaac would reject him. He would see disappointment in those wounded gray eyes.

Thinking this, Tank ducked his head and hesitated

while Isaac unlocked his apartment building.

Isaac was human, so Tank scrabbled for the language of the Castro and handkerchiefs. All that nonsense labeling humans loved so much, because they did not have pack to tell (or nose to smell) where they stood. Humans must define identity for themselves.

"I don't top, Isaac." Tank's voice was almost a whisper.

"No, you don't," replied Isaac, without any kind of surprise. "And it's not because you like the dark bite of the pain of being taken – although you do, don't you?"

Tank didn't answer, too relieved by the man's ready acceptance of his faults.

"And it's not because you're lazy, or a seeker of attention, or out to prove some point about heteronormative gender roles."

"Huh?"

Isaac pulled open the now-unlocked door. He hadn't looked at Tank while he spoke, but stayed focused on the fiddly deadbolt.

Inside, the hallway and the stairs were old, the carpet covering them threadbare and stained. The building smelled human, musty and ancient, with the bones of previous residents netted through the air – skin and sweat lingering like cigarette smoke. It made Tank think of unhealthy prey.

"You forget what I am, Tank."

"I do?" Tank followed Isaac up the stairs to another door and another lock. *Jesus, how many are there? How unsafe does he feel?*

"I'm the bartender that shifters visit because I understand how they think. You are you, and formed, I believe, to be made use of. You yearn for that."

"Yes," breathed out Tank. *Your foundation, please, let me be that. You can dig deep and build upon me, a home of wanting.*

Isaac's apartment was depressingly shabby. And the

door to Isaac's room, where Tank was led, hands still entwined, was also dead-bolted and locked.

"You don't trust your roommates?"

Isaac shrugged. "My roommates are fine. It's the tricks they bring home that I don't trust."

Tank wondered if Isaac tried to counsel someone once, trusted some werewolf shifter too much, or dated one in the past who abused him. "I would never push anything on you, Isaac, that you didn't want."

"Oh, I don't believe that's entirely true. I suspect what you want from me goes beyond this moment and *that* is scary. But right now, I don't care, for some reason. I just want it to be *this* – us – together. I want to do..." He swallowed.

Tank looked away, shy now that they were here. In Isaac's room. They stood awkwardly apart, leaning inadvertently toward one another, breathing almost in sync.

The scent of human was still around him but it was even fainter here, and beneath it – nothing. Nothing endemic to Isaac, nothing that told Tank anything more about the man. Nothing that spoke to his existence.

Here, truly, was a man without a scent.

It was a strange kind of blindness. Tank could smell only Isaac's arousal, salt sweet and musky sharp. Which caused his own cock, already iron hard, to twitch with need. Because it meant that Isaac must be dripping with want. But it was a generic scent, nothing unique to the tang, odd but more importantly right now, flattering.

He wants me. Me – dumb, and blundering, and needy.

"What do you want from me, Isaac?" Tank liked perimeters in place, so he knew exactly what to do and what not to do.

"Fuck." Isaac shuddered and closed his eyes. "I want to take and take and take and see how much you'll give me."

"Everything," said Tank, without hesitation. The skin

of his face prickled.

Isaac was on him then, his hands rough with want, ridding Tank of his clothing, sure and confident even as they trembled. Tank froze under his touch, holding his breath, afraid it might stop.

"I'm not going to remind you to breathe," remonstrated Isaac, with a sweet shake of his head. "I don't mind ordering you about, but that's taking it too far."

Tank nodded and gasped. He tried to regulate his breathing, so it would not distract Isaac again.

"Good." He was petted and praised for his efforts. "Be still for me now."

Tank was still. Still as he could be under those caressing hands. Hands that teased and weighed and stroked every part of him as it was revealed.

Isaac was efficient about stripping him, in a way that spoke of more experience than Tank wanted to think about. Tank, being a werewolf, wasn't wearing much clothing. He didn't get all that cold and he sneered at underwear. It behooved a man who shifted forms to have as few barriers as possible to his other self.

Isaac didn't seem to mind Tank's big, lumbering body. Tank always thought, at this juncture, that there was too much of him. It was overwhelming to some lovers, all muscle and hair, big balls and big cock. As if he'd been rough-hewn by some thoughtless sculptor out of mud rock but never refined. Abandoned incomplete. Here, in his naked human state, he was basic and unfinished, to be used and discarded. Well, the *used* part is always welcome.

Yet Isaac seemed to love Tank's body. The man's touch was appreciative and somewhat rough – which made Tank melt.

Tank was always gentle with others, mindful of his size, but he loved rough handling himself. Loved the idea that a lover might be overcome with passion, might need everything that Tank could possibly give. Might take it, whether Tank willed it or not. Delicious.

Isaac's gray eyes glittered silver and his hands were everywhere. Smoothing over Tank, almost reverent. They paused to pluck at Tank's nipples.

He gasped. Jerked a little, despite the order to be still. He leaked enough so he could smell himself now too.

"You like that."

Tank nodded. "They're sensitive."

Isaac did it again, scraped a nail through Tank's chest hair to the other nipple and across it.

Tank swallowed hard and clenched his fists, tensing his muscles not to react. He'd been told to stay still. It was sweet agony and so exactly right. He knew his place. He knew what was required of him. He was precisely where he was supposed to be.

"You're so responsive," whispered Isaac.

Tank glowed with it. Praise and forgiveness unasked. Such a gift from this beautiful man.

Isaac was breathing faster. His licked his lips. They were puffy and soft and glistening. Tank wanted to be kissed. But he also wanted the touches to continue. And he also wanted his own needs to be unimportant.

Isaac was still fully dressed. He'd discarded his jacket but was otherwise clothed. Tank whimpered at the discrepancy, the powerful difference between his own naked flesh and Isaac fully covered. Isaac's tight jeans strained over an impressive bulge.

Tank's eyes were riveted on the zipper, desperate to taste or to smell more.

Isaac followed his gaze and laughed low and delighted. "Of course, you'd be like this. Fucking A, *of course* you would. So goddamn perfect."

Tank didn't really hear him. There was a roaring buzz about his head. None of Isaac's words were an order or a suggestion or an instruction. Last he remembered, Tank had been told to be still – so he was still except for his gaze.

When he raised his eyes back to Isaac's glittering, intense stare, he knew his own were pleading.

"Kneel for me," ordered Isaac.

Oh, thank god. Tank folded to his knees with a clumsy jerk and a loud thump. He'd never be a graceful man, he wasn't even a very graceful wolf. But right now, none of that mattered. Right now, he had purpose.

Isaac was taller than most of Tank's previous lovers, but still Tank was a monster, so he must lean forward and down to nuzzle at the other man's fly. He inhaled.

Finally, Isaac had a smell. Not his own, nothing to mark him unique, but there was that overwhelming scent of arousal, the sharp acrid perfume of desire.

Tank simply knelt there, quivering, face pressed against Isaac's cock, absorbing him. Yearning for him.

"You want to get lost in me." Isaac's voice was full of wonder. "Go on, then."

Tentative and hesitant, because he hadn't been instructed explicitly, but he *needed* so badly, Tank reached to undo the zipper of Isaac's jeans. Isaac didn't stop him, just rested his hands lightly on Tank's head. Blessings upon the man, he wore no underwear, as if he too were a werewolf.

Tank reached, caressed, stroked – Isaac groaning over him – and pulled out the man's cock at last.

Isaac's dick was truly beautiful, uncut, a rarity in humans. It was darker than the rest of him, flushed almost purple. He was already so hard the foreskin was pulled back, the head glistening. Without even thinking about it, Tank bent to take him into his mouth.

Isaac stopped him with a hard grip to his hair and pulled a condom out of his back pocket.

Tank was a little disappointed he wouldn't get to taste, but humans could get this way about safety, and he liked that Isaac was protective. As a werewolf, he couldn't catch anything and he couldn't give anything, but Isaac didn't know that. And Isaac was in charge.

He watched, reverent, as Isaac sheathed himself and then, thank god, pressed into Tank's waiting mouth.

Isaac let out his breath in a rush as Tank swallowed him down. It was as if someone had pressed all the air out of his chest. Isaac was hot and hard and invasive, in a way Tank knew could become addictive.

Tank sucked him down easily, all the way to the root. Isaac muffled a shout of surprise. Tank held that perfect ridged cock in his mouth, the head down his throat, and swallowed around it. Isaac mumbled unintelligibly in dazed shock. Tank doubted there were many who could deep throat Isaac fully on the first try. But Tank was made to give everything to a lover, and that included his gag reflex.

Tank pulled off and then sucked Isaac down and swallowed again. And again. Slow and trance-like. Bathing in the feel of it. Isaac let him. Encouraged him. Enjoyed him.

He, Tank, was giving this beautiful, lonely, frightened man pleasure.

He glanced up, nose pressed against tightly curled pubic hair. Isaac's eyes were fixed on him. They were now more greedy than wounded. Tank was thrilled by the change he'd wrought.

"Let me," Isaac commanded.

Tank stopped moving. Isaac gripped his head and fucked his mouth, slow and steady and exactly right.

Used. Useful.

Tank's world went slack and formless. His whole being became one throbbing pulse beat. He melted into it, lost the worst of himself along with his doubts. His sense of self was gone. The best of him, the strength of him, was still present, still here in this shape, human and waiting. Care and obedience were all that were required now (and that's what he was best at).

Isaac's cock pillaged the depths of his mouth. Tank's tongue became the lone bastion of resistance – stroking and soothing and placating even as Tank screamed silently *more* and *faster*. Isaac was impossibly hard. Tank thought the man might be close to coming. He didn't want this to end so soon, but that didn't matter. The end wasn't the point. All he cared about was soaring through now.

"You would let me, wouldn't you?" Isaac's voice was loose and choppy. "Of course you would." He took a deep, stuttering breath. "You would let me take everything from you and leave you aching and wanting and empty." The gray eyes looked away from Tank's and further down, where Tank's own cock was stupid hard.

Under Isaac's hungry gaze, Tank's cock jumped and leaked. He'd forgotten about it. It wasn't important. *Isaac* was important. Isaac inside him. Isaac demanding. Isaac made powerful by desire, conquering and taking and pressing in with sweet force. Intoxicating to Tank's mouth, his eyes, his nose – every part of Tank was lost to this man. For this man.

"Or perhaps you can come just like this? No touch, no order, just my demands."

Tank figured that was a rhetorical question and kept sucking.

Isaac slowed his thrusting. The hands buried in Tank's hair relaxed, urging him with tiny pets once more into stillness. Tank obeyed the unspoken command without question. Although there might have been an involuntary (and very manly) whimper when that perfect cock was withdrawn.

Isaac explained. "Not yet. Not this way."

Tank jolted with anticipation.

Isaac was looking at him, head tilted to one side, fond and awed. "I really want to fuck you. Would you let me?"

Tank was confused. Of course he would. What sort of stupid question was that? *Oh yeah, first date.* Or not even really that. He'd forgotten all the nice little dances humans did around courting and sexual ritual. Tank nodded, then lowered his eyelids, hoping Isaac understood. Not only would he allow it, he needed it.

Isaac found lube somewhere and Tank found the bed somehow. Rising shakily to his feet and falling shakily back to his knees on an old worn blanket that had seen better days. Better years, really.

Isaac's big hand was tender, stroking the line of his spine, and Tank forgot about the blanket.

Isaac passed him the lube. "Prepare yourself. I want to watch you while I strip."

It would never have occurred to Tank to disobey and he was too far gone on the man to be embarrassed. He did as instructed, a familiar task, as he always preferred to be filled. Even alone, he had fingers or toys, sometimes both. It was never quite good enough – never quite *real* enough – when he did it to himself, but that was because he could not make use of himself, not in the right way.

He hung his head and performed the deed mechanically, trying not to take pleasure from it. Pleasure was not his to give to himself. That would be for Isaac, and with Isaac's permission.

He heard a little shift and moan and swiveled his eyes to see Isaac frozen, holding his shirt in one hand, staring at him. Starving. He'd never inspired such want before. The man looked like he might die without him. Gray eyes fixed on where Tank scissored three fingers, stretching and pushing in and out.

"Holy fucking Christ on a cracker," Isaac breathed. "I've never seen—" He choked on his words, suddenly a lanky flurry of activity as he stripped himself out of his jeans, tight enough to make him hop on one leg and flail slightly.

His gaze narrowed as if he expected Tank to chuckle. But Tank was breathing short and fast and hopeful, because Isaac was now gloriously naked.

Free of his clothing at last, Isaac stalked to Tank. His body big and lean and sculpted. He'd very little hair and all of it close and black and tightly curled. His eager cock jutted and Tank licked his lips.

Isaac fisted himself briefly, as though he could not help it. Or perhaps he was just spreading lube over the condom. Tank hoped not too much – he liked the burn.

Then Isaac was on him, folded over him, all soft silken flesh. He pulled Tank's own fingers out, and replaced them with the blunt head of that perfect cock. He pushed relentlessly in, no pause for Tank to adjust, no accommodation given for his size, just unending burning pressure.

Tank lived for this. Perhaps too much, he sometimes thought. The dark, aching glide of being taken. He trembled but held still, back arched slightly, loving every moment. Isaac was definitely one of the more endowed of his male lovers, but oh, so perfect. Tank felt, even as he was filled, that he was being shoved out of his own body, so that he floated above it in some warm safe other place, and looked down to see Isaac's dark back mounted above his pale one.

Isaac stilled for a long moment all the way in, absorbing Tank and gathering himself.

Tank hung his head and waited and willed himself not to come, not yet. He was skewered like the pack's full moon kill, hunted and sacrificed. Providing for his mate. Nourishment.

Isaac pulled back out just as slowly. Then came that relentless thrust forward again, a little faster. Isaac shifted his hips slightly this time, and pressed down on the small of Tank's back with one wide, firm hand, so he fell to his elbows and widened his thighs. Isaac's uncompromising cock pressed over his prostate. Tank shuddered and cried out.

Isaac pulled back a tiny bit and slid in again, and back and forth, until he was pulsing against Tank in tiny pushes exactly over that spot.

Tank shuddered and moaned and his cock strained and began to drip an endless milking stream, part orgasm, part agony, because Tank had not been told he could come, and he hadn't realized he was so close.

He started to shake, trying to hold it back, but Isaac was committed, and apparently getting off on Tank's whimpering.

"Please," Tank begged. Not sure if he was asking for relief, or persistence, or acquittal.

Whatever it was stopped the pulsing massage of his gland. Isaac began pounding into him, almost uncontrolled, his movements desperate. Now nothing else mattered but bracing himself and taking it.

It was utterly glorious, serving this man. The odd weightlessness of pure surrender. A suspension of all things but desire. Tank lost everything, head pressed to the ugly blanket, the slap of flesh echoing in his skull, the smell of arousal filling him to overflowing. There was only Isaac's body above him and in him and against him. Small, unintelligible words punctuated his thrusts, but nothing distinct, no orders, just praise. There was nothing else but this man and this moment.

Tank surprised himself with his own abrupt need to climax. He half thought it had been happening all along, his balls high and tight and tingling insistently. But suddenly, there it was, demanding he notice. It snapped him back into his own body. He whimpered at the loss of selflessness.

Isaac was deep inside him, jerking and crying out.

Tank managed a rough, broken "Can I—? Please. God, can I please—"

Isaac chocked out a despair-filled, "Yes," which might have been his own climax, but Tank took it as permission.

Then Tank was flying with release, transported out of himself by his own pleasure this time. There was a slight disappointment in the relief, except that he knew in his bones that Isaac was happy.

He'd made Isaac happy.

His man was a heavy, wrung-out, weight draped atop him. Tank relished the burden. He could take it, of course. Isaac was a big man, but Tank was bigger, and eager to hold him up even though his own knees were weak and his elbows trembled. Isaac remained inside him, limp and spent.

Tank wasn't sure what to do then. Wait? Fall? Roll? Leave? Already he was yearning for something more, some further intimacy. He felt perfectly used and inexplicably lonely – fragile. A tiny part of his soul felt rebuffed, some necessary connection absent, held apart by Isaac.

Then long, sweat-damp brown arms wrapped around him, and soft lips touched the nape of his neck. Isaac's weight tilted him to the side so they were resting, neither in Tank's wet spot, curled together.

Isaac trailed a hand over Tank's exposed side, from ribs to hip to ass and back up again.

Tank made a small noise of acceptance.

"Thank you." Isaac's voice was deepened by lust and some other emotion more complicated than gratitude.

That was, in some strange way, enough – to be acknowledged and held close.

CHAPTER EIGHT
Nude Awakenings

Isaac wasn't sure how he felt. Wrecked perhaps? Utterly vulnerable and impossibly powerful at the same time. He basked in it, and Tank's smell, all around him, all over him and in his space, citrus and brandy and warm winter spices, something freshly killed and lovingly set before him. Or perhaps it was he who had done the killing and providing and loving?

That thought shook him.

I need to get up and dispose of the condom.

Isaac had used a rubber for reasons of blow job, not fucking, of course. He may not smell like a werewolf, but he tasted like one, and another shifter would surely know the spicy flavor of his cum. He'd learned that the hard way, somewhere in New Mexico. Maybe Santa Fe?

He moved quietly out of his room to the bathroom. At some point his roommates had returned but they were now blessedly asleep. The house was quiet. He tossed the condom and cleaned himself up, then leaned on the ancient pedestal sink and stared into the speckled mirror at his own confused face. What had just happened?

He'd thought sex with Tank might be good, a kind of escape. And he liked escape.

But it had been perfect.

Not ideal, but perfect in that way the world sometimes gives you ice cream on a sunny day. Perhaps not the best brand or your favorite flavor of ice cream, but with the heat and the urge to lick before it melted, it becomes a momentary perfection.

Tank was unexpected. Isaac had thought him hot, in that way he had of always preferring bigger men. Some stupid instinct his wolf had forced upon him early and he'd never lost. Probably something to do with wanting an Alpha. Except Isaac's wolf's wires were crossed by his human's need to dominate. Tank had clearly liked that too.

Tank was sensitive to the needs of others and took orders so well at the club, Isaac suspected it would translate to the bedroom. It was in Isaac's nature to read people, so he could sense Tank's desire to serve. But the way Tank fell into it so easily? That too was perfect. *Flying,* someone at a BDSM club had once called it – *subspace,* said others.

On Tank it looked more like shifting forms. Only his mind had shifted without his body, rather than the other way around. Tank had lost himself so willingly, so eagerly, so committed to Isaac's desires. That kind of trust was humbling.

Isaac tried not to be awed by it. And he tried not to be frightened of it. His own life was already too much – the world burned and tortured, putting pressure on his lungs, suffocating. To be offered this man right now. Isaac wanted nothing more than to savor him. Tank could so easily be his solace.

Isaac thought about Tank lying in his bed, supine and sweet-smelling. *It must be some joke the universe is playing on me.* For the bitter pill at the center was always there. Isaac knew it even as he tasted perfection.

Tank was big, which Isaac found unbearably tasty. Tank was submissive, which Isaac found deliciously sweet. Tank was kind and loyal and so sexy.

Yet Tank was a werewolf.

Isaac stared at his own confused face and decided to allow himself one night to eat his fill. To appreciate perfection. There would be consequences for indulgence, there always were.

He just didn't realize how soon.

Isaac left the mirror and returned to his shabby room. The man mountain was curled like a child under his blankets, taking up most of the bed.

Isaac crouched to look at Tank's face, slack and peaceful. He'd used the man into exhaustion.

This wasn't Isaac's normal thing, a full-on ass-pounding on the first date. Or the first ride home. Or whatever form of first-forever this was. Usually, there was a pattern to Isaac's assignations. Hands. Hand jobs. Blow jobs. And only then did asses come into play, all previous encounters being acceptable.

Tank had made him want more so furiously. He'd been need-drunk. His wolf had risen up insisting that he take and claim, sink inside the man, so every particle of Tank's being might be filled with Isaac. The wolf had made Isaac ask Tank up in the first place.

It was weak of them both, primitive and animalistic. But Tank had been generous and yielding – every dream and every desire Isaac ever cherished in his worn old heart. To be made so profoundly necessary by one of his own kind. To be trusted and wanted so completely. Tank had given him everything without reservations.

Isaac climbed under the covers, pushing Tank gently over to make room. The man rolled instinctively, offering his ass again.

Isaac moaned only a little. His cock twitched hopefully, as if he hadn't just fucked them both into oblivion. Then he curled himself around Olympus and placed a soft kiss at the nape of Tank's neck. The werewolf made one of those little whimper pleasure noises that Isaac was rapidly coming to crave.

Isaac thought, on a startled moment, that he would give Tank anything. Even the truth. He owed him that. To have been made briefly whole because of something so basic as sex.

I did not know this is what it could be between werewolves. I did not know it could be easy and right.

His wolf said nothing but was smug. Curled somewhere deep within him, pacified for the first time ever.

Tank's voice, husky with longing, broke into Isaac's reverie. "I can stay?"

Isaac knew Tank was really asking: *Can I give you all my strength? Can we wind our souls together with no gaps?*

Isaac forced down the wolf inside him who had never wanted anything so badly as that.

Tank's big hand was gentle, smoothing along Isaac's draped arm.

That caress represented the sure warmth of home – an amorphous place of soft light, clean sheets, the sound of running paws, and all the things Isaac had never known to want. But his wolf knew. And his wolf wanted. Memories of another time, a past life, an impossible thing to force on this one man. This one other werewolf. Except, of course, that Tank could take it. Could take all of him. Had proved that.

Oh, not just Isaac's cock, but his darkness and demands – the uncertain parts of his soul that drove him to need. Need all the things he always knew he shouldn't – another man, another werewolf, a submissive beast. Bound to him and his will.

Isaac whispered into the back of Tank's neck, "What color is your wolf?"

Tank didn't seem surprised to be asked. He let out a rumble of amusement. "Humans. Always so interested in a shifter's second form. He's brown."

Isaac tightened his own brown arm against Tank's chest. "Like me?"

Tank bent his head and kissed Isaac's wrist. "No. Darker, almost black. People always think I'm pure black if they see me at night."

Isaac found this funny. His own wolf was nearly pure white. How unintuitive that that massive white dude should be a black wolf, and he the opposite.

Tank said, as if following his thoughts. "You are so fucking beautiful."

"You're sweet, but blind."

"I have excellent taste." Tank kissed Isaac's arm again.

They drifted into sleep. Isaac thought he might not be able to. It was rare for him to share a bed – usually he didn't feel safe. And yet...

He awoke sometime in early morning, only a few hours later. Difficult to tell the time, for he kept his room as dark as possible.

Tank was in the same position, as if he had been ordered into stillness, even in sleep. That perfect ass was pressed back against Isaac's now *very* interested cock.

He thought that might be what woke him. Tank made a tiny micro movement with his hips, brushing against him, trying, even in sleep, for greater closeness, for penetration.

Isaac's breath hitched. He ran the hand that had been resting, slack against the broad chest, down to wrap about Tank's eager cock.

How much he wanted this man.

Being with him was like remembering his own body existed and inhabiting it fully for the first time. Usually it was an internal struggle, his wolf making himself known only to test Isaac's control. The wolf was an unhappy tenant of Isaac's human body. Irony of ironies, the shifter shrink, who was really nothing more than a werewolf at war with himself. But in this bed, Isaac and his wolf were in accordance, they were liquid and prowling. Unified and predatory, they both wanted to press that unity into Tank.

The big man was awake now, arching back against him, then rocking forward into Isaac's stroking hand. *When did I start that?*

"May I?" asked Isaac, confident in his ability to take once permission was freely given.

"Please," begged Tank.

The word fell over Isaac like a blessing, breathy and wanting.

He twisted away. Tank keened at the loss.

"No touching yourself. That's mine," Isaac said, as he found the lube.

He didn't bother with a condom this time. Tank's ass couldn't taste him, not that way anyway. He coated himself liberally and slid back against that broad welcoming back.

Tank let out a long sigh of welcome.

Isaac closed his now slippery hand once more around that big lovely cock. Tank shuddered. Then the werewolf went perfectly still while Isaac pressed inside him. It was awkward. Isaac had to use the hand he was lying on to guide himself. But it was also hot and tight and perfect. His wolf was delighted to be bare inside his lover. The prospect of painting Tank's insides with cum triggering some primal need.

Isaac held his wolf in check, though, determined to make this good. Although Tank seemed happy with whatever Isaac did. His cock jerked and leaked in Isaac's hand with each slow, measured thrust. Isaac marveled at the willing eagerness, and then lost himself in it.

He bit and sucked on Tank's neck and shoulders, anything he could reach, both of them getting harder and harder and closer and closer until Tank began to pant and emit a little whimper with every withdrawal. The whimpers became "Please." Which might have been *please go faster*. Or *please go harder*. Or *please jack me more*. But was actually, Isaac knew, *please take me forever*. *Please give me your pleasure*. *Please use me like this, never stopping*.

He wished he could. He wanted to hold them both on that sweet pinpoint of *just before*. But Isaac's world had enough denial, so this time he wanted and he took. He moaned low and bit hard, though not so hard that he broke skin (he wasn't a complete idiot). He thought there was a good chance his eyes had shifted and his teeth were dropping because nothing had ever been this good. Nothing.

His cock buried deep and spurted hard. His mouth clamped down on the need to howl. Tank's shoulder became Isaac's gag. His wolf rose close to the surface, unsafe. His wolf told him this was like sinking teeth into the flesh of a kill. The warmth of life running out over his tongue. Total deadly satisfaction.

But Isaac's wolf had never killed anyone or anything. Had never hunted. Had never been allowed to by others and then never been allowed to by Isaac. This big man, vulnerable and willing, was as much his as that fantasy deer. In this moment, captured and held tight against Isaac, filled by his spend and his spent cock, Tank was his kill. Isaac thought, *This is that connection between death and love that the French are so foolish about, only worse, more deadly*.

His kill whimpered in denied satisfaction. "I can feel… Please, Isaac."

His name from those begging lips.

Isaac curled his hand, which had never stopped slowly jacking Tank, and twisted over the head of Tank's cock. He gave him a firmer grip, ran one of his short nails through the weeping slit and whispered, "Give it to me."

It might have been any one of those things, but Isaac

liked to believe it was his order, for Tank groaned and spurted his release, warm and satisfying.

They lay like that for a long time. Tank's softening dick in Isaac's hand, Isaac's softening dick in Tank's ass. Isaac had this weird sensation, as if the points of infinity throughout the universe had stretched and then snapped back, a sense of new wholeness, even knowing he was essentially unchanged.

Isaac thought it odd, that the world seemed to have shifted, and then returned to itself, and only he had noticed.

It was only relevant to him, anyway.

Early afternoon Isaac awoke still inside Tank and hard again.

This is utterly ridiculous. This need.

It was also distracting him from something, some unnatural stillness about the apartment, something *wrong*. Isaac, who'd been hunted more often than not, had developed some powerful instincts and spatial awareness as a result. He was a predator who'd become prey.

Isaac withdrew from his perfect werewolf, which was the very last thing he wanted to do. Tank whimpered at the loss even though he was asleep. Isaac resisted the urge to pet him.

Isaac dressed quickly, grabbed his go bag, always ready and always packed. *I never properly thanked him,* he thought. So sad it hurt his throat. But he was already straining to hear the enemy, the invaders, the hunters.

Someone was at his apartment door, which meant they'd gotten inside the building. His roommate's annoyed voice carried down the hall. No one ever came to their door – it's one of the reasons they all lived together.

"He's fucking asleep, of course. What the hell? Fuck you too and your early morning noise. Who does that?"

The kid was annoyed (clearly he'd been woken against his will). Isaac's roommate was a pretty little thing, go-go dancer, but tougher than glitter and twice as abrasive. Isaac always believed the boy hated him. Or at least feared him in that way pink humans had of associating darker skin tones with thuggish behavior. It was odd to hear him bitchy in Isaac's defense.

Isaac cracked his door and sniffed. He couldn't get anything through the haze of Tank's amazing scent, nutmeg brandy and salty sex. And belonging. Such perfect eager *belonging*. Isaac knew, without a shadow of a doubt, that he now smelled like Tank. *I will have to shower as soon as possible.*

All of Isaac's safety lay in *not* smelling like a werewolf. Himself or any other.

He sniffed again. Beyond that delightful scent there *was* something else coming through the house from the cracked front door. Jonny was no idiot to take the chain off. Whoever he was grumbling at, he was doing it through the crack. Bless his suspicious little heart.

"No, I won't go wake him up. I've no idea who you are and he never has visitors. Fuck off. Text or call like normal people."

Isaac revised his assessment. There was more than one person at the door. He also revised his opinion of his roommate. He'd thought the kid was a vain useless pothead who didn't like anyone but himself, but clearly he had a protective instinct.

He sniffed again and caught it then.

Shifter.

One was all honey, warm loamy soil, and deep forest caves, earthy... *bear*, his wolf categorized quickly. But not a friendly bear, not one he knew, like Kettil. The other smelled better, his wolf liked it – fields and fur and power – werewolf. *Unknown*, explained his wolf. *Not family, not enemy pack, not Tank, and not connected to him. But still another wolf, play, friend, connection. Hope. Alpha!*

Isaac shut that down quickly. *Stupid fucking wolf.*

Isaac made for the bathroom window. It was one of those inexplicable ones that faced nothing but another wall of another apartment building, designed to let out smell, he supposed, if nothing else. Although he hadn't thought humans built with such things in mind.

The window was big enough to squeeze through. He slung his pack over his back, braced himself in the gap between buildings, and shimmied down, landing in the tiny alleyway bruised and scraped.

He was running away, of course he was. But Isaac wondered if he was running from the shifters at his door or the shifter in his bed. He knew that while the one made him a survivor, the other made him a coward.

CHAPTER NINE
Trapper Keepers

Tank came awake fast and alert. He was alone in the bed and in the room. Isaac had left him. He knew that with complete certainty. Isaac was running from something. Probably him.

Tank had no idea *how* he knew, he just did. Inside he keened at the lost, panted with it, wanted to shift and track and be with and close and belong to Isaac all over again. But there was good reason for Isaac's flight, there must be. Tank had done something horrible and wrong last night. He struggled with his memories, fuzzy with that precious floating feeling. Had he done something not ordered, or said something unbidden?

He didn't *think* so. Isaac had made glorious and thorough use of him. Twice. He shivered, wishing he smelled like him. But he only smelled like himself. And sex. As if he had undertaken a whole evening of toy-ridden and cum-covered masturbation.

So, Isaac was gone because there was something else wrong?

Tank strained his supernatural senses.

There was a ruckus at the front door.

He lumbered out of bed and, in deference to the fact that

this was a house of humans, he pulled on his jeans from the night before. Nothing else necessary, he lumbered out of the room and padded down the narrow hallway.

A pretty boy with smeared mascara and a petulant mouth stood at the apartment's front door yelling at someone outside.

"And how the hell did you even get into the building?" There was a clinking rustle on the other side. "Oh badges, really? Badges? You think that does any good? I know those and you've got no jurisdiction here. No shifters in this…" He heard Tank then (finally! humans had such poor hearing) and whirled around.

His gorgeous green eyes bugged out of his face. "Who the fuck are you?"

Tank said nothing. The pretty boy turned back to the cracked door. The chain was still on it. "Okay, maybe there *is* a shifter here."

Tank arched a brow. He supposed it was a safe assumption for a human to make about him. A man his size and shape usually meant some kind of supernatural blood.

He crossed his arms and glared. Wondering what the hell was going on. Isaac had obviously run because of whoever was on the other side of that door. Which made Tank very much want to meet them, preferably with his teeth bared.

The boy slammed the door on whoever was outside it. Tank's nose told him berserker and a fellow werewolf. The wolf was female, Alpha, and only mildly upset. Impatient, probably, with the little human in her way. The bear was, well, a bear shifter. Difficult to read.

Those smeared mascara eyes turned to glare at Tank, not at all intimidated by his size.

Tank supposed it was a bit like being a kitsune. The little human must be accustomed to being smaller than everyone. Someone *that* much bigger, like Tank, was only really *that* much bigger than everyone else.

Tank figured he should say something by way of explanation, as presumably this was one of the roommates, and he was a guest in this house. "I came with Isaac."

The boy's eyes narrowed. "Yeah? He never brings tricks home."

Tank brightened. "No?"

"No."

"I work with him."

"I bet you do, beefcake."

"Just needed a place to crash." Tank tried to be noble with Isaac's reputation.

"I bet you did."

A hard fist banged on the door.

The boy flinched. "I think these fuckers are looking for you." He yelled at the door. "Fuck off, all y'all. I require my beauty rest."

Tank smiled suddenly. "No you don't, sweetheart, you're stunning enough already."

The boy gave a surprised bark of laughter. "Okay, I like you. Don't get killed or arrested. Just make them leave. I hate badges."

Tank nodded. He bet Isaac hated them too. He took a breath. He wasn't mighty fond of law enforcement himself.

Whoever was outside wasn't going anywhere. They banged on the door again.

"SBI. Open up!"

Ah, thought Tank, *trappers. Maybe they are after me.*

He cracked the door, just as pretty boy had done. Kept the chain on, although either one of those shifters could bust it easily.

The werewolf glared at him. "We're looking for a werewolf."

"Well," said Tank, "you found one."

She narrowed her eyes and sniffed him, ostentatiously. "You stink of sex and yourself."

"I should smell of something else?"

She narrowed her eyes. "No. Of course not."

He said, "Anything else, officers?"

"Oh, so much else. Get your ass out here. That one was human, but you're under our jurisdiction, sweetheart." She was not using Alpha VOICE. Still, best not to argue with a werewolf who so decidedly outranked him.

Tank didn't have to be nice about it though. He grunted. "Lemme get dressed."

He took a shower too, because fuck 'em.

Isaac had a contingency plan in place.

A gym membership.

It was, of course, under an assumed name, and more expensive than a man in his position ought to be able to afford. It was also in an entirely different part of the city. But all of that was the point. It was out of character for Isaac the man, or Isaac the werewolf, to belong to some fancy upmarket gym. The kind of gym that had a juice bar offering meat smoothies for shifter members. Isaac always salivated but never ordered anything.

He jogged there, because public transport was, well, *public*. And trackable. The gym never asked questions if he arrived sweaty. That was normal. It was a gym, after all.

Isaac had a personal locker with the rest of his go bag stashed there. It contained a new identity, money, snacks, that kind of thing. The gym also had nice showers and a full complement of soaps so he could wash away Tank's scent and smell like himself again, AKA nothing.

His wolf howled at him the entire time he washed. His wolf loved smelling like Tank, loved it too much. Ached and whined and pleaded with him about it. Didn't understand why they were running again. Why, if Isaac insisted on running, they were not running to Tank, to pack. They had *someone* now. They had refuge. They had other werewolves. There was a place for them to *be*. The wolf was confused. There was safety in pack. Go to pack!

Stupid, stupid wolf. Knows nothing, understands less.

Isaac took a long shower. It was the safest he was likely to be for a while. He might as well revel in luxury and cleanliness.

He quieted his anxious wolf by thinking about last night, which the wolf had enjoyed. Isaac was confused as to why both he and his wolf wanted Tank so badly. Even now when he knew he must run, all he wanted to do was hunt down Tank and devour him. He examined his own psyche. Was there some weird revenge fantasy mixed in? As one who had been abused by a big man, and then by packs of big men, did he want to have a big man subservient to him? He was a little revolted by that idea. It meant he'd taken advantage of Tank's giving nature.

This time his wolf thought *he* was being stupid. Isaac had always been dominant, despite his place in the pack hierarchy. He always liked to be in charge in bed; he got off on it. Not necessarily on pain, he wasn't a sadist, but he did like control. He needed control. Tank, on the other hand, obviously liked control taken away from him. Isaac wondered, miserably, if he would ever again meet a man better suited to his desires. They'd only just gotten started, but they had been so tasty together.

He finished his shower, dressed in his spare clothes, and checked over and consolidated his duffle bags. Then he sat a moment, staring at his hands, and wondered what to do next.

Flee town, probably. But where to go? North to Portland? Everyone else was doing that these days. He didn't think there was a Portland pack. But he'd been wrong about San Francisco. He could try for Canada.

"Hey, man."

Isaac looked up into the kindly eyes of Bruce, one of the gym dudes who spotted for him sometimes when he pretended to lift in the weight room. Bruce was always terribly impressed that Isaac could bench so much. Isaac always pretended to struggle more than he did. Supernatural strength could get a man into hot water at a gym.

They hadn't slept together, although Bruce had made the obligatory pass. Isaac had looked him up and down and said simply, "I'm a top. So are you."

Bruce had laughed and nodded. "Of course you are, should've known. Pity. Noodles?"

So they went and ate ramen together, as a sort of consolation prize, and that had been that. They'd stayed friendly, though they'd kept it to the gym ever since.

"You look a little low, dude, wanna grab some pho?"

Isaac thought, *why not?* Because he really didn't want to leave San Francisco.

He realized right then, for the first time, that he liked it. He liked the Bay Area and he liked Saucebox. He even liked his stupid prima-donna roommates and their dumb glitter that got *everywhere*. He liked Xavier and Lavish and Clara and Oscar and all his shifter clients who came in to see him because he could help them. And Tank, fuck, he really liked Tank.

I don't want to run, he thought. *For the first time in my life, I don't want to.*

Isaac could stay and fight, of course. He had done it in the past, once or twice. It always surprised people, but he could. He didn't enjoy doing it, and he wasn't sure what his wolf would do, now, if he let him out. It'd been so long.

His wolf snorted at him. *I would fight, of course. I would fight for us. Because we're one. You're the idiot who keeps us separate.*

Shut up, Isaac told his wolf.

He looked up at Bruce through his lashes. He was a good-looking guy, nice and muscled. But not Tank.

"Sure. Soup would be nice."

So they ended up at this pho place, getting the meat lovers special, because most places offered one now and it wasn't weird for human gym types to be all about the meat.

Bruce shared beloved memories of his childhood. How the first time he ate pho, his dad had ordered the tripe and then tried to pretend he actually liked it. It didn't ease Isaac's worries, but both of them enjoyed the nostalgia. And Isaac liked to be reminded there were good dads in the world.

"You're so easy to talk to, dude. I can't believe I remembered all that shit."

Isaac smiled. "Seems like you had a pretty cool childhood."

"Better than most." Bruce frowned at him. "So what happened to you? Boyfriend kick you out?"

Isaac blinked.

"I noticed the duffle."

"Something like that."

"Got a place to crash?"

Isaac only grunted. He didn't but he didn't want to lie, and he didn't want to leave himself open and vulnerable.

"I got a spare bed." Bruce seemed to surprise himself with the offer. Isaac suspected this was his weird empathy-powers working in his favor again. He tried to stifle down his wolf.

"Man," he grinned at Bruce, "I thought we went over this already."

Bruce blushed, looking a little overwhelmed. "I swear, you keep smiling and you make me wanna fool around regardless of preferences."

Isaac quirked a brow. "You switching for me?"

The man snorted a noodle.

"I thought not."

Bruce made puppy eyes at him and sighed. "Sometimes life ain't fair."

Isaac chuckled. "It's tough at the top."

"Very true."

There was a big hand on his knee. No malice in it. But it wasn't what Isaac wanted and some weird part of him, his wolf most likely, thought anything in that direction would be a betrayal of Tank's trust. *What the fuck, wolf? We just slept with the man once. Well, twice, but still.*

Isaac removed the hand and the invitation. "Decent of you, but I got this."

Bruce nodded. "Take my number, just in case."

Isaac didn't have his phone anymore. Too trackable. But he wrote the man's number down on a bit of napkin and was grateful for the thought, even if the offer came with expectations. He forgot, sometimes, that people could be kind.

"You a loner?"

Tank ignored the question and began walking. He had his motorcycle jacket on, not because he was cold but because he wanted both hands free. Also, the protection afforded by the thick leather was better than nothing, if one of them went after him with claws.

Although, it was full daylight, they'd have to be very strong to shift anything in direct sunlight.

He made his way out of the apartment building without answering any of the trapper's questions. He assumed they would follow him. Which they did. His only idea, at the moment, was to get them away from Isaac's home as fast as possible. Protected Isaac. His lover had run from them; therefore, they must be dangerous to Isaac.

Why a human man would flee trappers was totally mysterious. Then again, Isaac had that weird thing with shifters up in his business and confiding in him all the time. If he did have some kind of savage mage abilities that made him lure shifters, there was a chance he fell under SBI jurisdiction. Especially if the talent was on record.

Tank's brain went suddenly all conspiracy-theory wild. Was Isaac some kind of escaped government experiment? He did have strange moments when he seemed never to have been socialized, but Tank thought that was just humanity from a werewolf perspective. Was it possible Isaac was also legitimately weird for a human? Had he been raised in a lab or something creepy like that?

Tank wished he knew more. He wished he'd asked more questions about his lover's past before they fucked. Not that Isaac would have confided in him. But still, now Tank was faced with two SBI agents and he was working blind, his only goal to protect and to help as much as he could. He was certain of one thing, that he must not reveal any of the few facts he *did* know about Isaac.

If only Isaac had said something about being quarry, they could have gone to Alec. Or if not Alec, then Max. Max was a Magistar, no one could stop Max. Max was powerful enough to protect anyone. Maybe even go up against the SBI.

Tank was pleased to find his motorcycle still in one piece on the sidewalk, his helmet locked to the frame. Lower Mission was one of the worst parts of the city, even with gentrification. He turned, leaning slightly against his bike, crossed his arms and loomed.

It didn't work so well on these two. The berserker was bigger than he was, and the werewolf was an Alpha, so size didn't matter.

She was a fascinating-looking female. All muscle and sharp black hair. Her jaw was determined. She looked like she got her own way a lot. *Handsome*, he supposed, *rather than beautiful*. Her skin was dark, he thought maybe Mediterranean or Native American, or both. Her nose was prominent and her lips lush. She oozed command and dominance.

Tank was occasionally inclined toward women. He

thought she might be one of those in whose direction he would bend. Her control was iron and persuasive and it would be no hardship to kneel to her. Except he had Isaac still fresh inside him, and Isaac in all of his senses (except smell) and she had frightened his Isaac away. So the inclination to kneel was only some small secret at the back of his head that told him he could, not that he must.

The bear shifter was typical of the northern European stock. Massive and blond and to be blamed on the Vikings.

With Tank's attention finally on them, even though they were now in a public street mid-afternoon, the SBI officers started interrogating him. Or tried to.

The Alpha took point, possibly because Tank was her kind, or possibly because she always did most of the talking.

"You're a big one, pup. Enforcer?"

Tank shook his head.

"Loner, then?"

She had the right to ask. Werewolf loners were dangerous and as such, the social condition should be established up front. Loners could get erratic without the surety of a pack – emotional in the extreme, their actions unpredictable. It was one of the reasons SBI used Alphas to track, because it took an Alpha to control a loner.

"I don't see a pack at *your* back, Alpha." Tank challenged her gently. Knowing, of course, that the SBI *was* her pack.

She curled a lip at him. "SIT DOWN."

Tank's knees buckled slightly and he moved instantly to sit on his motorcycle. Then he realized what he was doing and locked his legs in place. *This is not Alec's command. This is not my Alpha.*

Around them several street humans, whose wills were muddled by drugs or loneliness or something worse, abruptly stopped whatever they were doing and sat down on the sidewalk.

The Alpha's eyes were fixed on Tank. She noticed, of course, that he fought off the need to obey. But she had also seen him start to follow VOICE.

This told her a great deal. "Solid resistance from a low rank," she said, possibly for the benefit of her partner. "So, you have a pack and Alpha already. And you're local, which means you belong to San Andreas."

Tank inclined his head.

"You do not live with them?"

Tank said nothing. *She thinks Isaac's apartment is mine? Interesting.* So they're looking for him but they don't know much about him.

The berserker looked at his partner, heavy brows furrowed. "This clearly isn't him."

"Clearly."

"So why are we bothering? We've tracking to do."

"This one is out of the ordinary. I don't like that."

"So far, everything we know about this San Andreas Pack is *out of the ordinary.*"

"He's so big, must be enforcer, but he doesn't show any of the signs."

Tank allowed himself to be talked about and ignored. Which she also noticed. Which was certainly not enforcer behavior.

She looked him up and down. "You really aren't, are you?"

"Nope. Just very big, not vicious."

The Alpha sighed. "I could make you talk."

"You could try. Alec might object."

She narrowed her eyes at him. "You think your Alpha is stronger than me?"

Alphas, always so fucking competitive. "Of course he is." Tank was nothing if not loyal.

"Because he's a dude?"

Tank actually laughed at that. This woman could bench press Alec, easily. Alpha strength was nothing to do with biological sex or physical prowess. "Because he's *Alec fucking Frederiksen.*"

She snorted.

"I take it you haven't met my Alpha yet?"

She snorted again.

Tank was pleased – that meant whatever werewolf they were chasing, it was nothing to do with his pack.

"You're after a loner, then?"

"How is it you are suddenly asking the questions of us?" The bear shifter wanted to know.

Tank explained, trying not to sound condescending. "If there is a loner in our territory, protocol demands you notify the local pack. Yet you haven't come to visit us. And here you stand *in our territory*. Seems to me, SBI, you're in violation of your own regulations." Like Alec would let them out of the house without knowing pack rights.

The berserker looked impressed. "Special dispensation for *this* loner."

Tank frowned. That meant the werewolf they were after was insane and either lost to his wolf form or psychotic, separated from it and stuck as a human. Either case made him a grave risk to himself and others. Or herself, although that was rare. Was the wolf after Isaac? Fixated maybe? Is that why the trackers were looking for him? But then, why would Isaac run?

"Moon-mad or beast-lost?" He hazarded a query.

The SBI looked at each other, but they remained close-mouthed. Clearly feeling they'd given Tank enough information. Perhaps Isaac knew something he shouldn't?

Tank gritted his teeth and spoke for his pack. "Come meet my Alpha."

The trappers looked at him. Suddenly thoughtful.

"Not yet, grunt," said the female, realizing at last exactly what he was – nothing important, just one of the pack. "We have another twenty-four hours before we're legally obliged to involve you. And you can't say anything about us being here."

"I won't need to."

Her eyes narrowed sharply. "Your Alpha knows we're in town already?"

Tank gave an expressive sort of shrug.

"Well, shit."

The bear shifter said, "We knew it was a risk when we hit the local DURPS for those records. There's almost always a leak to the local shifter community when we do."

"This pack has only been here six months. How'd they integrate so fucking quickly?" The Alpha wrinkled her nose, annoyed and impressed. "This isn't the kind of city to be all open arms and free love over werewolves. I can't see how a pack even functions in this town." She turned to glare at Tank.

Tank followed her reasoning completely. By all rights, the San Francisco Bay Area was the worst possible place for a pack of werewolves. Generally speaking, werewolves lived up to the shifter version of trailer trash. They were closed-minded, heterosexual, and pack-oriented, which was as close to *gang* as made no difference to the feds. (Those packs that the government didn't take advantage of by turning into military units, of course.) Most packs hung out in bars and on bikes (well, San Andreas fit *that* model), but those bars and bikes were rural, and their trailers were off-grid. Female Alphas happened, of course, but they tended to splinter off quickly, form their own packs with other women, or they went into government work. He understood this one's prejudice because it was based in reality. Their old pack had been pretty typical, although Fifi was a more understanding Alpha than most when Alec came along. He'd let them splinter and not fought them over the breach. Possibly because he knew that Alec was taking the weirdos and the malcontents with him – the homosexuals and the outrageous. Fifi had likely believed they weakened his pack. He certainly wouldn't want to see them breed into it, those few who were inclined.

"We aren't a normal pack." Tank swung to sit on his bike. Their DURPS records would have indicated *some* of this. Sexual orientation was a protected status, even among shifters. So these trappers wouldn't know from the records that the San Andreas Pack was mostly queer. Although if they read the files carefully they'd see that both Alec and Bryan had *domesticated* listed next to their names. Pair-bonded shifters tended to behave themselves slightly better than single ones, so a mating on record was considered a point of socialization and therefore *not* protected status. It wouldn't take much to learn both werewolves had been domesticated by males.

The trappers appeared, however, not to know. Not to have investigated San Andreas as thoroughly as they should have.

This told Tank, more than anything else, how little these two were interested in his pack. Whatever they were chasing, it wasn't anything to do with San Andreas.

Still, Alec would want Tank to press the pack's agenda. And Tank wanted to give the SBI something more to worry over than Isaac's whereabouts. So he forced his point. "When your grace period is up, I recommend you come visit us." He looked them up and down. Law enforcement, on the tail of a vagrant werewolf, they probably hadn't eaten properly, or hunted, in weeks. "Stop by and we'll feed you something," he paused significantly, "*fresh.*"

The two glared at him in silence for a long moment. Finally, the Alpha spoke because she had to pull the power back in her favor. "You're not leaving town anytime soon, are you Mr…?"

"Nope," said Tank, not offering his name. They'd never offered theirs. Besides, they could find his easily enough now that they knew he belonged to the San Andreas Pack. That's exactly what DURPS was for.

Then, because he wasn't Alpha, so it was no shame to

ask permission, Tank said, "Am I free to go?"

"Just not too far." She looked pleased to have been asked.

Tank knew how to play the game.

He pulled on his helmet, ostentatiously, blocking them out. He didn't respond and he didn't agree to stay. He'd leave town if that meant following Isaac, but he had to find him first.

CHAPTER TEN
Werewolf on the Lamb

Isaac ended up at Clara's place. It was the best he could think of at short notice. If they'd found him at his home, they likely could find him at work. Clara's, however, was somewhat less predictable. He assumed his previous pack (such as it was) was after him. They'd be hard-pressed to trace him to Clara's.

The Rocky Mountain Pack had no military or law enforcement connections to tap for aid. They were an off-grid pack with neither the resources, nor the intelligence, to run background checks on all his coworkers and then track each address down.

Unless, of course, it wasn't them. But who else wanted him that badly?

He turned up at Clara's only a few hours before they were supposed to go on shift together.

She let him in with a broad smile. "Hi, sugar! Come to do your nails? I got this fantastic turquoise – would look killer on your skin tone." He catalogued her mood automatically – happy and relaxed.

Then she really looked at his face. "Isaac, sugar, what's wrong? Did you not have fun with Tank last night?"

Isaac blinked at her.

"Oh, you *did* have fun. I thought you might. He is *mighty* fine. You should stick with that one for a bit. Is that the problem then, too much fun?"

"Clara, I'm not going to work tonight."

"You're not?"

"Can I crash here?"

"Sugar, what's going on? What happened?" She took his hands in hers and guided him to sit on her old worn corduroy couch.

Isaac was ready with his story. He hated to lie to her, but he couldn't possibly tell her the truth. "It's Hayden."

"Oh no, that asshole! Couldn't Tank, you know, stay and guard you and be all big and buff and protective and shit?"

"He can't be with me all the time. And I shouldn't need him to be."

"He can't? Pity. I imagine you'd like having him watch out for you, you know, all the parts of you." She licked her lips suggestively.

Isaac actually found himself laughing. "I think he would."

Clara waggled her brows. "There is something you aren't telling me. Did you two? Ooooo, you did! I want all the juicy details." She winced slightly. "Well, not juicy juicy. How about the Cliff Notes?"

"Can I stay here, just for tonight?"

Clara nodded, although there was a little fear in her eyes. Isaac hated himself for putting it there. There was a nasty piece of crap boyfriend in her past, years before Isaac knew her. But she was justifiably scared of anything that smacked of stalker.

Isaac looked at her full on. "I won't bring him down on you. He can't find me tonight and I'll be gone tomorrow, I promise."

"I don't wanna turn you out on the streets, not ever."

"But you need to protect yourself Clara, I get it. And

you've no guarantee he won't go through you to get to me. Please make sure Oscar walks you home tonight, okay?"

She nodded, "Okay. But it'll have to be the couch for you. I already got a friend in Mandy's bedroom. Mandy's at her boyfriend's for the weekend, bless her."

"Clara, I'm shocked, you have *other friends* besides me?" Isaac placed a hand to his chest and batted his eyelashes, vamping it up to make her feel better.

"I know, right? This one's special, she's a shifter. Sweetest little thing."

Isaac tensed. Waiting, holding his breath.

"Cat shifter. You'll like her and she'll adore you. They always do. We were at school together."

Isaac cocked his head. He didn't know much about Clara's past (humans didn't tend to spill their guts quite the same way as shifters did in his presence). But he did know that she'd been one of those true Southern belles with the debutante thing and the white dress and the private school and a ton of money. Something bad had happened, twisted it all, and she'd run, abandoning everything – including the money. Only to land in an apartment almost as shabby as his, in an almost as bad part of San Francisco.

Clara made a funny face and explained. "I went to one of those horrible all-girls high schools. Catholic. They took in charity cases and Jessie was one of them. Of course, she hadn't shifted yet. It was quite the scandal when they found out what her family really was. They kicked her out but we stayed in touch."

Isaac nodded. It explained a lot about Clara. Including why she wasn't weirded out when shifters started frequenting her bar, following Isaac. She'd had a shifter friend as a kid. That kind of thing made a difference with humans. "Will it weird her out to find me here?"

Clara nodded. "Probably. I'll let her know before I leave. Right now though, I'm starving." She made big hopeful eyes at him.

Isaac stood, glad to have purpose. "I'll make you something." Isaac enjoyed cooking. It'd been one of his duties at the cult. The only one he was actually good at. Now that he also got to choose what to make and how to make it, cooking was a true pleasure.

Clara clasped her hands in a pretend swoon. "I love you. Stay forever."

He gave her a sad smile and located her one skillet. "Me-style omelet?" He knew what was likely in her fridge – a dozen eggs, some optimistically acquired (now sad) vegetables, and twenty different types of cheese.

"Marry me?" she said. Clara couldn't cook anything, or at least she claimed she couldn't.

Isaac made her a quick open-faced omelet, cheese on top turned bubbly and crispy from the broiler. Clara always joked it was part omelet, part pizza, but it tasted delicious. Especially with a ton of hot sauce, which Clara put on everything. Isaac, who had nothing to prove where spicy was concerned, preferred his without.

She ate two helpings with gusto and then scampered off to work, promising to apologize to his *special friends* when they showed up for counseling. "But Xavier is all your problem to handle, sugar."

"Just tell him what's up, he'll get it."

She gave him a long-suffering arch of perfectly plucked brows, but left, and he knew she'd do as he asked.

Isaac was a night owl by nature and by profession. He stayed up, puttering about cleaning Clara's kitchen, and then her living room, and then most anything else he could clean. It occupied the time and made him feel useful and like he wasn't taking advantage of his friend by lying and hiding.

A couple hours later, Jessie appeared from the second bedroom looking sleepy and confused. She was bigger than Isaac expected, all striking sharp features, nose a little large, eyes huge and liquid black, skin a deep gold. Her

hair was a mane of brown with a million shades to it. He'd
thought when Clara said *cat* she meant *bakeneko*, which
meant small. But this woman was statuesque, which meant
she was a larger shifter. From the Arabic cast to her
features, his guess went to lion, but America being the
melting pot it was, the lines between source country and
shifter type were blurred.

She looked surprised and a little scared to see him,
because Clara had forgotten to warn her.

Isaac let his wolf rise to the surface, not in his eyes or
fur or skin, just in his nature. He pressed that out, the part
of him that made him comfortable to others, and presented
it to her, like some friendly gift – invisible warmth and
affection, low-rank, non-threatening.

She instantly relaxed and gave him an appraising look.
"Who're you?"

"Friend of Clara's. I'm Isaac. Another stray."

"Jessie." There was a wariness to her that could be cat
nature, or could be fear of men or fear of humans.

He nodded. "You went to school with Clara before you
were bitten." He was telling her he knew her story, that
Clara had trusted him with that.

She relaxed further. "You work with her at the club?"

"I do."

"Not tonight?" Her look turned flirtatious.

"Naw." He suspected she was one of those who felt her
worth partly justified by male admiration. His wolf wanted
to help her get over that.

"Why you here?"

"Boyfriend troubles. You?"

She smiled, a little disappointed. "The same."

Isaac's voice dropped instinctively to that mellow soft
burr that was as near to a purr as a werewolf could get. "I
made an omelet. Are you hungry?"

"Absolutely ravenous."

He cut a piece of the omelet and popped it in the

microwave. It beeped and he handed it over with hot sauce, which she declined, and a glass of milk, which she smiled over.

"She told you I was a cat shifter?"

He nodded. "I thought you'd be smaller."

She laughed. "I should be larger, but I'm not very big for my kind."

He offered his best guess. "Sekhmet?"

She nodded.

"So things okay with your pride?"

"Not so great, actually. The boyfriend was an arranged match, and there aren't enough of us for me to turn him down out of hand."

Isaac put the kettle on to make them both some tea. Hot milk would be better, but she was already drinking most of what Clara had in the fridge.

"Was it out of hand?"

She shook her head, looking sad.

"Well then, why don't you tell old Isaac all about it?" He let himself fall back into his role. There was comfort and peace in it for both of them. For all Isaac chafed against the reasons, he did love helping people, even when he couldn't help himself – especially then.

Tank went to bounce that evening hoping against hope that Isaac would show up for his shift, but he didn't. Of course he didn't. He was running scared, so he'd avoid all usual haunts.

Tank's churning stomach suggested that Isaac might not even be in San Francisco anymore. It hurt to already miss and mourn someone he'd known for such a comparatively short space of time.

The trappers *did* turn up, in plain clothes but still looking like cops in that way that people do when they're military trained. *You, civilian, me, protector – hoo-ah.* Or whatever.

They certainly weren't in clubbing gear. The bear shifter seemed to think khakis were acceptable. Which of course, they weren't. Ever. Even Tank knew that.

Tank grimaced at them and let them in, but kept a close eye on them.

They seemed startled to find him working the door, and engaged in a hissed back and forth that went something along the lines of, "Maybe it *is* him and we're totally off." "No, there must be another one. They just work together."

The trappers settled into a small booth to one side of the dance floor with a good view of the room and the bar. Tank reluctantly approved this choice. It was the spot he would have selected.

After that, everything was normal, except it didn't fill up as much as before. Isaac was certainly a draw.

Xavier came over to Tank at one point and asked, in an annoyed tone, what he'd done to his best bartender.

Tank gestured with his chin at the trappers, refusing to take the blame for Isaac running.

"Narcs?" Xavier noted their posture, position in the room, and general attitude.

The man didn't look scared for himself, only confused, which reassured Tank. He'd hate to think there was anything blatantly illegal going on at Saucebox. He was growing rather fond of the place and didn't want it to be shut down.

"Feds," said Tank. Not sure he wanted Xavier to know they were SBI. FBI was bad enough.

Xavier's nose wrinkled in disgust. "They're after Isaac? Why?"

Tank shrugged.

Lavish came sashaying over. "Tank, gorgeous, where's my honey?"

Tank lifted his chin at Xavier.

"Not that one. My pretty, pretty honey?"

Tank shrugged. "Not in tonight."

Lavish pouted. "But it's his shift. Isaac never misses his shift."

Xavier arched a brow. "Sure he does. Even Isaac gets sick occasionally."

Tank instantly stiffened. "How occasionally?"

"Don't you worry, big guy, there's nothing seriously wrong with your boy."

Lavish sighed. "It's pathetic here without him. No one knows what to do with themselves."

It was kind of true. The usually small trickle of after-work shifters had come, hoping to see Isaac, or having arranged for a consult. But there was no Isaac, so they milled about – lost, confused, and unhappy. Or they left.

Tank worried, of course he did. And he watched the trappers. He also kept Hayden out, when that asshole showed up, informing him curtly that Isaac wasn't even there.

Hayden spat in his face.

Tank decked him, breaking his nose. But that was basic posturing amongst predators. The nose would heal the moment the barghest shifted.

The trappers didn't even bother to look up at the brief fight. An Alpha could have sent Hayden running, tail between his legs, without doing anything. Clearly, she had other stuff on her mind, stuff that involved drinking a pink, foamy concoction and contemplating legal homicide of someone not Hayden.

The night continued.

Nothing else happened.

No Isaac.

The SBI Alpha eventually stood up, walked over, and slammed her hand to the bar top to get Clara's attention. The place had gotten crowded, although more so with humans than shifters.

"Where the fuck is he?"

Clara ignored her and no one else answered. The other SBI agent drank his sweet mead glumly.

As Tank had expected, they came after him at the end of the night, after the club had closed.

"You hiding him, grunt?" the Alpha wanted to know, clearly annoyed at the universe for stalling her hunt.

Tank rolled his eyes and turned to Oscar. "You walking Clara home?"

"For sure. You're off duty without your boy, or does the boss have something more for you?"

Trappers heard that. The bear shifter sniffed. "What boy is that?"

Oscar narrowed his eyes at the big blond. "Who the fuck are you?"

The berserker pulled out his SBI badge.

Oscar sneered at it. "I'm human and so is our boy, so I ain't gotta say nothing to you."

Clara turned up then, eyes sad and worried. Oscar took her arm and hustled her off, because the trappers might try talking to her too.

"Mistrustful of shifters, are they?" the Alpha asked Tank.

Tank resisted rolling his eyes. She was such an Alpha. "Nope, it's just your charming personality. Draws all the humans to your yard, I'm sure." He pulled on his motorcycle jacket. "You following me back to pack lands?"

It wasn't really a question. He could see it in their eyes. Their grace time was over and his pack had rights. Tank was heading home anyway – they might as well use him as an ambassador.

The trappers exchanged looks.

"Fuck it," said the Alpha.

The berserker laughed at her. "Werewolves, so touchy about territory."

CHAPTER ELEVEN
Teal Fire Balls

The trappers drove the ugliest car Tank had ever seen. Some kind of massive SUV thing. Tank supposed it had to be big for a bear shifter to fit inside, but it sure wasn't pretty. It looked like some Goth kid got hold of a brick in the 1980s, dressed it in metallic black, and stuck wheels on it. It shone more emo than evil under the streetlights.

Ha, thought Tank, *reminds me of a few Doms I know.*

Tank knew who would be home when he got there. Alec, because he kept daylight hours at his lab. Marvin, because he was on first shift with Coast Guard. Colin, because his classes started in the afternoon. Max and Bryan, because they worked in mysterious ways.

The enforcers were off on a Heavy Lifting gig, some sort of all-night selkie splash-and-shuffle. Lovejoy would have already left for his early morning bakery duties, feeding the Castro.

Tank parked his motorcycle and was entirely unsurprised to find Bryan on patrol in the pre-dawn light.

The Beta, who made for a massive dirty-cream-colored blob, came ghosting through the yard to greet him. When an SUV pulled up behind Tank's bike and disgorged strangers, Bryan immediately howled a warning.

The Beta approached the SUV cautiously, hackles up and teeth bared, until he stood next to Tank, ready to protect and defend.

Max slammed out of the apartment above the garage and came running down the steps. He might be human, but he knew his mate's howl. Bryan so rarely made a fuss about anything, it startled Max into injudicious motion. He was all angles and imminent disastrous stumble. His hoodie was half zipped, his sweats hung low and baggy off lean hips, and he was wearing those fuzzy socks, the kind with the rubber bits on the bottom.

Max looked the very opposite of a fearsome Magistar. A wet roll of toilet paper was more threatening and more dignified. Nevertheless, he joined them, quivering and glaring, hand on his mate's fluffy wolf head.

Tank explained. "They've come to make introductions. These are the trappers we were told about."

Bryan continued to rumble a warning. His eyes did not move off the female Alpha on their turf.

Moments later, alerted by the noise or by some Alpha instinct, Alec came gliding through the trees from the direction of the main house. He wore his work clothes – a button-up shirt and dark jeans. He did wear his lab coat at home sometimes, without anything else – it had snaps so it was easy to get out of and more dignified than a bathrobe. Marvin liked the look a lot too. Tank thought it was silly. Fortunately, Alec wasn't in that particular state of dress at the moment. With his glasses on and his hair sticking up, he looked like nothing so much as a geeky graduate student, with a head full of philosophy and dead poets. He was, as a result, very easy to underestimate.

Alec certainly didn't look like an Alpha. Slighter of frame than most, almost delicate when compared to the other Alphas. But he always thought like one. He'd left Colin and Marvin, the pack's weakest members, at the house where they were safest.

Tank missed the presence of their enforcers. Not that he didn't have complete faith in Alec's abilities. He'd never met an Alpha with stronger VOICE. And Alec could fight. He didn't enjoy it, but he was good at it.

Tank said to him, "Alpha. These are the two spooks who've been sniffing about our territory. They're tracking something or someone. Haven't told me what, exactly. Their grace period is up so I brought them to meet you, as protocol dictates."

Alec nodded. "So, introduce me."

Tank showed his neck briefly. "They've not told me their names, Alpha. I am afraid they must introduce themselves."

Alec's eyes narrowed – a breach in protocol, plus an insult to Tank. Not to mention the fact that they all knew the trappers were over their two days grace. Trickle had told them when the SBI first arrived in San Andreas territory.

Alec turned to face the interlopers. He didn't indicate that he was sniffing them, but he was. His unhurried gaze traced their faces, bodies, and muscles – the big Norseman and the other Alpha werewolf.

Then he waited.

Finally the berserker, clearly tired of wolf posturing, said, "I'm Special Agent Faste. This is Special Agent Lenis."

"Alec Frederiksen, Alpha." Alec gestured to Bryan, still in wolf form. "Bryan Frederiksen, my Beta."

Agent Lenis started at that. Clearly, she'd jumped to the usual conclusion, that a wolf as big as Bryan, out on patrol and as obviously powerful, was an enforcer.

Alec continued as if he hadn't noticed, although Tank knew him to be secretly pleased. Alec liked putting people off balance. "You know Tank."

Tank nodded at the agents, as if they hadn't been staring at each other across a crowded club all evening.

"And this is Max, Beta-mate." Alec didn't say what Max was. No point in giving away information about the pack's ace in the hole.

Max's fine sharp features looked particularly autocratic and cruel in the dawn light.

Alec assessed the two SBI agents. He gave them a contemplative once-over so slow it bordered on insulting. "Will you eat with us or walk the perimeter with me?" He was really asking: *Are you friends or emissaries? Will you build tethers in my territory or are you merely passing through?*

Because Alec was a smart man, and it was always better to be on the good side of cops, no matter what version they came packaged as, he tempted them further. "We have some venison, killed only a few days ago, plus homemade honey wine and local salmon."

The berserker looked both pleased and confused. "Fish?"

"Wolves will eat fish." Alec smiled. "But we have a cuter reason to keep our den well stocked with sea-life."

Agent Lenis seemed unhappy but interest-bound to take the peace offering. "We would gladly eat with you, Alpha."

Alec nodded at the capitulation. "Then we would gladly feed you, Alpha Lenis." He said her wolf title, not her government one, emphasizing colleagues in species, not the power imbalance between officer and civilian. "Follow me, if you would?"

Without having to be asked, Max and Bryan fell into step behind Alec. Max's hand rested lightly on Bryan's furry head. Contact between mage and familiar meant they could cast quintessence in an instant. Their Magistar clearly did not trust these visitors.

The trappers followed next, leaving Tank to bring up the rear. It was fair and there was no dishonor. The rear position was normally for an enforcer, guarding the flank.

Tank was being told by everyone there that he might have to fight, and he accepted it. He hoped if it came to it, he faced the bear rather than the other Alpha.

Through the vast overgrown yard and up the hill, the massive house loomed over them rather suddenly. Their two visitors regarded it with disconcerted eyes.

Alec opened the door and called out, "It's me and I've brought guests."

Code for: *It's safe to come out but use caution.*

Marvin and Colin emerged from upstairs.

The trappers looked even more confused.

Tank's smile went unseen. Everything about the San Andreas Pack would seem incongruous to them. Their Alpha, physically so slight and nerdy, especially compared to Tank. Their Beta not changing form to greet them, and nearly twice the size of most normal Betas. The fact that their Beta-mate was male and smelled of coolant and power and all things alien to pack. No mage should ever wish to live in the company of wolves. It would require weaker noses than theirs not to realize Max was a mage of some kind.

And now this.

Colin, ethereal and lovely with his strawberry blond hair and wounded green eyes. Marvin, lively and impossibly beautiful and smelling of the sea. Like two fragile fae princes from some ancient legend.

Alec introduced them, pride in his voice. "Colin, our youngest pack member, and Marvin, Alpha-mate. These are SBI reps, Special Agent Faste and Special Agent Lenis." For the benefit of Marvin and Max, whose sense of smell left much to be desired, he added, "Agent Lenis is a werewolf Alpha, government pack, I suspect. Agent Faste is a berserker, in case you hadn't guessed from his size."

Marvin moved to Alec's side. After a quick hug and a whispered reassurance from his mate, the merman was all bright smiles and warm, welcoming chatter. It was artifice, but Marvin was good at being charming, especially when nervous or under threat. In merfolk, charm was a survival trait. Luring sailors to their deaths using beauty and siren song wasn't all mythology. Marvin had simply moved onto luring locals to barbecues using throw pillows and canapés. Everyone needs a hobby.

Colin gave a shy smile and went instantly to the kitchen to get out food. If Alec had brought strangers *inside* the pack house they should be fed as a soon as possible, especially if one of them was a visiting werewolf. Etiquette demanded sustenance.

Alec said, "Venison for our werewolf guest, please Colin. And to drink?" He quirked a brow at Lenis.

She surprised them all with, "A beer if you've got it?"

Colin answered, soft and calm, "Of course. Stout or something lighter, IPA perhaps?" To drink beer was unusual in a werewolf, but to drink IPA was unheard of. Colin explained the IPA shyly, "We have humans visit regularly."

Tank wondered if that was why she'd asked. To check and see if they were this welcoming to the greater local community, or only when government spooks came to call.

"Stout's fine," said the Alpha, no hint as to whether this pleased her or not.

Alec turned to his mate. "And if you might spare some of your salmon, my love?"

Marvin inclined his pretty head. "With pleasure. Smoked, pickled, salted, poached, or raw, Agent Faste?"

The berserker's mouth dropped open. "You're a merman!"

"Yes, and as such, I have excellent taste in salmon. And most of it I caught myself."

"Raw, please," said the big man, ears pink under Marvin's amused regard.

Alec hid a smile. "And some honey wine, Agent? Or we have mead."

Faste's eyes were eager. "The wine, please."

Colin bustled about collecting what was needed. Usually it was Lovejoy in the kitchen, he considered it his domain, but when strangers were around Colin was always given something constructive to do. He didn't like making small talk and he wanted to be busy (then he did not have to socialize and he felt useful). Everyone in the pack understood that.

Max and Bryan went and sat in the den. Max in one of the solo armchairs, Bryan curled against his feet – still not feeling it was safe enough for human form.

Alec made a motion for the rest to join them.

Reluctantly, the trappers sat together on one of the settees. Marvin had recently arranged a series of teal sequined throw pillows around the seating area, the sight of which appeared to give Alpha Lenis heartburn.

Alec took the big couch opposite. Marvin snuggled in next to him.

Tank remained standing in the background, as an enforcer would.

Colin put a tray of artfully arranged venison, salmon, and cheesy crackers on the coffee table, and passed around small plates and cocktail forks. Then he returned to the kitchen for drinks. Unlike with humans, shifters always served meat before booze – blood was thicker than alcohol.

Alec said, "What brings you to my territory, special agents?"

"We're hunting someone." Agent Faste took the glass of wine with a nod. Colin blushed to be noticed.

"I figured you would be. Are they dangerous?" Alec drew all attention back to himself.

The trappers exchanged a look. It was a fair question. Alec was really asking if there was a werewolf loner or worse in his territory. Something that his pack might have to handle. Or if it was some other shifter risk, whether the pack might be called in as backup. By law, werewolf packs could be conscripted as short-term militia for shifter crises because they formed the most stable fighting units in any given area. It could be worse – in other countries packs were conscripted for long-term military service.

"He's not a threat to you or yours, Alpha. Although what's after him might be." Agent Lenis grimaced over her beer and then reached hurriedly for a piece of venison.

Agent Faste continued the explanation. "His name's Isaac and your big grunt there works with him."

"What did he do?" Alec's eyes flickered briefly to Tank.

I'll hear about it later, thought Tank, although most of him was now just more worried about Isaac. *What trouble is coming for my lovely man?*

"Nothing illegal," said Agent Faste.

Which made Tank profoundly relieved. At least Isaac wasn't in trouble with that side of the law.

Agent Lenis, oddly, seemed to leap to Isaac's defense. "Unless you count the crime of being born." She narrowed her eyes at Alec, Alpha to Alpha. "You never met him?"

"No."

"You swear it?"

"Are you questioning my integrity?" Alec bristled.

Agent Lenis flinched. She was worried or she wouldn't have spoken so rashly. Tank could see it.

Alec was too annoyed at being challenged by another Alpha in his own den to understand the reasons.

Tank stepped in to smooth things over, as Bryan was still in wolf form and could not do his Beta duty. "Isaac has never met this pack. So far as I could tell, the man is terrified of werewolves."

Agent Lenis gave a funny, sarcastic laugh. "So you *did* interact with him at the club."

Tank explained to his confused pack mates. "Isaac is one of the bartenders at Saucebox where I've been bouncing."

Alec's eyebrow lifted very subtly. *The one you were set to bodyguard?* Tank knew he was asking.

Tank inclined his head. *Yes, that one.*

They understood each other.

Agent Lenis's eyes narrowed on Tank. Not missing the interaction, but not understanding it either. Pack was pack and she was not one of them. She pressed Tank. "And you didn't notice anything odd about him?"

Tank shrugged. "Lots of people don't like werewolves."

Of course he'd noted tons of odd things about Isaac – no signature scent, all shifters attracted to him, so dominant and so afraid at the same time. But he wasn't going to offer up any of that. After all, he didn't know what they knew, and he'd no incentive to help them.

"That's not what I meant, and you know it." The other Alpha's voice was sharp. She knew Tank was hiding something.

Alec twitched, ready to defend his pack. The room got tense.

"Should I have noticed something odd?" Tank professed ignorance.

"Are you really that thick?" The berserker seemed genuinely curious. He was taken in by Tank's size and perceived slowness. Which, of course, he shouldn't have been, since it happened to bear shifters all the time.

Tank's face went blank. "That a rhetorical question?"

Alec understood what was happening.

Play along. Just poor, big, dumb Tank.

Max and Marvin both looked confused but they followed Alec's lead and allowed Tank to be thought an idiot.

Tank made his voice a little slow. "We were just work colleagues. Why on earth would I...?"

A narrowing of Lenis's eyes met that. "Why would you indeed?" The female Alpha looked disgusted.

Alec interceded. Anything that smacked of bullying raised his hackles. "Tank's only been at that job a few days. I don't see what you think he knows."

Just like that, things went rather rapidly south.

"We think he knows a great deal."

"We think he's slept with our prey."

"We think he knows where our prey's gone and we think that he believes he's protecting him by not talking."

"Do you have any idea what will happen if we don't get to him first?"

Tank blinked, feeling their anger and frustration roll over him.

Alec said, quietly, softly, "What? What will happen to him? Who else is after him?"

"You'd better be careful, new little Alpha." Agent Lenis curled her lip. "You might have a challenge on your hands."

Alec gave the woman a once-over. "From you?" Neutral tone, no contempt, just curiosity.

"If I have to for the sake of national security and the greater shifter community, yes."

"You think I'm not strong enough, that I can't fight you off?" Alec raised his eyebrows.

The bear shifter added. "Just look at you. You aren't exactly a threat."

Max spoke then, cold and sharp, "He has other fucking assets."

"Some of them quite mouthy." Alec micro-shook his head at his brother-in-law. Then he turned back to the trappers. "I'm stronger than I look."

"You're insane. You've no idea what's coming. You've a pack of misfits and a crown of ignorance." Alpha Lenis looked worried as well as mad.

"You could rectify part of that."

"How did you know we were in the area?" Agent Faste asked.

Alec paused at the switch of topic. Then gave a small smile, "As Max so succinctly put it: *I have other fucking assets.*"

Marvin spoke at that juncture, his eyes cold as the Pacific Ocean. "So, you come here to vaguely threaten us, and hint at something bad headed our direction. But you give us no particulars and you accuse us of hiding a man we've never met. Except Tank who worked with him a few times. Are we done now?"

The two trappers looked at the merman, who crossed his arms over his chest and rolled his gorgeous turquoise eyes at them.

"What, your so-called *other assets* can't inform you of the particulars?" Smug did not look good on Agent Lenis.

Her partner shook his head, sensing her patience was at its limit. The bear shifter stood, massive and looming in a way that was greater than even Tank could handle. "Fine, you won't tell us anything. Therefore, I'm legally bound to inform you that Alpha Alec Frederiksen may have a challenger within the week."

Everyone started and glared at Alpha Lenis, who continued to look smug.

Would the challenge really come from her? Tank wondered. *Or was yet another Alpha heading into their territory?*

Six months with no trouble at all from the greater werewolf community and now it's raining wolf shit?

Tank's mouth went dry. Thinking about Isaac: How Hayden had stalked him. How he was so ready to run. How shifters so desperately wanted to be near him.

Tank should have held his tongue, but he was worried about his lover. He hadn't noticed a bite mark anywhere on the man, but not all shifters showed ownership in the same way.

"Has Isaac been claimed?" Tank tried to keep the tremor out of his voice. From Alec's worried look he wasn't entirely successful.

There was no other way to tie a human to the shifter community but a mating mark. It was normally done to show protection. Max, who was already covered in scars, had a wolf's paw print tattooed on his neck, to indicate that he belonged with Bryan. Not that Max needed pack protection, but there was some small part of the snarky prickly man that needed to *belong*.

Marvin wore a platinum wolf emblem on a platinum chain about his neck. Platinum because gold clashed with his scales, and silver was obviously gauche around werewolves.

If Isaac had been claimed, it wasn't willingly. And that was certainly illegal. It would explain why SBI had been called in. Unless they were invested in returning Isaac to a mate he didn't want.

Tank drew himself up and glared at Agent Lenis. "Isaac is a free man!"

The Agents were both now standing and staring down at him.

"You have no idea what you're talking about," said the Alpha, sneering slightly.

"It's for his own good," stressed the berserker.

"Just tell us where he is," insisted his partner.

Tank shook his head. "I don't know where he is. Use VOICE if you need to. My answer won't be any different."

Alpha Lenis took a step closer to Tank. "You can't tell me you met him and didn't want to keep him. *Everyone* wants to keep him!"

Tank flinched. *No, I wanted* him *to keep me. But he didn't. I wasn't good enough. And that's fine because it's his choice!*

Tank took a deep breath. Alpha power stung his nose. She smelled of wolf and something else, something wild and desert-born, crossbreed perhaps? Was she more than just werewolf?

"Do *you* want to *keep* him, Alpha Lenis?" His voice was low, accusing.

The werewolf drew back her lips and growled at him. Tank flinched at the strength of it. He'd fight for Isaac if he had to, but she was Alpha. He wouldn't win.

Then Alec was standing by his side, his hand a firm touch on Tank's lower back. Support. Pack.

Bryan's big furry body was on his other side, pressing against his leg. Max was there, too, hand once more on his mate's head.

Alpha Lenis made to lunge at Tank.

Alec nodded at the mage.

Max twisted his hand forward, gathering the quintessence floating in the air around them into a powerful blue and green fireball. A Surge spell of immense intricacy and power.

Marvin said, "Not in the house, please, darling," in a very mild tone.

Alec said, equally mildly. "It was very nice to meet you both, Agents. Perhaps it is time for you to leave now?"

"He's a Surge!" Agent Lenis was impressed. Surges had the greatest amount of power and the least amount of control. They always impressed Alphas.

"Not quite," said Alec, proudly.

Max flicked the fireball up, then made a funny corkscrew gesture with one finger, pinning the sparking teal fire to dangle from the chandelier far above them, in a jaunty manner. Like hanging a Christmas bauble.

The quintessence stayed there, fixed in energy state. There was no manner of Surge that could do that. Surges had one skill and one skill only, the ability to take massive amounts of quintessence and turn it into a single blast of power. To fix quintessence into time took a Siphon, but Siphons could only handle small amounts of power, invisible to the naked eye.

What Max had just done was impossible by all

standards of quintessence study. Anyone who knew anything about civic mages would know that. Even savage mages couldn't do anything so powerful and precise at the same time. There was only one way to explain a dangling ball of teal fire.

Tank watched with no small amount of satisfaction as the realization dawned on the faces of the trappers in their midst.

"You're a Magistar."

Max rolled his eyes. "No, I'm a fucking rockstar with a sparkle addiction. Of course, I'm a goddamn Magistar. Christ, you dicks didn't read the file on this pack very carefully, did ya? I thought I was like a big red flag at the very top."

Agent Lenis's gaze jumped from the hanging fireball to Max, to Bryan, to Alec and back again. Bouncing around.

"Your Beta *mated a Magistar*?" Her voice shook only slightly. "How is that even possible?"

Alec lowered his eyelids like a coy debutant. A clear insult to the other Alpha. *You are nothing to me. I don't even need to keep watching you. My pack could take you, weaker Alpha.*

Tank puffed slightly with pride and then sagged a little in defeat. He was so not worth this kind of fuss. And he had caused all this posturing. Then he firmed his resolve. *Isaac, though. Isaac is worth it.*

Tank took a short, sharp breath and straightened his spine. Against his leg, Bryan was a reassuring presence.

We got this. The pack has got this.

Alec explained, because it was in the records on the San Andreas Pack that the SBI agents hadn't bothered to read. "Bryan is Max's familiar as well as my Beta."

Agent Faste said, "Weirdest fucking pack."

Agent Lenis swallowed. Then tilted her neck back infinitesimally, showing her throat to Alec. "But strong. Very fucking strong. Still, be ready for a challenge Alpha, the ones after our boy are stupid but strong in their own way."

With that, the SBI agents moved to the door.

Max said, "Shall we light the way?" And flicked his hand again, so the fireball zoomed toward the door, at his command.

Alec shook his head. "I think they can see themselves out. You've terrorized them enough for one evening. And they *are* government representatives. Wouldn't want to cause them too much bother. You should know how that goes."

Max gave a vicious grin, since he'd once worked for the government.

The trappers left. Tank ensured the door was closed and bolted behind them.

Max let the fireball spin into teal sparkles and then snap out of existence. The quintessence returned to its natural in-between invisible state with a loud *crack*.

"Very pretty," said Marvin.

Max grinned at him. "Did you like the color? I chose it to match your new throw pillows."

"How very thoughtful, sweetie." Marvin looked genuinely thrilled and complimented.

There was a sad crunching sound as Bryan shifted to stand, naked and human, next to his mate. "It's a new spell we've been practicing."

"I like it," said Alec. "You didn't singe anything or blow anything up. I call that a win."

Max moved to wrap his naked mate up in long, protective arms.

Bryan murmured, "Very pretty, baby." Then the Beta started, and hissed at the mate plastered against him, "Are you wearing a cock ring under those tight-ass jeans?"

Max whispered back, "It's getting cold in the evenings, hon, gotta wear layers."

All the werewolves around overheard this. Sometimes

Max forgot how good their ears were.

Alec rolled his eyes and went back to the den, dragging a confused Marvin behind him to sit amongst the sparkly cushions.

"What? What'd I miss? What'd Bryan say?"

Tank knew he was blushing bright pink. Colin was blushing even worse, because Colin was a redhead.

Alec said from his comfy seat, tone horribly cold and controlled. "Theodore Depeine, come here and explain to me everything you know about this Isaac person. RIGHT NOW."

Uh oh, VOICE command. Tank's feet started moving before he even registered the force of the power.

Marvin said, "Babes, be nice. He clearly didn't know this would happen. Tank, darling, would you like a drink?"

"SIT," commanded Alec, and then, "TALK."

Tank sat and talked.

CHAPTER TWELVE
Lamb on the Lam

Isaac should have left San Francisco the next morning, but he didn't. Something was keeping him there despite the risk to his continued freedom and safety. He refused to believe that something was large and submissive and Olympiad-perfect.

Since he couldn't stay at Clara's any longer (the last thing he wanted was to bring any trouble down on her), Isaac waited until midday, and then went to the only other person he could trust. Also, he was hoping to collect his final paycheck.

Xavier was supervising renovations on his hotel. Of course, the place was already perfect, but Xavier wanted it better tailored to the needs of a shifter clientele. He'd found his niche and it was lucrative.

The Minyas was the kind of hotel that ought to give a man dressed as casually as Isaac the stink eye. Except that most of its patrons arrived, if not less *well* dressed, definitely less *dressed*. When one was naked for ease of travel, one often had to reach for whatever was around upon arriving at a destination. In fact, the hotel boasted a massive cloakroom stocked with plush robes of all sizes, accessed by a discrete side entrance and presided over by an even more discrete attendant.

The Minyas boasted a marble lobby where visitors might spot a woman in a Savile Row bespoke suit one moment, and a gentleman in a silk kimono the next. The hotel even took pre-delivery of luggage, so shifters could don their own clothing as soon as they arrived. Since the prevailing attitude in the supernatural community was one of never judging by appearances, for obvious reasons, Isaac's sportswear was disregarded. The guest clerk greeted him with all courtesy.

"How may I be of assistance?" The clerk was an absolutely stunning woman with rich coppery hair and beautiful indigo eyes. The fact that she was whipping Isaac into mental poetry, despite his clear preference for cock, told him she was a mermaid. Xavier was a consummate businessman and a mermaid was the perfect choice for front of house during daytime. She would filter out non-shifters pretty fast, even if she hadn't the nose for it (humans tended to get tongue-tied around merfolk). Plus, she could freeze anyone in their tracks, if needed. It was a good physical position for her as well, with a view of the ocean right out the hotel's front door.

"Is the boss in yet this morning?" Isaac tried for harmless and timid when she looked up at him, smiling. "I'm one of his Saucebox employees and I'm trying to track him down, a matter of business."

She dropped her customer-ready expression and reached for a phone. "Let me just check."

Very nicely done. She didn't actually admit to whether Xavier was present or not.

She spoke into the phone. "Sir? There's a gentleman in the Minyas lobby from Saucebox. A Mr...?" She looked inquiringly at Isaac.

"Isaac, just say Isaac."

"Isaac no last name. Are you avail—" Her eyes widened as Xavier, on the other end of the line, interrupted her.

Isaac, with his werewolf hearing, could naturally make out both sides of the conversation perfectly.

"Isaac? Thank fuck. Send him up immediately. Don't let him leave."

Eyes wide, the mermaid put down the phone and said to Isaac. "He says to go up right away. You know where his office is?"

Isaac nodded. He'd worked a few shifts at the Minyas bar. He actually preferred it to Saucebox, more civilized. He might have requested a transfer, but the staff at the Minyas was a bit snooty for his taste, and it wasn't quite as comfortable for his clients. The atmosphere was a great deal less casual. And of course, at the Minyas he was more likely to encounter a werewolf traveling through.

Xavier pounced on Isaac the moment he entered the luxurious office. Normally so stoic, his boss was clearly relieved to see him, because he gave Isaac an awkward and unexpectedly demonstrative hug. He pulled back from it quickly.

"Come in, come in. Sit down. You in some kind of serious trouble, Isaac?"

Isaac flinched and then sat. "Someone came by the club last night?" he guessed. Otherwise Xavier would have just assumed he was sick. Something had happened to tip Xavier off to the fact that Isaac was on the lam.

Xavier nodded. "Couple of spooks. Feds, I think. Only I'm guessing they were shifters. At least one of them was too big to be anything else."

Isaac was quietly confused. *Shifters who worked government enforcement?* "Trappers? Why on earth would the SBI be after me?"

Now Xavier was confused. "They aren't what you're afraid of?"

Isaac shook his head, truly mystified. "I've only ever heard of trappers in passing. No idea why they're on my tail."

"Well then, who *are* you running from?"

Isaac wanted to tell him but he couldn't. It would be too much all at once: who he was, what he was, who he'd been, and why he was so afraid. Too much shame and too much wolf. "Something worse. But if trappers found me, others will follow. It's probably best if I take off."

Understanding was all over Xavier's harsh face. He'd come from the streets himself once. "You do this a lot?"

"What? Run?"

Xavier nodded.

Isaac felt inexplicably ashamed. Well, more ashamed than usual. "Yep."

Xavier offered, when he really didn't have to. "I could hide you." Silly human.

"Just store a bartender indefinitely in your attic?"

"Lavish adores you."

"Most women do."

Xavier's lips twisted into that small sharp sad smile of his. "Women and shifters. You've got the magic touch, Isaac. I'm sure glad you're gay. Is that the secret, then, magic?"

"You're asking if I'm some kind of savage mage?"

Xavier only stared at him, direct and questioning.

Isaac wrinkled his nose. "No."

Xavier nodded. Not convinced but also not pushing it. He, like most humans, understood very little about quintessence. Calling it *magic* was a dead giveaway. Not that Isaac was all schooled up in mage-craft himself. But he was shifter enough to know some stuff – savage abilities, after all, affected werewolves too. Supernatural creatures were the result of quintessence. His father had tried to keep Isaac in ignorance, but some of the cult members had talked a lot. Too much, as it turns out. Isaac had learned the hard way that he was no mage.

Isaac paused, hearing someone approach outside in the

hall – the tick tack of high heels on parquet.

He didn't say anything, but he also wasn't as startled as Xavier when Lavish burst into the office.

Xavier stood from his desk and went to greet her. All his attention off Isaac and focused on his lady-love. "Sweetheart, what you doing here?"

"Lunch date, darling. Remember? I told you I had a client meeting in the area." Lavish fussed over his shirt collar.

Isaac stood to say hello as well and Lavish registered who it was in the room with her man.

"Isaac, how perfect! Will you be joining us?"

Isaac smiled and shook his head.

She abandoned her boyfriend to give Isaac air kisses. "Of course you will, how delightful! You'll love the food at this little place I've found. Oh, but Isaac darling, where were you last night?"

Isaac cast Xavier a desperate look, but his boss was looking thoughtful.

"Yes. Isaac, would you like lunch? But I hope you don't mind too much, babydoll, I need to stay in the hotel. There's trouble brewing with that fresco I'm having done by the salt pool. I must stay close. How about we try out the new menu here, in the hotel?"

Isaac narrowed his eyes. *He wants to keep an eye on me and keep me safe.* "Oh, but I—"

Lavish instantly saw that Isaac was trying to escape. "My love, that's a charming idea. Isaac, it's a lovely restaurant, you'll adore it. It's not just for the shifter palate, the carpaccio is to die for."

Xavier nodded. "Would you mind heading up without me? I've a few things to finish here. I'll join you in a couple minutes."

Lavish linked her arm with Isaac's. "Not at all. We'll see you up there. Have you seen the roof garden, Isaac? It's amazing."

She led Isaac out and he went along obediently, enjoying her chatter. His supernatural hearing stretched back to catch Xavier pick up the phone and say, "Pearl? Get me Heavy Lifting, please. They should be in my personal directory under services."

The restaurant, though newly opened, had obviously already established a reputation. It was midweek, yet the place was packed. Lavish ordered for all of them, without Xavier, although he arrived soon enough. The food was sublime and Xavier and Lavish managed to keep the conversation light and charming. Isaac almost felt like he wasn't imposing at all.

Xavier begged off coffee to get back to work, but Lavish lingered.

"No major cases at the moment?" Isaac asked.

"Just finished the last one and it was a crap shoot. I actually took the rest of the day off, was going to get my nails done or something."

Isaac smiled encouragingly. "Self-care."

"You know what I really want?"

"A bubble bath, chocolate, champagne, and sappy movies?"

"Oh. My. God. How did you know?"

Isaac only chuckled. He'd hate to tell her women were predictable.

She gripped his arm, eyes shining. "Let's get a room here and do just that? Oh please, oh please. Just lie around and have a totally girly slacker day with me. You don't have to be anywhere else, do you?"

Yes. I do have to be anywhere else. But there was something haunting the air now, some tiny familiar scent lingering from someone else's drink in the restaurant. Brandy with lemon, and it made him feel safe. His wolf really wanted to stop and stay a while. *Stupid wolf.*

"Jane Austen movies?"

Lavish squealed at him. "We were separated at birth."

Isaac grinned. "Not quite. You can keep the chocolates and we're taking separate baths, but otherwise…"

Lavish clapped her hands and bounced. He doubted she ever let anyone else see this side of herself. "I'll get us a room."

"How do you know we can?"

"Don't be silly, my boyfriend owns the hotel."

Tank watched Isaac and the stunning black woman rise from their table, link arms, and head toward him where he held position by the restaurant entrance.

Isaac looked good. Tense and a little worn about the eyes, but all in one piece, thank fuck. *Safe. He's right there and he's safe.*

Thankfully, Xavier had called the pack in to provide security. No doubt it had something to do with Isaac hanging out with Xavier's girlfriend. Xavier wanted to protect Isaac, but he really wanted to protect Lavish from Isaac's mistakes. Heavy Lifting wasn't cheap at the best of times, and this was a last-minute call. Alec would charge the man top dollar.

Tank didn't care about the reason because Isaac was there, in front of him. Tank's stomach was queasy with relief. Also, Judd was with him for backup. One of the pack's enforcers, Judd breathed battle the way Alec breathed leadership. Tank could fight, but he didn't like it, and he wasn't especially good at it. He was just that much bigger than most, enough for things to fall in his favor when fists or teeth were involved. But Judd was bigger *and* meaner.

It was full daylight, so neither of them was as strong as they might be. And they couldn't shift. But Judd packed heat. It wasn't normal for a supernatural creature to carry weapons, especially not since Super Saturation and quintessence misfires put guns out of general favor. But Judd wasn't normal.

Tank signaled him in the hall. "They're headed down in the elevator."

"I'll take the other elevator."

Tank nodded. "I'll take the stairs."

Tank slipped out of the stairwell on the ground floor and skulked behind one of the massive potted ferns on the far side of the room. Judd gave him a look and then drifted outside to watch the street.

Isaac and the woman entered the lobby and, much to Tank's relief, didn't leave. Instead they seemed to negotiate checking into a room together.

Tank might have been confused, not to say jealous, except Isaac was decidedly gay. Far be it for Tank to discount bisexuality, but Isaac? No. His friendship with Xavier's girlfriend – *What was her name, Luxurious? Luscious?* – was intimate but not sexual. Besides which, having an affair inside her own boyfriend's hotel seemed extraordinarily ballsy.

The mermaid receptionist passed over a room key, gave them a cheeky grin, and said something about champagne, chocolate, and movies. Apparently, they were going into one of those vegetative states humans occasionally enjoyed when exposed to new video games or binge-watching vampire hunting parodies. Max did it occasionally. The pack's Magistar was extremely fond of a sitcom set in a mermaid pod called *Brining Women*. In Max's case, the hibernation pattern seemed to also require vast amounts of the ice cream flavor Berry Berry Nice, which Bryan complained was impossible to find.

Isaac and his lady friend returned to the elevators and Tank stuck his head outside to tell Judd what was going on. Then Tank called Xavier to request his authority in finding out which room Isaac now occupied.

Minutes later Tank was standing outside one of the

fancier suites on an upper floor, wishing he could smell if Isaac was actually in the room.

Even knowing his lover had no scent, Tank pressed his face to the tiny crack in the doorjamb. He got a whiff of vanilla peach and soap, bubble bath suds, perhaps.

About an hour into his vigil, the dulcet tones of posh British accents and classical music began drifting out. Tank stood for the next five hours, listening to what appeared to be an endless adaptation of *Pride and Prejudice*. Judd occasionally swung by to check on him.

"Humans. Their courting rituals are ridiculous." Judd kept his voice low just in case there were other shifters in the rooms nearby.

Tank nodded, gloomy. "Especially when written by Austen."

"Actually this is a pretty good adaptation," Judd said, to Tank's utter surprise, and then continued his circuit. He'd stopped offering to relieve Tank of door duty. Tank wasn't budging until he saw Isaac again.

Judd preferred to be in motion anyway.

Just as the sun began to set, the suite's door finally opened, and the man of the hour came sneaking out.

"Going somewhere?" Tank kept his voice low and calm.

Isaac started and then glared at him. "Of course, it's you out here." Emotions danced over his face, annoyance, pleasure, something carnal, something more profound. "Of course, it's you." He repeated as if to himself. "I felt safe all day in there. I'm such an idiot."

"Idiot, yes, far be it for me to gainsay your own assessment of yourself."

Isaac barked a surprised laugh.

There were a number of things Tank might have done at that juncture – yell at the man for disappearing or whine about being left alone after the best sex of his life. Instead Tank did what he wanted to do most, which was grab Isaac by the upper arms and drag him into a hug. Careful not to squeeze too hard (after all the man was only human).

"You frightened the shit out of me."

"How the hell did you find me?" Isaac pushed, looking around.

Tank hastened to reassure him. "I didn't track you. Xavier called me. Well, he called my pack. Hired us to come keep you safe."

Isaac's face suddenly cleared. "You're Heavy Lifting?"

"One part of it."

"I thought that call was something to do with the renovations."

Tank snickered. "I told Kevin the name sounded like a moving company. Sometimes I think that's the point."

Isaac relaxed and unconsciously moved back into Tank's eager arms. "It's not, is it? You're security. He's worried about Lavish because I was with her and he knows someone is after me."

Tank stroked Isaac's biceps, as if he were gentling a skittish pack mate. "Who is after you? Trappers? They don't seem so bad."

"No. I've no idea what they want."

Tank kept petting. Isaac didn't seem to mind. In fact, the man's hands began threading through Tank's short hair as if he couldn't help himself. Or he needed the reassurance. Perhaps he really wanted to tug. Only they were out in the hallway. *God, I hope he wants to tug.*

Tank pressed for answers. "Why is Hayden so fixated on you?"

Isaac looked around wild-eyed. "Fuck, is he here?"

Tank sighed. "No stalker. No trappers. No cops. Just me and one of my pack mates."

Isaac tensed. "Another werewolf?"

"Judd."

"Which one is that?"

Tank kept his touch gentle. "Enforcer."

That one word terrified Isaac. He twisted out of Tank's grasp. He was strong, much stronger than he should be. Much stronger than a human.

Tank grabbed Isaac's hand, holding fast and hard, grip werewolf-rough. Anchoring himself. Anchoring them both. Isaac didn't even flinch.

"What exactly *are* you, Isaac?"

But Isaac's gray eyes were panicked. "Enforcer? There's an enforcer *here*? I gotta go."

Tank couldn't stop himself from whimpering. "Isaac, no, please. Just come with me. Come with us. Judd's a good guy. He won't do anything. Just let us help you, protect you if you need it. My pack will look after you."

Isaac shook his head, crazy with fear. "No, they won't. You have no idea what you're talking about."

Werewolves. Werewolves is what he's running from. What has him so scared. We are what he's always been running from and what has always had him scared. I am his nightmare.

Tank tried again, desperate. "Isaac, we aren't all the same. I swear we aren't."

Isaac flinched and seemed to return to himself. Shaking off his terror, his gray eyes focused on Tank's face.

Isaac's free hand lifted, stroked the side of Tank's jaw – tentative as he'd never been before. Tank was desperate for him to be forceful, desperate for Isaac's confidence to return. Tank nuzzled in, tilted his head back slightly. *I'm yours. I'm no risk. I'm safe. God, what did my kind do to this man?*

"*You* are different." Isaac's smile was shaky. "You're something special, you know that?" Isaac's voice was thick. "I could sink into you and forget everything. You already made me stay longer than I should. I might have left yesterday, but fuck, I love the way you smell. And my—"

He paused, shook himself, then leaned forward, his

hand on Tank's jaw. Isaac moved his thumb to press down on Tank's lower lip, dipping inside slightly, forcing Tank's mouth open.

Isaac dove in and kissed him. Thoroughly and deep, claiming, and possessive.

"Ohmygod, that is so hot!" Xavier's girlfriend was in the doorway, dressed and looking ready to leave. Her eyes gleamed.

They jerked apart.

"Isaac, darling, I didn't know you had yourself a man. And look at the size of him. Extra large bonus yummy! Look, Xavier wants to go to dinner. You two can take the room if you like." She leered at them. "It's yours for the night if you need it."

She kissed Isaac's cheek and pressed a key card into his hand in an insistent manner. Either she was very invested in his sex life or she, like Tank, knew Isaac wanted to run, and was trying her best to keep him from going anywhere. "Ta ta, darlings!"

She gave Tank an indiscreet jerk of the head – *get him inside, stupid* – and marched off to the elevators swinging a leather purse Tank suspected was worth more than his motorcycle. "Is that a woman or a force of nature?"

Isaac glared at Tank. "She's great."

Tank snorted. "I think she's in love with you."

"Oh, right, and she somehow overlooked the whole gay thing?"

"Thinks you stumbled and fell into my ass."

"Or that any ass would do?"

Tank flinched. "Would it?"

Isaac sighed. "No, yours is awfully perfect. But I gotta go. I can't stay. Not if you've got an enforcer here."

Tank took the room card from him and opened the door. "Come back inside. He won't disturb us. No one else knows you're here."

"Apparently your whole goddam pack knows."

"Yeah, but we don't know why anyone is after you." Tank flipped the security latch on the door behind them, looked around with interest. The room was the height of opulence. "And we didn't tell the trappers anything."

"You didn't?"

"'Course not. Nothing to tell." Tank stripped quickly, losing t-shirt, jeans, and loafers. "You never said anything. And I wouldn't betray you even if you had." If him being naked was the only thing that might convince Isaac to stay longer, then naked he would be.

It seemed to work. Isaac's eyes dilated until they were almost black and his breath quickened.

Tank said, "You smell like fruit."

"Peach cobbler bath bombs."

"I don't know what that means, but I don't like it."

"You don't?"

"Nope. Now let me ride your cock and jizz all over your chest."

Isaac laughed, shocked but charmed. "Bossy bottom. You're awfully demanding for a sub. What does that have to do with bath bombs?"

Tank wrinkled his nose. "Then you'll smell like me instead of cobbler."

Isaac gave an involuntary little shudder at that. *Oh,* thought Tank, *he likes that idea. Whatever creature he is, smell is important to him too. Even though he doesn't have any scent of his own.*

Tank pressed his naked body against Isaac's clothed one. Feeling what his words had done. Isaac might pretend indifference but he wanted Tank every bit as badly as Tank wanted him.

"You like the way I smell, Isaac?"

"Fuck, yes." Isaac grabbed him then, hard and rough, and pressed his face against Tank's neck in a remarkably wolf-like gesture.

"What *are* you, Isaac?" Tank asked again, risking a

break in the mood.

"Not a good idea." Isaac was adept at being evasive. "God, why can't I resist you? What is it you do to me? And why did it have to be you?" He pushed Tank back onto the opulent bed.

Isaac had no idea what drove him. The instinct to flee had been tempered by Lavish with her dumb movie marathon and girly gossip. She'd distracted him with the mundane, suckered him into pretending that nothing was wrong.

Now Tank was holding him here, so big and warm and giving. All Isaac could think about was absorbing him into his soul one last time. Before they never saw each other again. *Melodramatic, much?*

Even with the risk of a pack enforcer here in this hotel, Isaac wanted to stay and do exactly as Tank demanded.

Maybe his pressing desire for this werewolf was *because* of the risk, and the fear, and the adrenaline. Tank was the only thing in Isaac's life that he could utterly control. What they did together? Isaac could dictate *that* perfectly. What little power Isaac had was all here, in a bed, with Tank. Everything else in his life was beyond him, spinning and reckless and chaotic. Always had been. But sex with Tank, there he could do exactly as he wished, exactly as he liked, exactly as they both needed.

He hadn't restraints or toys or anything useful with him, but he didn't really require them. Just words. Tank would do as he was told.

"You've been waiting outside this hotel room since lunch, haven't you?"

Tank lay back on the bed like a sacrifice, hard and eager, but holding himself to Isaac's will.

Isaac reached down and stroked the werewolf's cock, lightly, testing.

Tank shivered.

"Were you this hard while you waited?"

Tank's dark eyes twinkled. "Oh yeah, I'm so turned on by the dulcet tones of Jane Austen."

Isaac snorted. "Clearly you've never seen the diving-into-the-lake scene."

"Why are we talking again?"

Isaac climbed onto the bed and straddled him. Loving the power imbalance – him, still clothed, and Tank, utterly naked.

Isaac rubbed against the massive man, roughly, perhaps a little too rough, grinding his jean-covered groin down on that eager cock.

Tank winced and moaned and arched under him and Isaac ordered him to be still.

Tank froze, eyes desperate.

Isaac wanted to taste and bite, to fuck and take. His wolf was high on fear and flight and hope, riding him hard to mount and sink his teeth into the banquet of this man. Starving beast. Yearning for some foothold in reality. His wolf saw Tank as mate and savior and hope and resurrection all in one.

That realization, more than anything else, caused Isaac to rear back.

What is going on? He's just a plaything, a toy. A distraction.

Mine mine mineminemine, said the wolf in Isaac, grinding his teeth.

Isaac tumbled off his naked lover. "What the fuck? Me? I'm the weird one. What the hell are *you*?"

Tank levered himself up onto his elbows, looking dazed. He focused on Isaac and then his dark eyes turned sad. "Nothing special. Just a werewolf. Just a submissive. Just yours if you'd have me, but you won't, will you?"

Isaac backed away and stood staring at the massive naked man, in the huge beautiful bed, in one of the best luxury hotels in San Francisco and wondered how the hell had he gotten here. What was he thinking? What was he doing? And how the hell would he get away?

A loud hammering came on the room door.

Just like that, Isaac was out of time, and all his choices were gone.

CHAPTER THIRTEEN
Call of the Mild

"Tank, you in there?"

Isaac shuddered at the growl in the stranger's voice.

Tank jumped naked from the bed, unselfconscious. *Well he certainly has no reason to be ashamed.*

"Yeah."

"Our boy in there with you?"

"Yeah."

Before Isaac could stop him, because what reason would Tank have not to trust his own pack mate, the werewolf went to the door and opened it.

A big black man pushed his way in. His skin was darker than Isaac's own and he was way more muscled. His eyes were black and fierce. He looked mean and tough and exactly the way all werewolves always had looked. Until Tank.

Isaac was instantly on his guard and backing away.

Judd leered briefly at Tank. "Sorry, am I interrupting something?"

Tank only rolled his eyes and went back to lounging naked on the bed. Isaac was weirdly pleased to see he'd a knee up strategically so he wasn't totally showing off. Isaac's wolf agreed, *mine.*

Judd's gaze swung to Isaac.

He came forward, expression not unfriendly, hand outstretched in the manner of humans.

"Hi there. You're Isaac. We've been hired to look out for you. I'm Judd, enforcer for the San Andreas Pack, and—," he inhaled and froze. "Holy shit, what the fuck are you?"

The enforcer stood, poised, looking like he wasn't sure if he was about to kill or maim, but knowing he would be fighting something.

"He doesn't have a scent." Judd's gaze flicked to Tank.

"Yeah, I know."

"Like, *no scent*. At all. Nothing. Like he's a goddamn—" Judd seemed to choke on his own words. "Tank, you fucker! What the hell? You can't go around just hiding an *Omega*! Jesus Christ, how the fuck has he lasted this long without pack protection?"

Tank stood and with supernatural speed imposed his naked body between Isaac and his pack mate.

Isaac started to get déjà vu. *Here we go again. The moment a pack is around me, it fractures. Posturing, fighting, pain, death, hurt. Everyone arguing over me and no one asking me what I want.* Everyone wanting to take the Omega and keep him and trap him and hide him and… For no other reason than that he was an Omega.

Judd threw his hands in the air at Tank's protective posturing. "Of course, you're fucking sleeping with him. I always assumed you preferred to take it, not dish it out."

Tank rolled his eyes. "Who said I was topping?"

Judd looked like he couldn't keep taking the mental hits. "You're saying you're sleeping with an Omega. A male. An obviously gay male Omega and he's dominating you? I can't… what… fucking hell." Judd shook himself like the dog he wasn't and then straightened into enforcer stance – big and threatening.

"Obviously gay? Why *obviously*?" wondered Isaac,

because he couldn't keep his damn mouth shut.

Both Tank and Judd turned and stared at him.

Tank was bigger, but he was much less aggressive, even fully clothed. "Yeah. He could totally be bi or pan or…" Tank was ready to defend him no matter how ridiculous.

Judd growled in exasperation and stepped in toward his pack mate, chest out. "We gotta get him back to Alec. Right fucking now. We'll sort out how goddamn unlikely your sex life has gotten later."

Isaac crossed his arms. "You gonna involve me in your decision-making process or just bark orders and push me around like every other werewolf since I was fucking born?"

Judd only widened his eyes at him, somehow managing to look more dangerous than shocked. "Are you actually insane? Omegas just can't exist without pack. You *have* to come with us. You don't have to fucking stay with us, but you certainly can't go wandering around on your own. Hell! Why the fuck didn't the trappers tell us they were after an Omega? That goddamn Alpha probably wanted to claim you for herself."

Isaac could feel his skin prickling. *Here we go.* He glared at Tank. *You said your pack was different.* "You didn't tell me one of the trappers was an Alpha werewolf."

Tank let out his breath. "What's going on?"

Judd gestured at Isaac with his thumb. "Tank, you're *not* that thick. I know you're not."

Tank gritted his teeth. "Pretend. That. I. Am. Use short sentences, enforcer."

"This one is a werewolf Omega on the run. Omegas can't be without pack. I bet he's got every shifter in a twelve-mile radius panting after him. They come belly-up with big eyes and sob stories. He tries to fix 'em, right? Except the ones that go sour and turn psycho." Judd turned back to Isaac. Isaac was beginning to very much not like the man. "Is that how you netted our Tank?"

Tank bristled. "Now hold on there! No one netted anything. I'm not a fucking fish."

Judd put some enforcer power into his next statement. Isaac could feel it, shivering over his bones. "You two are coming with me, now. Alec should be home soon. This is so not the right place to do this." He turned on Isaac. "You thought it was a good idea to come to a *shifter* hotel? Just hang the fuck out. A loner Omega? Are you as dumb as Tank then? Well-fucking-suited."

Isaac's temper turned at that. *How dare he criticize Tank.* "You asshole! I've never had trouble from any shifters except werewolves. Tank's been the only exception to that reality. Ever. So forgive me if I don't do *anything* you ask. Or order."

Tank said tentatively, "What about Hayden?"

Isaac flinched. "Okay, maybe I've had issues with a barghest or two. But you all are like practically cousins."

"*You all.* But you're one of us." Judd let frustration leak into his voice.

Isaac wrinkled his upper lip. "Only by birth."

Judd looked both upset and desperate. "Only... *birth*? *Birth,* nothing more? Tank, get your man to come with us! This is ridiculous."

Tank crossed his arms, mimicking Isaac. "Isaac doesn't want to."

"That was not a request, grunt!"

Tank flinched at the slur.

Isaac bristled. His lover had taken the other insults with impunity but he didn't like that one. He held his ground, though. Isaac thought the worst thing was that Tank seemed to believe it was true. That he was nothing more than a grunt and didn't matter to his own pack. Which might be worse, thought Isaac, than not belonging to one at all.

Judd growled.

Isaac caught the slight tremble in his lover's massive

body. *Poor baby. It's against every part of his nature to stand against his own pack's enforcer.*

Isaac couldn't do that to him. Couldn't watch his big gentle wolf fight for him, fight a battle he couldn't win. Because Tank would try and Judd would take him down. Because Judd was an enforcer and Tank, well, wasn't.

Isaac took a shaky breath. Perhaps it was best to have this out. Perhaps it would be better if they were all witness to what happened next. How an Omega like him could destroy a pack, just by being inside it.

"Fine, I'll come."

Judd relaxed slightly. "Tank, get dressed."

Tank only sneered at him and in the next breath shifted into his wolf form. A massive dark brown beast, he looked far more incongruous in the luxury suite than a naked man.

Isaac was struck by a pang of regret. *I wish I'd had a chance to fuck him one last time.*

They walked through the hotel. Tank stayed a wolf and close to Isaac. He needed to touch him.

Tank couldn't really wrap his brain around it. Isaac was an Omega. It explained so much and not enough.

Well, I know now why he insisted on a condom for oral but not for fucking. He didn't want me to taste his jizz. Couldn't tell a werewolf from the way he fucked but you could from the way he tasted. Which only made Tank, now that he knew Isaac's species, want Isaac's cum filling his mouth. How spicy would it be? How much would it heat his tongue? Would it be sweet or bitter or if he was very lucky, both? Or were Omegas different from other werewolves in this as they were in so many other ways?

Tank knew almost nothing about Omegas. His old pack hadn't had one. Nor had the Red Paws mingled much with other werewolves. He'd never met an Omega in real life.

He knew that they were special. Highly valued by those packs lucky enough to have birthed one. Which put Isaac even more firmly out of his league as a mate, and way too far above him in pack hierarchy.

I should move away from him now, not act so proprietary. Besides which, as a dominant, Isaac probably didn't like him so close.

Except Isaac needed Tank's reassurance. He was headed into alien territory, confronting strange wolves. Tank was the only one he might trust, even a little.

Tank didn't want to move away. Couldn't.

He and Judd had driven one of the pickups to the hotel. For security's sake, Isaac should have been in the middle, but Tank wouldn't let him, cramming his wolf body into the cab first so he was between Isaac and Judd. He didn't want Isaac sitting next to a man who'd threatened him. It didn't matter that Tank knew Judd to be a good man – his instincts screamed to protect Isaac regardless.

Judd glared at him.

"I'm not going to run on you," said Isaac as he climbed in after Tank. "He's only trying to keep me happy."

Tank chuffed at them.

Isaac scratched behind his ear. It comforted them both.

"How the fuck did you even happen?" Judd asked, putting the truck into gear and peeling out into traffic.

"When a werewolf and a woman love each other very much—"

"Oh, I see, you're a punk-ass. You'll fit in well with this pack."

"You're not fucking keeping me. Why does everyone want to *keep* me?"

"Calm down, Omega," Judd said, as if it were obvious. "I only meant socially."

"You're an asshole."

"Well that's true. So you were born and then what, you ran away?"

"I was taken. Look, if I'm gonna have to tell this story I'd rather only do it once."

Judd grunted. "Music?"

Isaac grimaced. "Instead of talking? Hell, yes."

Judd twiddled with the radio until they had something resembling acceptable.

Tank couldn't help being pleased that Isaac was about to meet his pack at last. Tank was, if nothing else, a proper rule-abiding werewolf. He'd wanted to introduce Isaac to his pack from the start. Tank was also unhappy, because Isaac didn't want to be there. Isaac wasn't doing this of his own free will. Isaac didn't want them, which meant he didn't want Tank.

It took too long to get across the bridge, and then it wasn't long enough down Alexander into town and up the steep hill to the pack property.

Isaac jumped out of the truck and looked around, hunched and wary. All they could see from the parking area was the garage and the funny little apartment above it. The rest of the yard was too overgrown with trees and bushes.

"That's it?" Isaac looked suspiciously at the garage.

Judd snorted.

A large reddish wolf came bouncing up – Kevin. He exchanged nods with Judd and sniffs with Tank. He then approached Isaac, who hunched further into himself, as if trying to shrink, in obvious fear. Kev huffed at the stranger long enough that Tank started a low rumbling growl.

Kev stopped, flicked his ears at Tank, then looked up at Judd, head cocked to one side in utter confusion.

"I know, he has no scent and Tank's acting weird. We'll explain soon. You finish patrol and come in when Alec gets back. He's not home yet, is he?"

Kevin shook his head.

"Best we wait for the Alpha."

Kevin gave a bark and bounced off.

"Come on, then." Judd led them through the yard under the massive old oaks and young redwoods, until they arrived at the big house.

Tank glanced at his lover. Isaac was trying hard not to look impressed by the barn-like mansion. "Okay, this makes more sense."

Judd slammed in through the heavy front door. Tank nudged Isaac to follow, gently encouraging.

Isaac sighed. "Fuck my life."

Judd was already in the kitchen rummaging around for something to eat. The first thing the pack did when remodeling was knock out almost all of the downstairs walls, turning anything weight-bearing into pillars, so the whole thing was one big living area. Then they'd installed massive two-story windows that looked out over treetops and roofs to the ocean beyond. It was impressive and would be even more so when they finished the deck.

Tank loved it.

They were still remodeling the rest of the house, their private rooms and so forth. But this part, the pack den, was finished. Tank, who had done a lot of the heavy construction, was proud of it. More often than not because Max, who loathed the big house, was becoming comfortable on this floor at least. Because it was so changed. Tank was always pleased when his hard work brought others comfort.

Colin came down the stairs at the noise of their arrival. He looked nervous – but that was normal around Judd. "Oh, hello." He noticed Isaac. "It's you."

Isaac gave an embarrassed wave.

Colin looked at Tank. "What's he doing here?"

Judd answered since Tank couldn't. "Great. You met him too?" Judd's tone was off.

Colin blinked at the enforcer, who'd never been anything but gentle with him.

"He's an Omega, okay? And he has no smell. It's weird,

do you all not know how weird that is?"

Colin's big green eyes went wide. "Is he really? Cool. I've never met one before." He turned back to Isaac, looking almost eager. "Is that why you didn't want to talk to me?"

Judd looked at Tank. "I take it you never met one before?"

Tank shook his big shaggy head.

"Has Alec? Kevin? Lovejoy? Bryan?"

Colin turned and gave the enforcer a funny look. "Judd, we're all like a third your age. Possibly less, cause you never say how old you really are. When would we have had the chance? We never traveled as kids. Never even left our town. Most of us barely attended high school."

Judd crossed his arms, biceps bulging. "Just because I'm old doesn't mean I know that much more than you do about Omegas. They're basically a new species. Post-Saturation and all that."

Colin smiled softly, offering no possible challenge. "Except clearly, you do know more."

Judd looked poleaxed. Colin rarely smiled and almost never at him. Tank sniffed to test the pheromones in the air. But he couldn't get over his own eagerness at being near Isaac, who was still permitting him to press close.

Colin lowered his lashes and shrugged. "You've been wandering around, loner, post-Saturation, longer and more than we have. Did you forget how rare Omegas are? I did some research on them once. Nothing came up about their smell, though, or lack of."

Judd's expression shifted somewhere dark. "They should smell like pack. Wait, why were you researching Omegas?"

Colin flushed with embarrassment. "It's kinda silly."

Isaac waved a hand in the air. "I'll just go sit over there, shall I? While you talk about me like I'm not here."

Judd, as always, only had eyes for Colin, and Colin, for

once, was actually having a conversation with him.

Tank followed Isaac into the sunken sitting area. When Isaac settled into one of the armchairs, Tank flopped over his feet the way Bryan always did with Max.

He liked it too much. It felt right and good. He wondered what Isaac's wolf looked like. Isaac had asked him once, and then he'd laughed when Tank described himself in fur. *Why'd he do that?* Tank's mind was full of questions. But he knew he was less threatening to Isaac in this shape, more doglike and reassuring. He could wait to ask. Also, he still might have to fight one of his other pack mates. Better to stay a wolf.

Isaac petted his head and played with his ears as Colin talked to Judd. Tank knew that if he were a cat shifter he'd be purring.

Judd loomed over Colin. Enforcers, always slightly agro. "Fess up, pretty boy, how come you researched Omegas? I mean, I know you're all smart and shit, but why bother?"

Colin flushed and flinched back. "Look, I just thought maybe I *was* one for a little bit. Because I'm *this*." He gestured to himself. "Small and weak. Of course, I found out really quickly the one thing everybody knows about Omegas, they're *born* as well as made. Which means I can't be one. Since I was only made."

Tank bet that Isaac was really cute as a pup. He tried to imagine what that would be like, having shifting abilities as a child. *I would have gotten into so much trouble.*

The front door opened.

Alec came ambling in dressed for the lab. Kevin followed, shifting into naked human as he crossed the threshold.

Isaac said, "Well, he's hot."

Tank growled at him.

"Not as hot as you, baby. That's the other enforcer, right?"

Tank nodded.

"Definitely not my type." Isaac shifted his focus and stared at Alec. No surprise there, werewolves were always drawn to him. "Who's the pretty one?"

Judd stepped forward before Alec could do what he usually did upon getting home – head into the kitchen distractedly telling them all about his day with microorganisms, spill Meaty-O cereal over everything while he poured himself a bowl, and then wander aimlessly out onto the unfinished deck to look over his territory.

"Alpha, we have a visitor," explained Judd.

Alec looked over at Isaac with thick-lashed hazel eyes and an absentminded smile.

"You're the Alpha?"

Isaac jumped to his feet.

Tank stood as well, leaning against his leg.

"Yeah. Sorry about that. I'm never what anyone expects. Did you say I was *pretty*? That's very kind." Alec hurried over to greet their guest. "Are you a friend of Judd's? I didn't know Judd had friends. Welcome to the San Andreas Pack. But you have no food! Colin, would you get our visitor some—" And then, exactly like Judd in the hotel room, Alec hit scenting distance.

"Holy fuck, what are—?" And that was as far as Alec got before he, entirely without intent or control, began to shift forms.

"Holy shit," said Kevin. "What's he doing? Is that third form? Christ, grab his glasses, he'll break them with that size of head!"

"Is he gonna...? Oh, I think he is!" Colin blanched and took a step back, even though he was pretty far away.

Judd yelled, "Save the lamp! Marvin will kill us!"

Tank had no idea who anyone was yelling at. He swung around to defend Isaac, hackles up, teeth bared.

Isaac crouched behind him, making himself as small a target as possible. Isaac buried both hands into Tank's ruff, gripping as though Tank were the only thing anchoring him to the earth.

At that juncture, Marvin came home from work, wearing his Coast Guard bathrobe and looking tired. He took in the chaos in his living room at a glance.

"Is that Alec? What the *hell* is he doing? Is that third form? Alec, take it outside! Oh God no, there he goes. Save the throw pillows!"

Alec seemed to have registered what was happening and was trying to stop it. He was flickering between human and third form. It was a thing only Alphas could do, transform parts of themselves into wolf, while leaving the rest basically human. Third was the Alpha's breeding form. It was the shape a werewolf had to be to give a maker's bite – to turn a human into a werewolf.

So far as Tank knew, Alec had never used that form in its intended role. As a rule, being human was better for most activities and being a full wolf worked the rest of the time. If they ever had pups in the pack to grow up and take the bite, Alec would need third form then. Once or twice Tank had seen him use it to prove a point. Last month he put third form on for Halloween, to give the neighborhood kids a proper scare.

It was extremely weird for the Alpha to suddenly become a monster for no apparent reason. Tank had never known an Alpha to shift involuntarily.

He'd also never seen one fight against it so hard.

That was kind of the point, after all. Alphas were supposed to have the *most* control of any of them. Even on full moon.

Marvin, who had no fear, came rushing forward to his struggling mate. "Babe, what are you doing?"

Behind Tank, Isaac's breath quickened and he seemed to be close to hyperventilating. Tank whined. Isaac wanted to flee. Tank could feel the man quivering with it. Except that would be worse than anything, because then Alec would be overcome by the need to hunt.

Judd said, "Don't fight it, Alpha, just go all the way to wolf, then come back. It'll probably be easier."

Alec seemed to hear that. He flickered through his third form, which was oddly impressive, that true monster of werewolf legend – all massive head and claws but upright and bipedal, and then came out the other side as a smallish, lean but handsome wolf. Alec was a rangy beast, brown and cream with beautiful black markings that Tank envied.

Kevin said, "I'm just gonna go get Bryan. I'm thinking we need our Beta. Fuck, I hope he's home." He ran off, still naked. Kev's exhibitionist tendencies were one reason they never bothered much with trimming their yard.

Marvin let out a breath. "What an exciting thing to come home to." He noticed Isaac for the first time. "Oh, hello. Who are you?"

"I'm, uh, Isaac." Tank felt Isaac relax a little and then stand up. It was hard to stay terrified when one hundred and twenty pounds of willowy blond perfection was dimpling at you and acting like everything was perfectly normal.

Marvin always brushed off any and all werewolf fuss as being beyond his merman ken and not really worth worrying over. He glided through the couches and pecked Isaac on the cheek, as though they had known each other for years.

"Welcome, dear. You're Tank's special friend, aren't you? How nice. I was hoping he'd find someone."

Isaac was clearly both shocked and charmed. He was also confused enough to be no longer interested in running.

God bless mermen, thought Tank. Marvin was just so easy – easy to be around, easygoing, easy on the eyes.

Isaac was not flummoxed for long, though. "You must be Marvin the merman?"

"Oh, you've heard of me? Tank, darling, were you telling tail tales?"

Tank woofed at both him and his bad wordplay.

Marvin chuckled. "Yes, I'm Alec's mate. Sorry about that, terribly rude of him. Usually, he has better control."

"He makes for an attractive wolf," Isaac said, clearly at a loss for anything else.

"Oh, do you think so? I've always felt that." Marvin was oblivious to the oddness of Alec's recent behavior. He did not realize Alphas *never* lost control. They just didn't. "I think he'd like to be bigger, if he had the choice."

Alec only sat there, panting, trying to collect himself.

Isaac grinned and said to Marvin, "Well, I guess you're no size queen."

Marvin threw his stunning blond head back and laughed. Then, because Tank was still leaning protectively against Isaac, he replied with a gesture, "But clearly you are, honey."

Isaac gave a shocked snort.

A wet crunch sounded as Alec morphed back into human shape. He looked sadly down at his ruined clothing. "I was fond of those pants."

"Aw, sweetie, you have six pairs and they're all *exactly* the same." Marvin scooped up a throw blanket, went over and wrapped it around his mate's waist, like a skirt.

Alec sighed. He gave Isaac a look. "I think I'll stay over here, if you don't think it rude. The way you smell, or don't smell, pretty much drives me nuts."

Isaac nodded. "Appreciate it." Tank could hear the wonder in his voice. "Your self-control is remarkable."

"Really? Sure doesn't seem like it from here." Alec cocked his head. "Wait a second. You've had ample examples of werewolves who haven't any control around you, haven't you?"

"He's an Omega," explained Judd.

"Yes, I figured." Alec gave Isaac a funny bow, which caused Isaac to start.

Tank chuffed at him for comfort. Isaac fondled his ears.

Tank was proud of his Alpha, pleased he had manners and some control.

Alec cleared his throat and said, awkwardly, "It's an honor to meet you, Isaac. We had no Omega in our last pack, and that Alpha was not one to mingle much with other werewolves, so I never met one. None of us have." He glanced at Judd. "I don't *think*. Look, I'm sorry about that third form thing. I've never felt such a sensation before."

Isaac nodded. "You wanted to bite me? Or rough me up with marks? Or hold me down? Or lock me in your basement until I show you my neck?"

Alec looked genuinely appalled. He glanced at Marvin and swallowed hard. "Uh, just bite you, honest. And bite to change. Like for metamorphosis. A maker's bite. Nothing else, I assure you.

Is that what usually happens around Alphas, they try to maul and imprison you?"

And Tank understood, at last, why Isaac hated werewolves.

CHAPTER FOURTEEN
Shifters Temple Pastoral Gathering

Isaac nodded, feeling miserable. But also strangely hopeful. If Alec was telling the truth about only wanting to bite, then perhaps this really was a *different* kind of pack. Plus, Alec had already shown more self-control than any other Alpha he'd ever met.

Alec frowned. "Your previous encounters, were they mated, those Alphas?"

"No."

"And they probably weren't gay either."

Isaac shook his head.

"So they'd run into you, get overcome with all these blood urges, and probably go crazy. Because they wouldn't understand any of it. Not that that's an excuse, of course!" Alec was the strangest, talkiest Alpha Isaac had ever met.

Isaac nodded. "That's one way of putting it."

Alec was curious in an endearing geeky way. "But why? I mean, I've never heard of that being typical with Alphas and Omegas." He looked at Judd. "Is it? I mean, is it normal, this urge I have to bite him? Or does it have something to do with the fact that he's got no pack?"

Judd only shrugged.

Alec continued. "Why would I want to, you know, just

gnaw on him? It doesn't feel like claiming. Not really."

Tank growled.

Marvin whimpered.

Alec instantly put out an arm for his mate. "Come here, babe. It's okay, I honestly don't want him like that."

Marvin flew to him and nestled against his chest.

Alec looked worried and sheepish. "No insult intended, Isaac, you're hot and all." His frown cleared as he looked down at his mate. Alec kissed Marvin's temple. "Only you, babes. It's not that."

He looked Isaac up and down from a safe distance. "I don't want to fuck him. It's like my instinct is to fix him. I feel almost parental. Are you, uh, *broken*, Isaac?"

Isaac had the oddest sensation. It was as if his insides were hotter than his outsides, like his soul was trying to squeeze out of his skin in surprise.

It wasn't that Alec's reaction was unexpected. He'd assumed the Alpha would morph into third form and attack him (every other Alpha always had). Isaac had been prepared, if he had to, to use his wolf and defend himself. He hated to do it, but he would let his wolf free, if it meant protection.

But it had gone differently this time.

That ridiculous merman had sashayed in and smoothed everything over. The undersized Alpha had miraculously managed to shift back without pouncing on Isaac and mauling him. Now Alec was holding himself there, keeping himself human, and preventing himself from attacking. He was looking at Isaac with something approaching sympathy and a need to care, like a nurse.

Alec looked around. "Okay, let's just everyone be calm for a moment and see if we can't figure this out."

Then Alec began asking Isaac questions. Smart, gentle, appropriate questions, trying to understand the situation. There was no demand to them. No intent to trap. No intent to do anything to Isaac against his will.

Did Isaac have pack? (No.) Did Isaac have family? (Only nominally.) Where was Isaac from, originally? (Cleveland. Yes, people came from Cleveland to the Bay Area.)

It was almost enough to make Isaac relax.

Then the big red-headed enforcer came bursting back into the room, still naked. *Does he ever wear clothing?*

He was trailed by a large cream-colored wolf and an unfairly sexy Asian dude who smelled like coolant and power. These three were followed by a slender, cheerful Italian-looking fellow with slicked-back wavy hair and vaguely greaser clothing.

"Are we having a pack meeting?" asked this last arrival. "I didn't know."

Alec said, "Lovejoy, that's a great idea. Seeing as we're all here now. I'm gonna start over from the beginning." He looked for a long, thoughtful moment at Isaac and Tank. Tank was still a wolf and still leaning protectively against Isaac's legs.

Alec sucked his teeth, then issued orders. "Kevin, you stay near the door. And perhaps consider a bathrobe or something." For the first time, he sounded like an actual Alpha. "Judd, you're good where you are. Bryan, stay close to me. But both you and Tank, I want you in human form. We *all* need to talk about this."

Isaac gaped. *Talk? More?*

Imagine, a pack of werewolves who were just gonna sit around and discuss him. They weren't trying to eat him. Or fight him. Or fight *over* him. Or fuck him up. Or lock him up.

Marvin took a little breath and slid away from his mate's comforting embrace. He made his way to the kitchen. The Italian dude joined him there with a whispered, "What's going on?" Marvin shrugged and pointed him at the fridge. Apparently, they were getting snacks.

Isaac was both pleased and honored. Food meant welcome.

Isaac was also hungry. He hadn't eaten since the lunch with Lavish, a million years ago.

"Tank, Bryan, human form, *now*." There was steel in Alec's measured words. There was no VOICE to it, but finally Isaac felt Alec's true power. Both wolves instantly did as ordered.

Isaac found himself a little proprietary about the fact that Tank was now standing next to him in the middle of the living room in all his glory. Funny really, because they were werewolves and it happened a lot. Isaac pulled another throw off the back of a chair and wrapped it around Tank, much as Marvin had done with Alec. Tank looked delighted by the attention.

God, he so wants to belong to someone. I wish he were mine to keep. Isaac flinched at that thought. How horrible to want to do to Tank what so many had tried to do to him.

The throw was shades of teal and turquoise with a sequined fringe. It looked ever so slightly like a grass skirt, but Tank seemed perfectly comfortable in it.

Marvin came over with a tray of sliced meat and gave Isaac's possessive blanketing a nod of approval.

"Good. Well, yes, that makes sense. Tank, that's a lovely color on you. Now, sit and eat, Isaac. Tell us *everything*. And then tell us how we can fix it. Would you like a cocktail? I could make one, I think."

Alec looked genuinely confused. "We have booze?"

Marvin grinned. "We have gin!" He reached beneath the coffee table and produced a turquoise squarish bottle. "I got it 'cause it matched my cushions."

Alec remained puzzled. "What will you mix it with, babe?"

Marvin frowned then turned to ask the young redhead in the kitchen to check for mixers.

Colin stood a long moment with the fridge door open.

"We have milk."

Everyone winced. Isaac appreciated what the merman was doing – making himself ridiculous to lighten the mood.

The Italian came over with more food – little meatballs in some kind of sauce and cubes of cheese. "I'm Lovejoy," he said before heading back for napkins.

"Oh, goodness me!" Marvin set down the gin with a perturbed flutter of his hands. "How awful. I never made proper introductions. Now Isaac, who did you meet already? Oh never mind, let's start at the beginning."

Tank tugged Isaac to sit down.

Isaac found himself sharing a settee with his lover while the merman trotted about, arms swimming wildly through the air as he gestured at each werewolf. Isaac's own wolf, feeling odd and floaty and safe, stretched out his senses to follow along.

"Alec, you now know."

Isaac's wolf told him Alec was strong, beloved of his pack, and young in his leadership. His confidence was centered in his abilities as a scientist, the love of his mate, and care of his pack. But he was not yet fully settled into his authority.

Marvin continued for the sake of teasing his partner. "He's the rude one who apparently can't stop third forming all over the place."

"What? Third form? Why?" That came from the man who'd formerly been a cream-colored wolf. He was big, although not as big as Tank, with brown hair and long-lashed familiar-looking hazel eyes. *Alec's brother?*

"I'll explain in a moment. That's Bryan, he's pack Beta. I know he's too big for it, but Alec's not exactly your average Alpha."

Bryan said, "Should I make tea? This may call for tea."

"He's also obsessed with tea. Do please tell him what you like or you get something nasty and pungent."

Isaac could only shake his head when both Bryan and Marvin looked at him inquiringly. "No tea, thank you."

Bryan sniffed.

Isaac's wolf told him that the Beta was a still comfort, like the coastal redwood forests – the light that filtered through was valued, and he treasured those around him deeply. Where Alec was the head, Bryan was the heart of this pack. He would die for his Alpha, and they knew it and loved him for it.

Marvin continued. "The super sexy-mean one next to Bryan is Max, Bryan's mate."

Max was a hot Asian dude with a take-no-prisoners expression and the crackling of power around him. He left his lover's side and, totally fearless, came over to Isaac and stuck out a hand. "Yo yo."

Isaac shook it. His nose wrinkled involuntarily at the acrid sharpness of the man. "You're a *mage?*"

His wolf told him nothing, a blank on this man. Probably because he was cloaked in quintessence.

Max grinned. "Don't just say it out loud, everyone will know."

Marvin pressed on, stubborn. "Let's see... you met Judd, enforcer."

Isaac's wolf was no longer shaking in fear of the big black man, so he was able to inform Isaac that Judd was reserved, old, and lonely. Even here, surrounded by a pack that accepted him, Judd was guarded. Isaac stifled down his wolf's keening pity for the man, his need to explore that isolation and mend the divide.

"Kevin, the big redhead at the door, is our other enforcer." Kevin blew them a kiss. *Still naked.*

Isaac's wolf read Kevin as smooth and cheerful, his confidence brackish with old failure, worried about something dear, capable of great love, and extremely protective.

"That's Colin there. He's Kevin's brother, in case you

didn't guess."

Isaac didn't want to touch too closely on the boy. The jolt at the club had been bad enough, but his wolf perked up, reached out. *Mine heal mine help.* Damaged, then, and in desperate need of affection, but also frightened of it. Isaac could sympathize.

"Lovejoy is the one in the kitchen with too much gel in his hair. And then there's me, the prettiest."

Isaac's wolf thought Lovejoy was slightly uncomfortable with himself, but eager and interested in the world, cautious with things new and treasured.

And Marvin? Marvin wasn't a werewolf, but he was shifter enough to read – watery and light, all tangled tenderness and spikes of exasperation, with a sparkling overlay of adoration and easy amusement.

Lovejoy and Colin came to sit with them in the sunken living room area. Now only Kevin at the door, Judd opposite on guard, and Bryan next to Alec stayed standing and further away.

Isaac had no idea how it happened, but it was exactly the kind of arrangement that made him feel safest. The enforcers were furthest away from him and Alec was being tempered by a Beta who seemed quite strong. Isaac noticed Alec's breathing ease and his shoulders relax due to Bryan's proximity. The only pack members close to Isaac were all sitting and were also the weakest wolves and the non-werewolves. And his lover, of course, who even in his human form still preferred close, was offering comfort that Isaac found troubling but his wolf adored.

His wolf told him little about Tank except *mine mine mineminemine.*

Isaac took a small sip of air. He was hungry but too nervous to eat. "So hi, everyone, I'm Isaac." He felt a little like he was taking the podium in front of some alcohol addiction recovery meeting.

He glanced at Tank. *Make that* werewolf *addiction*

recovery meeting.

"I'm an Omega. I'm afraid I've been living in your territory for a while. I didn't realize. I thought there were no packs in the Bay Area. That's why I moved here. But I also didn't check with DURPS. Because, I... well, I didn't want to register myself. Anyway, I met Tank and I learned about you being here. I was going to leave. I swear I was!"

"It's okay." Alec clearly wanted to come over and comfort Isaac but he didn't move from his position. Instead he raised his palm in an awkward gesture of welcome. "We aren't upset about that. We aren't upset at all. We're delighted to meet you."

Isaac's wolf assured him that the Alpha was genuine.

"So, Isaac, you're a *born* Omega?" Alec was frowning hard and being careful with his words. Isaac had never seen an Alpha like that. Usually they were brash and prone to charging in teeth first, talk later.

"Yes sir," said Isaac.

Alec stumbled on. "Were you ever *made*? I mean, in adulthood have you ever been bitten by an Alpha in third form?"

Isaac felt his heart rate accelerate. "No!"

Tank's big hand slid behind Isaac on the couch and began to rub the small of Isaac's back.

Alec nodded. "Okay. So I think that's what's going on. Something in me is desperate to change you. The lack of smell, it's wrong. I think that I want to bite you so badly because then you would smell like pack. It's worse than any other instinct I've ever encountered."

Isaac nodded. "Every Alpha I've met has turned third form and attacked me. Or, if they aren't strong enough to have third, they locked me away or beat me up or both."

All the men around him looked unhappy.

Tank gave a sad little growling sigh and shifted closer, plastered against him, nuzzled his neck.

"I'm sorry, Isaac. We'll fix this." Tank lifted his head

and glared at his Alpha.

Alec nodded vigorously. "We will, somehow."

Tank continued. "So, my..." He coughed. "Isaac, why didn't your original pack Alpha bite you? I mean before you left them?"

Isaac winced. *Here we go.* "I was taken. As a kid. Before puberty and the bite." He decided he'd better spit it out as quickly as possible. "My father is, was, an enforcer. He left his pack, had this idea about the supremacy of werewolves, thought enforcer was strong enough, and basically started a cult. He kept me as a kind of mascot."

Judd squinted at him. "You father was Dominance Mercer? Holy shit."

Alec swung to look at his enforcer. "You know about this?"

"You don't?" Judd frowned. "The Shift Supremacist movement?"

Isaac winced. "I think Dad's official moniker was the Shifters Temple Pastoral Gathering."

It was Marvin who said, finally, "You mean the Smokey Suicides?" He instantly jumped to kneel next to Isaac. "Fuck. Honey, were you there?" He put a hand on Isaac's knee and looked up into his face with big teal eyes swimming in tears.

Isaac was instantly compelled to comfort. He shook his head and patted Marvin's hand. "Not at the end. I escaped years before that happened. But I was there at the beginning."

Tank's big solid hand petted down his back again, as though he were trying to gentle a skittish horse.

Judd was clearly irritated by all the blank looks from the rest of the pack. "It was basically the shifter version of Jonestown. This asshole enforcer, no offense, Isaac—"

"None taken. It aptly describes my father, although rather insults assholes."

Judd continued, "He loses his shit, leaves his pack,

starts a cult claiming werewolves should rule the world or some such crap, recruits a bunch of loners, low-rank wolves, other shifters, and a few of those human groupies who wanna be furry but don't have the genes for it, and starts a self-styled *utopia* in the Smokey Mountains. Ended up in a standoff with the SBI. Rather than be taken, Mercer shifted, killed whoever he could with his teeth, then had the rest swallow silver nitrite, including himself."

Everyone was now staring at Isaac. He grimaced. "Dear old Dad."

"Wow," said Max. "And I thought mine was a piece of work. Congratulations on drawing the shortest of short straws, dude."

"Thanks," said Isaac.

"It sucks to be the son of a man who has something to prove." Alec shook himself slightly. "So you were raised outside of both human and werewolf society? You were born Omega but never bitten after puberty, because there was no Alpha to do it. And you were how old when you got out, mid-teens?"

"Fifteen." Isaac twisted to look at Tank, feeling oddly desperate. He didn't care what the others thought, but he wanted Tank to understand. "You know the way everyone always trusts me instinctively?"

"It's called Omega empathy." A new voice spoke up at that juncture.

Everyone turned to stare at Colin, who flushed in embarrassment. "What? I know a bit."

"Of course, you do," said Kevin loyally. "You're the smart one."

"Hey!" Alec looked perturbed. "PhD, remember?"

"You're smart too, dear, but you're the Alpha."

"Which one am I?" wondered Lovejoy.

"You're the clown."

"I object!"

"Then stop putting so much gel in your hair. Judd is the

mysterious one. Bryan's the nice guy. Marvin's the pretty one."

"Aw, thanks, darling."

"Max is the sassy one."

Max snorted. "Snarky, please."

"And I'm the bad boy." Kevin finished his categories.

"Aw," said Alec, "it's sweet that you think so."

Isaac narrowed his eyes at Kevin. "Which one is Tank?"

Kevin blinked, as if he'd forgotten about Tank.

Isaac didn't like that at all, although Tank didn't seem the slightest bit perturbed.

Tank answered for his enforcer. "I'm the grunt, of course."

Alec looked at him, clearly startled by the dismissive tone. "No, you're the anchor. How do you not know that?"

Tank went pink about the ears. "I am?"

"Stable and boring," said Kev, in good fun, but a little nasty.

Isaac glared at the redhead. "Hey there, sparky. Stable is beautiful and sexy."

"It is?" Tank went even pinker.

Isaac tilted his head and raised his eyebrows. Tank should know this, how important stability was to Isaac. Especially Isaac, who had moved, and run, and drifted unmoored forever. To find a man who wanted to anchor him, not keep him, just be there if needed. That was amazing. Tank was amazing. How could he not know that? *I'll have to make it clear to him.*

Tank tugged on one ear and cleared his throat. "Ugh, could we get back to Colin being smart?"

"Thank you, Tank. So this Omega empathy thing? Colin, explain," ordered Alec.

"I read about it. It's a thing they do for their packs. It's why it is so nice to have one. It's like how Betas can calm Alphas, only it works on all of us. The whole pack."

Isaac was pleased to note that all the werewolves

around him were keeping position, trying to make certain he felt safe. No matter how interesting the conversation, the higher-ranked wolves hadn't moved any closer.

Alec nodded to Colin. "Thanks, sweetie. Isaac, would you continue with your history?"

"Sure. So I'm in this cult and able to change into a wolf from birth and then *that* empathy thing starts kicking in when I hit puberty. The cult started acting all weird around me, leaning in, gravitating toward me, asking me for advice. Dad felt his leadership was threatened and started locking me up." He didn't say where or how small the shed, or how hungry he had been *all the time*. He'd been twelve. The specifics were shameful, he'd been so weak and confused and afraid.

"Eventually I managed to escape and I just ran. I tried to research what it meant to be a werewolf. At libraries and online and stuff. I mean, I knew dad must be full of shit, couldn't trust anything he said, ever. So I wasn't gonna trust his explanation as to how the world worked. I didn't even know I was an Omega. Didn't know what ranks meant. I thought all wolves were born with the ability to shift right away."

Understanding flashed over Alec's face, making it beautiful with revelation. "And every pack you met after that, the Alpha would have basically gone mad. I bet the enforcers all tried to grab you and take you to their Alpha."

Isaac nodded. There'd been blood and worse, more often than not. Until he just avoided all werewolves.

Massive arms snaked around him and Tank squeezed him softly. "You went from one horror to another. And you were just a baby. You've been running ever since?"

"A long time."

Alec's eyes narrowed. "I could fix it. I mean, you wouldn't have to run anymore."

"How?" Isaac was careful with hope.

"Would you maybe let me just do it? You know, bite

you. If I was really gentle."

Isaac flinched.

Alec did as well, in response. "It's just there's such wrongness about you. It's like some existential wound. I'm desperate to heal you, knit you back together. And in classic werewolf fashion that seems to take the form of biting you."

Isaac's wolf agreed with this. Deep inside he could feel his beast, beaten down and frightened, nevertheless yearning for Alec. Straining toward the Alpha.

It was one of the reasons Isaac had stopped trusting his wolf. Always the creature was trying to take him toward pack. Toward Alpha. Yet Isaac had only ever suffered as a consequence.

Isaac looked down at his hands, risking taking his eyes off the Alpha as a gesture of trust. The man still hadn't moved. Truly, his control was extraordinary.

"My wolf would like it, I think. He has always wanted pack. But he is not to be trusted."

Around him all the werewolves seemed to inhale together, shocked by his words.

Isaac didn't understand. What had he said that was so awful?

"*What* did you just say?" Tank's voice, next to him, was low and frightened.

Isaac was confused. "I said that my wolf always wanted pack."

Alec whimpered. "Your wolf…" The Alpha paused and swallowed. "Your wolf is *separated* from you?"

Tank cleared his throat. "Isaac, look at me for a moment. Please."

Isaac turned, even more confused, and looked into Tank's big, worried brown eyes. "Yes, baby?"

Tank said, "You refer to your wolf as something apart from you. A different entity. Do you think of it – um, *him* – that way? Are you two separate beings?"

"Of course." Isaac was even more puzzled. "Don't you?"

Alec gave a funny whining noise but Isaac didn't look away from Tank's eyes, which were welling with tears.

"No, Isaac. There's only I. I am man and wolf, at the same time. There is no *we*. There is no human-me versus wolf-me. There's only one *me*."

Isaac shrugged. "Well, it's not like that in my head. He's separate, and let me tell you, we do not agree most of the time."

Tank winced and then pressed his face against Isaac's neck, trembling with strain as if he wanted to pull away but was forcing himself closer.

"Isaac," Judd this time, "how long has it been since you shifted?"

Isaac shrugged. "I needed him to get away from the last pack that got me, then I was on the run for a bit. Six months, maybe more?"

Someone made a gulping, retching noise. Kevin maybe.

"Six months." That was Alec's Beta. Bryan's voice was low and mellow and calming, as befitted a Beta. "Without a run. I need tea."

Tank nuzzled Isaac. "Poor baby."

Isaac did not like that he was now an object of pity. *I did fine. I'm fine. I'm alive, against the odds. I'm sane. At least I think I am.* "What's freaking you all out so much? It's all good. I'm in total control of my wolf!"

"Of course. He would see that as *good* because every fucking Alpha he's met is out of control." That was the Beta again. "Speaking of, Alec, get up."

Isaac turned away from Tank to see that the Alpha had fallen to his knees in anguish. He looked gray and ill.

Alec glanced up at his Beta. *Was he actually crying?* "Why did no one look after him?" He turned to Isaac, still maintaining a distance, but the yearning is his voice was unlike anything Isaac had ever heard. "Oh God, I'm so sorry. No one took care of you. Precious boy. No one ever took care."

The wolf in Isaac responded to the plea, howling, yearning to help his Alpha, to stop the pain on the other man's face.

Max, the only non-shifter in the room, was watching the whole thing with a mystified expression tempered by intellectual curiosity. *Impress me*, his attitude screamed.

Marvin still had a hand resting on Isaac's knee. Then in a clear bid to lighten the mood, he stood, pouted, and said in a huffy way, "Alec never calls *me* precious."

"That's because you're a pain in the ass," replied Max without any rancor at all.

"Stop being idiots, both of you." Bryan paused in his attempt to soothe his Alpha to glare at the mates. "Marvin, Alec isn't interested in Isaac in *that* way. Besides, can't you see that Isaac belongs to Tank? Or Tank belongs to Isaac, rather. This isn't about that. This is about fixing him."

"Isaac's actually broken?" Max clearly didn't trust Alec's assessment of the situation, but when Bryan spoke, he took it seriously. Isaac was getting the impression that Bryan rarely spoke. Good tactic for getting people to listen to you.

"I thought that was obvious, especially to you." Bryan gave his mate an exasperated look.

"Nothing is *ever* obvious to me, sweetcheeks, except your wood first thing in the morning," Max shot back.

Marvin lost his pout. "Oh my god, Max, we have a *guest!*"

Their silliness seemed to soothe Alec, who struggled back to his feet, still looking a little wounded.

He glanced desperately around at the rest of his pack. "We *have* to help him."

The two enforcers clearly wanted to move forward, no doubt to hold Isaac down by force if necessary while Alec administered the bite. But they had been told to stay back, so they did. Lovejoy and Colin merely angled to face Isaac, as if offering support through focused attention.

Tank returned his hand to Isaac's back where it resumed its soothing caress.

"I'm fine." Isaac tried not to scoff at all the ridiculous fuss. His wolf however, basked in it. Whatever this pack wished to do, Isaac had the sudden sinking sensation, his wolf would not fight them over it.

Tank's voice was pained. "No, Isaac, you're not fine."

Chapter Fifteen
In For Repairs

Tank wasn't sure how he could articulate to Isaac the depth of the wrongness in Isaac's words. To think of the wolf as something separate from yourself, it was like the werewolf version of multiple personality disorder. It was the kind of comment that made the hairs on the back of Tank's neck stand up. No wonder Isaac had no smell, he was neither man nor wolf.

"Please," he begged his lover... former lover, Tank supposed, since an Omega was so far above him it wasn't even funny. "Please. Let Alec bite you. Think about it? He'll be kind." He kept his body close, trying to offer comfort and hope and support.

Isaac just looked at them all.

Tank followed his gaze. The pack was clearly drawn to Isaac, but also horrified by what he'd said, the intimation of what he was, or might become. A werewolf who did not shift. A man who was neither fully one creature nor another. A true monster in their midst, to live in limbo like that. Tank's stomach went queasy.

Isaac turned and looked at him. Sitting so close, Tank could see the gray of Isaac's eyes had navy about the rim. *So beautiful.*

"You think that would help me, you know, with all the other werewolves?"

Isaac was trusting Tank, reaching for him for reassurance. This man, who'd had precious little reassurance over his lifetime.

Tank nodded. "My family has been with the Boston pack since before Saturation. I left them and that pack to follow Alec. I would trust him not only with my life, but with yours. Which is more important."

Isaac cocked his head. "How can you say that so soon?"

Tank shrugged. "You're you, special, Omega. And Alec is special too. Look at him, he's not a normal Alpha."

Alec's face was drawn and hungry and sad. His focus was hard and sure on Isaac. "Oh, I miscalculated."

"Miscalculated what?" Isaac's tone was shocked, no doubt unused to any Alpha admitting he was wrong.

"You don't need words, you need proof. You chose Tank. Of all the members of my pack, it's Tank you want. And he's all about proof in the doing, isn't he? In being there and helpful."

Tank wasn't sure how he felt about that. Was it criticism? It felt like praise. Was he, perhaps, important to his pack in a way he'd never noticed? He'd thought he was nothing, easily discarded. But in being there, in always showing up, in always supporting and helping and providing of himself, had that meant something? Had Alec noticed? Had the others? Was his submission to pack as much a gift as his submission to Isaac?

Alec continued. "So we follow Tank's example. I'll wait. I'll prove to you I'm different. That I'm stable. That this pack is stable and capable of self control and restraint. We will all prove it." He glared at the enforcers. "If you would like, Isaac, you can stay here. With us. Unbitten. In a guest bed or with Tank in his room. You can observe this pack in action. I won't push you or pressure you."

Isaac frowned, clearly thinking it over. He looked at

Judd, then Kevin, then back to Alec. Finally, he gave a curt nod. "A test?"

"A test."

"Okay then, with Tank is fine." Isaac sounded unsure of himself, but resolute.

Tank felt a prickle of relief.

Judd said, "Tank's room is upstairs near us. Is that wise?"

Alec nodded, jaw firm. "Judd and Kevin, you'll have to patrol the hall." Quickly he explained to Isaac. "Not to monitor you, to keep me under control. Sleepwalking could turn into sleep biting or what have you. I don't know exactly how I'll behave if I relax control even slightly." He looked at his brother.

Bryan sighed. "Fine, I'll stay. But I'm sleeping outside your door in wolf form, thank you very much. I'm too old for floors without fur."

Everyone breathed out in relief, then looked cautiously at Max.

"What? Oh." The Magistar rolled his blue eyes, "Oh noes, what will little ol' me do without my big strong boyfriend in my bed every single night? Forsaken and unfucked. The tragedy of it all." Silence. "Really, you sensitive dickwads, I'll be fine. I spent decades sleeping alone, I think I can handle it with my usual grace and aplomb."

Alec nodded, a small smile on his strained face. "Okay, good, we have a plan."

Tank looked hopefully at Isaac. The Omega was smiling too.

Without much further fuss, the pack went about their evening rituals. They were, Tank noticed, a little stiffer than usual. They made sure to say out loud, so Isaac could overhear, where they were going and what they were doing next and why. Especially Alec and the enforcers. No sudden movements.

Marvin and Lovejoy started puttering about making dinner. Well, Lovejoy did – Marvin hung out alongside sipping clam juice and gossiping. The pack house slowly filled with the smell of lasagna.

Tank sat as still as possible next to Isaac and tried to watch his reactions to pack activity without seeming to. Isaac was clearly a little awed, definitely uncomfortable, but he stayed seated on the couch. He sipped a glass of milk that Marvin brought him, gray eyes bright on the movement of those around him. Colin disappeared upstairs, then came and settled on the other couch, feet up and laptop out, working on a school paper. Normally, he'd hole up in his room until dinner. It might be Colin was trying to help Isaac feel welcome but Tank thought it was more likely the Omega thing was drawing Colin close.

The others drifted in and out. They were a noisy bunch, thumping about the house. Kevin, especially, had no apparent volume control. Tank couldn't help hoping that Isaac would tolerate it, even find it amusing.

Eventually Kev broke the stillness in the living room by swooping behind his brother, grabbing one of Marvin's beloved cushions, and bopping Colin on the head with it.

Colin batted it away in exasperation. "Fuck off! Now I have to fix my hair."

The artful muss of red locks took a great deal of product, if Colin's bathroom shelf was anything to go by. Tank couldn't imagine spending that much time on any part of his appearance, but Colin was a bit self-conscious.

The redhead left his laptop for the stairs with Kev loudly proclaiming that he could use some product himself, and what did Colin think of faux-hawks?

Isaac spoke at last. "He does that to distract?"

"Kevin? Distract from what?"

"The wrong kind of attention on his brother."

Tank considered. "You think he's still trying to save him?"

Isaac nodded.

A wave of sadness swept over Tank. "Even though they're safe now?"

Isaac's eyes were suspicious. "Are they? Are we? Am I? Does pack structure save anyone?"

Tank thought of his own willingness to sacrifice for his pack's greater good. *Cannon fodder.*

"We are all doing our best so far as our natures allow."

Isaac nodded. "That's what worries me."

"Our best or our natures?"

"Both."

Tank realized this was Isaac's version of Kevin's too-loud outrageousness. Kevin caused a scene to distract others, to draw attention to himself so his brother might hide his hurt. Isaac used Omega perception to shield himself. A weapon made of empathy and understanding. He saw too much in others, understood the soft underbelly of exposure. The thing he least wanted, therefore, was to roll over himself. Hence his fear of pack. Was that the reason for his dominance, or merely a contributing factor?

Tank stood and offered to show Isaac around.

He tried not to hope that Isaac liked the house despite its flaws. The upper floor hadn't yet been renovated. It was musty in that way old houses got, memories mixed with dust motes in the half-light. It had wall-to-wall carpeting, expensive and plush in the '80s, but it was no longer the '80s.

"Most of the bedrooms are up here. Alec and Marvin have the master bedroom at the front there with their own bathroom. Judd is on the ocean side, Kevin is opposite him."

Isaac nodded. "Enforcers bracket the Alpha."

"Colin's room is right in front of us." Tank pointed

down the opposite end of the hallway. "My room is there, land side, and Lovejoy is opposite me, ocean side. We all have to share a bathroom, so it can be a pain. Lovejoy and Kevin take *forever*."

He saw Isaac try to hide a smile. "Aren't they the straight ones?"

"Exactly." Tank opened the door to his room. "You can change in here if you like, or we've got a guest bedroom on the ground floor you can use. I know you said staying with me would be fine, but I don't want to pressure you." The Omega needed to know he was under no obligation at all. He was free to choose, free to stay or to go, to bite or be bitten.

Isaac dipped his head but said, gratifyingly quickly, "Here is good, if that's okay? I know Alec said it would be, but we didn't ask you and it's your room."

"Of course." *You can stay forever, if you want.*

Shutting the door behind them, Isaac visibly relaxed.

Tank felt himself beaming with relief. He loved that Isaac seemed most comfortable in his room. Probably the smell. But Tank also worked hard to make his space homey. Everything in his room, from furniture to bedding, was light and airy, in grays and blues and creams.

"I think the bathroom is free of Colin and his hair product reapplication, if you want to freshen up."

They'd borrowed something of Kevin's for Isaac to change into. Give him a break from gym clothes. Kevin was a touch more muscled, but preferred his clothing so tight that it fit Isaac comfortably.

"Maybe if your clothes weren't so tight you'd spend more time in them," commented Tank.

"Look at you developing claws in front of your man," was Kevin's only response.

Isaac took the stack and went to the bathroom.

Tank busied himself getting dressed and tidying up an already tidy room. He didn't have much stuff. His needs were as limited as his funds. The bottom two drawers of his dresser were already empty and he freed up hangers so Isaac could maybe hang clothing in the closet. They'd have to go get his stuff. Or was that too much like moving in? The drawers of his bedside table were full and he wondered if he should hide the toys. But the idea that Isaac might want to use them on him was so appealing, he decided he'd rather risk embarrassment.

Isaac returned wearing Kevin's jeans and t-shirt. His feet were bare. Tank really wanted to kneel and lick them. Now, of course, was not the time for that. Maybe later, if he was lucky.

He sniffed, cautious. Isaac smelled clean, of his soap, which pleased Tank because it meant he'd chosen that over the other offerings. "We can get your stuff from your apartment for you. Alec would send Judd or Kevin tonight if you wanted." He hoped Isaac was perceptive enough to understand the song beneath his words. *You are welcome, you are safe.*

Isaac shook his head. "I'm fine. I've always traveled light. None of it is important to me."

It hurt Tank to think on how transient Isaac's life had been. If he would not take the bite from Alec, at least the pack could offer shelter while dealing with trappers and hunters.

He wanted to ask if Isaac knew who was after him. But he also didn't want to break the mood. Isaac looked, if not yet comfortable, at least not in danger of imminent flight.

They made their way down to dinner. Where Lovejoy preened under lasagna accolades and pretended not to be even more delighted by the fact that Isaac ate two helpings.

Max was sharp and witty. Marvin was charming. Kevin was Kevin. And everyone else was calm and well-behaved (for werewolves). Tank was ridiculously proud of his pack. He could feel Isaac relaxing next to him.

Alec arranged the table so he sat as far away from Isaac

as possible. He picked at his food and looked at Isaac with hungry eyes, but he never once moved in his direction, and he never said a word out of place.

Tank's love for his Alpha in that moment was all-consuming. There was no other way to prove to Isaac they were a different kind of pack than to show him. Alec understood. *Good Alpha.*

Isaac found his first meal with a pack overwhelming. He was so sensitive to all the men at the table. Other werewolves. Except perhaps Max. But Max was so much woven into the fabric of Bryan that the Beta's quiet pleasure at Isaac's presence telegraphed to his Magistar.

Isaac found himself, more than once, the object of Max's sharp blue eyes. He was grateful that he had to guess what the man was feeling. The others were all too easy to read.

There was a general overlay of euphoria at Isaac's being with them, a sense of pride. To have attracted an Omega was an achievement, no matter how fraught or impermanent his presence among them.

It was flattering, although the innate sense of ownership troubled Isaac. They had said he could go free, if he wanted. He might need to test that vow. But during the meal they never once pressured him in word or deed. They treated him like an honored guest or a long-lost friend.

They kept the conversation light and fun, talking of friends Isaac didn't know, but in generalities so he might have an opinion on love lives and social habits, work choices and hobbies.

Isaac tried to push his fear aside. He understood that what they felt for an Omega was new and complicated, interweaving with the greater tapestry of pack.

It was that tapestry that interested Isaac's Omega

senses. *Is it tight and clear or loose and unstructured? Is it rotten or unsullied?*

While they talked and laughed and ate, he allowed the Omega part of him to follow the threads between the men at the table. It was exhausting and would take a lifetime to understand all the binds and knots and tangles within the weave. It was the melding of nine adults with strong personalities and long lives.

Isaac pretended that the tapestry itself depicted a wolf, Alec as its mind and Bryan as its heart. Judd and Kevin were the sharpness of teeth and claw, strength and defense. Tank and Lovejoy and Colin were the muscles and blood and tendons. Max and Marvin were there too, a brightness in the eyes, need and necessity, the reason to keep fighting.

Where does an Omega fit the beast? If the wolf is the pack and the pack is the wolf, what need then for one who sees both the parts and the whole?

Isaac smiled at his own whimsy. The idea made him feel frail and bereft. Under ordinary circumstances, when he felt formless and ungrounded he reached for dominance. But he thought that he might be too tired and overwhelmed for fucking. He hoped Tank would understand.

Apparently he did, for as the meal wound to a close, Tank extracted them both from further social obligations.

"Bed for me, I think. Isaac, would you care to join me?" Tank's offer was made sweet with uncertainty.

Tank would never presume. And he knew, of course, that Isaac would react badly to obligation or order.

Am I so predictable? Is this how others feel when I use my Omega wiles on them? Still he could not resist. Time away from the rest of the pack and their need for his validation would help. They desired not just his good opinion but his approval. They wanted so badly for him to choose them, for him to stay, it was exhausting.

Sleep would be good. Tank under him would be good. Just to rest, though, nothing more. Isaac felt stretched and incapable of anything more than cuddling.

Upstairs, he couldn't even admit to wanting that. But Tank sensed it, and was brave enough to reach for him first. Then Isaac could pretend he was snuggling for Tank's comfort and not his own.

They slept together, coiled and curled and mutually protective. Isaac was surprised to find that he didn't feel any lesser for it, as dominant man or an Omega wolf.

Isaac awoke groggy and grumpy. "What time is it?"

Fortunately for him, there was an amiable Olympian lump in the bed next to him.

"Good morning," husked the mountain, rolling over and nuzzling his neck, not answering his question.

"Christ, what day is it?"

"Tuesday," husked Tank. "You don't work on Tuesdays, do you?"

"No. Still, I might just call and check in. Let Xavier know I'm still alive and shit."

Tank cocked his head. "He's important to you?"

Isaac paused, then emitted a surprised huff noise. "They all are. No one ever really looked after me before Saucebox did."

"The lucky ones run and find themselves a family."

Isaac's voice was soft. "Is that what you did?"

Tank gave him a look. "You Omega-ing me?"

"Sorry. I can't always turn it off."

"Call your boss," suggested Tank.

"You giving me orders now?"

"Never," replied Tank, quickly and happily. "Here, use my phone."

Isaac laughed, took it, and dialed.

Xavier was gruff, but obviously pleased to hear Isaac's voice.

"Still alive, are you?"

"Yep."

"Miracles may never cease."

"What, you don't think I have innate survival skills?"

"Boy, you freak out if your mixer lids are swapped."

Xavier didn't ask where Isaac was holed up, he knew the drill. He did say that it would please Lavish to know Isaac was still whole, and that he'd expect him in on Thursday for the shifter mixer, unless he heard otherwise. He didn't ask why Isaac had decided to stay or where.

Isaac asked if Clara was all right, if anyone had gone by her apartment to check. Xavier said no one had but Oscar would. Isaac didn't know how to thank him.

So instead of gratitude, Isaac said he'd be in on Thursday and to give Lavish his love. He hung up, amused to realize that they used Xavier's girlfriend as a means to communicate their affection for each other.

"Macho is a weird thing, isn't it?"

Tank gestured at himself. "Never been one of my problems. I don't need to be, no one looks beyond the surface."

"Is that why you're submissive?"

Tank looked mildly offended. "Is a loathing of your birth rank the reason you're dominant?"

Isaac winced. "Ah, I see. Sorry. We are what we are."

Tank opened his hand in invitation.

Isaac instantly responded to the need in the gesture, covering and pressing down reassuringly with his own.

Tank let out a breath. "Why try to justify? I always end up convoluted with reasoning. It's like parents who wonder if they *did something* to make their kid queer."

Isaac nodded. "You're saying kinky is natural. Like being an Omega wolf or having black hair."

"We're supernatural."

Isaac grinned. "So you're what? Mr Super-sub? You want a little cape instead of a collar?"

Tank's breath hitched. Isaac liked that. The man wanted his collar, odd in a wolf. Difficult, too, as whatever Tank wore would have to transition with him through shape-shift. Isaac contemplated what might work. The symbolism of a chain bothered him. He'd been chained too often unwillingly.

Then he realized he was actually considering snapping a collar around this man – commitment, possession. He hadn't even decided to stay. He wasn't even sure he trusted Alec to bite him. Didn't know if he believed this strange pack could work for him. And Tank would never leave his pack.

Not that it mattered, he would never force Tank to choose.

Tank changed the subject. Isaac realized that Tank was as sensitive to Isaac's moods as Isaac was to everyone else's. Amazing.

"So, a cult, huh?"

Not that it was a much better topic, but Isaac could roll with it. "Asshole dad. You know how it goes."

Tank shrugged. "Mine's not so bad, actually."

"He know you sleep with dudes?"

"It never came up. But I did feel compelled to leave because of it." He shrugged his massive shoulders.

"He like you? I mean wolf-wise."

"Low rank and massive? Yeah. All of us Depeines come out that way." At Isaacs's confused look, Tank added, "There's nine of us boys in the family."

"Holy shit. All of you survived the bite?"

"Yeah."

"All your size?"

Tank laughed. "I'm pretty much the biggest, but they aren't that much smaller. Depeine males, the backbone of a pack. Together we basically form this big ol' defensive meat-wall."

"That's a lot of family to leave behind." Isaac only ever

had his father, although some of the cult had pretended to be family when he was young, before his dad's jealousy made his life hell.

"There's enough of them to fill even a hole the size I left behind."

"You didn't want to come out to them?"

"I didn't."

"Nice to be bi."

"Easy to be invisible. Not quite the same thing."

Isaac nodded.

Tank looked at him, dark eyes sharp. "You wouldn't have had the choice."

"That swishy, am I?"

Tank colored slightly. "Not what I meant."

Isaac wasn't mad. "I never hid my preferences. There was a time I thought it'd help, make me seem less of a threat to my father. Gay and not interested in any of his women. But an Omega can't disappear into the background. Too useful if you're a non-Alpha trying to hold a pack together. My father hated me, but he also needed me. I kept his followers calm. They stayed because of me, not him. 'Course, that too became a problem. He needed them to want only him, not scraps of attention from me. And I blame myself for them staying."

Tank sighed. "You and Max have a lot in common. Daddy issues."

"He's a weird one." Isaac was relieved to move away from his upbringing. He knew now, of course, that it was messed up. But the thing about being raised in a cult is that he never knew, until he was outside of it, just *how* messed up. He didn't like dwelling on it.

"You find Max difficult to read. Your stuff doesn't work on him, does it?" suggested Tank.

"My *stuff*?"

Tank smiled "That Omega thing you do that makes shifters lean in and say things they shouldn't."

"Oh, that *stuff*. To be fair, I didn't really try with your Magistar."

"Max is unlikely to give you the opportunity." Tank sounded confident.

Isaac tried not to feel like his abilities were in question. "He doesn't trust easily?"

"Prickly little thing."

"Not so little."

"Everyone is little to me." Tank gave an apologetic smile.

Isaac laughed. "His mate's an odd fit as Beta, too."

"I think it works because it's odd." Tank was being thoughtful, not defensive.

Isaac lifted Tank's massive hand and kissed the palm. "I get that."

"Yeah?" Such hopeful brown eyes.

"Yes. Tank, would you mind, while I decide about Alec biting me... Would you mind if we didn't, you know—?"

"Fuck?"

Isaac let out his breath, nodded.

Tank's face was soft with understanding. "That much of an influence, huh?"

"I think so, and while abstaining might make the wanting worse, there's something in topping that makes me too confident. I need to stay cautious. You affect me."

"You want to keep a clear head?"

"Exactly."

"We could just plain old fuck, nothing kinky?"

Isaac knew the truth in their dynamic. "I don't think that's possible with us."

"Good." So much joy in such a simple word.

Isaac made it an order. "You'll wait?"

"Of course. I've waited my whole life." Tank's big shoulders shrugged, his lashes lowered. "I'm honored you still even consider me."

"Don't be silly," Isaac scoffed. "I've been looking my

whole life."

Tank flushed in pleasure. He was so perfect Isaac immediately wanted to break his word and fuck him as hard as he could into the mattress, holding him a little too tight the entire time. So they both knew who they belonged to.

"I'm starving," Isaac said instead, surprised to realize it was true.

Isaac wasn't able to pinpoint the exact moment, but the decision crept over him slowly over the next few days. He supposed it was the pattern of them, the easy camaraderie, the notion that pack was a kind of chosen family, better than the real thing. Especially this pack.

They were vulnerable, too, broken in ways only Isaac could see, that he wanted to help fix. Colin with his nervous hesitancy. Kevin with his brash protective fear. Judd with his lonely anger. Alec with his new shaky confidence. Bryan's silence and Lovejoy's trying too hard. Max with all his prickles and Marvin with his complete lack of them. They fit so well, and yet they were missing something.

They were missing him.

And then there was Tank. Tank, who thought he wasn't necessary. Or missed that he was the reason for pack, their lynchpin and their fight. He was the one they all loved, they all teased, they all got along with. Yet somehow, they had lost him, forgotten to remind him of his worth.

All these things Isaac could see. He was needed. He could choose them, and it would be work. Like any relationship was work. This pack would be an exercise in balance, every day. And yes, he would belong to them, but also they would belong to him.

And best of all, he would *belong*.

They listened as he spoke. They let him cook and clean if he wanted. And he did, he liked cooking and he was a bit of a neat freak. He loved how they responded to him. How they delighted to be taken care of, reveled in his presence and his attention.

Alec stayed away as much as he could, running himself ragged to resist the urge to bite. He looked gaunt and Isaac doubted he was sleeping well. He certainly wasn't eating very well. But he got up and interacted with his pack and went to his job at a bio firm, of all things, and came home and kissed his mate like they were in some modern sitcom. Isaac scoffed at the cheesiness of it and secretly loved it. And eventually realized he was yearning for it all. Comfortable around them.

And that he trusted them. Which was terribly weak of him.

They were open-hearted. They were easy to predict. They did not try to trap him, not even in discussions. Which is not to say there weren't some heated discussions. Marvin had very strong feelings about shifter representation in film. They might have been all the stronger for his worrying over his mate's deteriorating condition. But he never lashed out at Isaac for it and he never blamed him.

The pack responded gently to all Isaac's needles and tests, his rebuffs and withdrawals. Each time he marched out of the house in a huff and just walked away, they let him go. They let him walk down into town or out into the open space of parkland alone. They did not follow. They waited. When he returned it was to see Tank's face brighten, his brown eyes fill with hope. The others were the same. Perhaps not quite so intense as Tank, but they wanted him to stay too.

Isaac found he was weak in the face of hope and kindness, where he could be strong in response to need and abuse. He began to think that perhaps his constantly running was no good thing. He had relied for so long on what kept him alive, he neglected to realize that's all it did. He wanted to live as well as be alive. He wanted to belong as well as stay. It was not weakness to trust. And it was not a horrible instinct to need a home.

CHAPTER SIXTEEN
Once and Future Kink

Things were going well, Tank felt. Isaac was looking startled, yet comfortable with them. With him. Alec was looking worse and Marvin was looking worried, but their Alpha was holding himself together. Even Bryan was showing a bit of strain – he brewed at least six cups of tea a day. And Max came every night to dinner, showing that he did actually miss his mate. But Isaac was still with them. Comfortable.

They were cleaning up after a pack dinner when it happened. Isaac was helping Tank scrub pans in companionable silence. Suddenly Isaac, up to his elbows in suds, turned and looked at the Alpha. Alec was sitting in the sunken living room helping Colin with his bio homework.

Isaac spoke, as if they had all been having a conversation with him in his head. Which they hadn't, so it was utterly out of the blue.

"Okay then, let's do it."

Dripping suds to the kitchen floor, Isaac sagged back against the sink, like some dam inside him had broken.

Everyone paused what they were doing and turned to stare at him. Collectively holding their breath.

Alec stood, trembling. "You mean?"

"I think you should bite me now."

"Oh, thank fuck," said Alec, sitting back down fast, as if his knees had given out.

Marvin clapped his hands.

Isaac added, so quickly the words almost ran together. "What's the best way, do you think? I mean, if I must be bitten, do we stand, lie down, sit? I don't know the right etiquette..."

He seemed so lost.

Marvin jumped in hurriedly, finger-pointed authoritatively at the deck. "Not in here, boys. You know how I feel about blood on my couches. Take it outside."

Tank thought that was a good idea. Isaac would be bitten under the stars with the trees and the ocean nearby. He would feel less trapped. It was also romantic. If one must be bitten...

Alec pouted at his mate. "Deck's bare wood."

Marvin sighed. "I might have some towels I'm willing to sacrifice."

Accordingly, Tank escorted Isaac outside and the others followed. Bryan had to help his Alpha, Alec was shaking so much, half starved and now pumped full of adrenaline. Tank hoped he was strong enough to do this carefully.

The deck was big and unfinished, one section to the side was nothing but support beams. Plus, there was no railing or anything.

"We aren't quite done with it," Tank apologized to his lover.

"Oh, but it's wonderful." Isaac looked about him, as if the view were not the same from the living room. As if he hadn't been staying with them for days. But Tank understood the awe, being up so high with such a vista all around and no barrier, not even glass.

Max had inherited the house when is father died, but

considered it ill-gotten gains, and consequently resented it. He'd given the pack carte blanche to do whatever they wished, so long as it was as different as possible from the gaudy monolithic opulence of the original building.

As a result, they'd kept very little but the basic barn shape and frame, putting in windows wherever possible to bring the outside in. They'd pulled out carpet and put in hardwood, pale and beach-toned, letting Marvin's ocean-modern aesthetic have free rein. They may be a pack of werewolves, but no one wanted to be on a merman's bad side when it came to interior design. The result inside was harmonious and airy. But outside, on the deck under the broad night sky, it was sheer magic.

The perfect place, thought Tank, *for a rebirth.*

Marvin followed them, carrying a big pile of old beach towels.

The pack assembled on the completed section of the deck, all of them sitting down, like children on a field trip.

Tank thought they looked properly pack-like. Judd and Kevin were twitchy, as if they wanted to jump into fur and attack Isaac. As if permission had been given for *them* to bite. Tank forced himself not to show teeth at the very idea. But Colin and Lovejoy seemed to instinctively understand that they must lean against the two enforcers, keeping them stable and distracted.

Marvin laid out the towels as if for a picnic and gestured for Isaac to sit. Isaac looked warily back and forth between Tank and the merman.

Tank sat first, opened his arms. He loved the precedent of this dynamic, him offering support to his lover.

Isaac stayed standing, head cocked, waiting for something.

Finally, Alec approached and knelt next to Tank. Bryan sat on his other side, big hand to his brother's shoulder.

Tank looked up. Only Max hadn't joined them outside. The Magistar remained in the house. He had a glass of wine and an imperious expression, watching them through the window as if he were at the aquarium. *Today, we will witness the biting rituals of the North American werewolf.*

Bryan followed Tank's gaze and rolled his eyes at his mate.

Max saluted them with his glass.

Red wine, of course. Tank hid a smile.

Alec snorted, looked up at Isaac. "You ready?"

Isaac nodded and sat, partly in Tank's lap, with his back to everyone else. Tank wrapped both arms around him, gentle and not too confining – support, not restriction.

Isaac's gave a tiny sigh and bent his head to Tank's shoulder, exposing and offering his neck to Alec sitting next to them.

This close, the sound of shifting into third form was gruesome. Even though it was just Alec's skull (and maybe a few other organs, no one was really certain), it made such a loud, wet crunching.

Then, like giving a child a shot, too fast for Isaac to get tense, Alec struck. His teeth clamped around the point where Isaac's neck and shoulder met. It was not a death bite, no intent to kill, but it was violent and raw.

"Saliva, Alec." Bryan's voice was low but firm. "You can't be too nice. You *must* get your saliva into him."

"That is so gross," said Marvin.

Everyone else was dignified and silent, as if observing a sacred ritual.

Tank was glad for Isaac's weight, and now Alec's too, pressed against Tank's side – both of them relying on him to steady them.

Tank had seen people take the maker bite before, of course he had. He'd witnessed the metamorphosis of many werewolves. But he'd never seen *Alec* administer the bite. His Alpha did it very neatly. Blood still leaked down Isaac's chest and back, soaking his shirt, but it could've been a lot worse.

Isaac sagged in the circle of Tank's arms. Tank would've worried, except he could hear Isaac's breathing, coarse and shallow, probably from pain.

Alec stopped finally, then leaned a little back and began to lick at the gaping wound in Isaac's neck.

Werewolves heal faster and better than humans, although Judd said it was nowhere near like it had been before Saturation. It would take most of the night and a day of rest before Isaac's bite mark turned pale and faint.

Usually, a prospective werewolf either survived metamorphosis or died just after the bite. A human without the genetic predisposition would bleed out, while one with werewolf genes would shift for the first time. None of them knew what would happen to an Omega. Isaac already had a wolf form, he already *was* a werewolf.

Alec sat back on his heels and stared. Still in third form, he cocked his shaggy head to one side, wolf eyes hopeful.

Isaac's scent shifted first. He went from smelling like nothing – absence – to smelling like home and pack and love and all good things. Them. All of them.

Tank inhaled deeply, relishing the joy in such a simple change.

Then Isaac began to shudder. His body became liquid, his bones breaking and reforming within Tank's tentative embrace. He writhed and twisted and screamed. It was horrible and not like any shift Tank had ever witnessed. Certainly, shifting was always painful, but never this bad. It was as if Isaac were fighting to stay human, and then fighting to be a wolf, flickering between the two – dancing in limbo with his own flesh.

Tank dropped him, afraid his hands would sink inside Isaac's body.

He looked at Alec, who was back to human form, and frowning.

"Alpha, do something!" *I promised him it would be okay. I told him to trust us!*

Alec shook his head, confused and worried.

Tank crouched helpless over his lover as Isaac thrashed. His beautiful dark skin went white, like a photo negative, then back to normal.

"TANK." Alec's VOICE cut through the horrible noise of bones breaking and flesh reforming over and over. Alpha command interrupted the fear throbbing in Tank's head.

He tore his eyes away from Isaac. "Yes, Alpha?"

"SHIFT."

Tank found himself shifting, unable to disobey a direct command. His will was utterly subsumed to his Alpha's will, and so he became wolf – big, dark, and strong.

His mate was there. His mate was in such pain. So tormented. So lonely.

Alec's voice came again. "Isaac, precious? See? See how easy? SHIFT. Like Tank, go on, you can do it. Just let it go, remember how it once was? SHIFT NOW."

There finally, lying on Marvin's old beach towels, bloody and shaking, was the panting form of a big white wolf.

Tank folded his own bigger body against him. He licked the wound still visible on Isaac's neck. He chuffed affection and welcome, buried his nose in the sweet-smelling ruff of his wonderful mate.

Isaac gave a long sad whine.

Tank pressed along the full length of him, comforting, lover, friend, home. *Together.*

Then Kevin was there, wolf form, all russet power and protection. Of course, it would be easiest for him to shift, as he was already naked. Then Bryan's big cream-colored shape, looking dirty next to the white of Isaac's coat. Then Judd, and then Lovejoy, and then even Colin, who rarely shifted outside of full moon.

Finally, Alec shifted too, immeasurably pleased, piled on top of them all, tongue lolling. They could feel the rolls of his happiness settling over them through their tethers.

They were one big puppy pile, each touching a small part of Isaac, warmth and safety and pack.

Isaac figured he must have fallen asleep, like an idiot. When he awoke, he didn't know where he was, but he was warm and the air was fresh about him – full of interesting evening scents. There was salt spray of ocean in the distance, and closer, that of fish mixed with man. There were a lot of wolves, too, but that did not scare him because it was pack. *Mine. My pack.*

Isaac stumbled to his feet and noticed they were big white paws. *Holy shit, I'm in fur.*

He felt...

What do I feel?

He felt... good?

He looked around, ears pricked forward, taking in the pile of fur, identifying and knowing each body. The large solid forms of the two enforcers – *guardians, protectors*. Swift to act, sometimes rash, he would need to temper them with caution. The smaller forms of Lovejoy and Colin. *Confidence*, Isaac thought. They showed their lack differently, but they both needed confidence. The steadying reassurance of the Beta pulsed slower, the heartbeat of the pack. But Bryan's focus was always Alpha first, mate second, pack third. As it should be. But the pack needed an Omega to knit them all together. To remind even the Beta that was one of many, and that the weight of cohesion and responsibility was not solely on him. There, at the center, was the beacon of Alpha – *power, sacrifice, responsibility*. Beneath it all, constant and calm, loving and waiting, was Tank. He was awake and watching Isaac, pale yellow eyes intent, ears pricked forward.

Isaac stretched into a lupine bow, an invitation to play.

Hesitant, wary, the massive brown wolf extracted himself from the pile and approached.

He chuffed a soft query.

Isaac chuffed back, tilted his head, and wagged his tail.

Tank tried a cautious nudge, nearly knocking Isaac over with his fat, fluffy head. Isaac bounced to the side, then up and forward, trying to tackle-hug Tank with his front paws.

Tank's ears twitched in the animal equivalent of extreme skepticism. Isaac couldn't possibly get the kind of leverage needed to topple a wolf of Tank's size.

Isaac yipped and pushed, undaunted.

Tank gave him a yellow-eyed look of *Are you quite crazy?* Then, slowly, humoring Isaac, he tipped to one side so Isaac could pounce on top of him.

They wrestled gently.

Isaac could tell Tank was holding everything back, scared of hurting him. He wondered if Tank spent his whole life scared of the world. Not because he feared what it might do to him, but because he feared the damage he could do to it.

They played until a throat clearing interrupted them. Isaac stopped and found that Alec and Colin had changed back to human form. The others were still wolves, relaxed but vigilant, watching them play, tongues out and ears perky.

Alec smiled. "Okay you two, change back, please. We aren't done talking. I'll go find some clothes."

Tank nudged at Isaac with his nose, clearly expecting him to shift first.

Isaac tried. He scrunched up his face, bared his teeth, and attempted to push himself into human form. It just wasn't there, like switching to a TV channel that was no longer available. Those few times he had shifted since puberty, he'd always seen his human body in his mind's eye, weak and pathetic, and curled in the recess of his wolf's control. He'd visualized himself diving into that form, as if diving down a deep well where his human self lay shivering at the bottom.

But that form wasn't there anymore. Neither was the well. Human Isaac was gone – not trapped, simply *absent*.

He whimpered and looked to Alec, who had paused in the act of going inside and was watching him.

Alec said, "Tank, show him."

Tank shifted. His dark, thick fur shrank short and then receded all over his body, until all that was left was on his head and chest and around the base of his pretty cock.

Isaac tilted his head and considered.

Tank said, "It's not a separate thing that you're hunting, Isaac. The human you is as much a part of you as the wolf. Simply slide from one to the other. Don't *try*, just be."

Isaac considered this. Instead of thinking of human Isaac as some captured separate thing, he visualized himself on two legs. He thought about wrapping his arms around Tank. He thought of skin against skin, no fur between them.

The pain arched through his body, shivering his bones, rending his flesh, and then he was standing, and stumbling a little, wobbly but back on two legs.

"Very nice!" said Alec. "Impressively fast."

Isaac couldn't stop himself from glowing at the praise from his Alpha.

"Inside, then?" Alec managed to make it sound not at all like an order. He turned to the rest of his pack still in fur. "You lot are going for a run, I take it?"

Judd barked.

"Good. Keep an eye for strangers. Trappers are still around. I saw them at the local cafe only yesterday."

A bark from Kevin this time. The enforcers took off 'round the back of the porch to the point where it was closest to the hillside and launched themselves off the edge, landing in the darkened yard below. Bryan and Lovejoy followed at a more sedate pace.

Back inside the house, and properly clothed, Colin joined Marvin to clatter in the kitchen.

"Time for second dinner," insisted Marvin. "They'll be starving when they get back."

"I'm starving now," whined Alec, throwing on a nice furry robe someone had set out for him.

The merman gave his mate a look of amused tolerance. "Finally, you want to eat. Good, most of your dinner is still waiting for you." He lifted a pot lid and passed over the mostly full plate that Alec had picked at earlier that evening. A lifetime ago.

Alec looked sadly at the congealed mess, but began chomping away quickly enough.

Max was already sitting in the den area, sipping his wine. "Would anyone like a glass?"

Isaac and Tank declined, but Alec and Colin each took one. It was so surreal and civilized as if the whole biting, forced change, slobbering, blood everywhere, deck incident hadn't happened at all.

"I'll find us robes." Tank trundled off.

Max eyed the man's fine ass appreciatively.

Isaac couldn't quite suppress a growl.

Max toasted him with his glass. "I'm mated, not blind. It's purely artistic voyeurism."

Isaac snorted. "We clearly have similar taste. Although mine's bigger."

Max arched an elegant bow. "Yours, is he?"

Tank returned, "Whose?"

Max sipped his wine. "Exactly."

"Enigmatic fucker," said Tank, without bitterness, tossing Isaac and Colin robes, and shrugging into his own.

"I'm practicing," said Max. "Magistar gravitas."

"You trying to be some kind of proper legendary wizard?" wondered Isaac and then hesitated – the robe was very clean and he was not.

Marvin hooted from the kitchen. "Can you imagine

Max as some kind of fairy godfather?"

Isaac's clothing had shredded off him during his shifts, and he was smeared with blood and dirt, as if a rather small murder had occurred somewhere on his person. *I am the crime scene.* He touched his neck gingerly – the bite was there, tender.

Tank understood. "It's okay to put it on, doesn't matter if it gets dirty."

Isaac nodded. "Those were Kevin's clothes."

Tank frowned. "We still need to collect your stuff from your apartment."

Alec slapped his forehead. "I suck, should have sent the enforcers to do it days ago."

"My roommates have probably chucked it all, or covered everything in glitter," said Isaac, morosely. "No offense, Marvin."

"What's that, honey?" The merman reappeared from rummaging in the pantry.

"Isaac was intimating you may have an unhealthy love of glitter." Alec continued inhaling his cold dinner.

"Sequins, darlings. Not glitter. Glitter is for infants. Real men wear sequins."

"I am suitably chastised and reassured," said Isaac. Oddly, he *was* feeling reassured. Banter was comforting, so was the robe. Everything seemed exactly as it had been before the bite. They were the same pack, the same people. He may have changed, but they had not. Well, Alec was more relaxed and peckish, but otherwise…

Isaac gingerly sat down next to Tank on one of the couches, close to the Alpha at last. He was careful not to touch anything with his skin, unwilling to leave blood smudges and risk the wrath of the merman.

I'm already bowing to his will, just like the rest of the pack. He wasn't sure how he felt about that. But he also didn't want to disappoint the beautiful, sparkling young man.

Max watched him with interest. "Like that, is it?"

The Alpha cleaned his plate and set it on the coffee table. He didn't lick it but he looked like he wanted to. He leaned forward, resting his elbows on his knees. "Well, that was fun."

"Was it?" wondered Isaac.

"No, not really. Still, it came out okay? You feel more…" Alec paused. "This will sound awfully woo-ie, but you feel more *at one with yourself* now, right?"

Isaac looked inside himself, expecting his wolf to be there, skulking. To be unhappy or eager or curious or hurt. To be ready to interrupt Isaac's thoughts with his lupine opinion. To be anything. Argumentative. But he wasn't. He wasn't there at all.

He was gone.

Isaac felt a terrible wash of loss and joy. This thing he'd struggled with his whole life was gone. His only friend, his greatest enemy, his protector, and his monthly torturer – just like that the beast had vanished.

Isaac found himself curled forward in a defensive crouch on the floor, face to his knees. Tank stroked him. Isaac could sense the man's surprise.

Tank, his wolf's favorite, his lover, his submissive. Isaac worried that he was meant to be the strong one in their nascent relationship. Lately, he'd been so weak.

"The wolf – my wolf – he's gone." Isaac's voice was small in his own ears.

Alec's big hazel eyes went soft and glassy with empathy. "No, precious. He's there. He's just *you*. He was always you. You splintered for a while, that's all." Tears spilled down Alec's cheeks. An Alpha showing pain.

It surprised Isaac enough into listening to him.

"You were walking around with an open wound. You only needed mending. I just stitched you back together again." Alec gave a small, self-deprecating shrug.

Isaac blinked, feeling awed and searching. He

straightened and sat back on the couch.

Alec sniffed, rubbed his eyes like a little boy. "You aren't separate. It's okay, he won't take over except on full moon. Right now you can just choose to be whichever form. Look, here…"

Isaac felt a gentle tug, not physical, not mental, and not even emotional. More like hunger or some other instinct. "What's that?"

Tank's voice rumbled close. "That's the tether, your connection to pack."

"You feel it too?"

"Of course. He can't distinguish between us. When he tugs like that, it pulls on us all." He looked to Alec. "Right?"

Alec nodded.

Isaac was awed despite himself. "And that connects to my wolf?"

Alec shook his head. "It connects to *you*. You are your wolf."

"It will take me a while to adjust." *Particularly my vocabulary.*

"Take all the time you need." Alec gave him a shy smile. "We're here for you. I'm here for you. And if you need to be let go, released from pack, I can do that too. But there is no harm in staying for a bit, if you want to."

Tank tensed beside him. Isaac turned. The big man's eyes were full of hope. Always so much hope.

Isaac looked back at the Alpha. He thought his own eyes might be full of hope too for a change.

Alec opened his arms.

Through no apparent will of his own, Isaac launched himself at the smaller man. It was odd, Alec had this nerd geek thing going on, it shouldn't feel strong and confident. Yet Isaac was being held, and healed, and reassured all at once.

It was everything he'd never known to want. Coming

home, being nurtured, being treasured.

Marvin said, "Are we back to hugging?"

Max slurped his wine. "Touchy feely lot, you wolves."

"Just because you're a cold fish." The merman's voice was a little rough.

"Who you calling a *fish*, Splashy McSplasherton?"

Isaac took a deep breath and extracted himself from his Alpha's arms, returning to the large mountain of worry and muscles.

"Okay?" wondered Tank.

"Strangely, yes," Isaac replied. Charmed and awed to find it was true.

"How do I smell?" he wondered.

"Like us," answered Tank, his voice full of joy.

Having felt the tether tug from their Alpha, the other pack members returned. They padded in, naked and smelling of salt air and wet grass.

Tank kept a close eye on Isaac to see how he handled the pack in full force of post-run euphoria. He hadn't had that with them yet. The Omega's brown eyes were wide, but Tank thought more for appreciation of the nudity than discomfort with the recent shift. Tank didn't want to, but he couldn't help hoping that Isaac would tolerate it, even *like it* enough to stay. To choose to belong to their pack. To choose to remain with Tank.

"So I smell like a mix of the pack now?" Isaac pressed.

"Yeah, not really yourself, no individual scent of your own. You know how we each have a signature scent. You don't."

"Like you're all brandy and lemon and nutmeg and fresh-killed meat."

"I am?" Tank was thrilled.

"Yes, delicious."

"You kidder." Tank pressed his lips together, to hide a grin.

Isaac bumped his shoulder. "I'll have to teach you to take a compliment."

Tank said, "All the shifters you meet will now know you're a werewolf."

Isaac looked sad. "Will they fear me, do you think?"

"No, you're still an Omega. That has to count for something."

"Does it? I thought it counted against a man."

Tank hadn't an answer for that. He knew so little of Omegas. And who was he to offer reassurance? He'd no rank at all.

He raised his head and looked about, at Alec's peaceful expression and Marvin's fussing. At Judd and Kevin and Lovejoy horsing around, and Colin reprimanding them. At Max and Bryan leaving for their apartment, together again all night long. He watched Isaac, who thought Tank smelled good. And he wondered if maybe it really mattered. Sure, he wasn't special, but perhaps he was necessary in his own right. Alec had called him an anchor, and Isaac had said that he was beautiful and sexy and stable. So perhaps, just perhaps, that made him important, too.

Isaac awoke the next morning feeling more himself than he had since childhood. More comfortable in his skin and with his own wants, and plastered up against the very lovely muscled backside of a man he was wildly attracted to. Who let him do things. Who yearned for him to do things.

Isaac allowed himself the luxury of time spent arousing slowly, caressing Tank's skin with appreciation and care. He inhaled the intoxicating scent of slumbering man – his man – aroused even as he slept.

Isaac let the rhythm of Tank's breathing soothe him, felt their heartbeats fall into sync. New sensations. Wolf sensations.

Tank woke with a tiny snuffle noise and Isaac was utterly charmed by it.

He pressed against him, urgent now. Tank arched back in eager response. Isaac could smell the spike in his desire.

"May I?"

"Always," Tank answered, voice torn with want and sleep.

"Pass me some lube."

Tank opened his bedside table and groped blindly in it, passing a bottle back over his shoulder.

Isaac coated himself and shifted to find leverage. He pressed inside Tank without pause or preparation, knowing that Tank wanted it as much as he did, possibly more – the relentlessness. They were both enthralled by the uncompromising nature of want.

The massive body shuddered against him. Tank let out an agonized cry of desperate need. He tried to push himself faster and harder onto Isaac's cock. Isaac slowed down rather than speeding up, drawing out both of their suffering. He could smell Tank was close to coming just from the denial.

Isaac bit down hard to give Tank pain and distract him from shooting off too soon. "Not without permission." Then he licked where he'd bitten to soothe it.

Every muscle in that big gorgeous body tensed as Tank tried desperately to obey.

Isaac took his time withdrawing slow and long, and then pushing back deep and measured, giving Tank no quarter. Tank yielded without question, shuddering for him, holding back for him, all of it *for him*. That knowledge turned Isaac on so much, his own control was tested.

"Stroke yourself," he ordered.

With tremendous effort, Tank unclenched one big fist from where he was mutilating pillows, and reached down to jack himself off.

"Tighter," Isaac ordered. He couldn't see over Tank's massive shoulder but he knew the man would be trying not to climax, his grip overly gentle.

Tank gave a low whine and clenched around Isaac's thrusting, clearly fighting against release.

Isaac was merciless. He changed his angle to glide again and again over Tank's prostate.

Tank's breath hitched. Isaac could smell the salt of tears. Tank did not want to disappoint Isaac, but the big man was reaching that edge where body trumped the will of even the best submissive.

"Now." Isaac gave him grace.

Tank writhed, emitted a relieved whimper, and began to come, his massive frame jerking so hard Isaac had to wrap his arm around him to hold him tight and still. The air was spiced with bitter salt and sweat and semen.

Eventually Tank relaxed, panting. Isaac did not pause his thrusting.

Isaac reached down to feel what he had wrought, to coat his hand in Tank's scent. Then brought his fingers to his mouth for a taste. There, yes, was that a hint of brandy mixed with the spicy bite that all werewolves had? *Delicious*.

Isaac came then, too, unexpectedly, without increasing his tempo, fierce and momentarily blinded by the suddenness of it.

The peace that settled over him after was a net woven of smell and flavor and warm skin. All parts of them connected and content, wolf and man, Omega and pack. It was a revelation. The comfort both welcome and terrifying.

"Oh." Isaac's voice was small and far away in his own ringing ears. "We really are mates?" He realized that before he could not fathom being one with another, because he had not been one with himself.

Tank's rumble was quiet and cautious, afraid of breaking something newly formed and fragile. "I think we must be."

"You don't know?" Isaac was surprised. Tank was, after all, much better at being a werewolf than he. Didn't they learn these things in werewolf school? Train for them, or something?

Tank gave a little shrug, still curled and looking away, then went still. "When we did this before, I always had this sensation of reaching out to you, trying to hold fast. But there was no touch-point."

Isaac tried hard not to cry at the pain in his lover's voice. "Locking my wolf away wounded you too?"

Tank would do anything not to hurt him, Isaac knew that. So he was not surprised when the big man said quickly, "I felt it just now, though."

"A tether?" Isaac wasn't certain how he would cope with such committed intimacy.

"I belong to you."

Well, Isaac certainly liked that idea. "And that means mate?"

"I guess so." Tank was being so very careful.

"No certainty?" Isaac pushed.

Tank's voice was hurt. "This is the first time I've felt this too, you know."

Oh, I'm being an asshole. And not the good kind. "I'm sorry, baby." Isaac examined the complexity of his feelings. The newness of his own pack-riddled scent. The sounds of morning – *or possibly early afternoon?* – in the big house. The mate in his arms. *Mate. Mine.*

"I like it," he said at last. Realizing it was true. "I like you belonging to me." The responsibility of it was a burden and a threat, but also a privilege and a relief. It was so utterly right, Isaac realized, to be bound to this man, any fear that he risked his heart was petty and unworthy of either of them.

CHAPTER SEVENTEEN
The Sound and the Furry

It turned out they had slept and fucked away most of the morning. Tank reassured Isaac that this was not considered rude in a pack of werewolves. Most supernaturals kept odd hours.

Isaac gifted him with a soft smile and said, "So do most gay men in San Francisco."

They came downstairs to find the pack either still in bed or gone off about various jobs or social obligations.

Only Lovejoy was present, puttering about the kitchen, having just gotten back from his shift at the local bakery. He was bright-eyed and bushy-tailed, although not literally. He welcomed them with an affable grin and shoved coffee at them.

Isaac snickered at his mug, which was emblazoned with the slogan: *Werewolves do it more than once a month!*

Lovejoy shrugged. "Not that caffeine is particularly effective on us but we like the sentiment."

Isaac nodded. "I hope there's not too much sentiment in the coffee or I'll take over making it."

Tank tried not to be thrilled by the casual comment. It gave the impression Isaac was planning to stick around.

Lovejoy pointed at a bag of misshapen baked goods.

"Rejects from my job, first come, first pick."

Tank opened it and held it out for Isaac to peer inside.

"Oooh, is that a savory éclair?" Isaac delved in.

"Salmon mousse," Lovejoy explained. "Good choice. They're super popular."

Tank chuckled at the éclair's misshapen appearance, bulbous one end, narrow the other. "You couldn't sell *that* in Castro? You could have marked it up and called it the aphrodisiac special."

Lovejoy laughed. "That's exactly what I said. My boss has no sense of humor."

Isaac paused before eating, a frown marring his beautiful face. "Is there another one for Marvin? If not, I should leave this for him."

"Aw, you're a sweetie." Lovejoy looked like he wanted to pinch Isaac's cheek. He gestured to a covered plate. "I already put one aside for him. They're his favorite."

"It's also dick-shaped?" Tank couldn't wait to see Marvin's expression.

Lovejoy nodded, eyes twinkling. "I might have made several of them. You know, *accidentally*."

Tank shook his head. "You're gonna be fired for being a prick who makes too many pricks." He chose one of the cheesy biscuit thingies that looked rather sad by comparison to everything else Lovejoy baked, but tasted just this side of salty heaven.

"But what a way to go." Lovejoy wiggled his eyebrows.

"I thought you were one of the not gay ones." Isaac bit into his éclair, squirting pink foam all over his chin. Tank wanted to lick it off him.

Lovejoy looked slightly disappointed at being accused of heterosexuality. "I don't come off as gay?"

Isaac clearly didn't know how to respond to that.

Tank understood the problem. How to tell a straight man that his pants were the wrong kind of tight? Lovejoy liked to think he was the most fashion-forward sexy

metrosexual ever. Mana hadn't beaten it out of him. Tank
secretly suspected she liked Lovejoy's weird sleazy Guido
style.

"No, you don't." Tank came to Isaac's rescue.

Lovejoy gave a perky smile. "Well, you're right, I don't
identify as gay. But I'm not opposed to dick on principal.
And, *come on*, a cock-shaped éclair filled with salty
salmon mousse? It's hilarious."

"Marketing genius if you ask me. And delicious." Isaac
finished said éclair and licked his fingers, carefully.

Tank lost his ability to speak and had to focus on his
coffee.

"My point, exactly! My boss never thinks like that. She
takes pastry so seriously. Just the other day…" Lovejoy
launched into gossip about his job, chattering happily
about various people neither Isaac nor Tank had ever met
but who apparently led very exciting lives. Hard to keep
them all straight, however, as Lovejoy was terrible with his
pronouns. Fortunately, it segued into Lovejoy telling Isaac
all about how he took up baking, his childhood, and even
his first kiss.

Tank could only be awed. Lovejoy was generally pretty
forthcoming but this was ridiculous. *The Omega strikes
again.* Isaac didn't really seem to do anything, yet Lovejoy
was visibly nostalgic and utterly relaxed in his presence,
pouring his silly shiny heart out.

The man eventually began talking slower and slower,
until Isaac suggested perhaps Lovejoy ought to get a nap
in. Lovejoy remembered he had a date that evening and
agreed.

Once he'd gone, they settled in the den with fresh
coffee.

"Date?" Isaac wondered idly.

Tank nodded. "He's seeing this kind of amazing shifter.
Far too good for him. Fortunately, he realizes that. She's
kitsune and very old. Very important 'round here. Very,

well, *very*."

Isaac frowned. "Not Gladiola?"

Tank chuckled. "No, not Gladiola. You won't have met this one."

"I won't? So confident."

Tank thought of Mana's eyes, full of other times and ancient worlds. "She would have known what you were, I think. And she would have come to us immediately. Besides, she's not the type to go to a shifter mixer at a midtown bar."

"She's not?"

"No, she's the type to own the bar."

Isaac nodded. "I know what you mean."

They made lunch together. Isaac openly mocked Tank's utter failure in the kitchen. Tank only said, "Fine. You tell me what to do. I'm good at following instructions." He played a willing sous chef, brushing against Isaac a little more than necessary.

Isaac enjoyed bossing him around the kitchen rather too much. Tank made the space seem small. He weaved the scent of brandy and spices in with their food. He offered warmth with his eyes and gratitude with his service.

Isaac got distracted once or twice. But the stew came out fine. The pack, as some began trickling back in late afternoon, were delighted by the smell and the offering of food from their newest member.

Isaac loved watching them eat what he'd cooked. In fact, he liked taking care of the pack too much. He had to step outside onto the porch and away from wolfish pleasure. The act of feeding them was even better than Omega empathy, and gave him the same jolt of satisfaction. Care and guardianship, nurturing, it shivered his bones as intensely as shifting, but much less painful.

The sun began to set.

Isaac turned his back on it and watched the pack through the big windows. The glass gave him objectivity, and relief from the alluring fragrance and grumbling noises of home. He was fascinated by how they all moved around each other, the innate division of labor.

Not all of them were there. Marvin and Alec were still at work – Alec at his lab, Marvin with the Coast Guard. Apparently, the cheeky little merman worked major crimes and special investigations whenever the authorities needed underwater reconnaissance. Made sense to Isaac. Besides, who wouldn't want Marvin around?

He noticed the moment Tank realized Isaac wasn't inside. His big body tensed until he saw Isaac out on the porch. He lifted one massive hand in a shy wave. Isaac blew him a kiss. Tank dipped his head to hide a blush but didn't follow him out. He hadn't been invited, and he knew Isaac needed space.

Feeling calmer just because of that, Isaac reentered the fray to find the pack getting ready for their nocturnal activities.

Kevin was out on patrol. Judd was preparing to relieve him. During the day, when it was hardest to shift, the enforcers tended to jog around the property, or just lurk in spots, doing yard work and exterior construction. Enforcers were naturally inclined to be outside, protecting everything.

The rest of the time, Judd and Kev ran the pack's security firm. Kevin had an assignment that very night to keep an eye on Clara.

"Your boss has Heavy Lifting on retainer right now. It's a good contract," Tank explained.

Bryan, it turned out, had a job as well as being a Magistar's familiar. The big quiet man ate Isaac's stew in appreciative silence and didn't bother to explain what his job might be.

"I'm on swing shift." He looked over at the clock. "Gotta go."

Lovejoy came downstairs smelling of hair oil and wearing a slick silver shirt with black stripes that was unbuttoned a little too low. He had the body for it, but it was a bit much.

"Hot date?" wondered Colin, who was packing up his backpack and heading out for an evening class.

"Mana's coming by." Lovejoy turned to Isaac. "You wanna maybe meet her?"

Isaac marveled at the varied emotions in the man's voice. He'd thought Lovejoy more simple than that, but a kitsune girlfriend obviously brought out something complex in his character.

Tank looked startled. "Don't you usually go to her place during the week?"

Lovejoy shrugged.

"This Mana is very important to you. I mean, more so than being just a lover." Isaac prodded, unable to help himself.

Lovejoy flushed and let out a nervous huff.

It was Tank who explained, saving his pack mate from embarrassment. "She's important to *every* local shifter."

Lovejoy cocked his head. "She won't need you, Isaac. Not like the rest of us do."

Isaac didn't know what to make of that. Every shifter he met wanted something from him, required his counsel. To take it or steal it or talk it out.

"That's why she's coming here? To meet Isaac?" Tank was endearingly confused.

Lovejoy got defensive. "It was Bryan's idea."

Isaac frowned. "Why?"

"He thinks you should meet Mana. Or Mana should meet you."

"Beta instinct?"

Lovejoy shrugged. "It's Bryan. I was lucky enough to

get *that* many words out of him."

Isaac was nervous. The rest of the pack was abandoning him, so he'd meet this mythical kitsune alone. Kevin left with Colin. Judd stripped, shifted, and went on patrol. Easier to do it in wolf form since the sun was now down.

Fine, not totally alone. Tank and Lovejoy were puttering about the huge den area.

"Where's Max? I mean, if Bryan is at work. What does Max do?" Isaac wondered. The Magistar hadn't come with Bryan to eat Isaac's stew.

"Snarks about. Goes running. Reads old books about lost spells. Complains a lot." Lovejoy did not revere their Magistar.

Isaac tried not to smile. What an odd group these men were.

Then it got odder.

Because there was a knock on the door, and Manifest Destiny strode into the house.

Tank was mildly terrified of Mana. She was too much all at once, with no predictable pattern and no reliable reactions. She changed from day to day, shifting her attitude, conversation, and appearance. To someone like Tank who craved both dominance and consistency, she was all one without the other, a dangerous force of mercurial avarice.

Tonight she wore a black and white checked suit, but cut like a Vietnamese áo dài. The long tunic was very tight, and worn off the shoulders in a wide fold. The pants were tailored perfectly, and she wore them with high black heels, and carried a small square bag with a discreet logo. Her hair, or probably wig, was a blunt-angled black bob. Her makeup was all red lip and strong cat's eye. She looked expensive and hard.

The clothing challenged Tank's calm. Mana looked slightly too powerful, she exuded charisma of the type that had once conquered whole courts with intrigue and manipulation. She dominated everything and everyone, yet she had come into the pack's lives and chosen Lovejoy instead of him. Lovejoy who, until Mana, had shown no inclination for submissiveness. Perhaps that was what she liked about him. Perhaps Tank would have been too easy. Nevertheless, it was challenging not to feel rejected.

Except there was part of Tank that understood. Mana would have been too much for him. Too shocking. Clearly, he was made for Isaac, anyway.

Didn't stop Tank from being intimidated by her.

Didn't stop him from feeling a fearful anticipation as to how Isaac might react to her.

"Hello darlings! My, where is everyone? Working, I suppose. So very droll of you all to have jobs like it matters. So diligent."

It was easy to forget that Manifest Destiny was diminutive, although not as small as most kitsune. She must have other shifter blood in her, or was born of a more ancient line. Despite her size, she could move oceans with her will.

Nine tails, Alec said once, reverently. As Alpha, Alec could respect Mana without risk to his own power.

"Even werewolves must make money, babe." Lovejoy explained the way the world worked to his girlfriend.

Mana dismissed such concerns as mere foibles of the modern age. "You need more kimonos, is what you *need.* Money is merely a shared cultural hallucination. A good kimono will last a lifetime."

She went to Lovejoy then. He bent so she might take his face in both her hands. "Hello, sweet boy." She kissed him, soft and lingering, ending with a sharp nip when he tried to deepen the embrace before she was ready.

Lovejoy gave a little whimper in his throat and stilled,

quivering beneath her touch.

Tank was sympathetic. He shuffled closer to Isaac, whether in a show of solidarity or as comfort, he wasn't certain. Isaac angled imperceptibly toward him, aware of Tank's need and welcoming him either way.

Mana's black eyes were on them instantly.

"This is the bartender? I've heard of you. Caused quite a stir." Mana had a pleasant voice with only the barest hint of an accent.

Isaac straightened under her regard. Tank glowed with pride, his man wasn't at all intimidated.

They circled each other, metaphorically speaking, like the two predators they were. Her examination of Isaac was painfully direct. Tank winced and she wasn't even looking at him.

Isaac didn't bare his throat or show any kind of deference to her power or her age.

"Omega? I never would have guessed."

"You wouldn't?" Tank blurted.

"Oh, I would have figured it out, but not from appearances or attitude. You're an odd one, aren't you? But it explains the sudden shifter fascination with that appalling Saucepot place."

"Saucebox." Isaac's voice was cooler than Tank had ever heard it.

"Whatever." Mana flapped a hand elegantly, as if it held a silk fan.

Isaac was being tested in a camp manner. It felt rude.

Unless. Is she teasing him?

Isaac's eyes narrowed. Then he did something, relaxed and opened himself somehow. Like he was warding off Mana's probing and looking beneath it. His examination of the kitsune was no less rude, but it was, somehow, more thorough.

"Oh!" He blinked. "You're scared too."

Isaac moved then, confident, and took one of Mana's

small hands in his. He led her toward a couch, pressed her to sit.

Startled, she did so.

Isaac sat too. Close, but on a separate love seat, and bent toward her, all concern and care. "I'm not after your position here, matriarch. It's not my purpose."

Mana blinked at him. "Oh, you're—" She swallowed. "That is *remarkable*."

"But not the same as you."

"No, not even slightly. I thought..." She shook her head. "Well, you can feel what I thought." She let out a little breath. "But you're so young."

"All Omegas are."

"You're one of the first I've ever met. Certainly, the first to enter my territory. You're brand new."

Tank thought he could guess at some of the undercurrents flying between them.

Lovejoy's face was a picture of confusion. "What's going on?" he whispered to Tank. They still stood near the door.

Tank said, uncaring that everyone could hear him. "Omegas came after Saturation, and Mana is from before. She is the keeper of this place, I think. In her way. Or has made herself so over the decades. Or perhaps the place chose her? I believe she thought Isaac might try to take that role away from her. Or take the responsibility of it, of all us Bay Area shifters."

Isaac smiled. "When, in fact, I'm merely a gardener, content to tend my small patch."

Lovejoy looked at Tank, eyes desperate. "Did he just call our pack a vegetable patch?"

Isaac grinned. "Rough metaphor. My bad."

Tank moved cautiously toward Mana and tried to explain the situation to her. Lovejoy had obviously done a bad job of it. "Isaac, if he stays, will stay for *us*. He is not a guardian, not really."

"What is he then?" Mana was looking at Tank with wonder on her face. He preened under it.

"He is solace."

Isaac rolled his eyes.

Mana gave Tank a small smile. "I made a mistake, didn't I, when I discounted you."

Tank felt only a little sad, he was accustomed to it. "It's normal for people to do that."

"So long as you don't discount yourself."

"I'm trying not to." *The anchor*, thought Tank, attempting to convince himself, *is important.*

Isaac gave him a funny look. And it occurred to Tank to wonder, for the first time, if their relationship made it hard for Isaac to read him.

Mana shook her head slightly and put a hand out for Lovejoy, who went to her instantly, crouching next to her rather than joining her on the couch.

Tank sat next to Isaac.

There was a slightly tense and awkward silence.

Finally the kitsune said, "So, I'm Mana, you may call me Mana. Although my stage name is Manifest Destiny."

"Isaac. Isaac Mercer."

"Mercer. Why is that familiar?" Long fake eyelashes fluttered a moment. "Ah, that dreadful cult thing?"

"Yes, my father."

Mana tapped her lip with one perfectly manicured fingertip. "Pity." Her eyes suddenly sharpened. "He used you, didn't he? To hold it together. I always wondered how it lasted so long under an enforcer."

Isaac shuddered slightly and inclined his head. "Now you know."

"You could start your own."

"Cult? Not really my thing."

Tank thought Isaac was handling Mana rather well.

Isaac assessed the stunningly beautiful drag queen, a fox sitting so calmly surrounded by werewolves. "So could you."

"Who's to say I haven't? Turns out, it's an awful lot of work to maintain cults. Not worth the bother, really."

"Tell me about it."

Mana laughed. "I've decided to like you. I think… yes. It would be good if you stayed. Are you staying?"

Isaac's eyes opened wide and he looked desperately at Tank.

Tank couldn't help him there, he wanted the same thing.

Then something shivered through the air, over them, around them. Something from outside. A sound.

Howling.

There were werewolves nearby, and they weren't San Andreas pack. Tank didn't know any of those voices.

He instantly went on alert and looked at Lovejoy. "Judd's on patrol. Everyone else is out."

Lovejoy nodded. "Leaves us."

Tank tilted his head. Perhaps the time had come to prove his worth to his pack, sooner than he'd thought. Perhaps he had to choose to be special. "You're more intimidating in wolf form."

Lovejoy sighed. "It took ages to get my hair to look like this."

Mana was watching them intently. "What are you boys…?"

Lovejoy gave her a little kiss on the temple. "Be right back, my heart. Just giving you a little visual taste of what's to come later tonight." He began stripping.

"If you're lucky," Mana snapped back, on instinct.

Lovejoy was fast out of his clothing and into his fur.

Isaac was looking at them with mixed fear and confusion.

Tank stayed in human form. He was intimidating enough in either guise, and someone needed to talk.

"Stay here, please," he said to the Omega and the kitsune. There was no real power to his request. He had no rank to back it up and they were both greater than he could ever be. But maybe they would let him try.

"Like hell," said the Omega, standing.

"Isaac," he growled, attempting reason, "you haven't fought alongside us before. You should stay safe. You're important. Please." *You haven't tried to fight at all. You're so new to being a true werewolf. To being comfortable in fur. You're Omega.*

Isaac's jaw went firm. "I'm the reason they're here."

"Yeah. Well, who are they, then?"

"My former pack."

Isaac knew it was an unfair bombshell to drop.

Tank looked hurt. Lovejoy whined in near physical pain. They didn't like the idea that he'd once belonged to some other pack, or worse, that some other pack once belonged to him. Yet it was the truth, in its awful way.

Isaac was ashamed to have brought this down on them. Humiliated by being caught, not once but several times. Ashamed that once a pack that trapped him had managed to keep him long enough to file paperwork, and now had managed to track him here.

He rushed to explain. "I didn't join them willingly, and I managed to avoid the Alpha biting me. You know that old adage? An unwilling bite won't stick. But they weren't the first to lock me up after I left the cult. Force my agreement. And they kept me the longest."

Tank winced, understanding at last. "They caged you, didn't they?"

Isaac inclined his head. "No other way I would have stayed."

"Fuck. I'm so sorry."

"Not your fault."

"No, but I won't let it happen now. Please stay in the

house."

"No, I'm coming."

Tank sighed. Then led the way out the door and through the yard toward the driveway. Isaac silently agreed that they were most likely to come from that direction. It was too close to sunset for them to have traveled very far as wolves, so they would be using human transport. Human roads.

The bile was hot and acrid at the back of Isaac's throat. He couldn't be taken again. He didn't think he'd survive captivity now that he was a whole werewolf. Before, he'd managed to suppress his frantic wolf and just be miserable and human. He no longer had that option.

"How many in this pack?" Tank asked.

"Eight." Isaac remembered each and every one of them. The way they smelled. The way they looked and acted – ashamed of their need for him, vicious in the execution of it. Pitiable if he had met them in another form, brutal because of what he was. "They will have ridden, I think. Motorcycles. Probably stopped at the bottom of the hill and shifted."

Tank nodded.

Suddenly there they were, all eight of the Rocky Mountain Pack. They were mean and harsh-looking, slovenly and ill-kempt, with shifty eyes and patchy pelts.

Their Alpha was typical of the breed, or what Isaac had always thought was typical until he met Alec – big and brash and angry. There was no peaceable leadership from Skulls. He ordered, and if his order wasn't instantly followed, then his fist did.

He'd only one enforcer now. Isaac had accidentally-on-purpose killed the other one. Or he assumed that's what had happened. He'd left the shack in flames and his once-guard locked into the cage that had been Isaac's home for nearly a year. The man's screams woke him up sometimes at night. Freedom always cost more than Isaac wanted to pay.

Isaac made introductions, because someone had to say something. "That big rangy one in the middle is Skulls, Alpha of the Rocky Mountain Pack. I can't really ID the others I only saw them in the dark inside and in human form. They never fully introduced themselves."

"Skulls, no last name?" wondered Tank.

Isaac shrugged and suggested, "Skulls Douchypants-Asshat the First?"

Judd appeared then, out of the shadows.

Isaac had never before been so glad to see an enforcer. As a wolf, Judd was almost solid black with bright orange eyes. Very Halloween. Size for size he matched Skulls, which was reassuring. Not that size mattered much when rank came into play.

Lovejoy moved to stand closer to Isaac. Lovejoy was a handsome wolf, not particularly big, with symmetrical gray markings of varying shades. His eyes were as blue in his wolf form as they were in his human.

Mana seemed to have sensibly vanished off somewhere. This wasn't her fight.

So the San Andreas Pack had three fighters. Isaac didn't count himself. It was a pitiful number against a full pack of eight.

Some of my pack might die today, because of me. These nice, warm, queer, weird werewolves with more love than sense, they're at risk, because of me.

I should have run. Why didn't I run? I could have drawn them away from my pack.

The enemy pack was all in fur, and none of them seemed inclined to transform to parlay.

"You're in our territory." Tank stated the obvious. "Protocol dictates you designate a voice, as you clearly have not brought an arbitrator. Have you a claim to this territory?"

It was the Alpha who shifted.

Skulls was a large man with an impressive beard and bulging muscles. He'd thought it weak to need an Omega, to want to bite him and keep him. Yet he couldn't resist the urge. And since Skulls hadn't the brains to handle an identity crisis over his own power, he'd taken it out on Isaac. Kept him naked and chained and touch-starved and alone, because if Isaac wouldn't yield to his bite, then obviously Isaac was the problem.

Isaac hated the man.

Skulls glared at Tank. "We ain't interested in your pansy-ass territory, grunt. We just want our Omega. We have us a prior claim."

"Oh, yeah?" Tank didn't flinch under the Alpha's regard. "I'm thinking it's our Alpha who bit him, so he stays with us. He chose us. You don't get to keep a pack mate just because you want to. Lupine protocol doesn't work that way."

Isaac didn't know the law. It was one of the reasons he always ran. His own ignorance of pack ways worked against him.

"Prior claim is prior claim. But if one of you wants to fight me for him…"

Judd stepped forward.

Tank said, "No. It's my fight."

Judd whined in distress.

"I need to do it, Judd, he's my mate."

Isaac couldn't bear it. That Tank would find his courage now, find his purpose and stand up for himself. Because of Isaac. In a battle he couldn't possibly win. Yet if Isaac begged Tank not to fight, his mate would feel diminished and rejected by Isaac's lack of confidence.

Skulls looked disgusted. "Males can't mate each other, and even if they could, Omegas should fuck Alphas or enforcers, not lowly grunts with no rank or function. You aren't good enough for him."

Tank shrugged. "He chose me. I'm his, so I must be

enough."

Isaac felt himself flush with pleasure. *He is mine, and if that helps him understand his worth, I'm doing something good by being with him.* The rightness of it made everything else around him all the more terrifying.

What kind of dominant lets himself be captured not once but several times? He wasn't strong enough to keep *himself* safe, let alone protect a mate. He didn't deserve Tank or Tank's submission, but apparently, he did need Tank to stand up for him and to fight. It was messed up.

"You think you're in control?" Skulls clearly didn't understand anything, this wasn't about control. The Alpha turned his steel gaze onto Isaac. "COME HERE, BOY."

Isaac swayed forward involuntarily, then flinched and dug in his heels.

It was harder to resist VOICE now that his wolf was unified with his human. Skulls' savage power was formed specifically to pull on pack obligations and werewolf tether. But it also worked against Skulls, because Isaac was tethered to a different Alpha. The threads that bound him to Alec were new, weak, and tangled, but they were there. Even though Alec was absent, Isaac trusted him in a way he never could trust Skulls, and that strengthened the bond.

At VOICE, all the wolves around moved toward Skulls, even Tank and Lovejoy and Judd.

Judd growled, fierce, trying to resist.

Tank said, "You can't use VOICE on wolves not of your pack. Are you mad?"

"He *is* my pack!"

"That can only be settled by arbitration."

"Or combat," insisted Skulls.

Tank looked resigned but ready.

Skulls pressed. "You will fight for him? Good, an easy win for me."

Isaac broke and turned to plead with Tank. "I'll just go with them."

Tank looked down at him, chocolate eyes soft.

Isaac leaned in close to whisper. "You can't win." Tank was massive and no doubt a strong fighter, but he hadn't a drop of Alpha in him.

Tank was calm and resigned, and he smelled of brandy and lost celebrations. "I don't have to win. I just have to hold out until Alec gets home."

Isaac felt his face tighten and tingle. "Better if Max came home." Max would have no care for pack protocols and would simply end whomever got in his way without remorse. Max was a *damn the consequences* kind of dude.

Tank twitched a smile. "He can't do anything until Bryan gets home too. Familiar, remember?"

"Somehow, I feel Max is effective even without his power."

Tank chuckled and began stripping. "You're probably right. He can flay you with his words alone." His movements were jerky. His laugh had no humor to it.

"Tank, are you angry?" Isaac hated how timid he sounded. He had questioned Tank's ability to fight, and therefore his newfound self-confidence.

"He caged you." Isaac hadn't thought his lover capable of sounding so cold. "I'm going to enjoy this."

"I didn't think you could get angry."

"I try not to. Isn't good in a man my size. Scares people."

"You're adorable. Please don't die."

"Also, not something you get when you're a man my size."

"What, death?"

"No, adorability."

Isaac's eyes burned. "I don't want you to fight but I understand why you must."

Chocolate eyes were on him, full of hope. "Yeah?"

"You are worthy of love, of your place in pack, but you don't know it. If this is a way to prove it to yourself, then I support you." What Isaac couldn't say, what he couldn't even imagine, was that if Alec didn't get home soon, then Tank would end up dying as a delaying tactic. Even werewolves could die from blood loss. Isaac could only hope that Mana was off making urgent phone calls to the rest of their pack.

"I thought you couldn't read me like you could the others." Tank was gloriously naked.

"Sometimes I don't need to be an Omega to know what's in someone's head."

"I'll be fine, Isaac. Just promise me, you'll stick around to make certain?"

He still thinks I'm gonna run away from this pack. "I'm staying, baby. Don't worry. It's just I'd rather you were whole and undamaged to properly appreciate me."

"I'll do my best." Tank transformed so that the end of his sentence turned into a growl.

Skulls also shifted back into fur.

The wolves formed a loose ring. Isaac, hesitating only a moment, also shifted. It was easier than it had been the night before and it hurt less. He still didn't love it, but he thought he might learn not to resent it – given time and practice.

Lovejoy pressed against his left side and Judd took his right. It was small comfort, three of them against the seven enemy wolves ranged on the opposite side of the ring.

Tank and Skulls took the middle, circling each other with slow deliberation.

CHAPTER EIGHTEEN
Sum of All Bears

It's a weird thing, thought Tank, *the knowledge that you're probably gonna die*. He was oddly at peace with it. He couldn't think of a better cause than Isaac's safety and well-being. It was the best kind of reason. And he would do it proving himself, proving he had value to his pack. Fighting for something meaningful.

Tank circled and postured as a delaying tactic until Skulls couldn't stand it any longer and charged.

Tank actually managed to dodge him a few times. But there was a lot of Tank and he wasn't fast, just big. Soon enough Skulls got teeth into him and then the fight was on.

Tank had fought challenges in the past. There was something about a big dude that made little angry ones want to prove themselves. He'd seen that kind of thing with a Great Dane and a dachshund. He wasn't human enough to just walk away from idiocy, so he ended up fighting the occasional dachshund.

Tank wasn't instantly defeated, he always sparred with enforcers when he had the chance. They always won, of course, because they were innately more vicious, but he had some practice above his rank. He'd never gone up against an Alpha, though, and it was a whole different game.

Tank was there, inside the wolf's head, but when it came to battle, he went on instinct. Enforcers were enforcers because they had the best instincts, but Alphas fought *smart*. It's like Alphas managed to keep all parts of themselves – wolf and man – in balance at all times. Their brains were some weird melding that made outward shape irrelevant. That was what made them Alpha and it was what made them dangerous in a fight.

Tank could only be *wolf* in a fight. He reared up when confronted, he lashed out when in pain, he looked for weakness and attacked, but he had no crafty tricks to call upon. He could not strategize or plan ahead.

Skulls was different. He was fast and strong and vicious, but very thoughtful about it. He got his teeth into Tank and though Tank shook him off, again and again and again, every time Tank lost a little more blood.

Tank managed one or two of his own bites, and with a bit of leverage he even heaved the Alpha over to the edge of the circle, where all the wolves snapped at Skulls to force him back to the center.

But that was the best Tank could do. The rest of the fight was him learning to take it, protecting his most vulnerable parts as much as he could. He had to lower his massive head to keep his neck protected, which limited his vision. Not that he could follow how fast Skulls moved. He had to flatten his tail down to keep his balls safe. All that while also keeping an eye to the white wolf who watched, trying to keep Isaac safe too.

Then Skulls did something crafty and unexpected and utterly human. He slid down under Tank and twisted, wedging himself onto his back. Instead of going for Tank's throat, the Alpha raked Tank's underbelly with his claws, deep and harsh.

Tank felt the blood gush, hot and wet, and wondered if he might be losing his insides. He didn't feel himself fall,

although he knew he must have. He hoped he had won
them enough time. The challenge had gone so quickly he
was horribly afraid he'd failed everyone. He was dizzy. His
sight telescoped inward and his ears were filled with his
own pulse, sea-song and rushing. He lost himself into
washed blackness, imagining he heard Isaac's voice,
calling to him.

Isaac suspected he was howling, frozen with eyes riveted
on Tank's collapsed form. He'd never seen so much blood
before. Did people really have that much inside them?
Tank's dark fur was matted with it. It stained the driveway.
It stained the air with a scent like shaved copper and salt
gravy.

Isaac jerked forward, desperate to get to his lover.

Judd got his teeth around the ruff of Isaac's neck and
yanked him back. Lovejoy body-checked Isaac, forcing
him to stay outside the circle, even as he whimpered and
keened for his injured friend.

A female voice said, "You cannot break the challenge
circle, white wolf, or your pack mate's life is forfeit."

Isaac thought, *What difference does it make, if he's
already dead? At least let me die fighting too.*

Skulls looked up, displayed fangs dripping with Tank's
blood, and growled at the intruder. Then he bent and
lunged, placing his teeth around Tank's throat, going in for
the kill.

"STOP." The woman was Alpha and strong with it.
VOICE command would not work on another Alpha, but it
was startling enough for Skulls to be confused and back off
Tank's neck.

"You haven't a kill-right, intruder," said a different
voice, a man's. With this voice came the smell of mulch in
the deep forest, of a cold country and sweet warm honey,

something bigger than wolf – bear.

The wolves in the circle all reacted to a predator in their midst, something larger and meaner than them.

The currents shifted.

Skulls shifted into human form, looking triumphant and covered in gore. "I win."

Tank wasn't moving.

Isaac couldn't stop straining to get to him.

The female voice said, "You're the Alpha of the Rocky Mountain Pack?"

Skulls inclined his head.

Isaac barely registered when the female Alpha came into view. She was power and patience and could've been comfort except that she did not smell of home. She had a shiny badge in her hand. Her hair was black and iron-straight. She seemed annoyed.

Isaac could only think of her as a distraction. He sank to his belly, wrenched hard away from his pack mates, and tried again to get to Tank.

Judd's hold on the scruff of his neck tightened.

Isaac whimpered in misery and frustration.

Just let me go to him.

The new Alpha looked at Skulls as if he was something under her boot. "Agreed, I pronounce you winner. The circle is no longer sacred."

Judd let go of Isaac.

Isaac lunged for Tank.

"NO. STAY BACK." That was Skulls' command VOICE.

Isaac was in wolf form and weak with fear. The power of VOICE froze him in his tracks. He couldn't even move his vocal cords to whine. All the other wolves froze as well. VOICE could be indiscriminate in its application. Skulls was particularly strong with it now, having just won a bloody fight. Victory resonated, making him that much more Alpha.

"You're mine now and should tend to me above all others, Omega." Skulls looked as if he might transform to third form and bite Isaac just to prove his point. Lay his mark over Alec's – carve away Isaac's neatly healing scar with his teeth, inject him with his own saliva and pack smell.

Isaac was ready to risk it. Risk his new home. Risk everything. Tank lay so still.

"What the hell is going on?" A new voice now, familiar, with the familiar scent of belonging. But also failure, because he hadn't done as he promised. He hadn't provided safety, not for Tank.

Alpha. My Alpha. Alec.

Alec Frederiksen was still in his lab coat. He looked worn and grim and tetchy. He smelled of chemicals and concern.

He pushed through the circle of frozen lesser wolves without care. He ran his hand over Isaac's back even as he moved to bend over Tank.

"Oh no." His voice was thick and sad. His hands shook as if he did not know where to touch or even if he should.

His hazel gaze moved to Skulls. "Couldn't pick on someone your own size?"

Skulls sneered at him.

Alec, Isaac suspected, would always fight with his mouth first.

"Aren't you a big bad Alpha? Such a great victory to win against an unranked wolf." Alec straightened, tone cool. "So, Alpha in *my territory*, have you always been a bully?"

The female Alpha was there then too, puffed up, pressing in between the two males. "Gentlemen!"

"You couldn't stop this?" Alec turned on her.

Isaac had never seen eyes so cold.

"I didn't get here in time."

"Fuck you, Trapper." Alec bent back over Tank,

insulting in that he presented the back of his neck to both the other Alphas. *I'm stronger than you,* he was saying. *I can protect myself. Vulnerability is irrelevant. You two are not even worth my attention.*

He pressed his face into Tank's bloody fur. "Shift, sweetie, please. Shift now, it'll help."

He's not dead, realized Isaac. So relieved he began shaking. Still unable to move, but trembling was involuntary, Skulls couldn't command that.

Tank wasn't out of danger. If he didn't shift, he wouldn't begin to heal. Even then, would it work with such a gaping wound in his belly?

"SHIFT, TANK," ordered Alec.

Tank's wolf form shimmered and contorted. He didn't even writhe or wince or react to the agony. Isaac supposed he must already be in too much pain to notice any more.

But then there he lay, Isaac's gentle man mountain, torn open and very still. Naked, blood-covered, and lying in the driveway.

Isaac *needed* to go to him. He threw everything he had against Skulls' VOICE. A command rarely lasted so long, but Skulls had been backed up by blood and adrenaline. All Isaac managed to squeeze out was a keening whine.

Alec finally noticed that all the rest of the wolves were frozen in place. "You're an asshole," he said to Skulls. "Let him go."

"No." The Rocky Mountain Alpha was proud of his ability. "He's mine now."

"Isaac Mercer is a member of *my pack.* I bit him to second shift. He is my Omega."

Great, thought Isaac, *here we go again. Everyone bickering over me and no one asking me what I want.*

"*You* bit him?" that was the female Alpha.

Alec glared at her. "Yes, I bit him, Agent Lenis! What did you expect me to do? He was all wrong, scentless and fractured. Someone had to do something to fix him."

"Did you have his permission?"

"Of course I did!"

The female Alpha pointed at Isaac. "That's him, the white wolf?"

Alec nodded then returned to Skulls. "Let Isaac go, you asshole. His mate is hurt."

My mate is dying!

"You aren't keeping him against his will?" The female Alpha could not seem to let that go.

Alec threw his hands up into the air. "I didn't do anything to Isaac but bite him when he asked, so he could stop being all were-schizophrenic." He glared at the two other Alphas. "You know it is possible to *control* your baser fucking Alpha instincts, you shitheads."

The berserker barked a laugh at that. Isaac had almost forgotten about the bear shifter.

"You're not helping, Faste," snapped the female Alpha at her partner.

Skulls said, "He's *my* pack. I fought and won the claim."

"Who cares? He was already bitten and a member of mine. By his own choice. Fuck off." Alec paused and looked at the female Alpha, "Legally?"

The woman wrinkled her rather prominent nose. "It's complicated."

Alec glared. "Isaac is a person! He has rights beyond being just a fucking Omega. Why don't we ask him what he wants?"

Thank you! thought Isaac.

The trapper shook her head. "He might be under your influence. How can he possibly be thinking clearly, if you bit him?"

Alec threw his hands into the air. "Great, so instead you do what? Take away all his agency and treat him like a child? No wonder he's running! You let him stand there under this asshole's VOICE as though Isaac's will is irrelevant. His mate is *dying*. Fuck this shit." Alec turned on Skulls. He looked almost slight, facing up to the massive hairy naked Rocky Mountain Alpha. "LET. HIM GO, YOU… PUTZ!"

He didn't really stick the landing. Isaac heard the berserker snort to suppress a laugh. And, of course, Alec's VOICE wasn't any good on another Alpha. Still Isaac appreciated the effort.

The female Alpha tried to be reasonable. "Technically, Rocky Mountain did have a prior claim, but they never provided proof of maker bite. They might have been waiting for him to decide and you stole him away, as they claim, or they kept the Omega against his will. Which isn't allowed. For now, their claim stands. They petitioned DURPS. San Andreas hasn't filed any paperwork on Mr Mercer."

"Because it just happened! And Isaac ran away from them! He hates them." Alec was getting frustrated.

"So you say," said the female Alpha.

"If this douche nozzle—" Alec gestured at Skulls "—lets Isaac free of VOICE, then he can tell you himself." Alec whirled on the other Alpha. "Drop the control, you fucker.

And all this time Tank lay right there, bleeding, and Isaac was almost close to him. He whined, or tried to.

Clearly frustrated beyond reason, Alec ripped off his lab coat and lunged at Skulls, transforming midair in a rather spectacular demonstration of Alpha ability. Skulls transformed too, although he was still bloodied and wounded. Tank hadn't gone quietly.

The two Alphas became a snapping mess of teeth and fur and claws, so much faster and more furious than anything Isaac had ever seen. Clearly, Skulls had merely toyed with Tank. It really had been no kind of challenge.

The female Alpha began yelling at them to stop in an exasperated voice.

Still it was enough of a distraction for Skulls' control to be broken. His VOICE command dropped, all the wolves were released, which was probably Alec's intent.

Isaac was free. He bounded to Tank.

But so did the Rocky wolves. They were coming to herd Isaac away, or intent on finishing off Tank, hard to tell which.

Lovejoy and Judd were quick to flank Isaac.

Everything became crazy and pain-filled and chaotic.

Teeth snapped. Claws flashed. Muzzles wet with blood, eyes turned dark and fierce.

Isaac had no idea what he was doing. His only goals were to protect his mate and to keep himself from being dragged away. He was trying to do what was necessary, but he was an Omega, he wasn't naturally very good at fighting.

A huge grunting snorting roar rent the air and a massive bear waded into their midst. He indiscriminately bashed and grabbed wolves. He hurled them hard onto the paved driveway. He tossed them into the street or against the garage door, denting it.

Wolves let out pain-filled yips.

Alec and Skulls didn't seem to notice, too intent on each other and too fast for a bear to catch. The Alphas tumbled together in a vicious embrace.

Isaac thought it was going to end with everyone dead or at least mortally wounded. And it was all his fault.

Lovejoy, next to him, whined and collapsed, partly on top of Tank's body.

Off to the side, someone screamed – a woman, high-pitched and broken-sounding.

Judd closed ranks with Isaac. It was just the two of them left, nose to tail fighting both sides, standing over the fallen forms of their pack mates.

Another creature joined them, worming her way through the battle – small and white and puffy-tailed, sharp-toothed and impossibly vicious. Coming in and down and under, she fought very smart, going for eyes and noses, almost catlike in her intensity. Ridiculous that a fox would even be in a wolf fight.

Isaac thought there was no way they could win. There were just too many of them. Even with the berserker playing wolf toss, the odds were not in their favor.

Isaac flagged.

The whole world flashed and he thought at first it was him, that he'd hit his head, but it was real. The evening was suffused with brightness, yellow and sharp and pure. The flash became a rainfall of light. Above them, heat exploded, and a voice that was all knives and arrogance said, "Now, now, now, fluffies. What's all this?"

Quintessence shifted and collected in the air. The awful cloying sweet chemical smell of mage-work surrounded them. So much of it. More than Isaac had thought to feel in his lifetime. Magistar's power – rare and immense and utterly terrifying.

Isaac smelled urine as some of the enemy pack pissed themselves in fear.

They all shrank away from it, trying to sink into the ground because quintessence was everywhere. Wolf tails curled hard against bodies, ears flattened.

"Which is which?" said Max, apparently to Bryan. Although Bryan would be in wolf form, so Max was carrying on a one-sided conversation with his familiar.

The Magistar continued, "They all just look like a bunch of blood-covered fur to me. How am I supposed to tell bad wolf from good wolf? I suppose that one is Alec. I'll just take care of his little issue first, shall I?"

There came a high-pitched yip, the smell of curling flame-singed fur. Skulls flew through the air, head over tail, into the street and down the hill.

"Alec, really, what possessed you? You hate fighting." Max sounded peevish. As if this were all a minor annoyance.

Isaac shivered under the flow of quintessence, afraid to move, the heat pressing on him. They were trapped in some poisonous bubble of Max's making, where any move would burn.

Max's voice continued. It was getting closer. "The white one is Isaac, isn't it? Hello Isaac. And is that Mana? Darling, I didn't know you fought. Isn't it totally beneath you? You'll break a nail. Lovely tail."

Then the wolves Isaac had been facing off against were lifted and pushed away by super-heated yellow dust. More singed fur scented the air. The wolves whined.

"And our two trapper friends. Big bear dude. Lady badass."

"Holy shit." The female Alpha was the only one to remain in human form. "That is so cool. I've never seen a Magistar really go to town before."

"Well, you wouldn't need to if you'd kept control of the situation, Agent." Max really could be an asshole.

Isaac wanted to scream at him. Because Tank and Lovejoy were hurt.

Enough of Max swanning about and bragging with his power. *Fix the pack first! Everything else is irrelevant when the pack is not well.*

Isaac threw his head back and howled.

He wasn't even sure it would work. How well sound would carry through quintessence. If Max even cared that much.

"Quite right," said Max to Isaac.

Tank awoke to the smell of quintessence clawing at his nostrils, acrid sweetness all around him. He sneezed.

That hurt. A lot.

"Hey, baby." *Isaac.* His head was in Isaac's lap and his

mate was petting him. He wanted those long fingers threading through his hair.

"Can't do that. Too much blood in it."

"I said that out loud?"

The voice of his Beta came then, deep and comforting. "He's fix-drunk, Isaac. I used quite a bit on him."

Tank coughed.

Isaac said, "You okay, Bryan?"

Bryan sounded amused and a little charmed. "Why wouldn't I be?"

"You went from familiar duties to a savage healing? It's not too much for you?"

Bryan's voice was gruff. "It's not too much. I'm fine. Thank you for your care, Omega."

Tank drifted. The voices were speaking to each other and not him. Bryan was Beta calm. Isaac was still petting him. Things must be fine.

"You'll do Lovejoy now?" *Is that Mana?* She sounded serious and worried and not flippant at all. *Weird.*

"He'll be okay. I think he just likes you fussing over him."

Bryan's tone suggested Lovejoy wasn't all that okay. *He's trying to make Mana feel better. I must be worse off, though, because otherwise Bryan would have fixed Lovejoy first.*

Tank rasped out, "I was hurt?"

"Yes, baby, you were bad." Isaac's voice was shredded.

"What happened?"

Isaac snorted in apparent disgust. "What didn't happen? Short version? You lost that dumb challenge."

Tank was crushed. He'd known he couldn't win but he'd hoped. *I did my very best and still failed. The first thing I try to do to prove myself, to help Isaac, and I lost. Couldn't even manage a noble death.*

Isaac was still explaining. "A couple of trappers showed up, one of them is a bear. Then Alec arrived, unhappy about everything. So he attacked Skulls. Then everyone attacked everyone else. Then Max came in with his *hand of God* bullshit. *I'm your all powerful Magistar, bow before me!* Blah blah blah."

Max's amused voice, "I wasn't that bad."

Judd's low grumble, "You kinda were."

"Well, it worked didn't it?" Max getting defensive.

Isaac continued, "And now Bryan is healing everyone."

Tank wheezed out, "Don't let him do too much."

Isaac shifted under him, picking up on the worry. "I take it he's prone to over-extending himself, in order to help people?"

Tank gave a small dip of his head. That hurt. Everything hurt. But he didn't feel the black numbness of total blood loss anymore, so Bryan had pulled him back from the worst of it.

"Caregiver syndrome." Without moving, Isaac took on the role of keeping Bryan from self-sacrifice. As any Omega should. "Bryan, don't bother with the other pack."

"But they're wounded too."

"Leave the fuckers, hon," said Max. "You'll undo all my hard work." *Not helping.*

Isaac pushed, "They're not in any real danger."

"But *we* did this." Bryan couldn't hide from guilt the way Max did.

"They deserved it," insisted Max. "Interlopers."

Isaac sighed in exasperation. "They'll be fine and better off suffering if it keeps them quiet and out of the way while we sort this all out."

"Okay." Bryan reappeared, looming over Tank.

Tank breathed in relief. Isaac knew how best to convince their Beta. Reasoning by virtue of the safety of the pack. The possibility of peace. These were Bryan's motivators. Isaac had realized this, without even moving from his position as Tank's pillow.

Isaac added, "Why don't you keep an eye on Alec, stop

it from happening again."

"Good idea." Bryan went off to be Beta to his Alpha.

Tank gave Isaac a hesitant smile. "I worry about him a bit."

Max was looming over them then, bright blue eyes visible, even in the dusky evening. "You worry, Tank? Christ. How on earth would this lot get along without you? Did it never occur to you that you too are a necessary part of this pack? How could you risk yourself like that?"

Tank closed his eyes.

"Oh, for fuck's sake," said Max.

Isaac growled. "Stop, Max. Let him recover. You'll never be able to understand Tank. You have too much ego, and he doesn't have enough. Besides, it's my fault. I brought them down on us."

Tank was sad for the guilt in Isaac's voice but happy for the use of the word *us*.

"Well, if you put it like that. Sorry, Tank. I guess you now see what my solution is to any problem?"

Judd said, sounding a little shaky. "You only have one setting, Max."

"Maximum?" joked Isaac.

Tank loved him.

"Oh, now who's a funny boy?" Max snarked back.

Tank opened his eyes in time to see Alec walking over to them, furious. Tank felt so guilty. How could he possibly have thought himself capable of fighting an Alpha challenge?

"Fuck, you guys!" said Alec, succinctly. "What the hell? And I thought the micro-organisms were difficult today, I gotta come home to this?"

"Sorry, Alpha," said Bryan and Judd in tandem.

"Sorry, Alpha," whispered Tank, his voice still giving him issues.

"Uh. Sorry, Alpha?" said Isaac, hopefully.

"My bad," said Max, grinning.

CHAPTER NINETEEN
Unclaimed Proper Tea

"You must come with us," insisted the female Alpha. *Agent Lenis*, Isaac remembered Alec calling her.

Now that his senses were less clouded by fright and fight, Isaac examined her closely. She had that Alpha air about her, but he wasn't intimidated, as he might have been a week ago. Isaac knew that he smelled like pack now, and when her nostrils flared he knew she realized it. *Not available for keeping*, his scent would say to her.

"Leave off the big guy for the moment," she insisted.

She turned to Skulls, who was lurk-creeping back up the hill toward them. "Back the fuck off, this is official business now." She flashed her badge. "SBI, motherfucker."

The berserker reappeared, obviously having gone off to change from bear back to man.

He was a behemoth Viking type, all blond Norse goodness. Isaac already liked his men big and this one was a particularly fine specimen. Except his eyes were blue, not chocolate, and he had that solitary warrior thing going that bear shifters seemed to cultivate. He'd a hard core without an ounce of bend to him. Not Isaac's type in the slightest, as it turned out. Not special like Tank was special.

The woman was intriguing, Alpha to the bones, striking rather than beautiful, with a hooked nose and fierce brows. She moved like the world was irrelevant. He liked her, but wasn't certain if that was the Omega in him or actual appeal.

It sucks to be a werewolf sometimes.

"You led us a merry dance." She steered Isaac into the overgrown yard, eventually finding a bench with a view of the driveway. "Sit."

Isaac sat and cocked his head. "How long you been tracking me?"

The bear grumbled. "SBI has been after you since that shit with your father's cult. We knew Dominance Mercer had an unregistered Omega with him. Of course, we thought you were female, most Omegas are. And we had no idea you were his own fucking kid. Made it hard to find you without those piddling details.

"My partner and I got the case a few years ago when old skull and cross-buckets there tipped us off registering a male Omega as part of his pack. No record of who you were, and SBI keeps close tabs on Omegas. We know every single one in the country. You weren't on record. His DURPS report put you at the right age to be part of the Mercer Massacre." Agent Lenis looked irritated. "But then he fucked it up and you were in the wind again."

Isaac nodded. "What do you need me for?"

She tugged on her ear, uncomfortable. "Well, that wasn't why we tracked you. We knew you never had an Alpha, so government figured you needed us or, more precisely, me."

Isaac understood. "You were sent to bite me?" He blinked. "You knew I needed it?"

"You were spliced out and scentless." She shrugged as if it were painfully obvious. "Of course you needed it. We are all a bit awed that you lasted as long as you did. Normally Omegas are bitten at puberty, Alphas can't resist.

If not, all the shifters around start acting emotion-drunk and desperate."

Isaac grinned. "Well, I was a bartender for shifters, hard to tell the difference."

"But they came and found you, didn't they? Everywhere you went."

Isaac nodded. "That going to stop now?"

She wrinkled her nose. "It'll tone down, but it's likely everyone will still want to overshare. We've no record of an Omega lasting as long as you did without a maker bite, so it's likely you developed a reliance on your Omega empathy. Overdeveloped the skill as a survival mechanism. Normally the effect rebounds just to pack after maker bite, but with you, who can say?"

"I might still be the best shifter-shrink-bartender in town?" Isaac knew he needed some kind of guidance. "So, what's expected of me now? Legally, I mean."

"You have options. You're properly bitten, so no longer in serious danger. You smell like a pack, no scent of your own, of course, but good to the nose. Werewolf Alphas won't go nuts around you anymore. I'm afraid, from what we know, you really can't be a loner. Pack scent would eventually evaporate and the cycle of Alpha aggression would resume. Frankly, no werewolf does very well alone, but Omegas just suck at it. I want it clearly known, however, that if neither of these packs works for you, we'll help get you settled wherever you like. So long as it is with some kind of pack. Mine, the government, would be delighted to have you."

Isaac breathed out long and slow. "I have a choice?"

She crossed her arms and nodded.

The berserker rumbled, "You better believe you have a choice. No goddamn Alpha gonna steal away your free will just because of old-fashioned shifter protocols."

"Oh my god, you are such a fucking bear." His partner glared at him. "But yes, he's right. Although, legally speaking, both packs do have a claim on you, you still get to pick. We just gotta make sure you're not doing so under duress. Speaking of, is Mr Depeine your mate?"

"Does that qualify as duress? It's like a minute old, this thing between us. But yes, I think so. I hope so. And that's the best thing happening to me right now, not the worst."

She looked annoyed. "He's hardly worthy."

"Fuck off." Isaac stood prepared to walk away.

"Whoa, there. Okay, perhaps he has hidden gifts."

"Damn straight. Or, not so straight." Isaac looked at the bear shifter. "Why do wolves have to make everything about rank?"

"I know, right?"

"Fine." Lenis gave a funny little bow. "Forgive me my judgey Alpha nature. Can we get back to what we're going to do with you, Mr Lone Omega?"

"I'm not alone. I have a pack now." Isaac kind of liked saying that.

"And they didn't coerce you? At all?"

"They didn't. They took huge steps not to. Alec starved himself to prove it."

Lenis sniffed. "I'm sure it was all very noble. And the previous Rocky claim was unwanted and unwarranted?"

"Entirely."

"I need to formally remind you that a claim must be acknowledged by both parties, and the proper paperwork filed with your local DURPS. If you say it was coercion, then Alpha Frederiksen can't hold you and neither can Alpha Skulls. We aren't savages. No matter what anyone thinks."

"Fine. Yes. I understand. But can I stay here, with the San Andreas Pack?"

She looked at him, thoughtful. "Is that what you really want?"

"Yes, it is." In saying those words, as if they were a vow, Isaac felt some kind of settling in his own mind. It was as if his acknowledgement was casting out tethers of its own, knitting him to this place and these people.

"It's a powerful pack, what with the Magistar and everything." Lenis looked concerned. "You're sure you aren't being unduly persuaded?"

Isaac winced. He would have to explain himself. He'd been running, and apparently, they'd been chasing, for a decade. He couldn't *stop* running without suspicion.

"I love my job here. I like this area and I've even made my own friends outside of pack, human friends. I know this pack seems weird and overwhelming, but they're kind. And fuck, I need that. I would like to try staying still for a change."

Alpha Lenis looked at him. He thought there was a little disappointment in her face. Perhaps she really had wanted an Omega of her own. "Okay, then, you stay. Follow my lead with the Rocky Mountain Pack, alright? It'll be a delicate business extracting you. It has to be done with no possibility of reprisal."

Isaac nodded. It was a big thing for her to ask of him, that he trust a strange government Alpha, but he liked her. And for once he decided he'd trust his instincts.

"And for fuck's sake, get your official local papers in order. You know how bureaucracy works, nothing means anything until the forms are filled out." Agent Lenis sounded annoyed with life.

Isaac remembered that Max had connections at DURPS. "I don't think we'll have too many problems there."

"Well, do it right away, okay?"

"Okay, Alpha."

Her big berserker partner was grinning at them.

"What's your name, by the way, bear dude?" wondered Isaac.

"Faste, Agent Faste."

"Cool. Nice, uh, you know, *tossing* back there."

"Thanks, man."

"You don't really enjoy it, though, do you, fighting?"

"Naw, but when you're big and have my upbringing, you learn to toss with the best of them. My old man used to say…" He petered off. "Dude. Wow. That's insane. I just wanna talk to you about *everything*."

Isaac winced. "Sorry. Omega-thingy."

"Don't take this wrong, but that shit's creepy."

"Enough chit-chat, boys."

"Oh, when *you're* talking, it's okay?" Faste joshed her.

Agent Lenis stood and led them back to the driveway, where a pseudo- standoff was in play.

The Rocky Pack was sitting and glaring at Alec and Judd. Max was slouched on the steps leading up to his apartment eating a bag of gummy wolf candy, biting the heads off with relish and staring hard at Skulls. Bryan was checking the enemy pack's wounds, although not healing any of them. Some had burns from Max, while others had bites and scratches from Judd, Lovejoy, Mana, and Isaac.

Isaac was weirdly proud. He'd fought as a wolf and as an Omega. And he'd done damage, even though he'd no idea what he was doing. He was also ashamed – it was not in him to hurt others like that. Administer discipline for mutual satisfaction in bed, sure, but not in battle.

He looked down at his hands and wondered at the strength in them.

Agent Faste said, "Alpha Skulls. The government recognizes your claim."

The Rocky Mountain Alpha stood up and smirked.

The berserker turned to look at Alec. "Alpha Frederiksen, the government recognizes your bite. You are commended on your self-control in the face of temptation, and we're pleased no damage was done to an unwilling Omega. Your claim is also recognized."

Alec walked over to stand near Isaac.

Isaac was terrified. This was not what he'd been led to

expect.

Alec opened his mouth but the bear shifter put up his hand.

"Wait. Let me finish. After due discussion we have determined that the Rocky Mountain claim was filed in error. Prior consent was not obtained from the Omega in question. The claim will be recorded as kidnapping cover-up and marked illegal in the territory of record. The government may decide to file criminal charges as a result." He looked viciously pleased as he said that and Skulls looked a hell of a lot less smug.

The bear shifter continued. "Accordingly, the Rocky Mountain Pack's presence in San Andreas territory is also illegal. Alpha Frederiksen may file a motion for removal, or he may challenge to defend his border. Given that there has already been bloodshed, we are shortening the grace period to one hour."

Alec looked thoughtful.

Agent Lenis spoke then, Alpha confidence in her tone. "We have determined Omega Mercer capable of making his own decision and uncorrupted by his circumstances."

Someone, Isaac thought it might be Mana, snorted rudely at that.

The female Alpha looked at Isaac. Her eyes were for him alone. "So make your decision, Omega. Rocky Mountain Pack or San Andreas?"

Isaac didn't even pause. "San Andreas."

She nodded, a tiny smile teasing her lips. "Alpha Skulls, you are dismissed."

"Wait. What?"

Agent Faste explained as if to a bratty child. "SBI has the power to act as adjudicator in cases of shifter-on-shifter conflict. You and yours should go now. *Without* the Omega."

"Fuck that noise!" Skulls really had no subtlety.

Agent Lenis kept her expression bland, even as she

bared her teeth. "You are in the territory of another pack with no valid claim and no broker for safe transit. You have an hour to get out." She turned ostentatiously to look at Alec.

Alec's grin was feral. "Alpha Skulls?"

The Rocky Mountain Alpha looked at him, dazed and frustrated and angry, as everything he wanted slid seamlessly though his paws.

Alec growled. "Get. Off. My. Fucking. Land."

"I'll kick your goddamn ass."

Alec was not the kind of Alpha who felt he had anything to prove. He only gestured with his chin.

"I don't think you formally met my family, did you? My brother and Beta, Bryan. My brother-in-law, his mate Max, our Magistar. Ever met a werewolf familiar before?"

Max stood, lazily chewing a gummy, and stepped forward. Bryan joined him, prepared to shift.

Skulls looked at them a long moment. Then he looked at Isaac.

Isaac said, "No. You can't keep me, and you never will."

Bryan shifted.

Max buried one hand in his familiar's thick cream-colored fur. He dropped the bag of candy and raised his other hand up.

Coolant smell filled the air, quintessence eddied around them. Max's open hand filled with blue flames.

"Shoo fly," said Max.

The Rocky Mountain Pack fled.

"Well, shit. I didn't even get to throw it at them." Max let his blue flame spiral up into the night where it cracked out of existence, the energy returning to its liminal state. "And I spilled my gummies. Isaac, you owe me gummies."

"Done," said Isaac.

Bryan shifted back to human and smiled softly. He would be pleased, sensed Isaac, that they had not had to hurt anyone again.

Mana said, "It's just all go go go with you lot, isn't it?"

"Werewolves," said Agent Faste, as if that explained everything.

"Agents? Would you like to come inside for tea?" asked Bryan.

"Come on, Max," said Alec, "I've got more gummies in the kitchen."

"Yeah!" said Max.

Isaac went to Tank. His lover's eyes were unexpectedly sad and confused.

"Thank you for staying. For choosing us." Tank spoke carefully, as if the words hurt.

I chose you, not just pack. Isaac wanted to say. *Don't thank me for this. Look at what I did. Look at you, injured defending me. That's my fault, I brought this on you.* Instead he flinched and nodded. "Let's get you inside, baby."

Of course, Tank was so weak he had to be helped into the house. He couldn't even do that right. Isaac was at his shoulders and Judd at his feet. Tank hated it. He'd gone from feeling useless to feeling worthless.

Bryan carried Lovejoy. Mana actually looked quite worried. Tank had always thought she didn't allow herself the luxury of concern. But then again, he vaguely remembered her actually fighting alongside them at one point. A white fox, vicious and oddly powerful for all her size.

She'd managed to shift from fox to human without anyone the wiser and was back to being fully clothed and entirely made up in a way that Isaac suspected had something to do with savage mage-craft because no one could just shift into false eyelashes like that. No one.

Tank found himself on the big couch and he looked around at the rest of his pack. He lost his self-pity briefly for concern. Worried that he couldn't quite remember who'd been there, and who'd fought, and who just wasn't home yet.

"Where's Colin?"

"He's at school, thank fuck." Judd had come through their ordeal none the worse for wear and quietly pleased with a battle in the manner of most enforcers. Tank envied him his confidence.

"Kevin?"

"He wasn't here, Tank, remember? He's working tonight." That was Isaac's voice.

Isaac was kneeling next to him. Isaac who'd chosen to stay with the pack, but who'd seen him fail them all. Isaac who was beautiful and special and Omega and too good for him and too close and it hurt a lot in a way that made Tank wish for more physical pain from his wounds, so they might distract him.

Tank didn't want to think about Isaac, so he kept worrying about his pack. "Is Alec okay? Did he have to fight that asshole? And Bryan, is Bryan here? Oh, wait. Bryan was healing us. He didn't do too much, did he?"

Isaac again, his voice clogged, "Everyone is fine, baby. Lovejoy took a few hits but he's on the couch next to you. You're the worst off. Everyone else is fine."

Tank shut his eyes.

Isaac was petting him now, just one finger down the side of his face, but that hurt too. He flinched away.

"Can I get you anything?" Isaac said.

Tank wanted to ask him to leave, but Isaac had chosen the pack, so he was staying. He needed to stay somewhere, to belong somewhere. Tank wasn't good enough to be part of that deal. Isaac should find someone better. Stronger.

"Let him rest, honey. Come sit by me." *Thank you, Mana.*

Tank got brave and cracked his lids in time to see Isaac reluctantly go sit on the other couch with Lovejoy, where Mana perched elegantly on the arm, keeping a careful eye on her lover.

Tank suspected she was tense because the two trappers had joined them. She wasn't the type to relax around strangers.

The trappers looked uncomfortable.

Bryan was attempting to make them feel welcome with tea. "Chamomile with honey for the bear."

"Thank you," rumbled Agent Faste.

"And pu-erh for the lady, after my own heart."

Agent Lenis took her stinky beverage with an inclination of the head.

Bryan disappeared again, returning to distribute mint tea to his brother, who sat in one of the armchairs, and a glass of some cloudy liquid to Mana, which Tank supposed was kombucha. Kitsune had a weird love of the foul stuff.

Bryan looked at the Omega. "Isaac?"

"Nothing for me, thanks. But Tank and Lovejoy? Should they have broth or something?"

"Broth?"

"You know, like wholesome bone broth full of nutrients to help them heal."

Bryan chuckled. "I'll get them milk if it'll make you feel better."

"Can I have the gin?" asked Lovejoy.

"Milk," said Bryan firmly.

Tank knew better than to protest. If Isaac and Bryan wanted him to drink milk, he'd drink the whole gallon.

Alec cleared his throat. "So that's it. Isaac stays with us?"

"Omegas can't be loners. You see what kind of shit happens," said Agent Lenis. "So long as you can guarantee that if he chooses to leave, he'll go to another pack, then our work here is done. Just, please, register him with

DURPS immediately."

Just like that? Tank was amazed. He was also certain that Alec wouldn't agree to that guarantee. The idea that Alec might keep Isaac against his will because he hadn't another pack lined up was appalling. But Alec would lie, because it was the right thing to do. Which is exactly what his Alpha did.

"I guarantee it."

Isaac shifted as if he would protest.

Alec shot him a subtle shake of the head and the Omega subsided.

They were already acting like pack.

Alec would perjure himself and let Isaac go, if necessary. Tank saw the moment Isaac realized that. His gray eyes widened with shock and then softened in hope.

Bryan was looking confusedly at a steaming mug in his hand. "Now whose was this? Did I make an extra?"

The front door opened.

Everyone tensed. Tank realized no one was out on patrol. They were all a little shell-shocked.

"Helllllooo, anybody home?"

Marvin.

Tank realized then that they were all sitting around the den clutching mugs of tea, naked and covered in gore.

"Fuzzy wuzzy darlings! What'd I miss?"

CHAPTER TWENTY
The Bun Also Rises

"I'm worried about him."

Tank woke from yet another nap to Isaac's voice in the hallway outside his room.

"He's quiet, even for him."

"He's still recovering." Judd's rumbled response.

"It's been three days. He's not speaking to me. He's not speaking to anybody."

"Can't you use your Omega wiles on him?"

"Doesn't work. I'm too emotionally invested."

Tank sighed and turned over in his bed, stared at the closed door. Wanting to see Isaac but also desperately not wanting it. *I'm pathetic.*

"Is he normally like this after a fight or an injury?" Isaac sounded frustrated and confused.

"Just bust in there and demand he tell you what's going on in that big fat head of his. You know he'd talk if you forced him to." Judd sounded annoyed with Isaac's whining.

"Oh, that's rich coming from you. You think I don't see how you are with your boy?"

Judd sounded prim. "I've no idea what you're talking about, Omega. Fine, let me try."

The door opened and a streak of light pierced Tank's safe, numb darkness.

"Go away," he said clearly.

"Tank, there's a barbecue later this afternoon."

Which meant it was daytime and the weekend. *Huh.*

"To welcome Isaac officially to the pack. Don't you think it's time you got up and joined the living?"

"No."

"Dude, it was just a challenge. Nice dust-up, really. No one cares that you lost."

Tank winced.

"You're all healed up. What's the wallowing for?"

"Fuck off, Judd."

"Well, I tried."

The door opened again and stayed that way. Tank could see the two men in the hallway.

"There it is. You talk to him."

"I can't even get that much out of him."

"He's your man mountain."

Isaac came in and closed the door behind him. Blessed darkness. He smelled good, of grass and home and comfort – slightly salty, like chicken soup. He smelled a bit of Tank too. And of Alec and Bryan and Judd. All of them. Tank didn't like that part as much, he wanted Isaac to smell mostly like him.

"Hey, baby, how you feeling today?" Isaac's voice was forcibly cheerful. "I got the evening off work so I could hang out with the pack. Marvin wants to introduce me to the neighborhood *in style*, he said. You sure you won't come down?"

Tank only blinked at him. It was dim in the room, but he could make out Isaac's face, dear and sweet.

Isaac puffed out his cheeks. "You know it's hard for me to read you, right? Other stuff is all tangled up in it."

"What stuff?"

Isaac tipped his head down. "You know, stuff I want to

do to you. How much you mean to me. Love."

"Oh. I wish you wouldn't. It'd probably be better if you got over that."

"Got over... Baby, what's going on in that head of yours?"

Tank couldn't say it.

Isaac sighed. "You're my mate, right? Aren't we supposed to talk to each other about this stuff? I'm sorry I don't quite know how it works."

Tank sat up. "What?"

Isaac looked pleased and taken aback to have gotten a reaction. "The mates thing? You know I've not had that before."

"I failed."

"The fight? You didn't fail me. I never expected... Oh wait, I see. You failed yourself. That's what's going on here."

Tank locked his jaw and rolled to stare at the ceiling.

"You stepped forward and you tried, and you think because you didn't win you aren't worthy? Or aren't important to pack? Or aren't special enough for me?"

Tank could feel Isaac's eyes on him.

"Or all of the above." *Isaac the bartender-shrink strikes again.*

The bed dipped. "Can I tell you something and ask you to listen? No demands or dominance or anything like that, please?"

Tank didn't like Isaac begging *him*, wrong way 'round. "Of course."

"I may have only been with this pack a few days, but you're vital. Yours isn't a concrete role like Alec's or Bryan's, or even like what I will eventually become. You're the purpose, don't you see? It's a simple thing that you do best – you're best at *being pack*. At being present and solid and reliable. That's not boring or unworthy, it's incredibly important. Otherwise, why would the rest of us bother?"

"Yeah?" The truth of it thrilled over him, because Isaac wouldn't lie. Not about this.

"Yeah."

Tank let out a huffed sigh. So relieved he actually felt ill. "Well, fuck."

Isaac tentatively put a hand on Tank's chest. "Believe me?"

Tank immediately coiled around (as much as his big frame would let him) and pressed his head into Isaac's lap, seeking comfort.

Isaac immediately began petting him. "Plus, mate-wise and sex-wise, you're pretty much specially designed exactly for me, why would I ever let that go? Even if you don't think you're good enough, I *know* you are."

Tank let out a watery chuckle. "Fierce Omega."

Isaac's voice turned hesitant. "While we're confessing, I have to ask. That's not why you like me is it? The Omega thing."

"That's not why. And I love you."

Isaac bent over him and nuzzled behind his ear, nibbled his neck. "I love you too. You'll have to give me time to learn how to do it properly. I don't have much of a grounding in it."

Tank smiled, remembering what he'd once thought about wanting to be Isaac's foundation. Turns out he was actually the whole pack's. "That's what I'm good for."

He could feel Isaac smile against his cheek. "I think about that sometimes. That Bryan and Max and Judd and Kevin are the walls of this place, and Alec is the roof over it, protecting us all."

"What's Marvin?" Tank wondered.

"The decorative throw pillows?"

Tank chuckled. "And me?"

"You're the foundation."

Tank was shocked at how closely Isaac mirrored his

inner thoughts.

Isaac pushed only a little. "Please don't forget how important that is."

Tank snorted. "Especially in earthquake country?"

"Tank, the pack doesn't exist without you. You're its essence."

"And what are you? The windows? Or are we losing the metaphor?"

Isaac sniffed. "It's long gone, baby."

"I really wondered why you would want me."

Isaac shifted under him, pressing his cock into the back of Tank's head to prove that *wanting* was obviously not a problem.

"Not want you?" Isaac wrapped one hand around Tank's throat, bracing it with gentle insistence and arousing him with subtle threat. "I want to collar you and keep you. I want to trap you and chain you, even knowing what that same thing did to me. Even hating that about myself."

"You can keep me." Tank was hardly able to get out the words, he was so excited to say them. For the first time he felt like he had something to offer. Like offering just himself was, in fact, good enough. Not throwaway. Not cannon fodder. "You can do it all." He curled in tighter and burrowed down.

Isaac hummed in approval and shifted his hips to rub his cock against Tank's cheek. Tank turned his head eagerly to mouth at it, losing himself in Isaac's new scents which were so strong there, delicious and musky with need. Not minding, now, that he smelled of all of them. Isaac smelled of pack, and Tank was pack.

Isaac pressed against the back of his neck with one hand and arched up against him, seeking friction. Then he drew back. Tank whimpered at the loss.

"Clearly we gotta work on our communication. Ask for what you want, baby."

Tank didn't want to. He wanted Isaac to take. But he hadn't any pride about it either. He'd beg if Isaac wanted that. "Can I taste you?"

"Not yet. Maybe later. Now I want you to strip and lay back, and wait a moment."

Tank did as he was told, trembling. He'd moved so fast from despair to shock, to relief, and now arousal. His head was spinning. But he *wanted* so badly.

Isaac locked the door and turned on the floor lamp in the far corner.

He returned and ended up standing next to Tank's bed, looming over him. Tank felt vulnerable, and needy, and useless. He went to move – to kneel, to offer, to crumble – but a hand was on his stomach, staying him.

"No, I like you there, laid out like a sacrifice."

Tank had been hard from the moment Isaac ordered him to lie back. These words made his cock jump and bead with moisture.

Isaac's chuckle was dark and pleased. "Stay."

Tank shivered, not from cold but from anticipation.

Isaac rustled about. Tank didn't move. He heard his bedside drawer open and a pleased grunt of discovery. Tank had a modest but thorough toy collection. It occurred to him to be embarrassed except, of course, Isaac already knew he liked all that stuff, and at least the toys were evidence that he wasn't giving himself away all willy-nilly to just anyone.

Isaac liberated Tank's desk chair from the pile of whatever was on it (half-worn clothing, probably) and pulled it up next to the bed. He sat close and looked down at Tank's long body. Tank shivered again.

Isaac's hands were on him and Tank knew what this was really about. Isaac wanted to learn him. Worship him in his dominating way. Understand every part, so he could better manipulate Tank's submission in future. But also prove to Tank that he was worthy of his attention.

Tank moaned, helpless.

He wasn't interested in this kind of play. He didn't like being the focus of pleasure, he wanted to be used and taken. Isaac should be the focus, not him.

Isaac knew this, of course. "You will lie there, and not try to control your reactions, and you will let me do exactly what I wish because this is what I desire. Understand?"

"Yessir."

"Good boy."

Tank felt himself flush with praise and approval.

Isaac began touching him then. Long sweeping strokes at first, feeling the textures that made up Tank – the thin smooth skin behind his elbows, the sparser hair of his thighs, the thicker hair on his chest, surprisingly soft, and the coarser hair at his groin.

Tank tried to do nothing more than breathe through it. He'd taken the lash once, at a club, just to see if it worked for him. Pain wasn't really his deal, but he used the same breathing techniques now to strive for endurance.

Isaac knew what he was doing, of course (the man was paying very careful attention).

He pinched one of Tank's nipples lightly. This was the kind of pain Tank liked. His nipples were terribly sensitive – with the right care, he might be able to climax just from them being tweaked. He bet Isaac would try.

Isaac played with them for a long while, because, as he told Tank, "You make such pretty, pretty noises." He changed the pressure and the type of pain, sometimes licking to soothe in between.

"You are so responsive, my mate." Isaac's words hitched and broke. "Do you know how amazing that is?"

Tank was starting to go to that in-between space where nothing mattered but being told what to do. He'd been instructed to lie still and feel. So he did. He'd never been able to get into sub space before, when he was the sole object of attention, when he was doing none of the work, but it seemed Isaac could put him there. Or maybe this was possible now that he let himself deserve it.

Isaac exploring again. He used his tongue and teeth this time. He laved and nipped at different parts of Tank's body, learning what made him twitch near to breaking (the divots around his hip bones were just too ticklish), and where he sighed in pure pleasure (the swell of his ass and all of his neck), and where he writhed and keened in pleasure pain (his inner thighs and upper back).

Isaac pushed and rolled him around, to get at places, but never flipped him over, and never touched his cock, just played the rest of him like an instrument he was tuning to his exact specifications. Tank hoped Isaac liked his noises, because he was making a lot of them.

At one point he opened his eyes to slits, Isaac had him on his side, facing him and was humming and licking and playing with the muscles near his abdomen.

Isaac was obviously enjoying himself.

His mate wore a t-shirt and sweats. His cock was so hard it created an obscene tent and damp spot at the front of the soft fabric. Tank wanted to taste so badly he contemplated begging. Except Isaac had instructed him to take this. To take the pleasure Isaac gave. To know he was worthy of it.

Maybe if he was very good, Isaac would still feed him his cock afterwards. Tank let out a long low moan at the idea.

Isaac sat back and saw what Tank was staring at.

Sexy bastard reached down and stroked himself over the material of his sweats.

"Pretty baby," he crooned at Tank, a term of endearment Tank might have flinched away from any other time but which he only registered as an affection in his floaty state.

"Still want this, do you?"

Tank nodded, hopeful.

Isaac chuckled that evil chuckle that Tank was beginning to suspect was both the best and worst noise ever.

"Maybe if you're very good."

Tank closed his eyes and nodded, and took another deep breath.

"Now lie back again and take it."

Isaac started all the fuck over then – with the petting and the licking and the biting and the scraping.

Pushed beyond frustration, Tank let go of his body. He floated and gave Isaac noises, moans and pleas and pants and whimpers. Isaac, delighted, drew them out of him.

Eventually, through his haze, Tank heard the pump of the lube, then something was pressed, thick and hard, into his ass.

Not Isaac's cock, he already knew that well, and this was slightly smaller and a great deal colder. *One of my toys?* The prostate massager perhaps? Or a dildo?

His cock, which must be dark red and very angry at this juncture (a thought which in and of itself made Tank nearly shoot, because he was a kinky fucker) throbbed at the invasion.

Isaac's voice was raw when he spoke. "Just look at you. I've never seen anything more beautiful."

Isaac wiggled the toy about, trying to find exactly the right spot. Because Tank's cock would probably never obey Tank again, only Isaac, the traitorous organ pulsed and wept the moment Isaac found his prostate.

"Jesus Christ," breathed Isaac and did it again. "I could fucking milk you."

Tank whimpered in acknowledgment. Yes, Isaac could do it, and yes, Tank would get off on it (boy would he ever) but it tested his control and his faith in himself. Which was likely part of the reason Isaac did it, manipulative fucker.

"You want me so badly." Isaac's voice was wrecked now. Tank could only just hear him over the throbbing of blood in his own ears, the heavy weighted fuzzy stillness of submission.

It was that sensation, and the certain knowledge that if Isaac continued to toy so dexterously with his ass that he would climax from that alone, that drove Tank to speak.

"Please, Isaac, I need—"

Isaac crooned at him, clearly delighted. "What do you need, baby, tell me? Maybe I'll give it to you."

"You. Please please please, just you. Any part of you."

Isaac's breath hitched and he was there, his face coming into view. He brushed Tank's cheek with his thumb, then fed him that and only that, one digit. It tasted oddly salty.

Tank realized that it was the flavor of his own tears on Isaac's flesh. He was crying, leaking hot needy drops, not sobbing, but yearning so hard.

Isaac cradled Tank's face and kissed his wet cheeks and murmured soothing words. Then covered his mouth and gave him his tongue, another piece of himself, another benediction.

Tank bucked, not too much, not rebellion, just an overload of need. But he was big enough for Isaac to be dislodged.

"I'm sorry! I'm sorry. I need to be of use to you. I can't just lie here. I'm not good at—"

"No no no no. Baby you're perfect. I pushed you because I wanted to. I need to know your limits, and we'll work on this. Because sometimes I'll want to do this more, just play, just see how far I can drive your pleasure, and you'll learn to let me. Because you are so very worthy of it."

Tank took a breath at the reminder. Isaac believed that he deserved this. *Oh,* he thought, *I do deserve it.*

Isaac's tone had gone clear and sharp. "You are exactly right, my mate, and I want to take you so badly I can hardly think. I'm stopping this now because it's my choice, not for anything you have done wrong. Is that clear?"

Tank took a deep breath and nodded.

"I'm done playing. You're mine."

Tank nodded again.

"On your knees, head down."

Tank scrambled to do as ordered.

"Wider."

Tank widened his legs.

The toy was tugged out of his ass and Isaac's cock was in its place, silken and hot. Everything snapped back into perfect rightness.

"Move for me," his mate instructed. "Do the work."

Tank moved, angling his hips for the smoothest glide, not to peg his own prostate. He searched for the motion that pleased Isaac best. That caused his mate's hands to fist iron-hard around Tank's hips. Isaac made truly glorious needy groans.

Soon enough neither of them could stand it any longer and Isaac took over. Driving into him. Words like *mine* and *mate* and *more* spilled from Isaac's lips. Tank writhed under them as if he were being barbed by hope.

Isaac bent forward, full contact while pounding into him. His mate's teeth were in Tank's neck, against his back, around his shoulder. Love bites, but hard and sharp – marking him. The physical memory of *mine* and *mate* and *more*.

Tank soared to that place where nothing was required of him but Isaac's needs. Simple. Beautiful. Beyond. He would spin free of the earth and drift, except for Isaac's weight on him, his hot cock inside him, anchoring him and spearing him with joy. And he was providing the same back, giving of himself in foundation and belonging and love. Tethered and mated and right.

So that *mine* met *yours,* and *mate* met *yes,* and *more* met *forever*.

Isaac admitted, to himself only, at being overwhelmed by the sheer number of people Marvin had managed to corral into *welcoming him to the neighborhood.*

By the time he and Tank made it downstairs, the barbecue was in full swing. There were tons of guests. They were loud and laughed a lot.

The whole pack was there, of course, but also assorted unexpected elements. The two trappers were a surprise. They looked uncomfortable and faintly overwhelmed. He wondered why they'd lingered in the area so long.

He saw Gladdy and Chrys trailing a whole collective of assorted humans and other shifters that he assumed must be friends and lovers, or more likely both.

Mana was there, keeping a close eye on Lovejoy, who basked in her attention.

Tank kept close to Isaac, on the auspices of explaining who everyone was, but really Isaac just wanted him near.

"Well, look who finally left his room!" Kevin came swaggering over, cheeky and full of cheer. "Man, what'd you do, Isaac? Use a crowbar?"

Isaac arched a brow at the redhead. "In a manner of speaking."

"Oh?"

"You really don't want the details."

"I don't? Oh. Oh! Yeah, no thanks. Lots of that going on these days. Oooo!" He spotted something leggy and curvy and went off in pursuit.

"Isaac, darling!" Lavish came swaying over on ridiculous heels for an outside event and wearing a fur coat, which among shifters was a bit of a faux pas.

"Hello, gorgeous." Isaac was pleased to see her. He hadn't since their girly fest at the fancy hotel. It seemed a long time ago now.

Xavier he'd seen at work last night, of course. His boss

took in the massive yard and huge house with professional interest. "Tight place, man."

Isaac actually looked around, seeing the property through the eyes of a stranger. The house was impressive – big and barnlike and looming. The yard was full of old oak trees and shrubs, more wild than carefully tended, but still welcoming. The fire pit was flaming merrily, surrounded by benches and camping chairs. Someone had put out folding tables which were covered in food. It was homey.

Gladdy came bouncing over. "Isaac, you'll never guess what I did at work on Friday!"

Isaac smiled down at her. "No, I won't. Gladdy, do you know Xavier and Lavish?"

The little kitsune turned and pounced. She tugged Lavish's hand until the statuesque woman bent so Gladdy could smack her on the lips. Before he could protest, Gladdy did it to Xavier too. Apparently tattoos, a fierce expression, and a dangerous attitude had no effect on kitsune.

"Now, where was I?"

Isaac felt Tank wind long arms about his waist and lean his chin on his shoulder. Isaac sighed and relaxed back against him. Oddly, he did not mind the show of ownership and support, or his own need for comfort. If he wanted to, he could take it out of Tank's hide or mouth, later. *His mouth, I didn't get to use his mouth. Tonight, after the party.* He smiled to himself.

"I was about to guess what you did at work on Friday."

"Oh, yes. Well, I processed a whole bunch of DURPS paperwork."

"That would've been my guess as it's, you know, your *job*."

Gladdy grinned and slapped Isaac's thigh playfully. "Cheeky. But you see it's the *kind* of paperwork that's important. Because…" She drew it out. "It was yours! Your application for residency and pack." Suddenly her big brown eyes got even bigger and welled with tears. "You're gonna stay with us."

"That's the rumor."

Another woman came up to them. "You better. Gladdy was crowing it all over the office. *We got us a legit Omega.* Not to mention the fact that those fucking trappers made a stink about getting it processed quicker than a witch's tits." The woman was huge, big as Tank, pale blond and almost aggressively plain.

"Isaac, you're settling here?" Lavish looked like she too might cry. "For good?"

Isaac rolled his eyes. "Ostensibly, that's what this party is about. It's a welcome-to-the-pack plus burn-meat-in-the-backyard dealy-bob."

"You want to stay?" Xavier would be fiercely protective forever.

Isaac smiled and leaned back to rub his nose in Tank's neck. "I want to stay."

"Okay, then." Xavier almost but not quite smiled.

Lavish took his arm and patted it. "Honey, you get to keep your best bartender."

"Hey, now!" Clara arrived in time to hear that. "I thought I was your best bartender. Hi, sugar." She smooched Isaac on the check. "Hi, bigger sugar." She smooched Tank.

Gladdy looked up at Clara. "Oooo, I like you. How do you feel about small Japanese females with the power of levitation?"

Clara looked down at her. "Uh, oddly positive?"

Gladdy took her hand. "Mr Tattooed-Human-Bad-Ass-Dude, I'm taking your best bartender over to meet the leash."

Xavier watched them wander away. "Was that meant to make sense?"

Isaac and Lavish laughed at him.

Tank said, "Have you all officially meet Ms Trickle?"

Xavier gave the massive female a very assessing look. "Do you bounce? I could use someone like you at the door since Tank stopped showing up."

Ms Trickle was evidently not amused. "I have a very good job, thank you. I used to order Max around."

"Max?" Poor Xavier, there were a lot of new people around.

"You called?" Max sidled up, looking gorgeous and suave and slightly fierce. Xavier clearly responded positively to that last bit. "Hello, former boss of my heart," Max said to Ms Trickle, bumping her with his shoulder.

Ms Trickle batted him off, twinkle in her eyes. "Asshole."

"Where's your nicer half?"

"Working, sadly."

Max said in a hushed tone, "So Gladdy said Jane from HR is sleeping with that sumage George from processing. Say it isn't so?"

"You know I don't keep track of the sex lives of peons," said Ms Trickle, who obviously knew everything that went on around her at all times. "But honestly, such bad taste."

Isaac was delighted with her. No idea who she was, or what she was, but *delighted.*

Max was also delighted. "Come along, woman, and tell me *everything.*" And he dragged her off toward the food.

"Who was that? What was that?" Poor Xavier.

Isaac could only feel sorry for him. He was outside the safety of his own domain and kingdom.

Tank said, "That's our kelpie friend. She's the head of Max's old department at DURPS."

"No, the other one."

Isaac chuckled. "Max? He's way more complicated."

Xavier pursed his lips. "Dangerous?"

"Very," said Isaac.

Xavier nodded like he'd guessed as much.

Tank clearly wanted to forestall matters. "Can I get you

a beer, Xavier?"

Xavier tried hard not to look relieved. "Just plain old beer? Nothing bloody or fermented with fish or anything?"

Tank laughed and let Isaac go. "IPA?"

"How'd you guess?"

"You seem like an IPA kinda dude."

"You're wasted on the door, ever consider bartending?"

"Come on, let's go see what's on ice."

Isaac was left alone with Lavish.

"You want some food or something?" Isaac offered. He couldn't seem to stop smiling.

Lavish took his arm and began to bodily pull him toward some chairs, nested away from the bulk of the crazy. "Don't be ridiculous, darling, I want gossip. Tell me everything! You're staying, you have a man, this is wonderful."

Of course, Hayden showed up. And was his usual stalker asshole self, despite the fact that Isaac smelled almost completely of Tank now.

He drove up, double-parked, slammed out of his car, then rushed the party shouting obscenities and generally making everyone uncomfortable. Tank hated the way Isaac shrank away from the awful man.

Tank didn't even have to kick him out. Looking like they were relieved to have something official to do, the two trappers summarily arrested the barghest and dragged him off for questioning.

Tank suspected they would never see the man again. *Good riddance.*

After that, the evening progressed in that magic-milling way of all good parties. Tank wasn't tipsy (that was pretty difficult for werewolves) but he was feeling lazy and content. Also horny, because Isaac kept pulling him off into dark corners of the yard and deliciously, if briefly, mauling him. Once, far away from the bustle, he'd pushed Tank to his knees and fed him his cock. Tank licked his lips hoping for some lingering flavor. He'd nearly cried when Isaac stopped it from going further.

"Tonight, my mate," the Omega had promised, and then led him back to the party, flushed and desperate. Tank stumbled along behind him, dazed, aching, and incandescently happy.

Eventually, the pack and any lingerers ended up around the fire pit. Isaac and Tank sat at the end of a crowded bench, with Tank in Isaac's lap. Which was absurd because Tank was way too big to sit in anyone's lap. But Isaac had tugged him there, and he was obedient to his mate's wishes.

Isaac teased him about it, of course. "You're squishing me, you big lug. I can't breathe."

Tank was feeling confident enough, after the blow job, to quip back, "Why you gotta be so needy?"

Isaac laughed and cuddled him. Judd was pressed against Isaac's other side. Alec was next to him with Marvin in his lap (a much more sensible arrangement). Lovejoy stood close by, too, with an arm slung over Mana, which she was tolerating for the moment. She was bitching loudly about having broken a nail during the fight. (Tank wasn't even sure manicures worked between shifted forms.) Kevin was laughing and flirting. Even Colin was there, perched in a camp chair looking more comfortable than Tank had seen him in a long while.

Tank heard someone on Marvin's right ask if he and Alec were going to have kids.

Marvin leaned forward, a little drunk and floppy, and explained that mermen were sterile. "Don't tell Alec," he whispered loud enough for nearly everyone to hear. "He *will* keep trying to get me pregnant."

"Marvin, honey, I think he knows you're a dude," said

someone.

Marvin whirled and with exaggerated care put both his hands over Alec's ears.

"Possibly," said the merman, pronouncing every syllable with great care. "But I don't want him to stop trying."

Nearly everyone laughed.

Alec flushed, removed his lover's webbed hands from his ears, and told him he was absurd and adorable.

Isaac shifted under Tank and sighed in contentment. "They're wonderful, aren't they?"

"Told ya," replied Tank.

Throughout the party, the werewolves had each gravitated toward Isaac at some point or another. Their focus remained on their Alpha, of course, as it always did when Alec was around. Alpha always caused a zing of awareness, all of them keeping him in their peripheral vision. It was almost, but not quite, like the vibration between submissive and dominant. Tank felt something similar for Isaac. An innate need to feel the man's eyes upon him, to know he had meaning, to know he was in Isaac's thoughts.

But what Isaac caused in the rest of the pack was different. If Alec was the current, strong and pulling them toward him, Isaac was like a pebble that had been dropped into the water, causing ripples of interest. It was less a disturbance than a delight, like a child skipping rocks. As if Isaac were there to remind them of pleasure in the water itself. *There is joy in the wholeness of pack.*

Of course, it was Lovejoy who remarked upon it, as the fire died and the waves of drunken laugher simmered into contented murmurs and snatches of song. Lovejoy, who had listened, pleased, when Isaac bitched about Tank sitting atop of him, while simultaneously keeping both arms wrapped tight about his mate.

"This is awesome!" said Lovejoy, throwing his hands

up and nearly falling over. Mana attempted to brace him.

"What is?" wondered Alec, turning to rest his head on Marvin's shoulder blade.

"Don't you feel it, Alpha? Isaac being here." Judd's smile was wistful.

"What? What does it feel like?" Marvin asked.

Max said, "Is that why you're all acting so goofy?"

Bryan sipped his mate's wine. Max poured a little more into his glass for him.

Kevin said, "It's like being high or something."

Tank pretended affront. "You calling my mate a drug?"

Gladiola whipped around at that. "Mate?" she squealed.

Isaac tensed under him.

Tank felt himself flush. *Whoops.* "Uh." He made a face over his shoulder at Isaac. "Were we not talking about that part?" His feelings of unworthiness returned in one big flood of shame. *He doesn't want to publicly claim me?*

Isaac squeezed him hard and said loud and bold with only a little tremor to his voice, "Mate." He and Gladdy exchanged a glare of understanding.

Isaac whispered into Tank's ear, "It's okay, baby, you can call me other things later. Or you can try to, but your mouth will be full."

Tank smiled into the light of the fire. *Okay, then, this is it. This is good.*

His pack was solid, if a little floppy around him. His mate was under him, warm and present and safe. Isaac smelled like brandy, and lemon, and spices. He smelled like Tank. He smelled like home. He reached up to touch the place where Isaac's hands were clasped about his stomach, and sighed with contentment.

"You're so very much mine." Isaac's voice was full of wonder, as if realizing it for the first time.

Tank nodded, and leaned back, and floated, and was very much his.

AUTHOR'S NOTE

Thank you so much for picking up *The Sumage Solution*. I hope you had as much fun reading it as I did writing it. If you would like more from the San Andreas Shifters, please say so in a review on Amazon or Goodreads. I'm grateful for the time you take to do so.

Even more welcome are donations to your local LBGTQ centers (time, attention, money, whatever you can give). Mine is the San Francisco LGBT Center, find them at sfcenter.org or @SFLGBTCenter on Twitter. Yes, that's the one Colin donates to in the story. We all spread magic in our own ways, and everyone needs a pack to come home to.

I have a silly gossipy newsletter called the Monthly Chirrup I promise: no spam, no fowl. (Well, maybe a little fowl.) Join it on my website.

gailcarriger.com

ABOUT THE WRITERBEAST

New York Times bestselling author Gail Carriger writes to cope with being raised in obscurity by an expatriate Brit and an incurable curmudgeon. She escaped small-town life and inadvertently acquired several degrees in higher learning, a fondness for cephalopods, and a chronic tea habit. She then traveled the historic cities of Europe, subsisting entirely on biscuits secreted in her handbag. She resides in the Colonies, surrounded by fantastic shoes, where she insists on tea imported from London.